THE CAPTIVE HEART

ANITA GORDON

J
JOVE BOOKS, NEW YORK

THE CAPTIVE HEART

A Jove Book / published by arrangement with
the author

PRINTING HISTORY
Jove edition / September 1995

ISBN: 0-515-11699-8

A JOVE BOOK®
Jove Books are published by The Berkley Publishing Group,
200 Madison Avenue, New York, New York 10016.
JOVE and the "J" design are trademarks
belonging to Jove Publications, Inc.

PRINTED IN THE UNITED STATES OF AMERICA

10 9 8 7 6 5 4 3 2 1

For my critique group
—never shy to share an opinion
and always generous in their support
—thank you, my friends:
Susie Brack, Dee Gordon, Christine Hyatt

And for a dear friend and the inspiration
for Héricourt's nursemaid, Felise
—Jenny Jones, bookseller extraordinaire!

AUTHOR'S APPRECIATION

Once again, a very special thanks to Jim Shellem for his nautical expertise.

Deepest appreciation to Suzanne Parnell for her guidance, aid, and advice on Anglo-Saxon England.

More thanks to Sand Toler for the geographical details of Ireland's Burren and peat bogs.

For my son, Scott Gordon, who, over the Heart trilogy, has helped "stage" many of the action scenes: a heart full of gratitude.

And for Linda Douglas, whom I should have thanked last time for her help in Lyting's and Deira's scene at Gelandri.

" . . . love knows no cost, nor faith any detriment,
and no distances on earth separate
those whom the bond of true love binds . . . "

—Fulco
Ninth Century

Prologue

"You have found her, then?"

Rhiannon rose in a fluid movement from her highseat and slid her gaze over the two men who stood before her.

"You have seen her with your own eyes?" she pressed, anticipation welling in her breast.

"Aye, Princess." The man with the pock-ravaged face stepped forward. "We located her as you directed, across the sea in the duchy of Normandy."

Rhiannon smiled, her nostrils flaring as she drew a breath and sensed triumph near at hand.

"At last." The words hissed from her lips.

Rhiannon averted her glance and looked with satisfaction to her well-muscled companion, Varya, who stood beside her highseat, his gold-cuffed arms crossed over his bare chest, a curved sword gleaming at his side.

She gave him a purposeful nod, then began to pace the chamber, exultation swirling through her veins.

What great fortune to have found word of her old adversary so soon upon her return to Ireland. She expected the she-dog to yet be enslaved in some distant land, conceivably dead. But according to accounts, she had lived these years past a free-woman in Normandy.

Rhiannon stayed her step and rounded abruptly, her eyes slicing back to the two hired men, Grimbold and Wimund, incising them with her gaze.

"You are sure 'tis she? There must be no mistake."

"There be none," assured Wimund, the shorter man with large bulbous eyes and receding chin. "She abides at Héricourt with her husband, the lord baron, and with their brood of children. Lady Ailinn . . ."

"Lady?" Rhiannon crowed a laugh. "She is no *lady*. She is naught but the lowly dropping of the Érainn, whose mother bewitched my uncle's heart and gained place for herself and her wretched daughter amongst my people. The bitch displaced me, presenting herself as my own person the morn we were seized by the Danes in their raid on Clonmel, *eighteen years past*."

Rhiannon steadied herself, moving to the highseat and grasping the elaborate carved back. She inhaled deeply and elevated her chin as grim memories rekindled in her breast.

"I, daughter of the *ruri ri*, Mór, princess of the Casil-Eóganachts, was fouled by their hands and enslaved that day—*my* wedding day."

The lines of her face hardened and her choler rose.

" 'Tis *she* they should have defiled. But instead, posing as myself, she was spared their brutal hands and rutting loins. Later, during our transport to the East, I was abducted by the barbarians of the Steppe. *That* I lay upon her head as well, as I do all I suffered, including this . . ."

Rhiannon swept back the veil that partially covered her face to reveal three bloodless lines, slashing straight and parallel across her left cheek. Her mouth twisted with a hard, black smile as she observed the men's predicted reaction, their eyes widening and their jaws slackening at the sight.

"Yes, look upon my scars, one gained for each attempt I made to escape those who sought to master me."

She drew off the veil completely then, exposing dark hair with a shock of white, and upon her neck a thick, puckered line, curving from beneath her chin to back under her ear.

"This last was meant to kill me and would have, had not Varya saved me."

Once again, Rhiannon waited on the men's reactions, which came as expected, their eyes flitting to her exotic companion and back again to the disfiguring marks that blighted her neck and face and forever despoiled her beauty.

"I have suffered much because of that conniving bitch, who thought to improve her lot at my expense. But now I am returned," she ground out, venom saturating every word. "And I shall have my revenge."

She moved off to her highseat, her back as straight and rigid as a rod. Yet when she turned and lowered herself to the broidered cushions, a narrow smile lifted the corners of her mouth.

" 'Tis why I engaged your services. And why I have further need of them still."

With a nod of her head, she bid Varya to bring forth the small, ornately carved chest he held in his hands. Then, drifting her gaze back over Grimbold and Wimund, she measured them closely as expectancy fired their eyes.

With great care had she chosen them. And while she trusted fully in their ability to carry out her dictates, she trusted them not at all where her treasure was concerned.

Presumably they knew the stories—how, upon her father's death, she had seized his riches, long hidden in an ancient, underground *souterrain*. Likely these two cutthroats hoped to gain the full of it—once they verified its existence—intending to use her as much as she intended to use them.

Rhiannon continued to gaze on them coolly. Varya would prevent any treachery attempted on their part. Meanwhile, she would bait them to her purposes. Both were familiar with the land, customs, and tongue of Francia. That assured they could travel with relative ease and gain entrance where needed. Both were unprincipled. That assured they would see her plans through without question or conscience.

She favored them with another smile. "You have done well in locating my stepcousin, and as promised, you shall enjoy a handsome reward."

At her gesture, Varya placed the chest on a narrow table beside her highseat, then repositioned it to sit between Rhiannon and the hired men.

Leaning forward, Rhiannon slid the elegant jeweled dagger from the brass fittings that secured the chest. Setting it aside, she opened the lid and reached for the leather pouch that lay within. This she held in Grimbold's and Wimund's view as she began to fill it with gleaming coins and sparkling jewels.

Rhiannon uplifted a brow at the men's avid looks. Grimbold's was intent, while Wimund appeared ready to salivate. Her lips curved, and her hands stilled to torment them just a touch further.

"Tell me. How fares my 'stepcousin'?" she drew out the last words with unsubtle distaste, then dropped a bright sapphire into the pouch, toying, tantalizing. "Have the fires of her hair dulled with age, and her waist thickened with childbirth? I'm amazed the chit was able to produce at all."

She suppressed the mental image of Ailinn coupling with the handsome Norman lord, Lyting Atlison. Ailinn had bewitched him, Rhiannon knew. 'Twas why he had chosen Ailinn and spurned her own self, years ago, upon the banks of the Dnieper. Ailinn, the low-birthed sow, was just like her mother to bind a man so.

"In truth," Grimbold spoke with some hesitancy as he watched several more jewels slip from Rhiannon's fingers into the growing purse, "your stepcousin is much as you described her as a younger woman. The dark red of her hair is indeed an exceptional shade. She is slender enough, I'd say." He shrugged, watching Rhiannon's hand dip once more into the chest. "More comely than expected . . ."

Rhiannon retracted her hand and stood to her feet, her mood shifting, tempest-quick. Jerking the drawstrings closed, she tossed the purse at the men.

"Enough! If you find my stepcousin so appealing, then return to Normandy and seize her from her pampered perch. Pleasure yourselves upon her to your content and consider it part of your reward. But do not tarry overlong. When you deliver her to me, the remainder of this treasure shall be yours."

Rhiannon reversed the chest, turning it round to fully expose its glittering contents.

Wimund's huge eyes distended. Overcome by the vision of such wealth, he lunged forward and thrust his hand into the chest, seizing up a fistful of jewels and coins.

Instantly Varya manacled Wimund's wrist in an iron grip. Riveting Wimund with an unyielding gaze, he increased the pressure, threatening to snap the bone. The precious booty trickled from Wimund's hand back into the chest.

Grimbold started forward, his hand seeking the knife in his belt. But before he could take another step, Varya freed his sword and shifted his stance to block him.

"Do not think to betray me," Rhiannon clipped out icily. "I did not survive the Steppe without some guile. And take heed. Varya is an Avar. Completely loyal to me."

The men's eyes shifted to Varya, taking in his dusky skin, the purplish-red birthmark covering the right half of his face, and his shaved head with its long swatch of jet-black hair hanging down at the back in a tangled mass. The Avar stood to a better-than-average height, his build hard, muscular, unclad above a wide leather belt that cinctured his waist tightly, making his shoulders and chest appear all the wider. As if nature had not attributed him enough, his eyes were keen as a serpent's and as black as death.

" 'Tis wiser to fear him above any Norseman, I can assure you.'' Rhiannon's voice broke through the men's concentration. At her look, Varya released Wimund, though he did not resheathe his blade.

"Be certain," she began again, "I intend my stepcousin pay for her sins and suffer all I have suffered in her stead. When she is in my possession, the treasure shall be yours. Fail and I shall find another who won't disappoint me."

Rhiannon grasped the chest's lid and slung it closed, shutting off the men's view of the prize.

"Return now to Héricourt and bring her to me."

Grimbold gave a curt nod, drawing Wimund back. "As you will, Princess, but we shall not take her from Héricourt."

Rhiannon's chin thrust upward, and she started to argue, but he stayed her with a hand.

" 'Tis too well garrisoned. Besides, the barons are to convene at Rouen in the coming weeks—a celebration of some order, devised around the anniversary of William Longsword's installment as duke. All of Normandy's noble families are to attend. With the press of people and distractions at the ducal court, 'twill be easier to snatch our prey right from beneath the noses of the proud Norman warriors."

The thought roused Rhiannon. She envisioned her stepcousin's entrapment at court. Envisioned the chit delivered into her hands at long last, then savored images of the retribution she would exact, slowly, painfully. The anticipation of it all surged through her anew, pounding in her veins and welling in her breast. Her breathing quickened, and the pulse at her temples and base of her throat began to throb. All she had suffered, all she had lost, would soon be avenged. The triumph would be hers.

Exhilarated beyond patience, Rhiannon's eyes swept to Grimbold and Wimund. "Why do you tarry? Be gone with you," she snapped, suddenly annoyed by their idleness.

Snatching up the jewel-hilted dagger from the table, she gestured them away.

"Bring her to me," she commanded with a burst of emotion, then stabbed the dagger downward into the lid of the chest, defiling its rich carvings. "Bring me Ailinn of the Érainn!"

Chapter One

Ailénor's dark red hair tumbled from her shoulders as she tipped back her head and looked straight upward into the canopy of leaves spread overhead.

High in the old pear tree, a fluffy white ball of fur clung tenaciously to a twiggy branch, its round golden eyes staring back at her as it gave a plaintive mew of distress.

"Cricket's going to fall," young Michan fretted at his sister's side and gave an anxious tug to her skirt.

Adelis, Brietta, and little Ena huddled beside him, each gasping in alarm every time the kitten lost her back footing or the bough swayed with the feline's shifting weight.

Nine-year-old Lucán stood tall and erect to Ailénor's left, his gaze fixed on the kitten, his brows drawn into the semblance of a scowl as he contemplated the animal's predicament.

"Really, Michan," Ailénor whispered. "I do think Cricket can manage. After all, she did climb up without difficulty, and her claws are quite sharp. She will back herself down. You will see." Ailénor sent up a quick mental prayer that the kitten was bright enough to do so.

As they continued to monitor Cricket's plight, the kitten edged, bit by bit, along the branch, toward the tree's trunk. Ailénor smiled inwardly. *Minette calée.* Smart kitty, she applauded silently.

Just then, a small purple finch flitted into the tree and perched on the branch, startling the kitten. Cricket drew back and tensed, her fur spiking. She postured to swat at the intruder with a tiny forepaw, only to upset her own balance.

Unimpressed with the show of aggression, the bird flittered off, leaving the kitten clutching the limb, her hindquarters dangling midair.

The girls squealed fitfully, jumping about, clasping one another, and squinching shut their eyes. Ailénor's heart flipped several times over. Blessedly, Cricket regained her hold, pawing her way onto the branch with her back legs.

The furrow on Lucán's brow deepened, as did the frown on his mouth. "I still say I can get her down. My wrist isn't that bad, Ailénor."

"Absolutely not." She glanced to his arm, immobilized with a narrow board and suspended in a linen sling at his side. "It has barely begun to mend from the spill you took from your palfrey yestermorn."

Lucán cast her a prickly look, plainly annoyed that she should voice aloud that particular embarrassment.

Several more piercing squeals issued from the girls as the kitten misstepped, now looking for all the world ready to drop from the tree any instant. Michan whimpered and tugged afresh at Ailénor, while Lucán darted her a sharp side glance.

"If Galen were here, he'd have the kitten down in the wink of an eye." He referred to the oldest of their brothers, younger to Ailénor by two years. "At least *he's* not afraid of heights, and he has a *man's* strength to make the climb as well."

Ailénor ignored Lucán's verbal jab at her aversion to heights and of his reproof of her gender. Lucán was at a mulish age, believing females—except their beloved *maman* and aunt—were only competent at cooking, sewing, and tending babies. Certainly not at climbing trees.

Still, Lucán's words nettled. Ailénor knew her brother provoked her apurpose, but she refused to be baited. Surely the kitten could manage the branch and then back herself safely to the ground.

Lucán gave a snort when Ailénor failed to respond.

"Girls," he muttered. "I'm going to find Richard and Kylan. They should still be in the practice yard. Best gain their aid before Cricket drops out of the tree and splats on the ground like overripe fruit."

Lucán emphasized his last words, giving Ailénor a pointed, just-see-if-I'm-not-right look, then hastened back toward the yard where their older twin cousins were likely engaged in swordplay.

Ailénor simmered, irritated with Lucán. But Michan's high-pitched whine drew her attention back, as did the gasps from the girls as Cricket shifted her position once more.

Michan's lips quivered, and his eyes brimmed with tears. "She's going to fall, Ailénor, and bust open just like Lucán said—like 'overripe fruit.' Then she'll be dead, and it will be all your fault."

"*My* fault?" Ailénor blurted, taken aback.

"You could climb the tree and save her, it you weren't so afraid."

"Felise will know what to do," Adelis declared in a rush, referring to their nursemaid. "We passed her in the flower garden when we came to the orchard."

Pale with concern, Adelis grasped little Ena by the hand, and together with Brietta, their cousin, the three hurried off toward the palace gates.

Michan, watching the spasmodic attempts of the kitten, began to cry in earnest, rubbing his fists into his eyes.

Exasperated, Ailénor vented a breath, then gave the kitten a querulous look. Why did the little beast have to get herself stuck up in a tree? And so high? A cat *should* be able to get itself down as easily as it got itself up. But, *non*. This one would probably fall just to spite her.

As Ailénor looked up at the white fur-puff, she couldn't help but soften. She knew she was more vexed with herself than with the kitten. 'Twas not that she was afraid of climbing trees or too feeble to do so. She had done that enough times as a small girl, much to her parents' dismay. 'Twas the height itself that afrighted her so.

But as Ailénor continued to gaze on the stranded kitten, her concern increased that the kitten might indeed fall. When Cricket stared straight at her with her perfectly round golden eyes and gave forth a small, distressed "mew," Ailénor's resistance melted along with her heart. She could not abandon Cricket in such a moment of need.

Shoring up her courage, Ailénor studied the tree to determine how best to pull herself up onto one of its lowermost branches. At the same time she engaged her mind with a constant, emboldening chatter. She was older now, she told herself, not the girl who once scaled trees without care. She would be cautious. Being overtall for a female, with long legs and a long reach, mayhap she need not climb so very high after all. Whatever was required of her, she must face. She would not have the demise of this little creature on her conscience, nor would she endure her siblings' and cousins' ridicule for failing the kitten in so simple a rescue.

Ailénor pondered the lowest branch. 'Twas a trifle high, even with the advantage of her height. Likewise, there was no place to gain footage to boost herself up. The aged pear tree reached to a remarkable height, its girth equally exceptional in width.

Ailénor refused to be defeated so easily. Glancing about

the orchard, she saw that most of the workers had already departed. 'Twas late afternoon, the harvesting finished for the day, and near to the dinner hour. At a nearby tree, she observed one workman in the process of lugging off a basket of golden pears, his ladder left behind, still propped against the tree trunk.

Ailénor smiled with grim determination. Mayhap this rescue would not prove so difficult after all.

"Come along, Michan, we shall save your kitty. But I shall need your man's strength to help me with yon ladder."

Michan palmed the wetness from his cheeks and followed Ailénor, animated by her words.

Procuring the ladder, Ailénor caught up the front to midsection, bearing the greater part of its weight, while Michan held the back, the end dragging somewhat.

"Hold it steady for me now," Ailénor instructed Michan moments later as she supported the ladder against the tree trunk.

Ailénor looked to the kitten in the upper limbs a trifle in dismay, then lifted her foot to the first rung. Immediately she stepped into the material of her dress.

Ailénor mumbled beneath her breath as she retrieved her foot, then glanced around to assure she and Michan were alone. Bending down, she reached through her legs, grabbed the hem of the back of her gown, and pulled the material through her legs to the front and upward. Securing the fabric in the leather cord of her girdle, she created "breeches" of sorts, baring her legs up to her midthighs.

Michan stared, wide-eyed. "Ailénor . . . What would Father Bruno say?"

"Don't you dare tell anyone, Michan. Most especially not Father. Nor *maman* or *papa*, either," she instructed sternly.

Ailénor removed her slippers, deeming them too slippery for the task, then once again set her foot to the ladder rungs and began the climb upward.

Sweet Virgin, do not let anyone see me, she prayed silently. The pain across her instep reminded her that she had not partaken of such sport for a very long time.

Ailénor spied the kitten above. Cricket had made her way along the limb to the trunk and now sat in the curve of the tree, where the two joined.

"Good, stay there," Ailénor commanded as if the cat could understand.

Planting her foot firmly on the first branch and grabbing hold of the limb directly above it, Ailénor pulled herself off the ladder and up into the tree. She steadied herself a moment, then stepped over and up again, onto another branch, at the same time exchanging her grasp of one limb for another.

Ailénor found herself immediately surrounded by leaves. Leaves in her face, leaves in her eyes, leaves swatting against her mouth. She blew at them and tackled the next branch.

"I'll get you, little one," she called to the kitten, as much to calm her own nerves as she braved the climb and mounted steadily higher. *"Un moment, minette,"* she prattled with forced cheerfulness, avoiding even a single glance downward. Gazing up, she saw that the little varmint had moved again.

"Restes! Stay put, I say!" she scolded.

Cricket gave a soft "mew," then, disregarding Ailénor's command, tested the trunk of the tree, sinking her sharp, needlelike claws into the bark, and ventured out. Ailénor ground her back teeth. Filled with determination, she lay hold to another branch, pulling herself up and scraping her foot in the process.

"Dratted cat," she muttered.

"Hurry, Ailénor," Michan bellowed from below as Cricket disappeared around to the back side of the tree.

A limb tore at Ailénor's dress, and another snagged her hair. Her temper warmed as she freed herself. She had no wish to get into a chase—with a cat—in a pear tree. Where would it end? She shuddered to think, glancing to the uppermost limbs. Ailénor continued to work her way higher in the tree, ignoring the insects she encountered and trying not to destroy any fruit.

Another "mew" told Ailénor that Cricket was just to the other side of the trunk. Carefully Ailénor made her way around, thankful for the sturdy limbs on the old tree. Gaining sight of the kitten once more, she smiled. Cricket was scarcely more than an arm's length away.

Mindful, Ailénor held on to the branch with one hand and leaned forward, stretching out her torso and opposite arm to grasp the white fur-ball. But even as she did, the kitten shied from her reach. Blinking her golden eyes, the kitten gave a placid "mew," then began backing down the trunk of the tree.

Ailénor gazed after the cat aghast. Cricket picked her way down without mishap, then, still a third of the way above the ground, turned herself around and dashed down the remainder of the trunk. Reaching the ground, she scampered a short distance, plopped her bottom on the ground, and started lazily licking her paw as though nothing of consequence had passed.

Ailénor boiled, feeling as though steam issued from every pore on her head.

Squeals of delight burst from Michan, startling the kitten as he rushed with open hands to snatch her up. Cricket bolted, with Michan trotting joyfully behind, intent on capturing her. Ailénor pressed her lips to a thin line, unamused as the two headed out of the orchard, leaving her abandoned in the pear tree.

"Wretched little beast," she groused after the cat. "Both of you," she tossed after Michan as well.

Ailénor felt hot and dirty and very disagreeable, especially as she spied ants and then a leggy spider on the underside of several leaves. Pushing back errant strands of dark red hair from her face, she made the mistake of looking directly below.

Ailénor clutched the branch, her knuckles whitening as the ground moved beneath her. She shuddered, her heart and stomach suddenly in her mouth. She had climbed much higher than she realized. All too vividly, Ailénor recalled the reason she had ceased climbing trees as a child. Likewise, she realized, 'twas not so much the height itself that afrighted her so, but the fear of falling. *That* she had nearly done at age five, from high in an oak tree. 'Twas her father who climbed to her rescue in that instance, she herself a lost kitten!

Heart beating hard and trepidation congealing the marrow of her bones, Ailénor began a shaky descent.

"Cricket, you better have nine lives," she warned beneath her breath. "Because you are going to need all of them when I catch up with you."

Garreth of Tamworth elongated his stride, greatly enjoying the stretch and pull of his muscles.

After having been cramped aboard a stocky little trading cog for three days, he now relished the simple act of walking, the stiffness diminishing from his joints and spine with each new exertion. He was amazed his legs hadn't folded beneath him, knotted and benumbed, when he first set foot to the dock.

But now, as he made his way through the twisting streets of Rouen, his muscles loosened, and the tension flowed out of them, replaced with a fresh resurgence of energy. He hoped his time here would meet with the same success he had just achieved in Paris.

Officially he traveled through Francia as an agent for his lord and sovereign, England's illustrious king, Athelstan. Like numerous other royal envoys currently scouring Europe and eastern lands, his task was to procure sacred relics and hallowed articles for the monarch's renowned collection.

The guise allowed him to travel about inconspicuously, without garnering undue attention. Moreover, in his capacity 'twas most natural and without suspicion that while in Paris he should serve as courier and deliver greetings to the king's sister, Eadhild, and to her husband, the Count of Paris—also know as "Hugh the Great" and "Duke of the Franks."

Count or duke, Hugh also happened to be the most powerful baron in the Frankish realm.

Garreth's lips lifted into a faint smile. His mission to

Paris—and now to the ducal court of Rouen—had less to do with sanctified bones than with the future of the throne of Francia.

Garreth proceeded along the narrow street, inhaling the pungent scents of the city and scanning the crowds milling there. Wattle-and-daub houses lined the way, decorated with a profusion of flowers, brightly colored pennants, and fluttery ribbons.

Clever of the duke to hold these celebrations and demand his barons be in attendance—given the events of the past months—Garreth thought. 'Twas convenient for himself, as well, that he might bear King Athelstan's wishes for the duke's rule—and all he might accomplish through it.

The street wound gently upward, reminding him that Rouen spread along the foot of high, forested hills. Garreth continued to follow the meandering lane, having been assured it cut through the heart of the city and would lead him directly toward the grounds of the ducal palace.

Progressing on, his gaze paused over a particularly flirtatious maid who lingered in an open doorway. He skimmed her shapely curves, giving her an appreciative smile.

He certainly wouldn't mind a dalliance while in Rouen. It had been sore long since he enjoyed a good tumble. His visit in Paris had been far too brief and too guarded to seek his pleasure in the softness of a woman. There would also be little chance to do so when he returned to England, for then he must choose a wife. Or rather, announce his choice of one.

With a sigh he gave a parting glance to the maid and pushed himself on, regretting his present mission must eclipse such indulgences for the moment.

A wife. The thought sent a prickle down the back of his neck. He held no complaint that he must espouse himself on his return, for at that time the king intended to reward his long service and friendship with handsome titles and lands, righting the wrong done him so may years past.

But being elevated from the status of royal *thegn* to the privileged rank of *ealdorman* would necessitate him to take a wife and begin seeding his own dynasty. To that end, Athelstan, king and "matchmaker," who had seen all his sisters wed to high places—save the ones who had escaped to monastery—had already proffered two distant cousins for his consideration.

Garreth had jested with the king at the time that he himself should take a wife. But, in truth, he was deeply honored and flattered by the king's gesture. Not only was his admiration for his sovereign unbounded, but no more steadfast a friend, nor truer "brother"—even of blood—could he ever hope to have than Athelstan.

Still, this business of a wife. As a royal *thegn* attached to the king's household, unencumbered these years by titles and lands and the need to make an advantageous marriage, he had entertained thoughts of choosing a mate for love rather than status. Despite his lack of lands, the king had seen him amply rewarded with wealth and privileges aplenty, advancing him to a high station within the royal circle.

Garreth looked on another fetching maid who flushed under his gaze as he passed. With a small flutter of lashes, she smiled at him with a shy, pretty seductiveness.

Rosalynd and Mora, the king's kinswomen, were not so pretty, he reflected, though acceptable enough and seemingly intelligent and capable. Mayhap affection would come with time, though from his few encounters with them, he suspected he would have little in common with either one he might choose beyond the marriage bed itself. Would that suffice through the years? A corner of his mouth pulled downward. Truth be known, it left a barren feeling in his heart.

Garreth shook the thoughts away as he passed through the postern gate of the city, the street turning from cobbles to dirt. In the far distance, left and right, he could make out the continuance of the wide, yawning ditches that surrounded Rouen, said to be filled with wolf traps. Along the banks of the Seine, of course, 'twas not ditches that protected the city, but miles of barbicaned walls, a legacy, presumably, of earlier Roman endeavors.

But now the road stretched on before him, winding and climbing the hillside, cutting through a sizable orchard, and terminating before the high limestone walls of the ducal palace.

Garreth leaned into his stride as the land sloped steeply upward, warming his leg muscles. Presently he traversed the distance and approached the orchard. It looked to have been long-standing, the trees mature and healthy in size, the foliage of the pears, apples, peaches, and plums densely full.

As he neared the edge of the orchard, an amusing sight caught his eye—that of a lad roughly five years of age, chasing after a small white kitten. The two trotted onto the road, dodging around an old man—a laborer from the looks of him—entering the grove.

The boy and kitten scampered ahead, while the man trod on and stopped in the midst of the trees. Doffing his cap, he scratched the thin wisps of hair on his head, looking from one tree to another as though he had misplaced something. He halted his motions as he spied a ladder leaning against a trunk several trees away. With a shrug and shake of his head, he trudged over and took hold of the piece. Hooking his arm and shoulder through the rungs, he carted off the ladder and departed the orchard.

Garreth watched the man with a mixture of amusement and compassion. Obviously the old fellow's faculties were slipping.

Garreth proceeded on, his gaze lingering a moment longer on the retreating back of the orchard worker, then drifting back over to the tree.

'Twas an exceptional tree, an ancient pear, lofty in height with stout bole, its leaves a glossy green. His stomach growled beneath his belt. As his gaze strayed over the tree, he wondered if it offered anything ripe for the plucking.

He started toward it, then halted abruptly as a long, bare, and very shapely leg appeared from the canopy of leaves.

Garreth stared in outright surprise, his boots taking root in the earth, his breath trapped in his chest. Slowly his gaze traveled over the trim foot and ankle, up the slender leg with its pleasingly rounded calf, on to the smooth knee and what promised to be the beginning of a tempting and equally bare thigh hidden behind the foliage.

Garreth took a long, hard swallow, feeling warmth rise from his toes to flood his whole being. He watched, entranced, as the leg stretched forth and the foot began to "search" the trunk of the tree. Several captivating moments later he came to himself, realizing with a start that the object of the search was obviously the ladder that the worker had just removed.

A wide grin stole across Garreth's face, and he chuckled, humor rumbling in his chest. The old man had not only forgotten where he left his ladder, but he had forgotten his helper in the tree. Gazing on the deliciously tempting leg, he wondered somewhat wickedly where it led.

As though the owner of the leg had overheard his thoughts, the leg folded back up on itself, disappearing behind the screen of leaves.

Garreth rubbed his jaw, wholly intrigued and most thoroughly tantalized. He remained lodged in place, waiting for the leg to reappear.

It did not.

Overcome by curiosity and unable to resist, he proceeded forward to discover for himself the secret of the pear tree.

Dear Lord, be kind to your servant and let it belong to a female and not some smooth-faced lad, he pleaded silently.

Garreth mounted the gentle slope to the tree with long strides. He spied a pair of ladies' slippers discarded on the grass.

Definitely female. His grin stretched the corners of his mouth farther, and his anticipation rose. Still, the leg remained hidden from sight. Dauntlessly Garreth stepped directly beneath the spreading pear tree and peered straight upward into the canopy of leaves.

His broad smile slackened with surprise. Perched above, amidst the foliage, on a smooth gray limb, sat a gorgeous nymph with fiery tresses, her long, sleek legs bare midway up her hips.

"By the Rood!" The words slipped from Garreth's lips, followed by a low whistle.

His gaze skimmed the silken legs upward to the slim waist and full, round breasts straining the fabric of her simple work dress. His gaze then lifted to the maid's hair, a most unusual shade—deep, rich red, mindful of the fires of autumn. The eyes gazing back at him were a crystalline blue, bordered with dark lashes. Garreth found the beauty of her delicate features to be utterly breath-stealing.

"Are you real, gentle maid?" he uttered softly, half to himself, half to the angelic vision above, fearing she might disappear in the next instant, the product of his happiest delirium.

Truly, he had been celibate far too long, for now he was entertaining fantasies. But the swelling response beneath his trousers was certainly not of any imagining.

Ailénor ceased to breathe as the dark-haired stranger appeared below her. His sheer handsomeness momentarily transfixed her. Though the light filtering through the canopy of leaves cast a dappling of shadows on him, she could see that the lines of his face were clean, straight, strong—most especially his jaw. Rich sable hair flowed to his shoulders, a shorter unruly piece curling over one brow. Ailénor's heart raced as his dark liquid eyes embraced her.

The stranger spoke, yet she did not quite grasp his words, for his mouth held the most irreverent of smiles, totally disarming her as, once more, his gaze began to roam over her.

Her body vibrated as those eyes touched her, vibrated with a thrilling, tingling awareness and a most disturbing unease. His gaze slid over her breasts, then grazed the full length of her legs only to return along the same path, retracing every inch.

Heat shimmered through Ailénor, and her bones dissolved. She gripped the limb all the tighter.

Striving to recover herself, Ailénor realized how scandalous she must appear, perched in a tree, naked to her hips. Her cheeks grew hot, while the stranger's lips remained spread with a wolfish grin, his dark eyes devouring her.

Garreth inclined his head. "Have you a voice, minx? A name?" he called to the exquisite creature above.

She gazed on him with large, wide eyes but did not respond.

" 'Twould seem your ladder has gone off. With the laborer, that is," he amended.

Still the beauty did not speak.

Garreth wondered if she could understand him. He assumed her to be one of the native Frankish villeins, and thus spoke that tongue. His own efforts were heavily accented, he knew.

But mayhap she was Dane. For the greater part, 'twas Danes who had settled Normandy and continued to do so with a steady influx of people from their homeland. Mayhap he should attempt to communicate in his native Saxon tongue. 'Twas the same root language as the Nordic one, their forebears belonging to the same stock of Baltic peoples. At home, Saxons and Danes communicated without great difficulty, the differences of their tongues being largely ones of dialect. Mayhap he should address her in Saxon.

But considering the maid, with her fine features and dark auburn hair, he decided 'twas more likely she was of mixed heritage, Danish and Frankish, and likely spoke the latter. Again he undertook to speak that tongue.

"Might I be of assistance?"

Understanding reflected in her eyes, but she appeared frightened and unready to trust him.

"Mayhap we need be properly introduced before an attempted rescue." He smiled easily. "I am Garreth of Tamworth. Have you a name, minx?"

He watched her take a small swallow, her hands tightening on the branch.

"Ailénor. Of Héricourt," she said in clear, pleasant tones.

"A lovely name, to be sure." His smile broadened, carrying warmth to his eyes. "Well now, Ailénor of Héricourt, 'twould appear that someone forgot you. The ladders have all been taken in for the day." He gestured to the empty orchard. "Certainly you cannot remain there till the workers return on the morrow."

The maid, Ailénor, listened attentively but made no response.

"Nor should you stay there through the night. No telling what beasts or ne'er-do-wells might lurk about in the dark outside the palace walls."

"Oh." Her mouth rounded into a perfect "O."

Garreth felt a jolt of desire to sample those lips and make them pliable beneath his own.

Ailénor stirred, looking appreciably disquieted by his last remark, and opened her mouth to speak.

"*Bien, messire.* How do you propose we manage it?"

Garreth groaned inwardly, thinking of what precisely he would like to manage with this damsel, be she made of flesh or dreams.

"You are already seated upon the lowermost branch."

Ailénor nodded, taking stock of her position.

"Now concentrate here, on the center of my chest."

Ailénor looked there. A ripple of warmth purled through her.

"And?"

"And . . . jump." He uplifted open arms to her.

"Jump?" Ailénor clung to the tree, her eyes rounding all the more.

Garreth caught the thread of panic racing through her voice.

"Truly. I shall catch you."

"Could you not seek out a ladder?"

"There be none, minx. And besides, 'twill be much quicker and easier this way."

Ailénor looked to his chest, then at the ground, then back to his solid and oh-so-disturbingly masculine chest and his outstretched arms. She shook her head.

"I would much prefer a ladder."

"My lady, you wound me," Garreth avowed, chuckling, then noticed how she clutched the limb, white-knuckled, and noted the paleness of her face. Ailénor, he suspected, possessed an acute fear of heights.

"As you might have noticed, I am a rather tall fellow," he cajoled. "The jump won't really be so far. It just appears so because, well, your head is higher than your lovely toes. Come now. 'Tis not so very terrifying. Why, if I were to leap up a mite, I could touch your feet."

The thought of this man touching her anywhere sent a shock of liquid fire up Ailénor's legs to burn warmly in her most secret of feminine places. She shifted restlessly. Below, Garreth widened his open arms to her, obviously believing her ready to make the leap.

"Loose your hold of the branch now," he called. "Give a little shove off and throw yourself at my chest."

"Your chest," Ailénor repeated, staring at that broad expanse and running the tip of her tongue over her lips.

Garreth's eyes followed the movement of her tongue over her lips, then suppressed his natural response and forced his concentration back to retrieving her safely from the tree. There would be time aplenty later to sample those lips and tongue.

He wiggled his fingers in a coaxing manner. "Now, Ailénor. At the count of three."

Ailénor gulped as she looked at the proposed target of his chest. He did look sturdy and solid. Nonetheless, 'twould likely be a hard landing.

"Loose your hold and drop down," he bid her. "Aim for my chest. One, two, thr . . ."

Ailénor pressed her lashes tight and shoved herself off the branch, casting herself at her rescuer.

A "whoof" left Garreth as Ailénor caught him high on the chest, compelling him backward. Together they tumbled, his arms wrapping instantly around her as they fell.

Thudding gracelessly to the ground, Garreth found his face suddenly buried between the soft pillows of her breasts. There was no help for it, for in the same instant they began to roll, over and over, down the slope, gaining considerable momentum and coming to a stop minutes later with Garreth atop of Ailénor, his nose and mouth still pressed intimately between her feminine contours.

Garreth started to raise himself, but Ailénor clung tight and pulled him back down.

"Am I . . . alive?" She panted for breath, wholly shaken.

Garreth muffled a response between her breasts, then managed to lift himself up partway. He felt the silken warmth of her flesh beneath his left hand, coming aware that that member now grasped her naked thigh, and that her leg twined about his like a lover, hooking him behind the knee.

"More than alive, from what I can tell." Garreth gasped for air and resisted the urge to sweep his hand upward and seek her bare backside. Instead he raised himself, bracing his arms on either side of her and gazed back down on the entrancing maid.

Her dark red hair spread about her, framing her exquisite beauty. Garreth felt a pang of desire pierce him anew and feared his unruly manhood would next burst from his *braies*. He could not help but favor their position, all the parts fitting so comfortably together. He promised himself he would see that their parts did so more completely, once they found a more secluded place. He had no mind to let this minx get away.

Eyes sparkling, Garreth began to feel along Ailénor's arms and then her legs.

"I trust nothing is broken. Does aught hurt? Here? Or here?"

Still somewhat dazed and tingling from his familiar inspection of her, Ailénor tried to focus on Garreth's darkly handsome features. He chose just then to shift upward. Bringing his face away from her breasts, he propped his elbows at the sides of her head, but in so doing, his groin pressed intimately against hers.

"*Mon Dieu!*" Ailénor gasped, her eyes flying to his face, heat shooting into her cheeks as she felt the hard bulge pressing against the mound of her womanhood—and, even more shockingly, a hot, pulsing response between her legs.

Before she could push him from her, a clamor rose off to the left—a mixture of voices and a scraping of steel. Ailénor turned her head enough to glimpse her older twin cousins, Richard and Kylan, running toward her, the children trailing behind with Felise, their nursemaid, who wore a thunderous scowl upon her face.

The twins' swords gleamed before them, their dark brows slashing over angry eyes fixed on Garreth, who yet hovered above her, pinning her to the ground.

Ailénor realized that Felise likewise perceived her virtue to be endangered. Felise snatched up a stick from the ground without slowing her trot, huffing indignantly as she bustled toward them.

The twins halted aside the entangled couple, their swords pointed at Garreth's back. But Felise did not stay her step and came at Garreth, amidst proclamations of outrage, and switched at him vigorously. But she quickly found difficulty in doing so without smiting Ailénor's bare legs as well. After a moment of indecision, she brought the stick down on Garreth's shoulders and head. Garreth, in turn, protected Ailénor, shielding her with his body.

"*Cochon!* Swine! Free my lamb at once!" Felise shrilled.

"Felise, *non!*" Ailénor cried from beneath Garreth, her lips against his throat. She shoved at him to move off her, but with their legs still entwined, they managed only to roll over together in unison.

Ailénor quickly shifted atop Garreth, briefly smothering his face with her breasts once again. Felise continued to circle the stranger and swat at him. Hastily Ailénor sat upright and rocked back, warding off the nursemaid with a flaying of hands, striving to knock the stick away.

Meanwhile, the parrying caused Ailénor to wiggle atop Garreth, bringing a groan from his lips. He glimpsed Ailénor's twin protectors exchange glances as the persecution continued. Between the stings of the stick and Ailénor's squirming upon his manhood, Garreth felt wholly tormented.

"*Non, non,* Felise!" Ailénor nabbed the stick, then scrambled off Garreth and stumbled to her feet. "Richard. Kylan. Put down your swords," she demanded and flung the offending stick away.

Aware that Garreth had shoved to his feet behind her, she backed toward him, her arms and hands outspread defensively. Their bodies came into instant contact, and Ailénor felt Garreth's hardness press against her backside. She jerked forward with a gasp, all word and thought deserting her tongue.

Taking in the amazed and expectant looks of the others, including Felise's disapproving gaze fixed on her bare legs, Ailénor yanked her gown free of her girdle and fortified herself with a deep breath. Gathering her frazzled thoughts, she started to launch into an explanation, but Garreth began with his own a fraction of a moment before, so that they overspoke one another.

"I had just arrived in Rouen . . . I was walking toward the palace gates."

"He found me in the pear tree."

"The worker carried off her ladder."

"I was trying to get Michan's kitten."

"A kitten? Really?" Garreth paused, tipping his head toward Ailénor. "Is that why . . . ?"

Ailénor ignored his question and raised her chin, looking back at the others. "It backed itself down, and Michan ran off . . ."

"As I was approaching, her leg appeared out of the tree . . . looking for the ladder. Well, I went to see . . ."

"And I jumped . . ."

"Well, yes, such as it was." Garreth rubbed the center of his chest. "We fell . . ."

"And rolled down the slope . . . together . . ."

"That's when you came . . ."

"We hadn't recovered ourselves yet . . ."

Garreth stopped and gazed down at Ailénor, the side of his mouth pulling into an infectious grin. "My dear minx. I doubt if I ever shall!"

Ailénor's eyes flew to his. At the same time Richard and Kylan split with laughter, their swords sagging before them.

Felise huffed, her large bosom heaving, while the children giggled beside her, excepting Michan who had the good grace to look embarrassed for having abandoned his sister and brought this mishap upon her. Cricket, now confined in a pouch suspended from Michan's belt, contributed a repentant "mew."

Wiping the mirthful tears from their eyes, Richard and Kylan resheathed their swords with some difficulty.

"Welcome to Rouen." Richard extended a hand and arm. "I am Richard, and this is my brother Kylan."

Garreth clasped arms with Richard, then Kylan. The two young men were identical with ebony hair and steel-blue eyes. He guessed them to be about twenty.

"I am Garreth of Tamworth, *thegn* of the royal court of King Athelstan of England."

"Athelstan," Kylan voiced the name with a note of awe. "We are indeed honored."

"Your business then brings you to see the duke?" Richard assessed him with sharp eyes.

Garreth hesitated at that look, concerned that the purpose of his real mission might be too easily surmised.

"In truth, I visit Rouen to procure a Psalter, commissioned for the king at St. Ouen. But I do bear my lord's greetings for your noble duke, William Longsword."

"To that end, we may be of assistance and can arrange an audience, if you so desire," Richard offered.

"In repayment for your kindness to Ailénor and for her damage to you," Kylan added with some merriment as he looked to Ailénor.

Garreth raised a brow, suspecting a little boasting on the part of these two. How was it that they could so easily arrange a meeting with the duke himself? How, too, did they know Ailénor, and why their fierce protectiveness of the maid? A briery patch of jealousy sprouted in his chest as he considered just what the nature of their interest in the beauty might be.

"I assume you have access to the duke, then?" Garreth could not wholly disguise his skepticism.

Felise snorted, miffed at his disbelief. "You Saxons need learn a few manners and show proper respect for the cousins of the Duke of Normandy," she scolded.

"You are cousins to Duke William?" Garreth looked to

Richard and Kylan in surprise.

"As is Lady Ailénor," Felise apprised, piqued by his ignorance.

"*Lady* Ailénor?" Garreth's glance skimmed over Ailénor's disheveled hair, worn gown, and bare feet. "I did not realize . . ." he offered, his tone apologetic.

Garreth reproached himself. He should have suspected as much when her defenders arrived—noblemen, to be sure, and a lady's maid. He recalled the slippers he found beneath the tree and chastised himself once more. They were fashioned of fine kid leather, obviously those of a lady. His eyes traveled to Ailénor again. Her simple gown and tousled locks did little to foster the impression of a lady.

Garreth's look was not lost on Ailénor. She realized at once that he thought her to be a commoner until this moment. The realization put a decided spin on her feelings, and she wished 'twas possible to simply melt into the ground and leave not a trace.

Her fingers trembled as she pulled grass and leaves from her hair, all too conscious of the virile man standing beside her. What had she seen in his eyes whilst they lay upon the ground entangled, their bodies pressed together? Had he thought her to be some easy maid? Were his thoughts ones of seduction? Ailénor glimpsed the Saxon from the corner of her eye. Never had a man looked on her as he had, as though ready to gobble her up.

At Felise's bidding, Ailénor quickened back to the pear tree to retrieve her slippers, then rejoined the others as they departed the orchard.

Richard and Kylan flanked Garreth and engaged him in a rousing conversation concerning the English court, causing Ailénor to trail behind the men with the children and Felise.

Once inside the palace gate, the twins directed Garreth toward the garrison quarters, while Felise escorted Ailénor and the children back toward the keep with a stern lecture on proprieties.

"What will your *maman* and *papa* say to find you so . . . so . . . compromised?" she tutted.

"Felise, please. Do not tell them," Ailénor pleaded.

"You must remember your station, Lady Ailénor," Felise continued with a decided sniff. "You are the daughter of the Comte and Comtesse de Héricourt. Never must you disgrace your parents, Lord Lyting and Lady Ailinn, but always bring honor to them. *Viens, maintenant.* Come along now. We must see you out of those clothes and dressed for dinner. And look at the wreckage of your hair . . . and the stains upon your clothes." Felise clucked her tongue as they mounted up the stairs of the keep.

"*Oui*, Felise." Ailénor sighed, then slipped a final glance in Garreth's direction, lingering over his splendid frame a moment longer than might be considered prudent for a lady.

Without warning, Garreth turned and looked back, straight at her, sending Ailénor a huge smile and a generous wink.

Ailénor's heart skittered wildly. She hastened to join Felise and the children, who were now disappearing through the door of the keep. As she gained the portal, she could scarce bridle her thoughts for, all too vividly, her senses overflowed with memories of the dark-haired Saxon.

Chapter Two

Garreth finished toweling his damp hair, feeling refreshed and infinitely grateful for the bath Richard and Kylan had managed to arrange.

Dropping the towel beside the half-barrel tub, he reached for his clean *braies*, folded neatly atop his other clothes on a small three-legged stool.

He was thankful his sea chest had been delivered from the ship. His traveling clothes had proven quite thoroughly stained from his roll in the orchard.

The image of Ailénor flooded to mind. He could not help but smile as he pulled on fawn-colored *braies* and tied them about his waist. He pictured the maid as he first saw her perched amidst the foliage, so stunningly beautiful. Briefly he allowed himself to relive the moment she cast herself from the tree—the sensation of her thudding against his chest, the feel of her supple body as he clasped her against his own and they rolled time and again down the incline pressed intimately together. Ailénor. He visioned her trapped beneath him, all feminine softness and loveliness, and so utterly beguiling—an enchantress.

Garreth heard a sigh escape his lips and wrested himself back to the moment. His gaze fell upon the shirt he now held in his hand, yet he couldn't recall having taken it up.

The maid has you behaving like quite the green fellow, he chided himself mentally, humor twitching the corner of his mouth. He drew on the shirt, then next reached for his tunic.

But with a will of their own, his thoughts bent back to Ailénor.

Ailénor. Such a captivating minx. He had desired a dalliance while in Francia—a "good tumble," he had phrased it to himself while walking the streets of Rouen. He certainly hadn't expected to have one thrust upon him quite so literally or so soon.

A liquid warmth spread through Garreth's chest as he considered the autumn-fire maid. He smiled inwardly. He'd favor a good tumble with the beauty—one of a much different nature than they had so recently shared. He desired nothing more than to sweep her away to some secluded haven and seduce her thoroughly. Even then, he doubted he would soon have his fill of her—not in one hour, one day, one . . .

He arrested his thoughts. There could be no dalliance with Ailénor. Not only was she a woman of gentle birth and noble breeding, but also she was kinswoman to Normandy's duke. That reality both frustrated him thoroughly and pleased him enormously. Frustrated him because he could not touch her. Pleased him because socially she was his equal.

Garreth regarded the tunic in his hands, a practical garment of sufficient, though not overly impressive quality. He was unsure how Ailénor might look on him. 'Twas necessary he present himself as a royal envoy, an agent of Athelstan's court and a man of indeterminate rank. To reveal his true station—or the one to which he would soon be elevated—could only bring suspicion upon himself and his king.

Verily, envoys of any kind drew suspicion in foreign lands. But a man of high rank would not be sent solely to quest for items to enhance the royal collection, be they of heaven or earth. Leastwise not without an accompanying delegation, and only for objects of considerable import.

Garreth looked again to the tunic in his hands—dark forest-green in color, unadorned about the neck and hem, with plain, close-fitting sleeves. The sleeves were not the fashionable, overlong cut, as was the current mode, so that one need push them back up over the hands, creating wrinkles of cloth above the wrist. Such indulgences, like other embellishments, would serve only to imply status.

Sorely, he wished to distinguish himself in Ailénor's eyes, but to do so by revealing himself would be a betrayal of his true mission and, thus, of his king. That he could not do. Never would he betray Athelstan.

Garreth vented a breath. He carried a sharp ache in his loins for the bewitching, untouchable maid. At least he could enjoy her presence while in Normandy. Likely he would be as hard as a rock his entire stay—a torturous state, but one he would willingly forbear. All too soon he must leave and bind himself elsewhere.

Garreth again took firm rein of his thoughts and chided himself for his fixation on the maid. Belting his tunic, he then drew on long woolen hose, pulling each to the knee and covering the end of his *braies*. Making quick work of the cross-gartering on each leg, he then slipped into his boots and tugged them up to midcalf.

Reflecting back on the past hours, Garreth deemed he had made substantial progress in little time. 'Twas providential, indeed, to have encountered the kinsmen—and kinswoman—of the duke. Richard and Kylan disclosed that they themselves were the sons of the Count of Valsemé, and Ailénor, the daughter of the Count of Héricourt. Their fathers—Rurik and Lyting Atlison—were both nephews of Normandy's first duke, Rollo, and thereby first cousins to Rollo's son and heir, William Longsword.

Garreth pondered that. From what he understood, the brothers Atlison had served Rollo since the founding of Normandy, twenty-two years past. He could not help but wonder where their personal loyalties lay in the matter of Francia's crown—with the exiled Carolingian or the Robertian usurpers.

Duke William himself had shifted his loyalties—something his sire had staunchly refused to do. Whilst Rollo lived, he and his barons had steadfastly supported the throne of the Carolingians, then held in the person of Charles the Simple—the same Charles who had granted Rollo his fiefdom in Francia and created him "duke."

Even when most other Frankish barons of the realm revolted and supplanted Charles, the Normans—along with the Acquitainians—remained faithful. But on the death of Rollo—and, soon after, that of Charles—the political landscape altered once more. The Robertians solidified their position, winning a crucial victory over the Norsemen of the Loire. The Acquitainians then swore fealty to the Robertians, soon followed by Normandy's new duke. In pledging their oaths, they turned their shoulders on Charles's son and rightful heir who dwelled in exile at the court of his uncle, King Athelstan.

The thought of the young Carolingian drew Garreth's thoughts back in time once more.

At the first of the uprising, Charles's queen and their small child, Louis, had remained in his eastern kingdom, that of Lorraine, the source of the king's problems. Charles had unwisely shown open favoritism for their people. When he replaced his high officials with Lorrainers, his barons revolted, led by Robert, the powerful Marquis of Neustria. Aiding Robert was another mighty baron—Robert's son-in-law, Raoul, Duke of Burgundy.

While Charles was engaged in Lorraine, Robert usurped the throne and saw himself crowned. Scarcely a year passed when Robert fell in battle against Charles at Soissons. Charles was routed in the combat, however, and the crown snatched up by Raoul.

'Twas at this time another grasping baron broke from the others and gave challenge to all—Herbert II, Count of Vermandois, and brother-in-law to Raoul. Through deceit, he entrapped Charles and imprisoned him. Queen Eadgifu fled with four-year-old Louis across the Channel to the court of her father, King Edward.

Charles later died, immured at Péronne. That was scarcely a year after Rollo's own death. But between the two deaths—just after Rollo's passing—Vermandois took Charles from his prison and forced William Longsword's allegiance.

Garreth rubbed his jaw. He guessed 'twas at that time William took Vermandois's daughter, Leutgarde, to wife, forming yet another bond of blood in the perfidy.

Not long after, interestingly enough, Hugh, son of the late king, Robert, also made an offer of marriage across the Channel—a move Garreth deemed infinitely wise.

Hugh himself—through his newly acquired titles as Count of Paris, Anjou, Blois, Touraine, and Marquis of Neustria—wielded, in actuality, more power than any other man in Francia, including King Raoul. Hugh had, in truth, refused the crown on his father's death, having no desire to hold, and then need defend, a much weakened throne in a fragmented kingdom.

Gauging the political airs, Hugh shrewdly sought an alliance with none other than Athelstan, Edward's successor and one of the most revered and well-connected sovereigns of the day. Through marriage alliances, Athelstan was already affiliated to many of the courts and thrones of Europe. He was also now guardian of the last of the Carolingians, Louis.

Garreth opened the door of the chamber and stood in its portal looking out on the grounds of the ducal palace.

Hugh, he believed, would support Louis when the time came. His informal exchanges with the man had been most encouraging while in Paris. But the restoration of Louis

would also require the support of another powerful baron—
that of Duke William Longsword.

Despite his changing loyalties, he might still prove himself to be the man his father was.

Originally, Garreth knew, the Norman barons had found
their new duke lacking. Not only was William dovish by
nature, but also as imprudent as the late Charles. He displayed open preference for the native people of Francia,
surrounding himself in court and council with Franks, re-
placing many of the faithful Norman warriors who had long
served his father. William reaped like results as had Charles
with his impolitic dealings. Earlier this year, and with few
exceptions, the barons of Normandy revolted against him.

But 'twas then, in the darkest hour of crisis, that the fires
of his Norse ancestors flamed to life in his breast. Heading
a handful of faithful barons and their troops, William
stormed out of Rouen and overwhelmed those who stood
against him.

In the midst of triumph, more good news awaited. The
duke's Breton mistress had given birth to a son.

The victory and the birth changed William. The dragon
had awakened. He now ruled with new authority, and his
barons rallied about him. Added to that, he recognized the
babe, Richard, as his heir—born not of the wife pressed
upon him and whose offspring would bind him eternally to
Vermandois, but born of a woman of his own choosing, his
mistress, Sprota.

'Twas difficult to say where William would place his
loyalties in time to come. Circumstance had driven him to
pay homage to Vermandois, then Raoul. But prior to those
coercions, he had supported his father in arms for the cause
of the Carolingians.

Wherever his loyalties now lay, Athelstan need know.

'Twas why, Garreth acknowledged, that he himself now
stood on Norman soil—come to test the temperature of the
ducal waters.

Garreth stepped outside the chamber and considered with
a wry twist of humor that 'twas lamentable Athelstan had
forged no marriage ties with the house of Normandy.

'Twould reinforce his mission here as it had in Paris. But the king was depleted of sisters, and the duke was still bound to Leutgarde, whether he bedded her or not.

Closing the door behind him, he started across the courtyard. Richard and Kylan had gone ahead to make his presence known. He was to join them in the Great Hall, where the court now gathered for the evening meal. He hoped the twins would be able to arrange for an early audience with the duke, if not an informal presentation this eve.

Garreth's thoughts quickened ahead—to the duke, to the court, and to the lovely and captivating Ailénor.

A cheery warmth blossomed in his chest, and he grew impatient to see her. Sweet Ailénor—the only woman to ever truly knock him from his feet.

Thoughts of Ailénor hummed in his mind as Garreth approached the palace, an impressive structure proclaiming the might and wealth of its duke. More a "tower keep" than traditional hall, it rose tall and square to a considerable height.

Garreth followed those others now converging on the hall and mounted the flight of timbered stairs leading to the entrance floor.

Upon entering the keep, he found himself on a level obviously occupied by the officers of the garrison. Many of the men whom he accompanied into the building—those of the soldiery—now separated from the others and headed down a passage, presumably to the Lesser Hall to take their meal with their comrades.

Following Richard's instructions, Garreth climbed a second set of stairs spiraling to the upper floor. Gaining the top of the flight, he passed through a barrel-headed doorway and entered the lower end of the Great Hall.

To the left rose columns, arched over and curtained between with costly painted fabrics, screening off the main hall from the drafts and the traffic of servants at the entrance end.

To his right, servants bustled back and forth with jugs of wine and rounds of bread from the buttery and the pantry. More servers hastened to and from the passageway that lay between the service rooms and obviously led down to the kitchens and likely a storage cellar as well.

Garreth made his way through the activity toward the main body of the hall, approached through two widely spaced and undraped pillars. His eyes strained ahead, skimming the gathering for a glimpse of rich auburn hair.

His gaze continued to travel the room as he entered. Stepping aside from the brisk flow of traffic to complete his search, he nearly blundered into two men, standing beside the column there.

Garreth began to pardon himself, but the words stilled on his tongue as he looked on them—hall servants who seemed oddly out of place, one with a pock-riddled face, the other with overly large and protruding eyes.

Neither man took notice of him, but continued to peer intently into the hall. Inexplicably disquieted by the men, Garreth looked to see if their interest might be held by the duke himself. He scanned the room—a spacious, high-raftered chamber, handsomely appointed, and crowded with brightly clad nobles and their equally resplendent ladies.

The dais stood at the far end, where the massive chair of the duke stood empty before the high table, beneath a canopy of crimson and gold.

Garreth beheld none to match the description he possessed of William Longsword. Still, the two servants continued to stare, their interest sharpened on something particular in the hall. Garreth followed their line of sight to the upper gallery that overlooked the hall. There a swath of scarlet and patch of green-blue caught his eye. A nobleman waited as his lady hurriedly joined him, settling her veil over her hair—a deep, dark, and very singular shade of red.

Ailénor. His heart leapt as his lips formed her name, yet he gave it no voice. He saw her face only a scant moment before she turned to the noble, giving her back to those below.

Garreth's eyes narrowed over the man. He was impressive in stature, tall and broad of shoulder, with striking silver-blond hair—not that of an aged man, but rather that rare Nordic white, bright and shining and whiter still where contrasted against his scarlet mantle.

The man was far from old, Garreth observed, though older than himself. To Garreth's consternation, he looked fit and vigorous and quite totally enamored of the lady who stood before him.

The man smiled warm and deep as he caught up the lady's fingers and pressed his lips to the back of her hand. Turning it over, he pressed a more intimate kiss to her palm, then her wrist, and higher still as he tugged her closer. She yielded with ease and spread her hands upon his chest. Pulling the veil from her rich auburn tresses, the noble trailed his fingertips down her spine to the small of her back, then drew her behind the pillar and out of sight.

Garreth bristled, taking a half step forward. A fusion of anger and jealousy surged through his veins, and his heart thudded hard and heavy. It pounded solid still as Ailénor moved back into sight, plainly affected by what had transpired behind the pillar. The noble's hand remained resting at her waist, while she smoothed order back to her hair.

Garreth caught her profile then. She smiled and laughed and gave a mock scolding with her forefinger before gracing her companion with a swift kiss upon his cheek, retrieving her veil as she did. Resettling the piece, she placed her hand on the noble's arm and accompanied him across the gallery toward the stairs. Though Garreth could no longer see her face, it seemed she carried contentment in her every step.

A storm of emotion crashed through Garreth. He stood unmoving, battling against the violence. Never had he considered Ailénor might be married. But then, at first, neither had he considered her a lady, given her state of dress and dishevelment, her unbound locks, and the very fact she had been climbing in a tree.

A brusque voice sounded beside him, jarring Garreth from his thoughts. He turned to find the head butler berating the two idle servants and ordering them off to fetch fresh casks of wine from the cellar. Unsmiling, the men moved away and followed their superior down the kitchen passage.

Garreth stepped farther into the hall, his pace much slowed, his spirit dampened. Threading through the press of people, his gaze impulsively sought Ailénor and the stairs she must now be ascending with her lover. Garreth spied a flight of steps rising just beyond an archway on the opposite side of the hall. 'Twas wrapped in shadows, and he could not help but wonder whether the couple lingered there.

Stabbed anew by the green horn of jealousy, he rebuked himself soundly and turned away. He had no claims on Ailénor or cause to behave thusly. 'Twas his own selfish interest and shortsightedness that led him to believe her to be a virginal maid. Quite obviously she was of marriageable age and likely wed. The man, then, would be her husband. Or possibly her betrothed. Or, if mayhap she were already widowed, a love interest. Recalling their ease and familiarity with one another stirred Garreth's blood to a bubble. Ailénor suited neither the image of a staid widow nor, did he wish to believe, a wanton one.

Garreth pondered the puzzle of Lady Ailénor. Would she be given to climbing trees for kittens in one instant, and in the next to sharing stolen moments of passion on balconies and stairways?

Garreth dismissed his vexatious thoughts. He forced the matter of Ailénor to the back of his mind and concentrated on his mission in Normandy. Restless and as irritable as a boar, his gaze ranged the hall for sight of the duke. But as it did so, a scarlet mantle and one of green-blue once more caught his eye, this time near the dais. There Ailénor and her noble approached a second couple—a man with golden hair and a woman with ebony plaits flowing over her shoulders.

Garreth pressed his lashes shut and opened them again, thinking his eyes played him a trick and that he saw double again. The golden-haired warrior stood a shade taller than the other, but facially the men's features were remarkably similar. Kinsmen to be sure. Brothers, he guessed, and from their attire men of import.

His gaze returned to Ailénor's back, trailing over the creamy veil covering her hair, then downward over the luminous green-blue mantle that so thoroughly concealed her form. He found himself wishing she would turn in his direction and take note of him.

"You appear better for your bath." A hand clamped Garreth firmly on the shoulder, and he recognized Richard's cheerful voice.

"I am much indebted." Garreth met him with a smile. "Not only to be clean, but the water's heat pulled the soreness from my bones. I vow, I rolled over more fruit than I realized and bear bruises aplenty."

Richard laughed, and as their smiles slackened, Garreth began to ask of the two noblemen where Ailénor stood. But Kylan chose that moment to appear, grinning widely, with a golden-haired maid on one arm and a raven-tressed one on the other, both beauties of exception.

"Word of your gallant rescue of the fair Ailénor has spread quickly, Garreth of Tamworth. Now all the ladies clamor to meet you." Kylan gave a mirthful wink and nodded first to one maid, then the other. "May I present to you our sisters, Marielle and Gisèle."

One after the other, the maids dipped into curtsies, their eyes grazing and fluttering over him as they did.

"And this," Richard added as he retreated a pace, widening the circle for another lady to join them, "is our cousin Etainn, Ailénor's sister."

A striking maid with an incredible snowfall of hair stepped forward. Upon her gloved hand, she carried a hooded goshawk, snowy white with a sprinkling of black across its feathers. She, too, dropped into a brief curtsy, regarding Garreth with crystal blue eyes, not unlike Ailénor's.

"You saved our dear cousin?" Marielle touched his arm lightly, drawing back his interest.

"Did you truly find her in a tree?" Gisèle abandoned Kylan's arm and pressed closer. "We are all so amazed that she should climb one."

"More, that she should *jump* from one," Etainn added

in a surprisingly low-pitched voice. She studied him closely as she stroked the bird's chest. "Tell me, do you hawk?"

Another maid pushed eagerly into their circle. "Do tell us of the Saxon court."

"And of His Majesty, King Athelstan . . ." Yet another joined, followed by more, all wreathed in smiles.

Garreth found himself suddenly surrounded amidst a bevy of court lovelies. Futilely he attempted a glance in Ailénor's direction to assure she was still there, but the others so engaged him, he could neither look to her nor ask his own questions of the man who held Ailénor's heart.

Besieged, Garreth looked helplessly to Richard and Kylan whose eyes crinkled with merriment and whose shoulders vibrated with unvoiced laughter.

"You've gained favor swiftly at Duke William's court," Richard tossed blithely.

"Best accept the burdens of fame graciously and savor them while you may." Kylan chuckled. "Who knows what the morrow brings."

But as the press of ladies filled Garreth's vision and hearing, he found his heart filled with Ailénor.

Ailénor tarried in her chamber. She smoothed imaginary wrinkles from her pale gold gown, restraightened the jeweled brooch securing her ivory mantle, then plucked up the disk of highly polished steel and observed herself for a hundreth time—checking hair, eyes, teeth, and the tiny scar beneath her chin to determine if it was truly noticeable.

She released a sigh of exasperation and set the mirror aside.

By now Garreth was in the Great Hall, drawing the attentions of the court maidens. Being so compellingly handsome and virile a man, she imagined 'twould take little time for the ladies there to lay claim to him.

The corner of Ailénor's mouth twisted with annoyance—annoyance with herself. She had dallied too long. But even had she accompanied Garreth into the hall, he would have likely soon forgotten her. The court was filled with comely women, a healthy portion unmarried. Then, too, there were her cousins and sister. As much as she loved them, she oftentimes felt inadequate by comparison.

Marielle, her cousin, was utterly beautiful and possessed a treasure of golden-blond hair. Blondes, of course, were the current ''ideal,'' and men pursued them avidly.

On the other hand, her cousin, Gisèle—though ebony-haired like her mother, Lady Brienne—was absolutely exquisite. She never wanted for suitors.

Etainn, her own sister, was exceptional—breathtaking, really, with her rare silver-white hair, the same as their father's. With a falcon ever present on her wrist, Etainn possessed an aura of mystery and magnetism that held men enthralled. Scarcely fourteen, Etainn seemed unaware of the spell she wove over them.

Ailénor took up the mirror again, feeling dismally inadequate to the moment. Her own hair shone of a deep, woody red—the same shade as her mother's. Personally she loved the color and oftentimes received compliments on it. But red was red, not blond. She also had to acknowledge that there were those men who simply did not favor red hair of any kind on a woman.

Added to that, she knew herself to be overly tall, which served only to intimidate men. If she observed correctly, men preferred their women more petite and fragile, who made them feel all the more manly and protective—and fired their possessive natures as well. Unfortunately for herself, she looked men of average height nearly in the eye. She could be thankful that among the full-blooded Norse who still comprised the significant portion of men in the duchy, many were on the tall side. Those she looked in the chin.

Considering herself in the mirror once again, she pressed her lips to a line and gave a small sigh, setting the piece aside. She feared the other maids would totally outshine her, captivating Garreth and leaving her to roam the hall forgotten.

''My lady, are you still here?'' Felise appeared in the portal of the adjoining chamber and, due to her affliction of shortsightedness, squinted to better see her charge. ''The horn will soon sound for supper, and you have yet to greet your parents. Lord Lyting arrived from the Contentin just a little while past and has been with your mother. Hurry now, they wait below.''

"*Oui*, Felise. Can I tell them of Ena? Does her stomach still ache?''

"*Non*. But she is slightly warm to the touch. I bathed her with herb waters, and she is sleeping comfortably. I will repeat the procedure in the coming hour as your aunt, Lady Brienne, suggested. You might tell your *maman* and *papa* that. Now best you be along.'' She gestured toward the door. "And mind you take care around that Saxon wolf.''

Ailénor chuckled. Crossing to her lifelong nursemaid, she gave her an affectionate hug.

"You worry for naught, Felise. There be ladies aplenty in the hall to consume his attention. Likely I've already melted from his thoughts completely.''

Ailénor tried to make light of the words, but inside her heart sank, believing her words to be true. She dropped her gaze away.

"But I see he has far from melted from your thoughts.'' Felise drew Ailénor's gaze back, placing a curled finger beneath her chin. "Guard your heart, child. I'd not see him bring you grief.'' She emphasized her words with a stern nod of her head, but her eyes held only concern. "Now, be along with you, before the servants are stacking away the trestles once more.''

Ailénor felt her heartstrings tangle, that Felise could so easily read her. She felt them tangle again at the prospect of facing Garreth. How completely he affected her.

Giving a final smoothing to her gown and adjustment to her mantle, she bid Felise good eve and departed the chamber.

Descending the stairs from the gallery, Ailénor lingered on the last step. Veiled in shadows, she directed her gaze through the arched pillars and into the hall, and scanned the vibrant sea of people collected there.

Garreth was not to be seen.

Ailénor's pulse slipped a beat, and she felt a sting of disappointment. But only a portion of the hall was visible from the stairs. Surely he was in attendance somewhere within. Leaving the steps, she crossed the small expanse and paused at the pillars. Straightening her spine and squaring her shoulders, she entered the Great Hall.

Ailénor's eyes swept left and right. She nodded greetings to several she knew, and proceeded on, searching the room for the handsome Saxon who had so suddenly invaded her life. Ailénor halted abruptly as her gaze locked on his tall figure across the room.

As predicted, a crush of women enveloped him. His dark head and shoulders towered above theirs, even as he bent to them in ardent conversation.

If her heart had bobbed on a low tide of self-confidence before, Ailénor felt as though an anchor had just attached itself and sank it completely to the bottom of her emotional soul.

Dispirited, she moved off to seek her parents.

Garreth lifted his head, laughing congenially at one of the women's witticisms. He took the opportunity to glance in the direction of the dais. The sight of a maiden moving toward it stayed his gaze completely.

She floated like a vision through the crowd, arrayed in a gown of pale gold and a mantle of ivory, her dark red hair rippling to her hips in fiery contrast. Ailénor. Was it she? His pulse quickened. Truly it must be. For the briefest of moments, she glanced in his direction—the most bewitching woman on earth.

Garreth watched as she approached the silver-blond warrior and his blue-mantled lady. As clearly as if the skies opened up and a bolt of lightning struck him straight through, he compassed the truth of the matter. The woman who now turned toward the maid, though lovely indeed, was not Ailénor. She could only be her mother.

His spirits shot heavenward. Darting a glance to Etainn, then back to the noble with star-white hair, he marked the family resemblances. Obviously this was Etainn's and Ailénor's father, Lyting Atlison, the Comte de Héricourt.

Garreth looked on as Ailénor embraced her parents. One by one, she kissed them on both cheeks, then turned and likewise greeted the other couple. Certain the men were brothers, Garreth concluded the second couple to be none other than the Comte and Comtesse de Valsemé, Ailénor's uncle and aunt.

Garreth felt buoyant and utterly the fool—albeit a happy one—for his mistake. He grinned hugely as he continued to look on Ailénor and her mother, where they stood side by side.

"I see Ailénor captures your eye, *mon ami*." Richard moved to his side. "But does she stir your humor as well?"

"You need forgive me." Garreth's smile did not flag. "I seem to be seeing double in the hall tonight—beside yourselves, and the amazing resemblance of your fathers, I mistook Ailénor's mother for herself."

"They do favor one another," Richard concurred. "But not so greatly when you observe them more closely."

"Mayhap we should warn you that likenesses run strong in our families." Kylan leaned closer. "You would be surprised."

"Really?" Garreth brushed glances with Kylan but did not follow out the thought. Instead he centered his interest on Ailénor.

"She is rather tall for a woman," he mused, then realized 'twas the very reason, when he lay sprawled atop her in the orchard, they fit together so perfectly.

"A fine attribute, indeed," he murmured with a wistful smile, vaguely aware of the twins exchanging glances.

"We have sorely missed your presence these past months at Héricourt, my sweet." Lyting smiled at his daughter. "Tell me, are you happy here at the court of Rouen?"

"*Oui, papa. Très heureuse.* Though I do miss you all hugely," Ailénor confessed.

It had been three long months since she left Héricourt and her beloved family. A week past, her mother and siblings arrived at court in anticipation of the ducal celebrations. Disappointingly, her father did not accompany them, having been summoned to some urgency in the Contentin. Now, elated to see him and overjoyed that her family was once more reunited, Ailénor felt tears burn the back of her eyes.

Her mother hugged her gently, understanding carried in the smiling warmth of her golden-brown eyes. "You know, your sister Etainn has been pressing us to allow her to join you and Marielle."

"As does our Gisèle," Brienne, her aunt, added with a light shake of her head and a sigh.

"Richard and Kylan have been keeping close watch of you two, I trust?" Rurik raised a meaningful brow.

"To a fault, Uncle." Ailénor gave a small inward laugh, remembering their swords, flashing in defense of her virtue just a short while ago. "Truly, you must not worry."

"Fathers ever worry over their daughters." Lyting smiled warmly, chiding, "Or did you not notice in recent years while you have been growing into such a lovely young woman?"

"Of course I have, *Papa*." Ailénor flushed under his praise and gave a squeeze to his arm. She looked again to her mother. "*Maman* looks radiant tonight, do you not think?"

Her mother always looked beautiful, Ailénor thought, but suspected her father was responsible for the present glow in her cheeks tonight.

"And such a glorious cloak. Is it new?" Ailénor fingered the luminous cloth, exceptional in its weave and its color most rare—a stunning blue yet green in its shadows. Given to the light the colors vied—a Nordic fjord and an emerald vale.

"A gift from your father just now." Ailinn raised loving eyes to Lyting.

"The color so complements your mother's hair, I could not resist," he confessed. "In truth, I purchased additional cloth and ordered a second made, knowing 'twould be equally stunning on you, Ailénor. 'Twill be delivered to your chamber during supper.''

"*Merci, Papa.*'' Ailénor pressed an impulsive kiss to his cheek.

The deep, mellow tones of an ivory horn sounded just then, signaling the arrival of the duke. Ailénor looked to see William Longsword and his three companions making their way toward the dais.

"I see the duke is entertaining the king's men this eve. Burgundians, are they not?'' Lyting directed his observations to his brother.

Rurik nodded grimly. "The three arrived this morn. Raoul keeps close watch of Normandy's duke.''

"As he does all those who move within the duchy.''

Ailénor detected the disapproval in her father's and uncle's voices. At the same time the reason for Garreth's presence in Normandy flickered through her mind.

"I see Leutgarde is still in absence from the court.'' Her father's voice disrupted her thoughts.

"Shh, love. They grow near,'' Ailinn cautioned, then added, "Leutgarde summers at Bayeux.''

"And Sprota at Fécamp with the babe, Richard,'' Brienne whispered with a tilt of the brow.

Listening, Ailénor found she could not help but feel sorry for Leutgarde, a pawn in the games of men. She hoped for a more agreeable marriage for herself, one like her parents' or that of her aunt and uncle. Theirs were ones of rare happiness.

As Duke William approached with the Burgundians, Ailénor observed a subtle stiffness pervade her father's and uncle's stances. Even the smiles on her mother's and aunt's lips seemed a trifle cool as they presented themselves to Raoul's men.

"Cousin,'' Duke William greeted Ailénor as she dipped into a curtsy before him. A tall man with golden hair, much like her uncle's, the duke was a passably handsome man, Ailénor believed, and though he wielded great power and authority, he was but eight and twenty years.

The Burgundians followed with greetings of their own, each bowing over the ladies' hands, the last man, named

Faron, tarrying a trifle overlong over Ailénor's.

"The beauty of the court doth blind this eve, Duke William." Faron measured Ailénor with undue interest.

Ailénor fought her disgust. The oily little man revulsed her, especially when his eyes slid to her breasts.

Judging him to be of less than average height, she took distinct and unrepentant pleasure in rising from her curtsy to the full of her own, and then staring back down upon him.

A trill of pipes signaled the commencement of supper. Ailénor's heart skipped as she reclaimed her hand from the Burgundian, fearing he might insist on sharing her trencher. Mercifully, Kylan chose that moment to appear.

"I believe you promised to share a place at table with me this eve, cousin Ailénor." He bowed graciously, a mischievous twinkle in his eyes, then slipped a glance at his father.

Rurik gave a faint nod of his head, approval reflected in his eyes.

Kylan maneuvered Ailénor quickly and deftly away from the dais and escorted her toward the far side of the hall.

"You need not remove me to the kitchens to save me from the Burgundians." Ailénor laughed, seeing they neared the entrance end.

"Was I?" Merriment laced his words.

"Were you not?"

Kylan stole a glance back toward the dais. "*Vraiment. Ici*, here. The others hold us a place at table just ahead."

Good for his word, their numerous siblings gathered at the next trestle, draped in a snowy white linen and set with goblets, spoons, and rounds of bread trenchers stacked at the ends. Kylan conducted her to an open space beside Richard and Marielle. At the familiar trill of the pipes, signaling the blessing, they stood with heads bowed before their places.

A moment later, benediction complete, Kylan stepped back, allowing Ailénor additional room to seat herself.

She was still settling herself when the edge of her vision caught a blur of dark forest-green. She glanced toward it and found Garreth dropping down beside her.

Ailénor started, rising off her seat in surprise. Deftly Garreth caught her elbow and drew her back down.

"Forgive me for startling you, Lady Ailénor. I did not know until this moment what your cousins were about."

He glanced at Richard and Kylan who were chuckling to themselves, Kylan now seating himself with Gisèle, to the other side of him.

Garreth returned his interest to Ailénor. " 'Twould seem they are intent on our sharing a cup and trencher this eve. If it pleases you, I know it pleases me, and I promise to be most attentive."

He disarmed her with the most engaging of smiles, and Ailénor felt a small thrill pass through her. Swiftly it turned to a jolt as their thighs chanced to brush, recalling to Ailénor their previous, more intimate entanglements.

"Pardon," he murmured.

"*Mais, oui.*" She gave a quick nod, her heart skipping madly. Happy as she was to sup with Garreth, she shivered at the thought of the coming hours she would share with him. It promised to be a very long meal indeed.

Servants rapidly appeared with ewers, basins, and towels. Ailénor thrust her fingers over the bowl a trifle too quickly, bumping them into Garreth's. She began to pull back, but he caught the tips of them, then drew them into the bowl with his and held them there.

Cool, fragrant water, perfumed with rose petals, poured over their joined hands, a soothing sensation of silken liquid over warm skin. A fragile pink petal caught between their fingers.

Releasing his hold of Ailénor, Garreth captured the fragile treasure on a fingertip and lay it in the palm of her hand, gifting her with it. Ailénor sucked in her breath as his fingertip pulled away, grazing the sensitive flesh of her palm. She avoided his gaze altogether and reached for the towel on the server's arm, her palm still tingling. A very long meal indeed!

Additional servants now appeared to fill the goblets with spiced wine and distribute the trenchers of day-old bread along the table, one to each couple.

"You look greatly changed since last I saw you," Garreth commented, a smile tilting his lips. "I can only wonder if you possess as many bruises as I."

Ailénor warmed under his admiring gaze and thought of a few unmentionable places where she did have bruises. She began to reply, but at that precise moment another pair of cousins, Brand and Delling, installed themselves directly across from herself and Garreth.

Garreth's brows shot upward. Two golden-haired men, possessing identical features and appearing only slightly younger than Richard and Kylan, regarded him closely from where they sat opposite. In coloring and countenance, they greatly favored Marielle.

Laughter rippled along the table.

"We tried to warn you," Kylan reminded. "And there be more still."

"More?" Garreth voiced with amazement.

"Aimery and Tyr," Richard supplied. "But they are not present tonight. They are delayed at Ivry where they are in fosterage to the castellan, Ketil, and his wife Aleth."

"Our father begat his sons in sets of two, and the girls singly," Kylan added blithely.

"Mind you, our uncle begat near as many children, doing so one by one," Brand added in a rich voice.

"But never was he known to complain," Delling rejoined with devilish good humor and brought a gasped response from the ladies.

Garreth glanced the length of the table in both directions and, noting the marked similarities there, realized that he and Ailénor would be sharing their trencher under the scrutiny of nearly her entire combined family.

Ailénor's cousins quickly caught him up in introductions. Brand and Delling proved second oldest to Richard and Kylan. Next came Marielle, then Gisèle, both of whom he had already met. The other set of twins, Aimery and Tyr, as explained, were in absence. The youngest daughters, Brietta and baby Linette, took their meal in an upper chamber with their nursemaid.

Ailénor next presented her side of the family, directing his attention to where Etainn sat, her hawk resting on a perch behind her. Beside Etainn sat Galen, their brother, who bore the same striking silver-white hair as Etainn. Galen, Ailénor informed, was eldest after she herself. Farther down the table sat her younger brothers—Brenden, Lucán, and Michan, who seemed occupied trying to quiet faint mewling sounds coming from beneath the table.

"My sister Adelis is sleeping with Brietta tonight," Ailénor continued. "You will most often find them together, hand in hand, for they are the best of friends. The littlest, Ena, is not feeling well and stays with Felise upstairs. I believe you met most of the younger ones in the orchard today."

"So I did." *And the aggressive nursemaid as well*, Garreth thought to himself. "An impressive family."

"And you?"

"I have none."

"No family? None at all?" Ailénor's brows twinged upward.

"My parents and sister died some years past." Garreth diverted his gaze. He wouldn't mention his half siblings or the stepmother who had cheated him out of his titles and lands.

The pipes sounded once more, signaling the first course. Servers bore great platters from the kitchens, parading through the hall to first present them at the high table. Meanwhile, butlers reappeared to top off the goblets with more wine.

Supper commenced, each course announced with a trill of notes. Being the last meal of the day, 'twas of lighter fare and fewer courses. Still, meat and fowl were served in variety, some sauced, some in pasties. Added to this were leek and onion dishes, eel, a vegetable pottage, fresh bread, and a compote of walnuts and pears pickled in honey.

Ailénor found Garreth proved most attentive, selecting choice morsels of meat, offering her their goblet before he drank, and entertaining her with a steady stream of light repartee. In truth, the banter that passed up and down the table made the entire meal seem a great family occasion, as those often shared at Héricourt and Valsemé—one that easily embraced the Saxon, who was, for all purposes, yet a stranger.

As evening deepened and their conversations took diverse paths, Ailénor came to realize that despite being surrounded by her beautiful sister and cousins, Garreth's interest remained concentrated upon her own self. This pleased her immensely. And caused her to tremble like a custard—acutely self-conscious, and so very aware of the potent man beside her.

Garreth's eyes traveled to Ailénor for the hundredth time this night. He steeled himself when she suddenly bent to retrieve a fallen napkin, causing the neckline of her dress to drop slightly away from her breasts, allowing him—from his height—a most tantalizing glimpse of cleavage. Garreth drew a stabilizing breath. He was as rock-hard as he knew he would be.

Ailénor looked up just then, her eyes colliding with his. She began to straighten, but he didn't withdraw his gaze.

"I cannot imagine how such a beautiful maid could escape the marital knot without getting caught before now," Garreth remarked, their eyes still locked.

Ailénor stilled, astonished by his words, and at the same time mindful the others watched them. Judging from his tone, she believed he meant to flatter her, that his words were meant as no insult or to emphasize the fact that she was yet unmarried. Still, lost in his liquid brown gaze, she could scarce form a response.

Richard came to her rescue. "Our fathers are Danish by birth and, though protective of all their women, hold to the customs of the North. There, women are given a voice in the choice of a husband."

Garreth blinked in surprise. "Women may accept or refuse their suitors?"

The others nodded along the table.

Turning back to Ailénor, a teasing grin stole up to his eyes. "And did you refuse all your suitors? Or have you a husband or a betrothed lurking somewhere?" He plucked up the tablecloth sportively and pretended to look beneath.

"*Non.* No husband." Ailénor whisked the cloth from his fingers with an admonishing look, wondering if he sought a glimpse of ankle. "Or bethrothed. There have been suitors, of course," she added quickly lest he think her wanting in some wise.

"Of course." He grinned.

"And offers for my hand."

"I am not at all surprised." He waited a moment, but she held silent. "Might I ask what became of them?"

"Well, the first died on campaign of . . . well, of . . ." She cleared her throat. "Dysentery." She reached for the goblet and took a quick sip of wine.

"Dysentery." Garreth coughed into his hand. "Tragic. Many a good man has succumbed to the disease."

Ailénor saw that he shook his head with compassion, yet somehow he did not appear in the least bit remorseful for the man's plight. She lifted her chin and continued.

"The second died during an engagement against Flanders."

"He died in battle?"

She nodded, nibbling her lip, then cleared her throat once more. "He fell from his horse, and the beast took an arrow and fell atop him. Well . . ." She waved the remembered accounts of that event away with her hand and took up the goblet once more.

"The horse fell . . . I see." Garreth considered her words. "The Normans battle on horses—to advantage and disadvantage."

He caught Brand's and Delling's look. They were grinning as irreverently as were Richard and Kylan.

He glanced back to Ailénor. "Were there others?"

She hesitated a moment. "Actually, after having lost two prospective husbands, I thought perchance the Good Lord meant me to serve him as a religious. My family agreed that I go to the monastery of Levroux. Only we found I am not well suited for the religious life either."

Garreth tipped his head, intrigued. "And why was that, minx? Did the abbess catch you in her tree?"

Ailénor's eyes swung to his, and she found him grinning with that heart-quickening smile of his. She smiled, too. In truth, until that moment she had quite forgotten her reasons for leaving Levroux. But now recalling them, she knew there was no way she could confess them and risk his re-action or that of her many kindred who listened so intently at the table.

Certes. She was *not* well suited to the rigors of monastic life and the discipline required. But her shortcomings had been more than ones of tardiness at services or woefully wandering thoughts during prayer.

Increasingly there had come upon her a strong sense of fate, of destiny. A destiny that lay heavily upon her heart, bidding her beyond the convent walls.

Then, too, there followed vivid, recurring dreams, pos-sessing an eerie realism. Dreams of a man who swept into her life and changed it forevermore. She could never quite see his face. Still, the feeling, the strong pull to leave, re-mained until it became so overpowering that she finally succumbed and returned home.

No sooner there, word came that Marielle wished to join her brothers, Richard and Kylan, at the ducal court. Ailé-nor's parents encouraged her to join her cousin for a change, and so she did.

Coming back to herself, Ailénor found Garreth still wait-ing for her reply. She gazed on him pensively, through new eyes, a fluttery feeling building in her stomach and rising to her chest.

She groped for his question. He had wondered why she left the monastery.

"The Lord directs our paths, Garreth, wherever they lead. 'Twould seem, for now, mine leads to Rouen."

"As doth mine." Garreth's smile eased to a more sober look, his dark eyes reflective with something she could not name, but which caused her to flush. His smile returned, slowly lifting the corners of his mouth. "And to good pur-pose this day, I deem. Should ever you be in need of res-cuing again, my fair Ailénor, I promise to come promptly to your assistance."

Holding her gaze, he took up the goblet they shared, then, turning it round, sipped from the very place her lips had just touched.

Rurik drew on his goblet as he listened to a congenial dispute among the duke and the Burgundians as to whether elephants' legs were jointless or not.

Knowing Lyting and Ailinn had once seen one in Constantinople, he turned to his left to ask them of it. He found Lyting engrossed, staring across the hall, his interest fixed on Ailénor and the dark-haired Saxon.

"His name is Garreth of Tamworth." Rurik leaned slightly forward, speaking across Ailinn. "Richard and Kylan say he is a *thegn* of King Athelstan, a royal agent purchasing relics and holy objects in Francia."

"Do you believe that?" Lyting took a draft of ale, not taking his eyes from the couple.

"I am not certain. Richard and Kylan say he also bears his king's greetings to the duke. Anywise, they perceive no threat."

"Do our guests know of his presence?" Lyting indicated with a tip of his head toward the Burgundians, where they now rose with the duke and began to move from the dais.

" *Nei*. William is informed but thought not to bring attention to the Saxon while the king's hawks circle. Best see what he is about first. For the present, Richard and Kylan keep close watch of him. His visit here could be as he says. I dispatched a messenger to St. Ouen. The monks have, indeed, a completed Psalter in readiness, commissioned by the English monarch."

"What know you of these *thegns* of the royal household?" Lyting brought his eyes from the couple to Rurik's.

"Only that they are nobly born and of diverse ranks."

Lyting's gaze returned to the hall. "Garreth of Tamworth certainly does not look like a mere 'hall-*thegn*' to my eyes. He has too much presence about him."

Ailinn, who sat between the two men listening silently, smiled at this last and laid her hand to her husband's arm. "You look so grim, my darling. Do you fear the Saxon's mission here is to carry off our daughter as well?''

Lyting darted Ailinn a quick, stormy look. She burst into laughter and placed her hand to his chest. ''Do not worry, my love. After all, they are more than well chaperoned. What maid could enjoy even the slightest flirtation with such a brood hovering?''

Seeing that Lyting appeared yet unswayed, Ailinn patted his hand. ''Well, you continue your watch, but I must slip upstairs to check on Ena's fever.''

''I shall join you.'' Brienne rose from her chair. ''Ena was playing with Brietta and Adelis earlier. I need check on them and Linette as well.''

Taking leave of Rurik, Brienne caressed his arm with her fingers, which he promptly covered with his own hand and gave a gentle squeeze.

''I'll watch over Lyting while you ladies are gone.'' Rurik grinned, giving Brienne a spirited wink. His eyes fell to a spot on her gown as she began to move off.

''*Ástin mín.* You have stained your dress,'' he called after her. She stopped and examined the front of her skirt. ''Mayhap I should have fed you,'' he teased.

Brienne glanced up and caught Rurik's look. ''Later . . .'' She gave a wink back to him, a bright smile breaking over her face.

Brienne joined Ailinn, and they made their way across the hall, discussing the best method to remove mustard sauce from fabric. As they passed beneath the arched columns, leading to the stairs, Ailinn's eyes hesitated over a man standing a short distance away—a man with huge, bulbous eyes. Slowly he shifted the cask of wine from his shoulder and set it down. His great eyes continued to follow her.

A chill spilled down Ailinn's spine as she ascended the stairs with Brienne. Feeling his gaze continue to bore into her, she slowed her step, then stayed it altogether. Pivoting in place, she tossed her glance back down.

The man was gone. As was the cask.

''Is something amiss?'' Brienne halted on the step above her and followed the direction of her gaze.

Ailinn's brows gathered over her eyes as she scanned the vacant space below. Had her imagination run wholly rampant?

"*Non*. Naught is amiss." Ailinn dismissed the incident, not wishing to concern Brienne.

Turning, she followed her up the stairs, but a wintry cold spread through her bones.

Descending the stairs, Ailinn thought to herself how precious the children looked asleep. Ena rested cool and comfortable now, and Adelis and Brietta shared a pallet. The two should have been twins.

Brienne remained in her chamber, treating the stain on her gown, but she bid Ailinn to go on ahead and rejoin their husbands. She would be down momentarily.

Ailinn roused from her musing, a hushed voice catching her ear. She thought it spoke in the Gaelic tongue of her native homeland.

Halting at the bottom of the shadowy stairs, she glanced about only to find herself alone. She then looked toward the hall, through the portal, where the meal had ended and the tables were being disassembled.

A scraping sound brought her gaze back. She turned toward it, to behind the staircase. There, wrapped in deep shadows, a servant bent, stacking a dismantled trestle against the wall. It struck her as odd, yet she abandoned the thought as the servant moved into the torchlight, revealing a pock-ravaged face.

Ailinn stilled. His eyes burned into hers, then traveled past her shoulder. She heard a soft scuffing of shoes from behind. Slowly she turned, her stomach twisting into a fist-tight knot. A second man stood behind her, bearing another trestle from the hall—the man with the huge, protruding eyes.

A cold rush swept through her. She glanced from one to the other. Their eyes seemed to fix on her, intent and filled with purpose.

The man with the trestle started toward her. From the corner of her eye, she glimpsed the other coming forward from behind the stairs as well.

A small sound escaped Ailinn as the space shrank between them. She dropped back a pace, her retreat abruptly halted as her heel hit the step behind her.

Ailinn's breath left her, and her legs threatened to go liquid as the men continued their approach. She wondered wildly if her mind played her false. Servants stalking her? Why?

She lifted her foot, backing up one step, then another, clumsily catching her gown with her heel and hearing the fabric tear. She cared not at all.

Her pulse points throbbed fiercely as she watched the men close in on her. A rushing sound filled her ears, while a speckling of inky spots suddenly danced in her vision. Ailinn fought her light-headedness.

"*Elskan mín?* There you are." Lyting's voice broke through the haze enveloping her. He appeared in the archway, accompanied by Rurik.

Ailinn's eyes leapt to him as he came forward, the servants no longer there. She looked to the side and found them stacking the trestle with the other, behind the stairs.

Ailinn rushed down the few steps to the security of Lyting and slipped her arms about him. Just then Brienne appeared on the stairs above and began her descent.

"*Elskan mín*, your hands are as ice." Lyting covered hers with his own and began rubbing heat into them. "I shall have to warm you thoroughly, I see," he teased, then noted the distress in her face. "Does aught disturb you, my love?"

Seeing the servants move harmlessly away in the direction of the hall for more trestles, Ailinn thought she must be unsound to have imagined they were stalking her.

"I . . . *Non. C'est bien, mon amour.* I am fine. Though I could do with some fresh air, I think."

"An inspired suggestion," Rurik interjected, seeing Lyting pause and glance back through the portal. "Lyting could use a walk himself, to take his mind from Ailénor. At the moment, she is playing a game of *merles* with the Saxon. Lyting has been stewing that their heads are too close over the board. It matters not that her siblings and cousins still surround them.''

Brienne joined them, coming to Rurik's side, amused by his words. ''A walk sounds like a splendid idea. I can think of a few good reasons of my own.'' Her eyes sparkled mischievously.

Rurik grinned, for oftentimes he and Brienne took evening strolls at Valsemé, many of them ending most enjoyably at their secluded lake.

As they followed Lyting and Ailinn toward the hall's entrance, Rurik skimmed a final glance back toward the stairs. Something nettled at the edges of his mind. He could not recall ever seeing trestles stacked behind the staircase. Mayhap 'twas temporary. With the ducal celebrations about to officially commence, the keep burgeoned with guests. Additional tables crowded the halls. 'Twas likely storage space was scarce.

Still . . . Trestles stored behind the hall's stairs? Rurik could not banish a nagging apprehension that continued to climb through his senses.

''Come, my heart.'' Brienne slipped her arm through his. ''We have yet to discover whether the duke secretes a lake on these grounds. 'Twould be regrettable if there be none.

Rurik smiled into her eyes as he escorted her through the entrance portal. ''All the more reason to take our leave as soon as we may and repair to Valsemé.''

Wimund and Grimbold emerged from the shadows of the alcove, watching the foursome depart.

''We nearly had her,'' Wimund groused.

''Do not worry. She cannot have people about her all the time. There will be a better moment.''

Wimund's lips spread to a grin over stained teeth. ''A better moment and time aplenty to have our sport on her. Time aplenty to deliver her to the 'princess.' ''

''Patience,'' Grimbold counseled. ''She shall yet be ours. Count on it.''

Chapter Three

Garreth stood watching the Normans in the practice yard, intent on their methods of training.

Earlier, Lord Rurik demonstrated varied stratagems with spears. One particular feat—catching the weapon in flight and returning it without pause—left Garreth in total awe.

Now, as the Normans exercised their blades, his own hand itched to take up a length of steel and test his skill against them. Regrettably, he could not. To do so would reveal himself as a man of the sword and belie his purpose here.

Instead he directed his interest to the adjacent field where mounted soldiers—*chevaliers*—drilled with horses and sundry equipment. The Frankish penchant for mounted warfare ever fascinated Garreth. In England a man rode to battle but dismounted for the engagement itself. In Francia a *chevalier* remained horsed, the man and the beast becoming a single fighting unit in combat.

Surveying the field, he saw, to one side, that the younger aspiring *chevaliers* practiced with wooden horses. These they mounted without use of their hands—first unarmed, then burdened with shields and swords and, at times, long poles. The more proficient took turns leaping on and off the timbered forms from diverse directions—right, left, and from the rear. Only the most advanced worked with the live animals, vaulting into the saddles without touching the stirrups and with their blades drawn.

In the far right quadrant of the field, Garreth observed horsemen drill with lances, casting them at targets like spears, stabbing groundward to run through stuffed sacks, and charging straw opponents on wooden horses at speed, thrusting upward at the last moment to unsaddle their "foe."

Garreth rubbed his jaw, impressed, then came aware of Richard's approach.

One side of Richard's mouth kicked into a smile as he nodded toward the far field. "Would you care to test your skill with the lance?"

"And risk making a fool of myself? Nay, I think not." Garreth gave a small laugh, but wondered that Richard should think to make the suggestion for thus far he had presented himself to be no more than a royal collector of hallowed bones and sacred antiquities.

A slip of the tongue? A snare, perchance? Might Richard suspect his true station? Or did he simply offer genial conversation in a spirit of friendship?

Garreth chose to redirect matters.

" 'Tis said the duke stables the finest horseflesh in Francia. I would favor seeing the famed *destriers* of Normandy. 'Tis my understanding the warhorses are bred to great size and trained in specific war maneuvers."

"That they are," Richard returned with pride. "The stallions have already been put through their paces this morn, but if it interests you, we can visit the stables. Come.''

Together the two men headed back in the direction of the keep, passing near the archery range as they went. There Lord Lyting and his son, Galen, sharpened their skills with bows and arrows.

"You might enjoy this." Richard slowed his pace and came to a halt. "Galen grows better by the day, and my uncle's renown as an archer is excelled only by his repute as a seaman."

Garreth directed a glance to Richard at the last of his comment, but looked back in time to see Galen's arrow streak to the target and pierce dead center.

Lord Lyting stepped to his son's side, smiling, and bestowed his praise. For a moment their silver-blond heads bent together, discussing some point of bowmanship. Lyting then nocked an arrow, gestured to the one embedded in the target, and appeared to explain an aiming technique.

Galen stepped away as Lyting took up his stance. Drawing smoothly back on the string, Lyting anchored his aim, released, and, with a blur of wood and feathers, split the shaft of Galen's arrow in two.

Garreth's jaw slackened. Galen, for his part, only shook his head and grinned at his father, obviously having witnessed his sire's extraordinary skill many a time before.

Father and son launched into another discussion as they strode to the target and inspected the hit, unmindful of their spectators.

"He is called *Skarp-Øje*, 'Sharp-eye,' " Richard explained as he bid Garreth on.

Garreth fell into an easy stride beside him. "You say his ability as a seaman surpasses his mastery as an archer?"

"Upon the waters, he is known as 'Sjorefurinn,' the 'Sea Fox.' Lady Ailinn renders the best version of the tale that gained him that title. You might seek her out and ask her of it."

Garreth nodded thoughtfully, then his lips pulled into a smile, and he gave a shake of his head. "From what I beheld earlier of Lord Rurik's prowess with spears, and now that of Lord Lyting's with a bow and arrow, I vow I hold no desire to ever tangle with the brothers Atlison. Od's blood, I cringe to think what they must wreak with a sword.''

Richard chuckled. ''From one who *has* crossed steel with them in the practice yard, I would say the word 'cringe' is well put.''

As they closed upon the stable complex, Richard pointed out the various structures that housed a broad collection of horses from coursers, pacing horses, and trotters to rouncies, hobbies, and packhorses. The war stallions occupied a building of their own, while the brood mares were segregated in a separate enclosure, partitioned round with sturdy palings to forestall any untimely visits from overly zealous males.

Garreth's gaze alighted on a stable lad drawing open the gate to the mare enclosure. In the next instant a sight greeted his eyes that set his heart to racing—Ailénor riding atop a splendid golden courser, leading her brothers Brenden and Lucán out of the compound.

Seeing him, she smiled brightly and waved but did not slow her steed. Instead she reined the horse to the right and touched its flank, setting it to a light gallop as she conducted her brothers in the direction of the practice field and the palace gate beyond.

Garreth watched enrapt, unable to pull his eyes from her, nor possessing a desire to do so. 'Twas exhilarating simply to watch her for she moved with supreme grace and fluidity, one with the creature in glorious abandon.

The mare's legs reached out, slender and swift. The breeze its passage stirred lifted its flaxen mane and tail on the wind, as it did Ailénor's rich auburn tresses to flow out behind her.

Garreth's heart caught in his soul, and he recognized in that moment that he wanted her to remain in his life—for now and for all time.

''I thought 'twas the *destriers* that interested you,'' Richard uttered in a voice filled with levity as he matched the direction of Garreth's gaze.

"*Destriers* . . . Aye." Try as he might, Garreth could scarce form a coherent thought apart from Ailénor. " 'Tis unusual she rides a courser, is it not? I mean, 'tis a large animal for a woman, though she sits it well."

"Be not concerned. Ailénor is an excellent horsewoman. My uncle breeds horses of all manner at Héricourt, including *destriers*. He took Ailénor up in the saddle while she still wore swaddling cloths. Nowadays she requires a sizable mount due to her height and the length of her legs. Wouldn't want her slippers to drag on the ground riding a palfrey," Richard jested.

The memory of Ailénor's long silken legs, entwined about his in the orchard, flashed through Garreth's mind and sent a hot jolt to his loins. He cleared his throat.

"From what you have told me, I would have thought Lord Lyting would be more involved in sea ventures than horse breeding."

"He is, in part," Richard allowed. "He designs ships for my father, who maintains a number of vessels that trade regularly with England—from such places as Jorvik, Lindum, and Lundenburh. Now that the Contentin is part of Normandy, he is more preoccupied with improving the duchy's stock of warhorses. My uncle foresees the region as a prime place to raise *destriers* due to the limestone plains that will produce horses of strength and size."

Garreth knew the Contentin, along with the Avranchin, was a recent "gift" from King Raoul. The price of Norman fealty? he wondered, but did not dwell on it, giving his attention to Ailénor instead.

Beside him, Richard continued to remark upon Lord Lyting's experiments with crossbreeding, disclosing how his uncle had recently acquired a Barb from Spain to put to Héricourt's mares.

But Garreth only half heard, his concentration so absorbed with Ailénor. Disparate thoughts collided in his brain, rapidly realigning themselves and broaching a course he had yet to consider.

As Garreth faced the truth of his heart and the future that stretched before him, he knew, with sudden, pulse-pounding clarity, all he must do and the inexpressible rightness of it.

His decision made, he felt vitalized, awash with joy and brimming with purpose. Just when his heart was like to burst with excitement, Kylan's voice fractured his thoughts.

"Good news, Garreth!" Kylan bellowed as he approached. "Duke William will grant you an audience this coming hour. My father will meet you on the steps of the keep and accompany you to the ducal council chamber."

Heartened by this news, Garreth cast a last, longing look at Ailénor as she passed through the gate on her gilded steed.

He must collect himself, he knew—fulfill his mission and bring it to conclusion. Mayhap he could remain in Rouen an additional day or two, but then he must carry his accounts back to Athelstan and have done with his shaded involvement in the matters of the Frankish throne.

Once in England, he would need delay committing himself to a bride and explain his intentions to the king—tactfully and without offense to the sovereign's kinswomen. Then, upon the conferral of his new titles and lands, he intended to return to Francia, present himself to Ailénor and her family, and offer for her hand in marriage.

Ideas clicking through his mind, Garreth took leave of the twins and strode back toward his chamber to prepare for his imminent meeting with Duke William Longsword.

Lord Rurik conducted Garreth to the upper portion of the tower keep and proceeded to a massive oak door, banded with iron and flanked by two men-at-arms.

Acknowledging the Comte de Valsemé, the guards moved promptly to open the heavy door, obviously expecting the two men.

The council chamber proved stark in comparison to the Great Hall below, Garreth thought. Lime-washed walls glared at him, white and naked. Directly opposite stood the duke's imposing highseat, positioned at the head of a column of simpler, low-backed chairs that faced one another in two strict lines. In a far corner squatted a brass brazier, unlit in this warm season, and against the wall, beside the entrance portal, sat a small service table holding a tray of fruits and a glazed pitcher of wine.

Garreth's gaze traveled across the chamber to the room's single window. There stood William Longsword, Count of Rouen, Duke of Normandy.

He turned at their entry, one arm still bent behind his back, the other half raised, a goblet in hand. Garreth had seen Duke William at a distance last night, but now, viewing him in close proximity, he realized the man to be younger than he guessed, younger than even himself.

Their eyes met, and Garreth felt the duke's needle-sharp scrutiny. It lasted for but an instant, then William's countenance altered. The crease between his brows dissolved, and his mouth eased into the semblance of a smile.

"Ah, the Saxon who saved our dear Ailénor from her plight in the pear tree—Athelstan's *thegn*."

"Garreth of Tamworth, Your Grace." Garreth gave a short bow from the waist.

"Tamworth." William considered that, coming forward partway across the room. "King Athelstan grew to manhood at Tamworth, I am told, raised up by his aunt, the famed 'Lady of the Mercians.' "

"Aye, Your Grace. Athelflaed was King Edward's sister and wife to Athelred, Lord of Mercia. Truly a remarkable woman."

" 'Remarkable'?" William choked out. "I understand she was utterly formidable. Fierce as a griffin!"

Garreth repressed the smile that threatened to curl the corners of his mouth at the accuracy of that statement.

William downed a mouthful of wine and regarded Garreth with a close, penetrating look. "You also were raised and schooled at Tamworth, were you not? You must have known Athelstan when he was yet an *atheling*, a prince."

"Aye." Garreth shielded his surprise at William's knowledge, instantly wary.

"Interesting." William tapped a thoughtful finger on the side of his goblet. "You are Mercian, then?"

"At heart," Garreth allowed, deflecting the query for it riddled deep into his soul.

In truth, his father had been a Kentish nobleman—the *heah gerefa*, high reeve of Aylesbury—his mother, a Mercian lady who once attended Athelflaed herself. Garreth's mother died soon after he had been placed in fosterage at Tamworth. In time his father remarried and begat other sons. Who could have foreseen the events to follow?

Upon his father's death, the second wife contested the validity of her husband's first marriage and, with the support of her powerful Kentish kinsmen, successfully seized her late husband's estates and titles for her own offspring, disclaiming Garreth.

Inflamed by the deceit of the woman and the injustice of the Kentmen, and disdaining the assault upon her former lady-in-waiting, Athelflaed sheltered young Garreth beneath her wing, refusing to return him to Kent and providing for him from her own coffers when his stepmother would not.

Aye, a true griffiness was Athelflaed, Garreth reminisced —part eagle, part lioness—furiously protective and ready to deliver a swift, sharp justice to anyone deserving of it. Athelflaed's power did not extend to Kent, however, and she could do naught to help him regain his rightful lands.

"Mercian at heart," William echoed Garreth's evasive words, then folded them to mind. "And how fares your lord, Athelstan?"

"He enjoys robust health, and prays the Duke of Normandy does as well."

"And Louis?"

Garreth hesitated. William, once again, moved swift to the mark.

"Come now." William incised him with his gaze. "Surely you have not traveled to Normandy solely for relics and courtesies. You might have wished to evade Raoul's notice as you moved about Francia, but I see no reason for pretense between us now. Besides . . ." William released a breath akin to a sigh. "After spending nigh on to two days in the company of the king's men, I have had quite enough of parrying with words.'' His eyes bore into Garreth. "Shall we be blunt?''

"As you please.'' Garreth felt as though a noose had just been slipped in place about his neck and tightened.

"Then tell me of the young Carolingian.''

"Louis is fine and strong, grown fourteen years into his manhood and waxing impatient to claim his rightful crown,'' he replied with a directness he believed William sought.

William lifted a golden brow at that. "Then 'tis best Louis exercise prudence and patience a time longer.''

Garreth stiffened. "And how much 'longer' might that be, Your Grace?''

"Mayhap months. Mayhap years. Mayhap forever. 'Tis difficult to augur the future in these turbulent times.'' William began to turn away.

"Maybe not so much so if Louis could depend on the loyalty of those who faithfully served his father.''

The duke shot Garreth back a glance. "Charles is dead,'' he emphasized sternly. "And much has transpired in Francia since that event. Be the whelp anxious to claim a tottery throne only to promptly lose it again? Would Athelstan, in his wisdom, assist his nephew to such a foredoomed fate?''

"With the collective support of his key barons, Louis's throne could be shorn up,'' Garreth retorted. " 'Twould be no need to see it forfeit again.''

William barked a laugh. "And who do you believe would be so foolish to hasten to his banner at this time? Hugh? Despite what he might have said to you—and, *oui*, I know you are fresh from Paris and no doubt have spoken with him—nonetheless, Hugh will first and foremost solidify his own holdings, mark my words. Raoul is strong in his power. To whom else may Louis turn? The Lorrainers?'' William gave a snort. "They have neither the numbers nor the strength to support him, and the Acquitainians are in Raoul's palm. You will not soon find them flocking to Louis's cause.''

"And what of Normandy?'' Garreth pressed, his own choler rising. "Or is Normandy's duke swayed by the richness of Raoul's gifts?'' He caught William's eye at that. ''You wish to be blunt? The English court is well aware of the recent grant of the Contentin and Avranchin at the time you pledged your oath to Raoul.''

William's face flushed with anger, and he took a quick pace forward.

''Listen well, Garreth of Tamworth, and impress upon your celebrated sovereign—however you Saxons wish to interpret that particular grant, or my motivations for accepting it—Francia is a much splintered kingdom. She needs no green, untried child-king to challenge the likes of Raoul. The barons of Francia recognize this full well, for their energies are occupied securing their own borders. The time is ill-starred for Louis's return.''

''And when will it be favorable?''

William offered no response.

''Or will it ever?'' Garreth dared, his meaning unmistakable.

William scowled blackly. ''Naught binds me to Athelstan. Nor Louis.''

''Not even the oath of fidelity your father pledged Charles and the honor of Normandy?''

''Charles is dead.''

''Louis is not. Have the Normans in their achievements forgotten they hold their lands of the Carolingians, not of the Robertian usurpers?''

William's mouth thinned. ''Those lands granted at St. Clair-sur-Epte were already in my father's control *before* the king made his conferral.''

''Rollo might have dominated the land, but he did not create himself duke. That Charles did, ennobling him and raising him to a place within the Frankish aristocracy.''

William did not answer, but turned and directed his gaze out the chamber's small window. A muscle worked along his jaw. His ire sharpened his features and heightened his color.

''Your father faithfully supported the Carolingians,'' Garreth added in a more subdued tone. ''Once also did you.''

William paused, then turned slowly round, his eyes unreadable. He held Garreth's gaze for a moment longer. When he spoke he measured out each word.

"Advise Athelstan—bring back Louis now, or a year from now, and he will not succeed. A Carolingian cannot long hold the throne, with or without my aid. Take a lesson from Hugh. For all the power he wields, he rightly chose to decline the crown. 'Twould endanger all that he holds to accept it.''

"But if Hugh stands with Louis?"

"Open your eyes and ears, Saxon.'' William's patience burst. "Whatever Hugh might have promised you in secret, he is no fool. Even should he aid Louis's return, he will guard first what is his, and abet Louis second. Given these times, that support can be only minimal at best.''

Deeming the audience at an end, William crossed the chamber to leave, handing off his goblet to Rurik who yet stood by the portal, having remained there silent and attentive throughout the interview.

"And if the times should change?'' Garreth addressed the duke's retreating back, challenge in his tone.

William halted, then pivoted, fire kindling in the depths of his eyes. Garreth feared he had pressed the duke too far.

"*Should* the time come for Louis's return, I shall do what I must—for Francia, to be sure, but foremost for Normandy. When you report our conversation to Athelstan, give him to realize that in the breast of William Longsword beats a heart, neither Carolingian nor Robertian, but Norman. And it beats for Normandy.''

With that, William turned on his heel and strode from the chamber.

Garreth clamped his jaw tight and then quit the room as well. Rurik followed, setting aside the goblet on the small table beside the door.

In silence, Garreth and Rurik descended the stairs to the entrance level of the tower keep, then paused atop the outer flight of steps.

Garreth's stomach roiled, upset by the encounter, his nerves scraped raw. He had intended only to test William's bent of mind on the matter of young Louis, not sink into an argument and openly contest him. How had their exchange disintegrated into one of confrontation?

Garreth began to descend the stairs, but Rurik stayed him with a hand to his arm, locking steel-blue eyes with his.

"You might not care for what the duke voiced just now, but do not discount the validity of his words. My brother Lyting and I fought alongside Charles at Soissons, and I can assure you unseating Raoul will be no easy matter."

By his words, Lord Rurik revealed himself and his brother as Carolingians, giving Garreth one of the answers he sought. He could only wonder that the count chose to do so.

Lord Rurik continued. "After the recent turmoil in Normandy, William is most interested in solidifying his position and strengthening the duchy from within." Garreth knew he referred to the revolt of William's barons. "This colors his view, but his opinion on the matter of the crown is one shared. There is as much upheaval outside the duchy as within, and the other barons must protect their own interests. A Carolingian throne would be too weak to endure."

"And so you also counsel patience for another day?" Garreth felt his spirit deflate a bit further.

Lord Rurik did not answer immediately but measured Garreth behind steel-blue eyes as he considered his next words.

"*Já*. But I would add that William is more like his father than many give credence. When the time comes for Louis's return, I feel certain Duke William Longsword will be at his side and support him fully, all the way to the throne."

At midday, Garreth stood before the iron gates of the church-monastery of St. Ouen.

He tempered his features, knowing they must reflect the dour mood that pervaded his bones. Compelling a smile to his lips, he waited as the spindly Brother Ansfrey bent to the gate's cumbersome lock and worked his key.

With a solid clunk, the mechanism disengaged. Beaming,

the monk hauled the gate open against a screaky protest and welcomed Garreth of Tamworth, royal *thegn* and representative of England's great monarch and patron, come to procure the precious Psalter of Metz.

Garreth moderated his pace to match that of Brother Ansfrey as they proceeded toward the complex of monastic buildings and exchanged further cordialities. A blunt pain pulsed to life at Garreth's temples. Try as he might to concentrate on the monk's converse, a portion of his brain persistently strayed back to his earlier clash with the duke, striving to recapture and dissect every word, look, and gesture.

He felt his smile slip and lifted it back in place, just as he came aware of the approach of another, more sturdy member of the community. This proved to be Abbot Berengar.

Additional greetings and pleasantries flowed while the ache along the sides of Garreth's head spread its fingers upward to his crown.

Ailénor. He must find her, speak with her. Given the troubling outcome of his audience with the duke, Garreth knew he could no longer remain at court. Once he completed the king's business at St. Ouen, he would need leave Normandy—and Ailénor—and return to England forthwith.

His heart slumped. His head pounded. How could he expl . . . ?

"Come, my son." Abbot Berengar motioned to the ponderous limestone building that hunkered on the path before them, directly ahead. " 'Twould be our distinct pleasure to guide you through St. Ouen's workshops before we attend to our business."

The churchmen's shining faces mirrored their enthusiasm. Garreth realized he would grievously offend Abbot Berengar and Brother Ansfrey should he decline such a privileged offer and thus allowed them to usher him into the building that, they explained, housed the scriptorium, bindery, and library.

The back of Garreth's mind still churned with possibilities of what he might or might not have said to Duke

William when he stepped into the scriptorium, an especially large room, tomblike for its hushed quiet and muted rustlings.

"Here, as you can see, our labors are quite diverse," Brother Ansfrey informed in a voice that was a little above a whisper, gesturing to the workroom with a sweep of his hand.

Crossing to the far end, they watched the brothers finish the preparation of new parchments, pumicing them smooth and chalking them. Garreth gazed on the process attentively, though even as he did, images of Ailénor appeared before his mind's eye and projected themselves against the creamy sheets.

Ailénor in the pear tree, her legs bare to the hips.

Ailénor beneath him on the ground, her fiery hair spilled bewitchingly about her.

Ailénor beside him at dinner, laughter shimmering in her eyes.

Ailénor atop her golden courser, riding to the distance, full of life and passion, her shapely form so tantalizingly profiled.

Ailénor . . .

His thoughts deflected against a wall of reality. They would part by sunrise tomorrow, he sailing for England, she remaining in Francia. But he *would* return, he swore to himself. And soon.

A small inner voice nettled. He had earned the duke's displeasure this day. Conceivably William would impede his suit for Ailénor's hand. Would her family dismiss him as well? He had sensed no antagonism from Lord Rurik, but what of Ailénor's father, the Comte de Héricourt? The man had watched them both like a hawk last night.

"Here you will see how the leaves are cut to size, then pricked and ruled for the copyists." Abbot Berengar steered them around long worktables, situated in the center of the room where more men bent to their tasks. Finally he brought them to where the scribes, rubricators, and illuminators populated their desks amidst scrolls, quills, inkpots, brushes, and paints.

Garreth watched as one worker scraped an error from the parchment with a small knife and re-inked the letter, but his thoughts continued to flicker back to Ailénor. He must seek her out directly, as soon as he departed the monastery.

Moving on to the bindery, Garreth and his companions made a brief tour and were subsequently greeted in the library by Brother Gilbert. Immediately the monk brought forth a sizable package wrapped in leather. This he placed upon a stand with great care and stepped back, allowing the abbot to uncover the piece.

"Now, my son, gaze for yourself upon the Psalter of Metz."

As he slipped the book from its wrapper, jewels flashed on a ground of gold.

"The cover is called a 'treasure' binding. The plaque, at the center, is of the finest ivory, carved over a century ago at the famed workshops of Metz." He indicated the large inset, a superb relief, depicting Christ in majesty.

Garreth's brows rose. Thoroughly impressed, he gave his attention to the exceptional workmanship.

Abbot Berengar opened the heavy cover, explaining its core to be of beech, the edges beveled and cambered beneath its gold overlay. Turning to an exquisitely decorated leaf, he paused for Garreth's inspection.

"The codex has been painstakingly restored. 'Twas originally inscribed at Metz, but as is sometimes the custom, the work was forwarded to another abbey so that a particular artist might complete the illuminations. In this instance, 'twas the Abbey of Liège and the artist a man named Rimpert.

"Alas." The abbot sighed. "Norsemen ravaged and burnt the abbey some fifty years past. Rimpert fled with the unfinished Psalter and hid it well. Too well, actually. Rimpert died in his flight of the wounds he bore. Only in this last decade has the book been rediscovered. 'Tis a great prize."

Garreth nodded, awed and totally consumed as he scanned the pages, all rendered in neat, uncluttered minuscule, the initial letters elaborate and brightly colored.

At his elbow, Abbot Berengar expounded on how the monks of St. Ouen completed the decorations begun by Rimpert, recopied the damaged leaves, and added their own full-page illuminations, lavishly touched with gold.

For the next hour Garreth studied the dazzling work and more fully appreciated Athelstan's desire to possess it.

" 'Tis magnificent," he uttered. "A masterpiece," he pronounced several pages later. "King Athelstan will be highly pleased."

Smiles broke over the monks' faces. Removing the Psalter to Abbot Berengar's office, Garreth settled the king's account. The abbot then insisted they seal their transaction in the cellar with a sampling of Brother Fiacre's superb apple brandy. Garreth found the drink potent but smooth, with a distinctive bite. The first small cup fired a trail from his lips to his heels. The second dissolved the remnants of his headache and replaced it with a pleasant glow.

At the tolling of the abbey bell high above, Abbot Berengar took leave of Garreth and Brother Ansfrey to say his daily office. Brother Ansfrey, in turn, led Garreth from the cellar depths and directed him to the church, assuming he would wish to see its fine improvements under the Norman dukes and spend time before the altar, praying for safe travel to England.

Passing through a series of connected chambers and the vestry, they emerged at the rear of the church in the central nave. Garreth thanked the good brother a final time and, with the precious Psalter in arm, crossed to the altar.

No sooner had he knelt and closed his eyes than voices drifted to his ears from the front of the church. He tucked his head down to better center his thoughts in prayer, but the high-pitched whisperings of children shattered his concentration.

Casting a glance past his shoulder, his gaze fell immediately upon several young children and two women, clustered to one side at the entrance end and partially obscured by a column. The children he recognized at once, as he did their stern nurse, who stood conversing with one of the brothers, a stack of embroidered altar linens in her arms.

The other woman now moved from the column and into full view, robed in a brilliant green-blue mantle. Though her face remained averted, her deep auburn hair glimpsed from along the edges of her snowy veil. The Comtesse de Héricourt, Garreth bethought. But looking again and marking her height, he realized with a start 'twas Ailénor.

His heart jarred in place, and he rose to his feet. Outside the open doors, he spotted Brand and Delling waiting for the women and children, obviously their escorts. He brought his gaze back to Ailénor, wondering how he might gain her attention and draw her aside. But in that very moment, she turned and glanced toward the altar.

Vivid blue eyes collided with dark brown.

Ailénor gasped her surprise, and he saw her lips pronounce his name.

"Garreth," Ailénor murmured on a soft breath. Her heart capered. The nave stood empty but an instant ago. From whence did he materialize?

Her eyes remained coupled with his, and she felt a warm, sweet joy stealing through her. Jesu, but he was a handsome man. She wavered a trifle under the intensity of his look, then sent him a smile.

Last evening was one of the happiest she could recall. They had lingered long over their dinner, trading good-humored raillery with her siblings and cousins, then dallied over *merles* for hours more, rapt with each other's company and forgetting their "guardians" who dwindled away one by one. Ailénor recognized she must possess a wanton side for she fervently hoped Garreth and she might again share a trencher and the evening hours that lay ahead. Would that they could find a small space of time to themselves, away from the eyes of so many.

Ailénor collected herself, remembering the children and Felise, who was now debating the best methods for removing wine stains from altar cloths with Brother Eustache.

Ailénor excused herself on the pretext of going to light a devotional candle before the statue of the Virgin. Traversing the nave to the side chapel, she brushed gazes with

Garreth as she went, her pulse accelerating, and prayed he would join her.

Ailénor flamed a candle and waited. Moments later she perceived Garreth's presence towering behind her. A thrilling, vibrating sensation spangled through her at his closeness and settled low in her abdomen. Her every nerve stood on end, sensually aware of him.

Turning, she cast up a sunny glance only to meet with his somber expression, a touch of sadness in his face. Her smile faltered.

"Ailénor . . ." He hesitated, then his gaze traveled over her face, as if tracing her features to memory. "My business in Rouen is at an end." Again he paused, seeming to search for words. A muscle leapt in his jaw. "On the morrow I must sail at first light."

Ailénor's smile slipped from her lips and fell to the floor of her heart. All gladness left her. She bit the inside of her cheek against a sudden rush of emotion.

" 'Twould seem you are to leave my life as abruptly as you entered it," she offered in a small, dry voice, attempting a smile but failing miserably.

"Not by choice." Garreth lifted a hand to stroke back a wayward strand of hair from her cheek. "Ailénor, I would not leave so soon if matters were otherwise. Believe that."

She caught her bottom lip with her teeth, the hopes and fantasies concealed in her maiden's heart crumbling. "There be only this day left to us, then?"

Garreth bowed his head. "Not even that. I need arrange my passage and make the necessary preparations. I regret I shall be unable to join you in the hall this eve."

An unseen hand squeezed her heart. "Am I never to see you again?" Unexpected tears pricked the back of her eyes.

Garreth quickly closed the space and pressed a finger to her lips. "Never is a harsh word, fair Ailénor, and one I refuse to use where it concerns the two of us."

She trembled beneath his touch and wondered at his words. His hand dropped and enclosed hers in its warmth. He began to speak again, but the children's voices sounded their approach—Adelis's, Michan's, and Ena's—reminding them they were not alone.

Garreth drew Ailénor over to one of the church's lofty columns. He could not give her up to the others yet. Their time was near to an end. One last moment must be theirs. He continued to enfold her hand in his palm, his other arm still encumbered with the heavy Psalter. His gaze poured over her, hot, consuming.

"The children . . ." Ailénor fretted as they neared.

"Here. Look to examine this." Garreth placed the Psalter in her hands, unable to think of aught else he might do. Aiding Ailénor, he helped brace the book's weight from beneath, but did not move to withdraw the leather wrappings.

Again his gaze spilled over her. How could he leave her when everything in him clamored to stay? And yet he must. He could not reveal those things yet hidden about himself. Not at this time.

Beneath the Psalter, Garreth's hand slipped over Ailénor's. He believed her discontent to be as great as his, for she wore her heart in her eyes.

" 'Tis my most ardent wish to return to you, sweet Ailénor. I vow, to that end I shall faithfully strive."

Mayhap 'twas the moisture that glistened in her eyes and so tore at his heart, or mayhap the brothers' fine brandy that prompted him to boldness, but he knew he could not depart Normandy without seeing her again.

"If 'tis in your heart, then meet me on the morrow, before I sail." His mind rapidly cast about for a place where they might do so, near to the keep.

Ailénor's free hand sought his beneath the book. "*Oui,* Garreth. At the stone bench in the rose garden."

"The stone bench," he repeated, the corners of his mouth lifting. " 'Twould please me greatly if you would grant me your token then. I shall carry it with me, until again we meet."

Ailénor nodded, a single tear slipping from her eye. His heart compressed, stirring Garreth to draw one of her hands from beneath the Psalter and press his lips against its back.

Ailénor swayed toward him, pressing into the edge of the book, a cumbersome barrier. He raised his head to gaze on her, but heard a shuffling accompanied by a distinctive "mew" nearby.

Garreth and Ailénor glanced down in unison to find young Michan sitting on the floor next to the stand of candles, his hand tucked inside the pouch at his waist where white fur and a small pink nose peeked out. How long the child had watched them, he could not guess, but Garreth pulled Ailénor along with him, behind the column and out of sight.

"Wait for me, Ailénor." He spoke in a rush, knowing their time had run dry. "I pray God returns me swiftly to your arms. Know I will do all in my power to hasten the advent of that day."

Encircling her with his arm, he swept her to him, the Psalter folding between them. He covered her mouth with his and kissed her deeply, urgently. His fingers pressed against her spine, then slid upward to tangle in her hair and send her veil askew.

Beneath Garreth's searing lips, Ailénor felt a fire ignite inside her and flame upward, bright and white-hot. She met his passion and answered it fully, her mouth parting beneath his. She jolted momentarily at the invasion of his tongue, then welcomed its questing, silken warmth. Their breaths mingled, their tongues mated and danced, scandalously, passionately, their fervid kiss becoming one of longing and parting and bittersweet anguish.

Footsteps echoed across the nave, rupturing their passion-clogged haze. Garreth released her, and they panted for breath.

"Until the dawn, my heart." His dark eyes shone with unspoken emotion.

Seizing a final kiss, hard and swift, he unloosed his hold on her, pivoted, and left, leaving her tottery and groping for the solidity of the column.

Garreth crossed the nave in long, rapid strides, nodding tersely to the monk and Felise whose brows flew upward at his appearance, while the children chittered amongst themselves.

Ailénor watched Garreth pass out of the church, her heart pounding, her lips burning. The force of her newly awakened desires and her hunger for Garreth startled her. No promise lay beyond the morrow, yet she knew she would wait for him.

"Until the dawn," she whispered after him as he disappeared from sight.

Ailénor rose in the early-morning dark.

Drawing on her gown and slippers, she made her way around the pallets of her cousins and retrieved her mantle from its peg on the wall.

Cloaking herself, she moved into the outer chamber where Felise slept deeply with the young ones, her soft snores filling the air. Soundlessly Ailénor crossed to the door and emerged onto the upper gallery that overlooked the Great Hall.

Following the passageway to the far end, she gained the stairs and began her descent. Torches blazed in their iron brackets, spilling gamboling pools of light over the steps and distending shadows to dance upon the walls.

Reaching the bottom, she paused in the alcove and peered through the archway, into the Great Hall. Her heart beat high in her chest. With so many guests at the palace, she feared some might sleep in the hall. Unable to distinguish forms in the inky darkness there, and not wishing to chance discovery, she continued on toward the entrance end, keeping close to the wall.

She hesitated. Never had she wandered the keep at night, but guessed there to be guards posted throughout. Likely before the portal to the Great Hall itself. Certainly on the level below that quartered the high-ranking *chevaliers*. And without doubt, outside, securing the main stairway to the keep.

Diverting her course, Ailénor followed the partition of curtained columns, paused long enough to look about for men-at-arms, then, finding none, dashed the distance to the entrance of the kitchen passage.

With a sigh of relief, she quickened her pace along the corridor and closed on two sets of stairs, one leading to the wine cellar, the other to the kitchens that lay just outside the tower keep. She hastened down the latter, her anticipation mounting. 'Twould be a matter of minutes before she reached the garden and Garreth.

Rounding the steps at their turn, her gaze fell to the bottom of the steps. She froze in place. A guard stood below, his back confronting her. How could she hope to steal past him?

The man bent his head forward and appeared to speak to someone, hidden before his bulk. Ailénor's eyes widened as a feminine hand slid around his waist and began to caress his back. At that encouragement, he ushered his companion into an adjoining storage room that projected off the corridor and closed the door.

A part of Ailénor wished to rail at the man for abandoning his post. Another part praised Heaven above for his timeliness, which opened her way to slip from the keep unseen. Rushing down the remainder of the steps, she escaped outside and into the yard.

Servants stirred about the kitchen buildings, laying in the fires and beginning preparations of the keep's main meal that would be served at ten.

A man bearing firewood to one kitchen halted outside the door and stared pointedly at her. Again Ailénor feared discovery. Yet there was something in his look that chilled her blood. Or was it his pock-scarred face that so disquieted her?

Ailénor upbraided herself for her narrowness of spirit. She broke the gaze and headed in the direction of the garden, persuading herself she need not worry. Servants might gossip amongst themselves, but their buzzings usually stayed within their own ranks. She highly doubted the man would inform the officials of the keep or seek out her parents, even if he knew who they might be.

Drawing into her green-blue mantle, cocooning herself against her unease, Ailénor continued to the arbor.

A fine mist hugged the ground, dampening Ailénor's slippers and the hems of her cloak and gown. Entering the low-walled garden, she found it empty. She had left her chamber somewhat early to arrive in advance of Garreth. With that achieved, she now found herself anxious that he arrive directly and undelayed.

Ailénor paced the confines of the garden restively, then seated herself on the cold stone bench. The early-morning chill seeped into her bones.

Somewhere behind, a twig snapped, causing her to jump. She scanned the area but found naught. A bird fluttered into a tree nearby and began to chirp out a melody—a mockingbird, reciting his lengthy repertoire. He finished a flourish of notes, then switched abruptly to a discordant cawing, as though to drive her from the garden or warn her away.

Ailénor pulled her mantle snug about her and rubbed warmth into her arms. "Garreth," she whispered. Did aught detain him? Had something occurred since yestereve to prevent his coming this morn?

Ailénor touched her fingers to her lips, remembering his kiss and the heat of his mouth, and how he called her "his heart."

Above, the sky began to lift from a pitch-black to a deep, lambent blue. Of a sudden, Garreth's request for a token leapt to mind. Ailénor meant to gift him with a particular ring, but in her eagerness to meet him, she forgot to retrieve it from her chest. And yet . . .

She fingered the brooch securing her mantle. 'Twas a fine piece and a worthy token. She smiled. Working the pin at its back, she unfastened it and slid it from the cloth.

Ailénor started to secure the pin when she heard distinctive sounds, just past her right shoulder and directly behind—footfalls and a swishing of cloth. Ice shot up her spine, instinct telling her 'twas not Garreth. The mocker flew past, forsaking the garden. Ailénor shoved from the bench but had only half risen when a hand snaked from behind and fastened over her mouth.

A scream scaled Ailénor's throat. She tore at the hand

and battled the solid strength that forced her back down. In a panic she wrenched beneath the entrapping hands, twisting violently as she lurched forward and partially freed herself. Driving upward, she regained her footing. Yet her attacker overpowered her efforts and caught her in a crushing grip, one hand still afixed over her mouth.

Twisting, she caught sight of the man's pocked face. Her heart nearly stopped beating. Another form emerged, seemingly from nowhere, and grabbed for her legs.

Terror possessed Ailénor. She kicked out. Remembering the brooch in her palm, she hardened her grip and stabbed backward, sinking its long pin into the thigh of the man who held her. He shouted and swore blackly, then, in a fit of anger, struck the brooch from her hand, sending it into the grass. The two men trammeled her next efforts and hauled her toward a hedge of bushes, terrifying her nearly beyond her senses. Would they rape her right here?

Garreth! Garreth! Her mind screamed out to him.

Ailénor fought with all her remaining strength but to no avail. Her cloak dropped from her shoulders and snarled at her feet. The morning cool rushed over her, swathing her as she bit, kicked, and scratched. Tearing one hand free, she clawed for the man's face. He snared her wrist and gave it a twist, but in the struggle her knee jerked upward and connected with his groin, shocking herself and incensing him. Fury fired his eyes. Doubling back his fist, he struck out.

Pain exploded along Ailénor's jaw, while her head burst with a brilliant shattering of light.

Crumpling, she fell into a well of darkness.

Grimbold worked quickly to bind the comtesse's hands and gag her. He had not anticipated so much pluck or fight from a noblewoman. He smiled darkly. She should make for some stimulating sport later.

"Help me with this," he barked at Wimund.

Together they pulled a hemp sack over her, one of size, filched from the kitchen. Enshrouding her fully, they hauled her upward.

"Get the cart and meet me at the west gate," Grimbold ordered.

Wimund started to argue the arrangement, but harnessed his tongue and trudged off.

Shouldering the comtesse's unconscious form, Grimbold took up her weight and vanished into the shadows that yet lingered before the dawn.

Garreth strode toward the garden, eager to see Ailénor. Eager to hold her in his arms and claim one last kiss before he took leave of her for England.

Entering the rose arbor, he found no sign of Ailénor. All lay still and silent.

Garreth removed the cumbrous Psalter from beneath his arm and placed it on the stone bench in the heart of the garden. He stood waiting, watching. His nerves knotted up.

As loath as he was to leave Ailénor, he found himself anxious to be away so he might return all the sooner. More strongly than ever, he felt sure of his intentions, sure of his feelings, for the autumn-fire maid of Normandy. If the king would have him choose a wife, he would choose Ailénor. Even if the king did not urge him to the altar, 'twas a journey he would gladly embrace with this fair damsel.

Pale fingers of pink and lavender streaked the sky. Still Ailénor did not appear. Tension coiled through Garreth. The boatswain would not delay the ship for long, he had made himself clear. Even now Garreth knew he must hasten his pace to the docks.

Young Michan came to mind. Yesterday in the church the boy overheard the details of his and Ailénor's plans. Had the lad informed his nursemaid? Or his parents? Had they prevented Ailénor from coming this morn?

Garreth's heart plummeted.

He doubted not at all her feelings toward him, not if he judged by her passionate response beneath his kiss yesterday. How keenly he wished to see her before his leave-taking.

Long minutes passed while the sky continued to lighten. He could wait no longer. He did not have time to seek her out, and disappointment weighted his chest like granite. Until he returned to Francia, he would neither see Ailénor again nor have further communication with her.

Taking up the Psalter, he withdrew from the garden and crossed the ducal grounds. At the gate Garreth identified himself to the guards, completed the formalities, then gave a single glance back toward the tower keep.

Ailénor. Where are you? he called to her mentally. Only the vacancy of the morn answered back.

Releasing a long, frustrated breath, he directed himself to the demands of the day that lay ahead and forced himself to depart.

Garreth arrived at the dock to find the boatswain pacing the plankings. Seeing Garreth, the man quickened forward.

"All is in readiness. Your trunk arrived earlier and is stowed aboard."

The boatswain twitched several glances back to the ship and licked his dry lips.

"We . . . ah . . . have some unanticipated company for the crossing—two men bound for Ireland. 'Twill not delay you one whit, I assure you," he added in a rush. "They paid right handsomely, they did, and extra, too. But I made it clear to 'em both I'd first be delivering you to Hamwih. They have no problem with that."

Garreth flicked a glance at the men who waited in the ship, drawn into their cloaks and hoods. In truth, he had paid quite handsomely himself for a swift and direct passage, convincing the boatswain to forgo all stops save the requisite one on the coast at Harfleur.

"Then I have no problem either," he muttered in assent, his greater concern still residing with Ailénor.

Climbing into the ship, he afforded the men a nod, then stepped to the cargo hold where the decking opened to the hull amidship. Casks of ale and provisions of food crowded the mast there, while the remainder of the space was only partially loaded. Garreth spied his chest positioned beneath the foredecking. It struck him as odd that it should be stored apart of the other goods, but he leapt down the short distance, thinking to store the Psalter there as well and protect it from the elements at sea.

As he squatted before the trunk, he heard a scuffing of boots on the deck astern, but paid it little thought. Instead he slipped the precious book in its waterproof wrappings behind the trunk. He encountered something there, firm but with "give." He noticed the end of a hemp sack then. Grain? he wondered. Again he deemed it odd but thought whatever the sack contained, 'twould buffer the Psalter nicely and keep it from sliding about.

Rising Garreth found the two men watching him from deep within their hoods. One had stood to his feet and now stared down at him. Garreth felt a prickling feeling move along his neck. There was something about his eyes, yet the shadows obscured them . . .

Garreth gave another slight nod of the head, then joined them on the half deck astern and settled himself where he could keep his valuables in view.

The boatswain cast off the mooring lines and trimmed the sail to take advantage of the light breeze.

As the ship glided from port, Garreth looked back to Rouen and the distant tower keep, outlined against the hills. There his gaze remained as the expanse steadily widened between himself and the maid who had so captured his heart.

Chapter Four

Felise's stomach churned as she mounted the stairs to the gallery and huffed along the corridor to the bedchambers.

Ailénor. Where was the girl? She had neither appeared at chapel nor again when the castle folk broke their fast in the Great Hall.

Lady Ailinn and Lord Lyting grew deeply concerned, particularly when Etainn and her cousins just now revealed that Ailénor's pallet lay cold when they awakened at dawn.

Ailénor *had* to have passed through the outer chamber where she herself slept, Felise reflected. That knowledge tormented her no end.

Entering the first of the rooms, Felise continued directly

across to the one that lay beyond. She halted just inside the portal. Squinting to see better, she began to pace the chamber slowly, seeking some detail that might suggest what became of her ward.

The oak peg that normally held Ailénor's cloak thrust naked from the wall. The floor below it stared up just as vacant, her slippers likewise gone.

Felise moved on to Ailénor's pallet. The servants had yet to tidy these particular chambers, being occupied cleaning those of the higher-ranking lords first. The pallet lay as Ailénor left it, with the blanket folded back. On the floor beside it lay her rich corded girdle in a snarl.

Felise bent to pick it up. 'Twas the one she wore yesterday. Had Ailénor dressed hurriedly and not thought to put on the belt? Or mayhap it fell to the floor unnoticed, or she could not locate it in the dark.

Crossing to Ailénor's clothes chest, Felise opened it and checked through the neatly folded gowns. The ivory dress was missing.

Felise bit her thumbnail, winnowing her thoughts, unsure this told her anything. Turning, she skimmed another glance over the room. Her gaze came to rest on young Michan who crouched by the door, his fluffy white companion filling his arms. He watched her with intent eyes, round as the kitten's.

Felise cocked her head to one side. "*Mon petit*, have you seen your *soeur*, Ailénor, this morn?" she asked in a milky tone, striving to mask her anxiety.

Strangely, Michan scooted back from the portal, clutching the kitten high against his chin, half hiding his face behind it. Guilt pooled in his eyes.

"*Qu'est-ce que c'est?* What is this?" Felise's brows parted upward.

Going to the boy, she studied his expression. Drawing on her long experience as nursemaid to the numerous *enfants de Héricourt*, she placed a hand to her hip, elevated an eyebrow in a practiced arch, and partially shuttered one eye. She then began to tap her foot upon the floorboards.

"If you know something, *mon petit*, you had best be out

with it. Your parents grow fierce worried for your sister and will soon have the entire guard out searching for her."

"She is not here," Michan asserted in a small voice.

Felise blinked. "This I can see with my own eyes." She gestured back to the room with an open palm, her patience slipping.

"I mean, Ailénor is not in the keep."

"Not in the . . . *Donc.* She has gone out onto the palace grounds? And pray, where might she have taken herself? Do you know, child?"

Michan avoided Felise's eyes and took a visible swallow.

"*M-i-c-h-a-n . . .*" Her voice climbed, drawing out his name with measured sternness.

"Ailénor went to meet Garreth. Well, I think she did." He screwed his face and shrugged. "I heard them talking in the church yesterday. You remember, Felise. You saw him there, too."

Felise compressed her lips, preferring to forget. The man materialized from nowhere, though she suspected he had just been . . .

"They agreed to meet in secret just before dawn at the stone bench in the rose garden."

"Did they indeed?" Felise harumphed. She squared her shoulders and stiffened her spine. "*Alors.* We shall just see about this . . . this . . . *rendezvous.* I shall have a word with your sister and a switch for that Saxon wolf who prowls ever about her."

Uplifting her chin, Felise marched through the portal, intent for the garden. Michan hurried behind, his kitten clutched firmly in his arms.

Minutes later they entered the garden, only to find it empty. Piqued by the entire matter, Felise cast an irritable glance about. Where had they gotten to now? 'Twas not a stick but a cane—a very big cane—she would take to Garreth of Tamworth.

In the same moment Cricket leapt from Michan's arms and scampered off behind a hedge of bushes. Michan scurried after the feline. Instantly he reappeared, his face gone pale.

"Felise . . ." he called anxiously, his voice rising on a thread of alarm. "Felise . . ." It rose again, higher, thinner. Unable to utter more than her name, he pointed a shaky finger toward a place behind the hedge.

Felise hastened to his side, a testament of peppery caveats and rebukes she planned to give the Saxon forming on her tongue.

She halted abruptly, gasping as her gaze fell upon a lustrous green-blue cloak, lying in a tangled heap upon the ground. Taking it up, she found it to be thoroughly soiled as though it had been trampled underfoot.

"Felise . . ." Michan pulled at her sleeve, uncertain but fearful. "Look at how the ground is churned."

Felise covered her mouth, seeing what he said to be true. "My lamb . . . *non* . . ."

A grave foreboding gripped her, and she shook her head. In so doing, a gleam of sunlight caught her eye, reflecting off something hidden in the grass a short distance away.

Felise hugged the mantle to her breast and warily approached what looked to be a metal object. Reaching down, she retrieved it. And recognized it at once. 'Twas Ailénor's brooch, a lavish piece gifted to her this Christmastide past by her parents.

Nearly pricking herself on its underpin, she turned the brooch over. Her heart stopped midbeat. Dark red blood coated the pin's shaft.

Felise cried out. Clutching the brooch and mantle, she bustled back toward the keep, wailing for her lord and lady, Michan and his kitten heeling behind.

Garreth watched the two men surreptitiously as he took up his skin of wine and raised it to his lips.

He had recognized the two a while past, when they cast off their concealing hoods in the full light of day. He remembered them from two nights ago, when they tarried in the Great Hall of the ducal palace, watching Ailénor's parents on the gallery above.

If their sharp interest in the count and countess did not strike him as odd then, it did now as he called it to mind.

'Twas equally curious that they would leave their positions in the duke's household to sail for Ireland. Of course, considering the altercation with the head butler over their idleness in the hall, mayhap they no longer enjoyed employment at the palace.

Garreth downed another swallow of wine and watched the soaring flight of a gull. Something rankled deep in his bones, but he could not quite lay a finger to it.

He sifted through what little he knew. The men had paid the boatswain a hearty sum for transport to the Irish isle. That did not bespeak of men needing to scrimp their earnings for lack of a gainful position. Rather, it suggested precipitous arrangements, made with an urgency to be away.

But an urgency to what purpose? To return to Ireland, or to depart Francia? He tumbled the thoughts in his mind.

Garreth held fairly certain the two were of Irish blood, not only by their looks but by the distinctive Gaelic tongue in which they had been quietly conversing—a tongue he could identify readily enough, though he was at a loss to comprehend a single word.

Now that he pondered it, the pair were apparently fluent in tongues. 'Twas reasonable they would need speak Frankish in order to procure positions at the palace. They certainly had exhibited no difficulty in understanding the irate butler. Just a little while past, they had addressed the boatswain, a Kent man. In that instance, the man with the disfiguring scars spoke in accented Saxon.

As though the man heard his thoughts, he chose that precise moment to glance over at Garreth. His eyes were not overlarge and protruding like his friend's, but small and flat, reflecting no light in their depths—cold pebbles of jade, hard and inscrutable.

The man shifted his gaze out over the winding Seine. If he and his companion recognized him, they gave no indication. Garreth could not recall whether either had actually taken note of him when they stood side by side in the Great Hall. Nor was he sure that it mattered.

A small inner voice warned that it did.

The man with the huge eyes and weak chin rose and

made his way to the fore of the ship. There he relieved himself over the bow before making his way back.

He paused before the cargo hold, scrubbed his face with his hand, then stepped down into the space and ladled up a dipperful of ale from the barrel at the mast. After slaking his thirst and recovering the cask, he made a point to ramble about the hold, pausing near Garreth's chest and the hide-covered package beside it.

Garreth's brows drew together. 'Twas not the first time one or the other visited the hold or lingered before his belongings. Did they know of the Psalter of Metz?

How could they? he argued with himself. 'Twas possible only if a member of the monastic community of St. Ouen had alerted them. He rejected the notion soundly.

Another thought nettled. Earlier, when he himself visited the hold to check on his trunk and the Psalter, the men's looks instantly darkened. They watched him closely the entire time, of that he was sure. As to why, he had yet to fathom.

Garreth scanned the cloudless sky. The two were a grim pair. He had a gnawing feeling 'twas a mistake for the boatswain to have taken them on. If they posed a problem, they still could be put ashore at Harfleur before beginning the Channel crossing. After that, there was no recourse till they landed in England.

As he secured the skin of wine, he cast another glance toward his goods, sheltered just below the half deck and visible from where he sat.

His hands stilled as his eyes alighted upon the hemp sack, projecting out about a foot's length from behind the chest. He rubbed his eyes, sure that the day's bright sun meddled with his vision.

His gaze wandered back to the sack once more. It lay stock-still, as one would expect. Yet the moment before, he thought to have seen it move.

Ailinn paced the far side of the chamber, wringing her hands in silent anguish, while Felise sat on a chair in the corner weeping into her apron, thoroughly distraught.

Brienne moved between the two, offering what solace she could.

Lyting brought his gaze from the scene. He carried a dark fury in his soul but counseled the grimness from his features as he crouched before Michan and questioned him for an untold time, sifting every word, every detail, for some clue to Ailénor's disappearance.

"That is all I know, *Papa. En vérité.* Truly. Garreth told Ailénor he had to leave and sail for England. That upset her greatly. I think she had tears in her eyes. She said she would meet him in the rose garden just before dawn, and he asked that she give him something to remember her by. A token." Michan concluded his tale, then wrinkled up his brows. "Did she run away with Garreth, *Papa*?"

Lyting squeezed his eyes shut, bowing his head as he pinched the bridge of his nose between his thumb and forefinger. He no longer knew what to think or say.

"Of course not, Michan," Brienne soothed when Lyting did not respond. "It does not make sense now, does it?"

Ailinn turned from the narrow window where she stood, and Lyting glanced over his shoulder, lifting his eyes to his sister-in-law. Felise stopped her sniffling.

Finding herself suddenly the center of interest, Brienne felt a flutter to her pulse. She had said too much. Lord, she did not wish to bring up painful matters. Still, the others waited. She moistened her lips.

"Well, it does not make sense that there is blood on the brooch and her cloak was left crumpled on the ground if she went willingly with Garreth."

"And what if she went unwillingly?" Lyting posed, his voice taut.

"Surely you do not believe he forced her?" Brienne met with unconvinced stares. "The two seemed enamored of one another." More unblinking stares challenged her. "To what purpose, then? He might be an impulsive young man but certainly not foolish. Would he kidnap Ailénor, who is not only your daughter but kinswoman to the Duke of Normandy, thus risking the wrath of William and his powerful allies, not to mention the displeasure of his own sovereign?

Athelstan is not a king given to kidnapping innocent women, or condoning it. I cannot believe it.''

"I must agree with Brienne." Rurik's rich voice carried from the portal as he entered. "The guards who held first watch at the main gate have verified Garreth passed through at dawn. Alone. He bore no visible marks upon his person—no wounds, no scratches, no stains of blood upon his clothing. He appeared hale, though in a brooding mood. From other reports gathered, 'twould seem he went straight to the docks and boarded a small cargo vessel with two other men and a boatswain, their ship bound for England. 'Tis also confirmed no women departed the palace grounds in the first hours of dawn—noblewomen or servants.''

"Where does that leave us, then?" Lyting gave a reassuring squeeze to Michan's shoulder and rose to his feet.

Rurik locked a somber gaze with Lyting. "We know Ailénor passed through the kitchens just before dawn, presumably on her way to meet Garreth. One of the cooks spied her crossing the yard in the direction of the garden. 'Tis unclear whether she and Garreth actually met. But since he left alone, 'tis possible she came to harm afterward.''

"Or before," Lyting added.

Rurik nodded in agreement. "We cannot be certain of the sequence of events. What we know suggests she is still on the palace grounds, yet they have been thoroughly searched and the buildings turned out. The guards have accounted for all those who have passed through the gates this day, male and female alike. Those within the palace confines are being questioned. A number of wagons and carts are known to have passed out of the gates at varied times. Those are being sought. As to ships, only two others departed at dawn, upriver, bound for Paris. Again, no women were reported aboard.''

"So, we have naught but speculations." Lyting vented his frustration on a long breath. "If we eliminate Garreth, we must ask who else would abduct her—if she has been abducted—and why? I cannot believe they could hide her this long upon the grounds." Lyting dropped his gaze to the floor, a muscle working in his cheek. "What enemy have I, to do so monstrous a thing?"

"Mayhap not an enemy of yours, *broFir*," Rurik offered, "but of our noble cousin. William has adversaries aplenty, both within and without the duchy. We might better ask who would seek to strike out at him in this way?"

"But why Ailénor?" Ailinn stood before the window, her features stark.

Lyting went at once to her side and slipped his arms about her. She sank her head against his chest.

"Dear God, who would do this to our daughter? Why, why?" Ailinn's voice broke with a sob, and she began to shake against Lyting.

He felt her pain. A pain resurrected from long past for them both, but most especially for Ailinn. She had once been abducted in a raid on her homeland in Ireland. Lyting embraced her all the tighter, wishing to shield her against the misery of that nightmare, remembering her great trials, for he had accompanied her into that captivity, seeking to free her as they voyaged to Byzantium. This time he vowed he would not be trammeled by inaction as he had been when he fought to save Ailinn. He pressed his lips to her hair.

"I shall find her, *elskan mín*. And when I do, whoever brought her the least grief shall repent the day he was born."

Just then, one of the soldiers materialized at the door. "My lords, a cart has been found abandoned a short distance from the west gate. 'Tis full of stale rushes, removed from the hall last eve. The cart passed through the gates this morn, at dawn, driven by two men. We are seeking to identify them. They could have traveled in any number of directions by now—no telling where in Francia."

Lyting turned to Ailinn. Their eyes touched a single aching moment. He gave her a swift, hard kiss, then followed the soldier out the door. Rurik embraced Brienne and likewise was gone.

Brienne moved to Ailinn's side at the window and encompassed her with a comforting arm. Together they gazed out the narrow slit.

"Merciful Lord, watch over them all," Ailinn prayed, her voice breaking. "Wherever Ailénor may be, grant her Thy protection even as You did me, so many years ago."

Great tears stole over Ailinn's cheeks. Tasting again of the dark terror she once had known, a deadly cold swept through her, and fresh fear for her daughter convulsed her heart. Clenching her hands to fists, she brought them down against the window sash.

"Oh, Ailénor, Ailénor! Where are you, my darling?"

Ailénor parted her lashes. And met with darkness.

She blinked and refocused. 'Twas not a pitch-black that confronted her but an umbery brown, pricked with a hundred pinpoints of light.

Her nose twitched at the close air and the coarse material that rasped her face. By degrees, her brain registered the musty smell of hemp, the gag in her mouth, and the bindings that constrained her hands and feet. The floor beneath her rose and fell in a steady rhythm.

Ailénor jerked upward, her heart slamming against her ribs as she recognized the motion. Instantly pain stabbed through her head and twinged along her tender jaw. She winced and dropped back down to the hard boards, then lay listening to the rhythm of her blood pound in her ears.

Mon Dieu, she was aboard a ship, inside a sack, being borne to she-knew-not-where but certainly away from Rouen.

How long had she lain unconscious? How far had the ship traveled? And to where?

Her head throbbed as questions assaulted her. After enduring several panicky minutes, she grasped hold of herself with a firm mental shake. She must rely upon her wits and clear thinking if she was to survive this ordeal.

Ailénor's thoughts vaulted back to the palace garden, her last memory being that of the pock-faced man who attacked her. A second man aided him. He had grunted and clutched at her with clumsy hands, his features shrouded in shadow.

If the two meant to despoil her, why had they not done so before now in the garden and been done with it? Why had they taken her captive and sailed with her from Rouen?

She shoved the questions to the back of her mind. 'Twould be a futile, sapping effort to even begin to reason it out. Instead she gave her thoughts over to the great Seine that flowed beneath the hull. It offered only two possible courses—upriver toward Paris, or downriver toward the coast, and from there La Manche, the Channel, and the open sea beyond.

The image brought her up short. Was she to be enslaved in a foreign land?

Her heart sprinted. Composing herself with effort, her thoughts turned to Garreth. Had he waited in the vacant garden, thinking she had forgotten or rebuffed him outright? Worse, had he encountered the scoundrels as they removed her from the grounds? Had they dealt him some harm?

Concern welled in her breast, but the scuffing of feet and rumble of male voices arrested her thoughts. Two men approached and halted nearby.

Ailénor took a tiny swallow. She held herself perfectly still, alarm skidding along her nerves. One of them spoke in a gritty voice. Her inner ear sharpened as she caught his words—Gaelic words. He spoke the native tongue of her mother.

Ailénor concentrated, attuning her ear. She was grateful her parents had insisted on raising their children to speak the tongues of their own birth lands—Ireland and Danmark—as well as that of Francia. Ailénor sent up a quick prayer of gratitude that they had, her attention shifting to the second man as he made a reply.

"She should have wakened by now. You hit her too hard, Grimbold, and probably suffocated her in that sack in the bargain. I say we open it and have a look. She best be alive." His voice took on a tone of warning.

"Quiet yourself, Wimund. You draw the others' attention. True, I slogged her good and solid, but she'll not smother in the sack. 'Tis a loose weave with breathing holes aplenty, and I cut a few extra. I suspect she'll be blacked out a time longer being a noblewoman, fragile and all. Less trouble for us, I say. Now, leave Lady Ailinn to her rest. She'll be needing it soon enough, eh?'' He gave a coarse, suggestive laugh, and the other man sniggered as well.

Ailénor stiffened at the implication, then again as she realized they knew her name.

The second man's humor driveled away. ''She's a pretty piece, she is. You said I could have her first, Grimbold. On a vow you did, and I'll be holding you to it. I ride Lady Ailinn first.''

Ice shot through Ailénor's veins as she realized 'twas not her name but her mother's they spoke. Shocked and horrified, her whole being revolted. The thugs believed they had abducted her dear *maman* and had done so with every intention of ravishing her!

Why, why, why? her mind screamed. 'Twas too appalling to compass.

''How long might we keep her? The princess warned not to tarry overlong or she'd give over the treasure to another.''

''Wimund, you worry like an old woman,'' Grimbold groused. ''There be sufficient time to take our pleasures, deliver our prize, *and* reap our reward.''

Wimund fell silent a moment. ''What think you of Rhiannon? Is she truly a princess, as she claims? A real one, I mean.''

''Does it matter?'' Grimbold riposted. ''The treasure is real enough.''

Rhiannon. The name spread its tentacles through Ailénor's mind, then coiled around her heart. 'Twas a name rarely uttered in her parents' household, a name filled with dark and grievous memories for them both.

Could it be the same woman? Had Rhiannon survived the perils of the Steppe?

Rhiannon was one of her mother's three stepcousins— princess of the Eóganacht clan. All four had been seized that ill-starred day when the Norsemen ravaged Clonmel.

By her own connivances, Rhiannon devised for Ailinn to be mistaken for herself during the attack so that she, Rhiannon, might be spared. But her schemes failed, and Rhiannon suffered no less than any other—save Ailinn who, due to a twist of fate, remained undefiled.

Later, during their transport to the East, Rhiannon brought about the death of their cousin, Deira. Later still, Rhiannon sought to save herself once more at Ailinn's expense. Amidst a fierce Petcheneg attack, Rhiannon cast Ailinn into the path of oncoming horsemen while she herself fled for safety. But Lyting rescued and defended Ailinn. Meanwhile, the heathens snared Rhiannon and carried her off into the immense plain of the Steppe.

Ailénor knew her parents assumed Rhiannon to be dead. She had overheard them speak of it with Lia, her mother's other stepcousin, Deira's surviving sister. Given the harsh conditions of the Steppe and the nomadic life of the tribesmen, they agreed 'twould be a miracle for Rhiannon to survive.

But Ailénor now knew she had survived and had returned to seek some distorted form of vengeance upon her mother. As impossible as it might seem, who else could it be? The men spoke of an Irish princess named Rhiannon, who promised them treasure to specifically abduct her mother. It *had* to be the same woman. Ailénor felt it in her soul.

"How much longer do we have?" Wimund's voice broke through her thoughts.

"We shall make the Frankish coast tonight, England's late tomorrow," Grimbold advised. "Then we need sail on to Erin and round the southwestern coast. Our time is good, so we can keep the *comtesse* to ourselves a few days longer before taking her on to the hill-fort at Cahercommaun."

"Can I have her tonight, Grimbold?"

"Patience, friend. The boatswain has yet to discover the true nature of the goods he carries. Though I expect no great trouble from him, our other companion concerns me more. Best wait until we put him off tomorrow, or leastwise until we are partway across the Channel and away from land. We can make our own rules then, eh?" He chuckled.

Ailénor strained to hear more but only caught the hollow sound of boot falls fading across the boards of the ship.

She digested the men's latest exchange, then folded her thoughts inward and tried to calm the rapid beat of her heart. She must let them continue to believe they held the right woman. As long as they did, there would be no danger they might return to Rouen to seize her *maman* or attempt to barter the daughter for the mother.

Ailénor doubted that they would free her once they discovered their mistake. At least this way she could protect her mother and, for the time, place her out of danger—no matter the personal cost. Ailénor determined to take on Rhiannon herself, if need be. The witch would not harm her mother again!

Ailénor continued to lie very still, hoping Rhiannon's hirelings would believe her to be yet unconscious. 'Twould be best if they did not see her in the light of day—if it were day—and risk their realizing their error. Even so, she and her mother favored one another. Mayhap they would not immediately realize the difference.

Somehow she must escape. Or get word to her family. There was little hope for either while she was trussed up in a sack in the bottom of a ship, sailing down the Seine.

Ailénor lay motionless, aware of the pitch and roll of the ship. 'Twas best to reserve her strength and fortify herself with rest for the time to come. Could she depend on the boatswain's help? Or that of the other passenger mentioned? The cold truth was, she had only herself upon whom to rely.

Lord, I need a miracle, she prayed silently as she closed her eyes and inhaled a breath of stale air. *If only Garreth were here.*

From beneath his lashes, Garreth watched the man with the bulbous eyes sniff about the cargo hold for an untold time this day. Predictably, he stopped before the sea chest and the parcel that contained the Psalter. Rubbing his jaw, he cast a glance back in Garreth's direction.

Garreth dropped his lashes to give the appearance he

dozed. When he cracked them open a moment later, he observed the man squatting before the chest and reaching behind it.

Garreth restrained his impulse. Hours past, he realized 'twas neither the trunk nor the Psalter that elicited the Irishmen's interest. 'Twas the sack that lay hidden behind them.

What had the men smuggled aboard? What could draw so much concern, demand so much vigilance? The two were as restless as ants, ever crawling about the hold and inspecting the sack as though it contained something . . . live.

Garreth's eyes flew open before he could halt his reaction. *God's breath. Of course.*

Having revealed himself to be awake, he straightened upright and made a show of stretching and yawning. As he stood to his feet, he gauged the deepening blue sky overhead, then ambled casually astern to where the boatswain sat at the tiller. He engaged in small talk while keeping an eye on the Irishmen, and learned they were to reach Harfleur in the coming hour. Meanwhile, the man with the enormous eyes climbed from the hold and moved off to join his companion.

Garreth strolled toward the fore of the ship, exercising his legs and slipping several more looks at the other two men. For the moment they busied themselves with a skin of drink and hard-baked biscuits. Mindful they would mark his movements, Garreth dropped down into the hold and strode toward his chest.

Crouching down, he withdrew the wrapped Psalter from behind the trunk and set it aside. He then took hold of the trunk and dragged it out from beneath the decking. Garreth could veritably feel the Irishmen's eyes spearing holes in his back as he unlocked the chest and opened its lid.

He spent several more minutes rummaging inside the piece. At the same time, he continued to steal glimpses at the hemp sack. He felt a cold knot form in his stomach as he realized, from the look of it, 'twas likely no animal in the sack, but a human.

Garreth decided his course, then closed the lid and shoved the trunk back under the decking, purposely ramming it into the sack. A feminine yelp escaped the sack, and it jerked sharply.

A woman! Garreth's thoughts jolted in surprise. Relinquishing all thought of the other men, he shouldered the trunk aside, pulled on the knife at his belt, and slit the drawstrings securing the sack. Hastily he yanked open the sack's mouth and next spied the top of the girl's head, her disheveled tresses spilling out. Their color remained indeterminate in the deep shadows, and still . . .

The knot in his stomach went to ice as he yanked the hemp down farther, exposing a pale forehead, then familiar eyes.

All flashed in a blinding white light as the back of Garreth's head exploded in pain. The light died, and he toppled forward into a black abyss.

Garreth groped his way to consciousness. The rhythmic rise and fall of the ship heightened the throbbing in his head. Still he fought on. Breaking through the shadowy barrier, he hauled open his lids.

The ribs of the ship's hull came slowly into focus, then the wood planking overhead. Judging by its outline, he knew he lay beneath the ship's foredeck.

Garreth started to rise but came instantly aware his hands and feet were tied. Twisting to one side, he forced himself up on his elbow. A pair of slippered feet came into view, issuing from beneath a lady's skirt.

Garreth froze. His gaze traveled upward over the gowned legs to a slender waist, the lady's arms being drawn behind her back as though bound. His gaze traveled farther to high, round breasts and slightly broad shoulders, all framed with a bountiful spill of dark red hair. His gaze vaulted to the woman's face, and his breath left him.

"Ailénor!"

Ailénor's heart beat hard and fast as Garreth's eyes locked with hers and he spoke her name. Fiercely worried about him these many hours, she smiled for joy. "Garreth, you are all right?"

"What are . . . How did . . . ?" He squeezed his eyes shut. "Please. Tell me I am dreaming. Tell me you are not here but safe in Rouen."

"*Alors.* We are on La Manche now. We sailed before dawn and are partway across."

Garreth opened his eyes, wincing as he moved his head.

"*Attention.* Careful. Wimund hit you quite hard."

"Wimund?"

"One of the men who abducted me. The other is called Grimbold. He is the more dangerous one, I believe."

"Sweet Jesu, Ailénor. Have they hurt you?" Garreth dragged himself upright, concern filling his features.

"*Non*, thanks to the boatswain. He saved us both." At Garreth's puzzled look she continued. "The other two would have killed you outright, but the boatswain argued you are a nobleman and worth a healthy ransom. This led Grimbold and Wimund to open your trunk and the package beside it. When they saw the weave of your garments and the magnificent book you transported, they realized the boatswain spoke true."

"The Psalter of Metz?" He stiffened. "Where is it now?"

"Wimund has it." Ailénor leaned forward and nodded toward the rear of the ship. "There, on the deck astern."

Garreth followed her line of sight leaning forward. His pulse jumped as he beheld the chinless, bug-eyed churl bent over the Psalter with a knife in hand, prying the jewels from their settings and slipping them into a pouch at his belt. Garreth swore blackly beneath his breath.

"Grimbold, the one with the scarred face, seemed to recognize you."

"Probably from the ducal hall," Garreth muttered without explanation, drawing his gaze back to Ailénor. He stilled, seeing the bruise spread along her jaw. Anger shot through his veins. "They did hurt you."

"Shh. They will hear," she calmed. "I am all right. I gained this when they first seized me, but they have dealt me no harm since. Actually the boatswain abetted me—in his own way.'' A smile tugged at her lips. ''He made a great complaint of my presence onboard, grumbling 'women brought bad luck at sea,' and 'had he known they had a female in the sack,' he would never have allowed them aboard. He warned if they gave any trouble he would put them ashore at Harfleur to find another ship.''

''And they did as he said and left you alone, without argument?'' Garreth asked, incredulous. ''They seem naught but cutthroats.''

Worry creased Ailénor's eyes. ''*Oui.* But I suspect they know little of ships and need the boatswain. As to myself, I feigned illness from the ship's constant motion. They have not bothered me. Wimund appears to suffer a touchy stomach himself, and Grimbold has been busied keeping watch of the boatswain. We anchored off the shores of Harfleur last night and sailed before light.''

Garreth glanced again to Wimund who now scrutinized the book's ivory plaque and gold covering as though looking for a way to pull them off. Garreth ground his teeth.

''There is naught we can do for now,'' he conceded finally. ''Best save our strength for the trials to come.''

Garreth scanned the bright sky overhead and the tops of puffy white clouds visible in the distance. Easing down on his side, he worked at the ropes binding his wrists and pondered their situation.

Ailénor dozed lightly for a time, then came suddenly awake as she sensed the ship moving rougher, swifter.

''We've picked up a good clip of wind. Do you feel it?'' she asked Garreth, leaning forward to glimpse the sky from beneath the decking. Clouds skated overhead, stringing out before the wind, naught but wisps of white.

''You know of ships and the sea?'' He followed her gaze.

''My father is a master seaman.''

''Ah, the 'Sea Fox,' Sjorefurinn. Your cousin Richard said I should ask your mother of how he came by the name.''

''You should.'' She tossed a smile, then returned her

attention skyward. A bud of hope expanded in her heart.

Hours slipped past. As Ailénor expected, the clouds grew gray, the water choppy. If only she could look out over the water to gauge its swell and see whether wavelets had begun to form or if they showed white.

Garreth, too, watched as the clouds darkened further. His efforts with his ropes had proven futile. Now, as he sat hunched beneath the half deck, he hoped for a miracle. Wimund, he noted, had abandoned the Psalter to join Grimbold. They stood astern with the boatswain who frowned deeply as he gazed to the south.

"Move the goods beneath the decks and lash everything down," he barked above the din of the sea. "We'll soon have a witches' brew."

Grimbold took exception to the seaman's orders, but Wimund's eyes grew to saucers as he stared at the horizon. He plucked at his companion's sleeve. "Best do as he says."

Grudgingly Grimbold joined Wimund and began shifting crates from the mast and stowing them underneath the half decks. As he looked on Garreth and Ailénor, he drew his knife from his belt.

"Out." He gestured with the tip of the blade, then cut the ropes binding their ankles.

"What are you doing?" Wimund cried and rushed over.

"Wouldn't want our prize captives to be crushed should the chests come loose. Tie them to the mast."

Ailénor tucked her head down as she emerged, lest they realize by her youth she was not the Comtesse de Héricourt. Her hair whipped about her in the wind, further veiling her features as Wimund tugged her and Garreth to their feet and led them to the mast. As he bound them, she looked south.

"Merciful Jesus," Ailénor uttered as she saw the bank of black clouds scowling on the horizon. She shifted her gaze to the water and saw how the swells were long, carrying sizable waves atop them, capped with white. As they broke, they threw up spray, wetting anyone near the ship's sides.

Grimbold and Wimund finished securing the goods as the clouds darkened to iron-gray.

"Reef the sails!" the boatswain bellowed.

"Reef them yourself!" Grimbold snarled. "I'm no seaman. 'Tis why we paid you to take us across."

"Then say your prayers if you remember how," the boatswain snapped back. "This vessel may be naught but a *sentine*, but she still requires two to sail her, and you've trussed up the man who was to assist me. Now cut him free or aid me yourself, but be quick about it. These storms barrel up the Channel fast and turn the waters into a boiling cauldron. They'll drag a ship straight to the bottom if not handled right. We need to reduce the sail area *now*, unless you want to be feeding the creatures down below."

"W-what creatures?" Wimund cast a nervous glance to the heaving waters. "What's down there?"

The boatswain turned to Wimund and grinned darkly. "No one knows, but 'tis deep enough to hold anything *you* can imagine. Now start reefing."

The ship rose and plunged dramatically as the waves grew bigger and the wind stiffer. Ailénor pressed against the mast to steady her stance, as did Garreth. He strained the ropes to lean closer as the waters buffeted the ship and sent sheets of spray onto the deck and into the hold.

When Grimbold and Wimund bungled their efforts to draw up the sail, the boatswain cursed vividly. He stationed Grimbold on the tiller, then saw to the task himself as he bawled directions to Wimund. Barely had they finished when a large wave broke over the ship's side, drenching everyone and covering the planks with foam.

The boatswain lurched toward the aft deck. Crouching down, he hauled out several implements and buckets. Making his way back to the mast where Wimund still stood, he thrust a wooden, shovel-shaped tool in his hand. " 'Tis a bailer," he called out. "Start bailing."

Obviously shaken, Wimund hastened to do as he had been told. The boatswain next turned to Garreth and Ailénor, released the knife from his belt, and cut them free. This brought a furious shout from Grimbold and caused

Wimund to turn back, but the mettlesome boatswain stood fast.

"We need every hand to see this through, including the woman who brought this piece of bad luck. They are going nowhere. Now, watch that rudder till I get there. The rest of you ship water." Thrusting the buckets into Garreth's and Ailénor's hands he made his way astern.

Garreth and Ailénor worked side by side, as did Wimund and Grimbold nearby. Huge waves continued to break over the ship's side, bringing frothing waters and making it difficult to stand or see. At one point, Ailénor slipped and fell, but Garreth quickly caught her up.

"I thought you were the one with the sea legs," he teased as he set her to her feet.

As he held her against him, they looked in unison at the squall line as it drove toward them, filled with fury and lightning. Ailénor pulled the sopping, draggled hair from her face and peered through the sheeting waters. In the distance she saw the loom of watch fires.

"Look!" she cried out, pointing toward the lights and what could only be land.

Making out the fires, the boatswain nodded brusquely. "We'll beat for the lights and try to outrun the worst of the storm. Reef the sail," he shouted to Garreth. "Not too far or we'll lose our steerage way."

"I will help you." Ailénor moved to Garreth's side, disregarding the boatswain's sharp glare that bespoke what he thought of a woman touching his sail. Together, she and Garreth took up the sail another foot.

As the minutes passed, the storm closed steadily upon them. Sighting the fires proved difficult and intermittent.

"Where are we?" Garreth shouted to the boatswain.

"Selsey is my guess. Unless 'tis the Isle of Wight that lies off the coast. Either way, we need head between the two and slip into the estuary."

The news heartened Garreth, for if 'twas true, they still held to their original course and could make it to Hamwih, however badly they limped into its port.

The ship fought on through the violent waters, driving

toward the loom of light off starboard. But as they approached their objective, the line of the storm hit full force, the great black cloud swallowing them whole.

Wimund shrieked in the ensuing darkness. Garreth grabbed Ailénor and pulled her down to the floor of the hold, searching at the same time for something solid to grip on to. His hand met with a shot of line attached to the gunwale. Seizing upon it, he wrapped it about his wrist and held fast.

Lightning flashed, revealing Wimund where he clung to the mast and Grimbold holding on to a rib of the underdecking. The boatswain rode the storm at the tiller. Thunder reverberated in their ears, followed by cold, pelting rain filled with chunks of hail. Garreth loosed his soggy mantle and covered Ailénor against the stinging onslaught.

As the ship pitched amongst the waves and the storm moved over them, the rains began to fall vertically. At the same time, Ailénor detected a shift in the wind.

"We are catching the back winds," she shouted to Garreth.

They climbed to their feet and sought the lights. Several moments later they located them. The fires appeared brighter but were no longer off starboard. Rather, they shone off to the left, port side, the winds' circular pattern having driven them southward.

The boatswain looked momentarily uncertain of their position, then made alterations and drove hard toward the land. The others resumed bailing despite their weariness, but the storm had yet to lose its teeth.

Suddenly the boatswain rose and pointed toward the land. " 'Tis the north edge of the Isle. Someone, get to the fore and look for the shoals."

Garreth started forward, but as Ailénor watched, she saw a huge rogue wave rise like an arm from the sea and crash down upon the *sentine*, swamping its deck, knocking Garreth back, and sweeping the boatswain overboard. The vessel lost all its way and bobbed like a cork on the sea. Wimund wailed and hugged the mast, while Grimbold scrambled for the tiller. Grasping it, he pulled it back hard.

"*Arretez!* Stop!" Ailénor screamed, seeing his mistake. "You'll drive us onto the rocks. Push the *other* way."

Garreth regained his feet and lunged toward the aft deck. Climbing up, he shoved Grimbold aside and seized the tiller, thrusting it out and putting the wind on beam.

Grimbold started to give challenge, but Garreth faced him down. "We do as she says. She knows more of ships than we, and I know the waters. There are rocks and sandbanks all along here. Unless you can navigate the tiller and follow her instructions, then you best make yourself useful on the foredeck and look for the shoals."

Grimbold reluctantly went to the fore. Garreth, in turn, motioned for Ailénor to join him. With Ailénor's help, he held the vessel on a rough course. He had no intention of risking a landing on the island or a desire to wait out the storm there. Hamwih was a better choice, especially to rid themselves of the Irish cutthroats.

Garreth followed Wight's shore to its northern tip, then steered the ship straight north across the Solent to the deep harbor known as Hamtun Water. Half an hour later, amidst driving rains and nerve-grating thunder and lightning, Hamwih's lights came mercifully into view.

Garreth sighted the wharf, a thin gray line barely visible through the raging storm. He looked to Ailénor.

"Support me in this," he said swiftly, without explanation, then shouted to Grimbold. "The shoals are treacherous here. We are going to try to sail in alongside the wharf, but we have too much way to make a safe approach. Get Wimund to drop the sail to slow us. We'll still have momentum. Be ready on the fore of the deck with the mooring lines. When we come in parallel with the wharf, jump onto it and get the line around one of the pilings."

"That's insane!" Grimbold yelled.

"You must try." Ailénor feigned desperation. "We have too much speed to run the ship ashore. We can only hope to lash onto the wharf and use it as a brake."

Grimbold mouthed his displeasure but leapt into the hold to rouse Wimund. Ailénor turned to Garreth.

"Do you really intend to attempt this?"

"No." Garreth kept his eyes determinedly ahead. "I intend to run us aground." He heard her gasp. "Brace yourself and be ready to jump when the time comes."

As the distance diminished between the ship and the pier, Garreth held the ship on course. He watched Wimund fumble with the sail but make no progress. 'Twould be a rougher grounding than he planned. With Grimbold poised on the foredeck, the lines in hand, Garreth drove for the wharf. The distance rapidly shrank, but at the last moment he pulled hard on the tiller, taking the ship off the wind and veering onto the rocky shoals.

The ship jumped forward, its bow splintering on the rocks, then heeling to its port side. Garreth lost his footing on the slick deck but saw Grimbold knocked overboard in a tangle of rope.

Garreth mounted the starboard rail and reached out his hand to Ailénor. As he did, he caught sight of Wimund clambering up out of the hold and forging toward them like an enraged bull.

Ailénor followed Garreth's gaze. Her heart turned over, but at the same time the corner of her eye caught sight of the Psalter that had been sliding about the deck. She lay hold of the weighty book and hefted it shoulder high. Aiming for Wimund's head, she swung and clouted him solidly in the jaw, cracking the aged ivory panel.

Wimund staggered, then struck out, hitting the book from Ailénor's hands and sending it spinning through the air and overboard into the waters.

Garreth followed the path of the priceless Psalter with a sickening feeling. But as Wimund lunged for Ailénor, he jumped from the rail and slugged him straight on. Wimund reeled backward, plunging into the hold unconscious.

"Let's get out of here," Garreth panted, grabbing Ailénor's hand.

Together they leapt from the ship into the shallows. Stumbling through the surging waves, they fled for the lights of Hamwih.

Chapter Five

The storm raged unabated as Garreth and Ailénor made their way up the sloping shore through sheeting rains.

A heavy roll of thunder resounded overhead, followed by an earsplitting crack and a brilliant flash of light that illumined the town in an eerie, false daylight.

Ailénor tucked close to Garreth. At once his arm encircled her, and his hand fastened about her waist. She, too, compassed him, instantly aware of the lean hardness and warm line of his body beneath her hand. Forcing her thoughts and herself ahead, she gripped up the sodden weight of her gown and fought the mud that clutched at her slippers.

Again lightning crackled sharply and fissured the skies, branching outward in a great display. Before the light died, Garreth pointed to a graveled street that led from the shore toward the town and directed her there.

"Where are we?" Ailénor called above the din.

"Hamwih." His response coincided with a clap of thunder.

"Where?" she repeated, squinting against another blinding flash.

"Hamwih. Come. We need to find shelter."

And safety, Garreth added mentally. Safety, not only from the convulsing storm, but from the miscreants who might be close at their backs. Surely when the two recovered they would be after them again like hounds on a scent. There would be no rest until he and Ailénor reached the security of the royal palace at Winchester. By God, he'd not let anything more befall her.

His thoughts circled back to their more immediate needs. Fortunately he had a passing knowledge of the town, having sailed from Hamwih's port a number of times, as recently as July. He now pulled on memory for a place where they might take refuge.

The town sprawled to a considerable size, yet half its area lay abandoned or in ruin. Hamwih was a dying town. Over the last decades the once thriving port and market center had been gradually displaced by Hamtun, a more favored site on the west side of the peninsula, situated on the River Test. Added to that, the town had never fully recovered from the Norse raid of the century past. Large tracts of land lay derelict, offering no more than weeds and traces of foundations.

As Garreth guided Ailénor past a collection of sheds, shops, and animal stalls, he swiftly considered, then dismissed, a number of possibilities that might offer them a safe haven.

Hamwih boasted an inn, but if the wastrels closed hot upon their trail, they would easily find them there. Most of the deserted buildings he could recall were no more than shells—single-roomed, ground-floor structures with no place to conceal two people in the event of a search. Given the sundry states of their neglect, the buildings themselves might prove as hazardous to tarry in as the storm itself.

Garreth felt Ailénor shudder at his side and perceived the lag in her step. The rain lashed down on them, cold and unremitting. He must find a place directly, even if they need retreat elsewhere once the storm lessened.

The sky fired afresh with light, and his eye caught sight of a familiar outline in the near distance—the answer to an unvoiced prayer. He smiled, then chided himself for not having thought of it first off. Sending his thanks heavenward, he conducted Ailénor toward the east side of town that lay along the River Itchen.

They found their way easily, following the straight and regular streets. With a wry, inward smile, he remembered his last visit to Hamwih, when he embarked for Francia. He had arrived amidst wedding festivities that the townfolk celebrated with great joy. The revelers had promptly adopted him and plied him with drink. It seemed Hamwih's widowed miller married its widowed ale-wife. Ale flowed aplenty that day—an exceptionally fine ale as he recalled.

He reined in his thoughts as the mill and the miller's cottage came into sight, standing apart of and a stretch beyond the end of the tenement-lined street. He scanned the three-storied mill, and his mood cheered. 'Twould serve their purposes well.

Garreth pointed out the miller's snug cottage to Ailénor, a welcoming sight. Light flowed about the cracks of its door, and a ribbon of smoke battled the rain as it escaped the center of the thick, thatched roof. They hastened toward it, and in the next instant Garreth knocked firmly on the door.

Ailénor shivered and nestled closer to Garreth. He gave her a reassuring squeeze and knocked again, this time calling out a greeting in his Saxon tongue.

Ailénor clearly recognized several words, including his use of the king's name. That she should understand aught surprised her, but she had scant time to ponder it as the door wedged open and buttery light spilled from the cottage.

A man's whiskered face appeared in the space, the top of his head no higher than Ailénor's cheekbones. Past his shoulder, she spied a small, plump woman standing by an open hearth, her protective arms encircling two children, a lanky lad who looked much like the miller and a girl who obviously favored her mother. All four appeared dubious of their late-night visitors.

As Garreth spoke in rapid Saxon, the man's expression altered, and the lines puckering his forehead and mouth began to relax. Likewise, the woman's face brightened, as though she recognized Garreth. Unexpectedly, the man drew wide the door and motioned the soggy travelers to step inside out of the rain. To Ailénor's dismay, Garreth declined with a shake of his head but gestured toward the mill and spoke further with the miller.

Again, Ailénor comprehended a number of words. Her thoughts skipped back to conversations she had had with her Uncle Rurik in the past. His ships traded regularly with England. Ever he maintained 'twas entirely possible for his Nordic Crewmen to converse with the Saxons. Their peoples shared a common Baltic ancestry and a common tongue. Nowadays, the differences of language were more like those of a thick dialect. Much could be compassed if one but listened with care.

She directed her full attention back to the two men, grateful a second time in as many days that she spoke the tongues of her parents' birth lands. Her knowledge of Danish would serve her well while in England, however briefly.

But she found the men had concluded their exchange, and Garreth now drew a leather pouch from his tunic. Ailénor's brows winged upward as he filled the man's palm with silver coins. At once, the miller gave over the silver to his wife, directing her to some task, then grabbed his mantle and ring of keys from a wall peg. Joining Garreth and Ailénor in the downpour, he led them to the mill.

Keeping in step with Garreth, Ailénor peered through her spiky-wet lashes to the building ahead. Her spirits lifted.

'Twas a charming structure, timber built over a stone foundation, deeply thatched, and possessing a great water-wheel that now creaked in protest against the bruising storm.

The miller shoved his hefty iron key into the lock of the stout oak door, and in the next instant they found them-selves standing inside the ground floor of the mill, dripping and shivering but out of the jaw of the storm.

The miller moved off for a moment, then Ailénor heard the sound of steel striking flint. A small flame appeared, puncturing the darkness, then a second. The miller rejoined them, offering one of two rushlights to Garreth, then guided them toward a staircase that flanked the inside wall.

Ailénor could see little. The narrow light played off the oaken floor, thick posts, and massive overhead beams. Darkness swallowed the room beyond the flame's imme-diate reach, though she could make out the waterwheel's shaft where it entered the building and a hint of the mill's machinery.

At Garreth's urging, Ailénor followed the miller up the stairs with Garreth joining them directly behind. The steps proved steep, and she climbed with some difficulty in the dragging weight of her rain-soaked gown.

The next floor lay in impervious blackness, like the first, excepting where the rushlights drove it back. The hollow echo of their footsteps told her 'twas a large, open space—a workroom of some sort, she presumed. All floors would be utilized in the milling process. Naught would be allowed to remain idle.

The miller led them up another flight of stairs, these much steeper than the ones before, so that Ailénor had to clutch hold of the railing and, in part, pull herself up. Her muscles burned in protest, and she feared she might slip and fall back atop Garreth. Several long, winded moments later she gained the top and stood on the uppermost level of the mill.

She inhaled deeply, swiftly, trying not to pant outright as she evened her breaths. Garreth finished his climb and moved beside her. He enclosed her at once within the circle of his arm and held forth the small rush lamp to inspect their surroundings. As he did, he stroked her upper arm with the pad of his thumb. 'Twas a gentle, reassuring movement meant to soothe, yet it stirred a most disconcerting and pleasurable sensation deep within her. Ailénor's breathing pattern broke all over again.

"Look there." Garreth nodded to the room as the miller flamed an oil lamp, suspended in an iron ring from a wall bracket.

She followed his gaze to discover large, upright frames congesting the floor space, each filled with a length of material stretched on tenter hooks. With a start Ailénor realized 'twas not a grist mill in which they stood, but a fulling mill for the finishing of wool cloth.

The miller's voice netted back Ailénor's attention. He addressed Garreth while pointing to the rafters above. She lifted her gaze to match theirs. Above, planking overlaid a wide portion of the cross beams, creating a loft over the central part of the room, evidently intended for storage.

Without further comment, the miller disappeared into the ebony depths of the room and returned with a long, narrow ladder. Bracing it in place against the rafters, he tested it, then scaled it straight up with the agility of a squirrel.

Ailénor watched, her jaw dropping open.

"We will pass the night in the loft," Garreth apprised, bending to her ear.

Ailénor's lashes flew wide, and she swiveled to face him. "Up *there*?" The second word came out several notes higher than the first.

He tipped his head in affirmation. " 'Tis a fine place to secrete ourselves from the scoundrels who dog us."

A shaft of fear arrowed through her. "Surely you do not believe they follow us still?"

Garreth's gaze held hers, calm but cautioning. "For whatever reasons they abducted you, 'twas with purpose and likely for profit. They are not the sort of men to be easily discouraged."

Ailénor's mouth went dry, knowing the truth of his words and recalling Wimund's mention of a promised treasure. She glanced again to the ladder, then to the boards creaking overhead with the miller's weight. Her stomach clenched in a rock-solid knot. After the trying events of the last two days, she held no wish to undertake yet another ordeal, especially not one involving heights. But neither did she wish to encounter Rhiannon's hired men *ever* again.

She worried her lower lip with her teeth as her gaze traveled to the ladder. "Even should we hide in the loft, what of the miller and his family? Can we trust them to keep silent as to our whereabouts?"

Garreth nodded thoughtfully. "I believe so. They seem good, honest people. In any case, I have compensated them amply for their troubles, and they, in turn, have agreed to shelter us and keep watch for our Irish 'hounds.' "

"But what if our 'hounds' tempt them with even greater riches?"

Garreth brought his eyes to her, their deep brown now black as midnight as they shone in the light. "The men who pursue us are foreign to these shores and naturally suspect to the villagers here. Like most Saxons, the miller and his wife prefer to succor their own kindred before any outsider of questionable ilk."

"But, Garreth, I, too, am for . . ."

He laid a finger to her lips. The warmth of his touch traveled through her, shimmering to the tips of her breasts and down to her toes.

"It matters not, sweet Ailénor. You are in my care. In truth, I have met the couple once before, and they know I am a member of the royal court. Since we are together, they consider us both under the grace and protection of the king."

Garreth withdrew his finger. Turning his hand, he lightly brushed Ailénor's cheek with the back of his knuckles and smiled. Her pulse fluttered erratically. Before she could recover herself, the miller descended the ladder, turned, and urged them to climb aloft.

Ailénor glanced to the ladder, then skimmed its length to the platform above. Her pulse fluttered again, but this time the reaction had naught to do with the warm stirrings of the moment before. To the contrary, she felt a sharp chill reach into her bones.

Ailénor shored up her nerve and stiffened her resolve, knowing what she must do. But as she continued to mark the height, her spirit flagged miserably. She shrank back and shook her head.

"Oh, Garreth, I cannot do this. Truly, I cannot."

Garreth's breath stilled in his chest as Ailénor transferred her gaze to him. Her normally blue eyes looked huge and dark and filled with dread, all the more so set against her waxen features. His heart tightened. Would that he could spare her this trial. But for her own safety, he could not.

"As I recall, you managed quite admirably in the pear tree," he said gently, gathering her to him and radiating his most captivating smile.

She started to counter his words, but he stayed her. "Trust me in this, Ailénor. I shall climb with you every step, every rung of the way. I'll not let you fall. Upon my sacred vow. Trust me."

Their gazes mingled and held as she absorbed his words and deliberated them in the depths of her eyes. Beneath his fingers, he felt the tension locked in her spine. But suddenly her trepidation seemed to subside, like the tide returning to the sea. Her body softened, and she relaxed against him, ceding with a small nod.

"Come," he prompted, his voice calm and steady and full of assurance.

Guiding her to the ladder, he encouraged her to mount the first few crosspieces. With that accomplished, he gave over the rush lamp to the miller and joined her, stepping onto the rung directly below the one she stood upon. As he gripped hold of the sides of the ladder, the length of his body blanketed hers.

"Do not look down," he said at her ear, his head even with hers. "I am here. I'll not let you fall."

Warmth rippled through Ailénor as Garreth's breath grazed the shell of her ear and skimmed along the edges of her senses. Together they began their ascent, with Ailénor first progressing a rung, then Garreth. The feel and movement of his body against hers distracted her thoroughly. Unmindful, she stepped into the folds of her gown and trammeled her foot.

Ailénor attempted to kick away the material with a swat of her toe, but to no avail. The cloth hung wet and heavy. When she attempted to position her foot on the next crosspiece, she succeeded only in further entangling her foot.

Charily, Ailénor loosed the grip of her left hand, reached down, and yanked the fabric free. This achieved, she caught her skirt up above her ankles, enough to execute the next step upward. Garreth moved with her, their bodies continuously touching and brushing and rubbing against one another.

Ailénor paused and fortified herself with a deep breath. Painstakingly she repeated the process. Shifting her weight, she switched the grip of her hands and dragged up the right side of her gown. Unavoidably, she rubbed against Garreth once more as she secured her foothold on the next rung and began to mount.

Garreth suddenly caught her hip with a hand and stayed her movements. "Ailénor . . ." he rasped, his voice oddly tight. "Allow me."

Shockingly, Garreth gathered up her skirt and draped its length over the crook of his arm, raising Ailénor's gown to a scandalous height. She gasped aloud.

At Ailénor's intake of breath, Garreth remembered the miller below, standing silently at the foot of the ladder.

"I do not think he can see," he assured. "My body covers yours and obstructs his view."

Ailénor did not respond, her lashes fluttering down to her cheeks. Her color appeared heightened in the dim light.

"Do you have a better solution?" He inclined his head.

"Non." Ailénor moistened her lips. "But 'twas not he who concerned me."

Garreth chuckled at her admission, but then realized, where he gripped the rail, his forearm, wrist, and the back of his thumb pressed intimately against her naked flesh. The realization sent a rush of heat lancing straight to his loins.

He steeled himself. With all Ailénor's wiggling and rubbing against him, she had already roused him to a most uncomfortable state. If she continued to do so much longer, he would surely embarrass them both with his bold and undisguisable need.

His thoughts flickered back to their first encounter in the orchard of Rouen. Truly the maid excelled at torturing him in the most singular of ways.

Garreth bent his thoughts back to their present task. Haltering his burgeoning impulses, he coaxed, encouraged, and talked Ailénor up the remainder of the ladder with as much celerity as he dared.

Gaining the top, Ailénor stilled. The rails of the ladder did not extend much above the platform itself.

" 'Tis all right," Garreth assured. "I'll hand you up." He moved his hand to her waist, outspreading his fingers to support her by the side and ribs and to better steady her.

Ailénor, in turn, placed her hands flat on the platform and, after a fractional pause, mounted the next two rungs with decided caution. Her upward advance caused Garreth's hand to slip from the curve of her waist to the roundness of her hips. As Ailénor drew up her knee and placed it on the platform, Garreth found himself staring at her curvaceous backside and at his fingers where they molded that lovely creation. He took a deep swallow.

"Garreth. The boards . . . Will they shift?" Apprehension threaded her voice, and she twisted to glance back at him over her shoulder.

Garreth snapped his gaze away from the delectable vision she so innocently presented him and wrenched his thoughts into line. He cleared his throat, aware of the state of his anatomy below his belt that currently ignored all mental commands. He cleared his voice twice more.

"The planks are nailed fast, according to the miller. Be not concerned."

The lines smoothed from Ailénor's forehead. Heedless of the placement of his hand, she returned her attention to the loft and crawled forward, moving away from the edge and leaving Garreth with his hand upraised, cupping thin air.

Garreth released a long, ragged breath as he lowered his hand and mounted the last of the rungs. Composing himself, he joined Ailénor and crouched down beside her.

"You were very brave, my heart." He smiled. "Are you all right?"

He yearned to touch her but restrained himself with appreciable effort. Oblivious to his condition, Ailénor leaned forward and laid her hand upon his. Flesh fired flesh.

"Thanks to you, I am more than all right." Her eyes shone with appreciation. She gave a squeeze to his hand, then withdrew her fingers. They trailed away in a butterfly-light caress.

Garreth's breath wedged in his throat, and his loins ached in response. His smile faltered, and he lifted it back in place as he rose and moved apart. Aware of the rapid rhythm of his heart, he compelled his attention to their night's lodging.

Large chests occupied the loft, some stacked atop others. Two had been pulled over and opened. Next to them, the miller had fashioned a makeshift pallet.

Stepping toward them, Garreth found the chest to be packed with wool cloth. This did not surprise him. 'Twas common for millers to receive a portion of the goods they processed in exchange for their services.

Examining the bed, he found it to be fashioned of dense, unfulled fabric, folded many times over into a thick padding. This was overlaid with softer, milled cloth, natural in color, having yet to be dyed. Additional fabric layered the top.

" 'Twould seem the miller has prepared a fine pallet." Garreth called over to Ailénor, avoiding comment on there being a single pallet to share. He debated whether to lay out a second.

A feminine voice sounded from below, dispersing his thoughts. Crossing to the brink of the loft, Garreth looked down.

" 'Tis the miller's wife," he informed Ailénor, then saw she held her breath at his nearness to the edge of the boarding. He stepped back. "She has brought us food and drink.

Make yourself comfortable. I shall go down for them and return in a moment. I need to have a few more words with the couple about those 'hounds' who track us.'' He flashed her a grin.

As he started to descend the ladder, the woman's voice sounded again from below. Garreth paused and looked back at Ailénor.

"She says to toss down your wet clothes. She will dry them in the cottage overnight by the hearth. There are ample lengths of wool cloth in the chests. She says to use what you need. They will serve as fine blankets.''

Ailénor watched the top of Garreth's dark head disappear beyond the edge of the floorboards. She waited several minutes, then gingerly crawled forward and peeked over the planking. The miller's wife waited directly below. Nearby, cloaked part in shadow, part in light, Garreth stood speaking with her husband.

Seeing Ailénor, the woman motioned for her to undress and drop down her garments. Ailénor gave a nod of understanding and backed from the edge of the loft. She rose to her feet and, with a wobble in her step, went to the pallet and open chests.

Of a sudden, she felt quivery and trembly inside, but whether 'twas from the cold, the climb, simple fatigue, or the thought of Garreth returning too soon and discovering her stark naked, she could not say.

Ailénor worked apace. She removed her ruined slippers, then peeled away her sodden gown, exposing pebbly gooseflesh, damp and chill, the tips of her breasts beaded tight. Quickly she snatched an ell of cloth from the chest and wrapped it about her. Balling the soggy gown, she crossed the flooring gingerly, then knelt down and eased toward the edge.

She peered below. The distance sent an instant shiver of fear sleeting down her spine. The miller's wife glanced up just then and gestured for her to drop the gown. Ailénor complied, pushing the wad of fabric to the end of the boards and shoving it over. Several seconds later the dull slap of wet cloth sounded on the wood floor.

Ailénor scooted back, then returned to the pallet. Catching up another length of cloth from the chest, she sat upon the bedding and toweled her hair. Readjusting the fabric that enwrapped her, she slipped between the layers of wool covers. Though the simple pallet could not compare to her fine eiderdown mattress at Héricourt, it seemed every bit as heavenly this night. She rolled to her side and tucked up her feet. They were as ice.

Curling deeper into a ball, she lay listening to the sounds of the mill—the creaks and groans, the steady drum of the rain on the thatching overhead. The murmur of voices drifted from below, while in the distance thunder rumbled as it moved away.

Ailénor's lids grew heavy as she waited for Garreth, a bone-deep exhaustion claiming her. Her lashes slid downward, and she sank into a velvet sleep, her last thoughts of Garreth, her gallant champion.

Garreth gained the top of the ladder and hefted the earthen pitcher he carried onto the planking. Extracting a small sack from his tunic, he set it beside the pitcher and finished his climb.

"We have food and ale aplenty," he said with cheer, skimming a glance at Ailénor's back as he caught up the items and strode toward the pallet where she lay.

Kneeling beside her, he unknotted the sack and withdrew a wooden cup, a meat pasty, a wedge of cheese, an apple, and a pear. He also retrieved a flint and steel and set them out. Again Garreth reached into his tunic.

"And, for my lady's pleasure, a small luxury . . ."

He produced a slim, tallow-dipped candle fitted on a small spiked stand. The item brought no response from Ailénor. He pondered the back of her head and wondered whether she listened. Flaming the candle and filling the cup with ale, he moved to the other side of the pallet and gazed down on her.

His lips curved as he discovered her fast asleep, her head propped on her arm and her pale, delicate features profiled against her dark red tangle of hair. He felt another throb in his loins. Lord, but she was ravishing.

He absorbed the sight of her a moment longer, before setting aside the candle and cup and returning to the ladder. Drawing it up, he lay it on the floorboards. No sooner had he finished the task than the miller's wife called to him from below. She wanted his clothes.

Garreth darted a glance at Ailénor. She appeared to sleep soundly enough. He feared shocking her maidenly innocence clear to the core if she should awaken at an inopportune moment.

Plucking a wool cloth from the open chest, he retreated into the shadows and began to slough off his wet, clingy garments. Cloaking his lower torso, he bundled his wet clothes and headed back toward the edge of the loft. Signaling the miller's wife, he tossed them down, followed by a wave of thanks.

With that, the couple bade him good night. They extinguished the oil lamp and departed, leaving him in darkness, save for the light of the solitary candle.

As their footsteps faded below, Garreth moved to Ailénor's side. He stood in pensive silence, gazing on her elegant features in the flickering light. She slept deeply now and, to his eyes, peacefully. Only the dark smudges beneath her lashes betrayed her exhaustion and hinted of the trials she had endured these last two days.

Garreth lowered himself to the pallet. Spying the cup of ale, he took it up and sipped it thoughtfully as he continued to watch Ailénor and contemplate the tumultuous events they had just survived.

Verily, there were moments this day he had questioned whether he could gain the advantage before Ailénor came to harm. Such powerlessness in the face of Ailénor's peril had ignited a white-hot anger in him. And a dread—nay, a fear staggering and soul-devouring—that she might be defiled before he could . . .

Garreth extinguished the thought, unable, even now, to face the possibility. He allowed his thoughts to drift back to their last morning in Rouen. What *had* befallen Ailénor in the ducal garden? How did she come to be on the ship?

And what dire fate had awaited her in Ireland?

He brushed back Ailénor's hair from her temple. By God's providence, their paths continued to entwine. 'Twas that providence that saw them both upon the same ship out of Rouen and safely to this mill tonight. He deemed it a favorable portent—a divine blessing—not only for the past and present hours, but also for the future days he and Ailénor would share.

Danger still shadowed them, Garreth knew. On the morrow he would conduct Ailénor to the most well-fortified *burh* in all England—the royal capital of Winchester.

Draining the cup, he set it aside, slipped beneath the covers, and blew out the candle. Stretching alongside but just behind Ailénor, he conformed his length to the curve of hers and draped his arm over her waist.

Their bodies quickly warmed one another. Ailénor stirred and turned over, then nestled against his chest. A gladsome warmth spread through Garreth's heart. He lay his head atop hers.

"Rest, my darling," he whispered into her hair. "I am here and I vow ever to keep you safe."

He came again. Riding from the mists, tall and broad-shouldered, astride a fine silver stallion.

His mantle billowed from the powerful lines of his body, and his locks flowed free with no helmet to constrain them or otherwise mask his face. His features remained vague, however, as ever they did. Yet Ailénor felt the heat of his eyes. They penetrated her straight through as he entreated her with unspoken thoughts.

He came again, as he had so many nights before, circling the ancient abbey, waiting just beyond the wall, bidding her to come away with him into the pearly mists.

Round and round he rode, the hooves of his stallion pounding beneath him, pounding in perfect unison with the beats of her heart and the heavy pulse in her veins.

Ailénor felt a compelling, irresistible urge to join him. Destiny beckoned and beguiled, yet she knew instinctively the choice remained hers.

The warrior reined his fine stallion before the age-old gate and waited upon her decision. Again she felt a deep pull within her soul, like a lodestone drawing her to him. In previous times she had vacillated too long, until he returned to the mists and left her aching with regret.

Tonight, however, she did not hesitate, for at last she knew truly the longings of her heart.

Nipping up her gown, she rushed on slippered feet down an endless, winding flight of steps. On and on she hurried, descending to the bottom, then escaped her confines and emerged onto the grounds. Hastily she sought the gate, but when she looked about, all had changed. She found herself enclosed in a hedged garden with no retreat—a garden that seemed familiar yet somehow discrepant in the abbey complex.

She moved toward the stone bench at the center of the garden to consider what next to do. Scarce had she sat upon its edge than a sound caught her ear. A sound distinctive and vibrating with memory. A sound just past her right shoulder—footfalls and the swishing of cloth. She turned toward it, but before she could identify its source, a hand slid out and grasped her from behind.

Ailénor screamed open-throated, but her exertions found no voice. Struggling to gain her feet, she grappled with her attacker, twisting in his hold and battling his restraining hands. He forced her down till suddenly she no longer stood but lay flat upon her back, writhing beneath him. Again she struck out with all her might, this time contacting a solid wall of flesh. The attacker trapped her hands, and another scream climbed her throat. Fiercely she struggled.

"Ailénor! Ailénor!" A voice sounded in her ears.

She sought its source, then to her amazement she beheld the mystic warrior.

He came for her, astride his silvery steed. Riding the mist like a cresting wave, he stole over the ancient walls and into the garden, scattering her foe at his onrush. He leaned out and caught her up in one arm. Setting her before him, he held her fast against his hardened body, then turned his mount into the pearly mists.

Ailénor's heart beat madly. She shifted her position to slip her arms about the warrior and clasp him tight. No mail shirt did her hands meet, nor corslet of leather, but bare skin, hot and smooth and wholly unclad. She awoke with a jolt.

"Ailénor . . . Ailénor." The voice sounded at her ear, gloved in darkness.

Ailénor blinked against the wall of pitch-black, momentarily disoriented but instantly aware of the hard, muscled body pressed against hers.

"I have you, my heart. You are safe. 'Twas but a dream."

"Garreth," she whispered, recognizing his voice, the realm of her dream dissolving into reality.

Her heart skipped several beats. *The warrior . . . Garreth . . .*

" 'Tis you," she said softly in a tone touched with recognition and awe.

"Aye, 'tis I. None other," he assured.

Ailénor lifted her hand in the dark and found his cheek. She explored his beard-roughened jaw, the fine ridge of his cheekbones, then feathered her fingers through his hair. Happiness welled in her breast.

"Truly, you are real."

"As real as a man can be." He chuckled softly. Drawing her hand from his hair, he gave her fingers a kiss and a squeeze. "A moment."

He rolled apart. Ailénor heard steel striking flint. A flame sparked brightly to life against the night as he lit a small candle beside the pallet. Turning back, Garreth braced himself up on one elbow and smiled down upon her.

Ailénor's breath caught as the light illumined his impossibly handsome features and accentuated the virile lines of his half-naked body.

Her heart thumped in her breast. Slowly she drew her gaze downward over the sturdy column of his neck to the base of his throat, then skimmed the width of his powerful shoulders, and drank in the sight of his chest, broad and sculpted and covered with dark, crisp curls.

She took a swallow, then remembered to breathe. Garreth. Her warrior come to life. The man who held her future as well as her present. A dizzying rush of emotions surged through Ailénor. Lifting an unsteady hand, she placed it over his heart and felt its beat.

"Truly, 'tis you, one and the same." She raised her gaze to mingle with his, then, approving her fate, broke into a deep smile.

Garreth's heart jarred beneath Ailénor's searing touch. Jarred twice more as she embraced him with a stunning smile, all the while looking much as she did the day she lay beneath him in the orchard, her autumn-fire hair spilling entrancingly about her, kindling his blood with desire.

He felt himself harden. But at the same moment a crease appeared between Ailénor's brows, and her smile dimmed.

"I was so frightened." Her eyes clouded with memory.

Garreth gathered her to him, settling her against his chest as he eased back down on the pallet. 'Twas unclear whether she spoke of the dream that had awakened her or the ordeal of her abduction.

"I was frightened for you." He dropped a kiss atop her head.

"Oh, Garreth, 'twas horrible."

He felt a shudder pass through her. But before he could comfort her, she turned in his arms and raised herself up, leaning half over him.

"I waited for you in the garden," she said, intent with her thoughts, oblivious to the disorder of the blanket that enwrapped her and how it gaped from her breasts. "The men seized me . . ."

Garreth followed her tale, yet his mouth went dry as he glimpsed the ripe swell of her flesh, the deep valley between, all bewitchingly enhanced by candlelight.

"But 'twas a mistake," she continued. "They mistook me for my mother."

Garreth pulled his gaze from the enticement of her breasts as the last of her statement brought him up short. Surely he did not hear aright.

"Your mother is safe in Rouen," he soothed, drawing

Ailénor down against him and tucking her blanket chastely about her.

How he craved to cup the fullness of her breasts and quest their sweet beaded tips. He shackled his rampaging impulse.

"'Twas but a dream," he becalmed.

"*Non*, Garreth. Not a dream." Ailénor thrust upright once more, her eyes wide.

Tossing the length of her hair over her bare shoulder, she caught the blanket just before it fell to her lap and exposed her fully. Garreth's pulse leapt, his eyes fixed on the blanket and the movements of her hands. Much tormented, he tore his gaze away and pushed to a sitting position. Rearranging the snarl of blankets that entangled them and concealing his arousal, he concentrated on Ailénor's words.

Briefly she recounted what had passed in the garden— how Grimbold seized her and struck her unconscious, and how she awakened hours later aboard ship.

Anger flared in Garreth as he listened, overriding his passion of the moment before. He examined Ailénor's jaw as she related Grimbold's and Wimund's conversation, and how they prided themselves on carrying off the Comtesse de Héricourt.

"They intended to deliver *maman*—me—to my mother's stepcousin, Rhiannon, at Cahercommaun. She must be an evil, twisted woman to contrive such villainy. In truth, my family thought her to be long dead."

Garreth listened closely to the incredible tale, then bowed his head, filled with guilt and fury.

"Forgive me, Ailénor. 'Tis my fault and my failing that you suffered as you did, and that you are here now. 'Twas my suggestion we meet at dawn. Had I not tarried in my chamber, I would have been present in the garden to protect you."

For the first time, he thought bitterly of the Psalter. He had taken pains to wrap it in a waterproof covering for the crossing. 'Twas that which delayed him, to Ailénor's detriment.

Surprised that Garreth should assume any guilt, Ailénor

caught his hands in hers. "*Non, non.* I came early. How could you know? Rhiannon's creatures saw me pass through the grounds and followed me, believing me to be my mother." He appeared unconvinced. She gave a squeeze to his hands. "Why, had they not seized me when they did, they would still be lurking in Rouen and perhaps by now have truly seized *maman.*"

"I somehow cannot imagine their succeeding with your father and the rest of your kin about." Garreth shook his head. "Nay, I brought this misfortune upon you, all to have you selfishly to myself a last moment before I sailed."

"Ah, Garreth." She smiled gently. " 'Tis not misfortune that has befallen us, but destiny."

He paused at her words and lifted his dark eyes to hers.

She wet her lips, a fluttery feeling filling her heart. "You asked me once why I left cloister. 'Twas a dream—a portent—that brought me from the monastery, the same dream I dreamt again tonight as I awakened in your arms."

Carefully she detailed the dream to Garreth with all its ominous and prefiguring aspects, describing, as she finished, how, this night, dream and reality merged to one.

"Methinks all that has passed is exactly as 'twas meant to be," she said earnestly, her blue eyes melding with his. "Even this mill—your chancing upon the couple's wedding—'twas all part of God's design. Only 'twas not chance at all," she added softly, almost breathless. "Do you not see, Garreth? I was meant to be taken in my mother's stead, as much as we are meant to be here tonight, in this loft, at this very moment in time."

Garreth went very still, his heart picking up its pace as he absorbed all that Ailénor spoke. His blood began to thrum in his veins. The powerful attraction that ever existed between them charged the air, multiplying a hundredfold till it fairly crackled with its potency. Instincts stirred strong and deep, ancient and ageless. Instincts to protect Ailénor, and to meld with her, body and soul.

Garreth lifted his hands from hers and threaded his fingers through the wealth of her hair. Its highlights shone of gold in the candlelight, firing his senses further still. He tipped her face to his, traced her elegant beauty with his eyes, then drifted his gaze downward over the creamy sweep of her neck to the pulsing hollow of her throat.

He bent his head and pressed his lips there, his blood flowing hot and thick. He heard her soft gasp, then felt her yield toward him. Dropping his hands, he encircled her at once and drew her to him. His breath came short as he trailed several kisses upward, then paused over her lips.

"Whether 'tis destiny or dreams that bind us, I know not," he said raggedly. "Only 'tis a force too powerful to deny. Nor have I the least desire to do so, Ailénor, for I would that you were mine."

His lips descended over hers, claiming them in a deep and hungry kiss.

Ailénor's passion spiraled to meet his as their mouths blended and fused. Fire spread through her limbs and swept along her senses, enlivening every inch of her skin. She parted her lips, welcoming, nay, urging his invasion. He did not disappoint but plundered at once and ravished her thoroughly, mating her tongue with his, stroking her to a fine madness.

Ailénor went to liquid beneath his possession. The fire that sang in her veins migrated to the tips of her breasts and centered there, awakening them with an aching, urgent need she scarce understood.

Garreth lowered her to the pallet as he continued his ravishment. Their lips coupled impatiently, and their breaths mingled. Leaving her mouth burning with kisses, he trailed a path of fire over her throat to the valley between her breasts. Cool air rushed over one breast as he pushed the blanket aside, followed by the intense heat of his mouth as his lips closed over her nipple.

Ailénor arched upward, gasping as he swirled his tongue over the sensitive peak and then suckled it. Again he circled her nipple—and again—until it contracted to a tight bud and begged with want. Baring her other breast, he laved it erect with equal attention and care, triggering a hot, throbbing response between her thighs. Ailénor wantonly reveled in his seduction, experiencing both joyous fragility and power.

His mouth returned and covered hers. She grew bold beneath his caresses, experiencing a fierce craving of her own to touch and taste and explore.

As his tongue delved into the recesses of her mouth, she met him stroke for silken stroke. When his hands fondled and kneaded her breasts, hers strayed over his chest and shoulders, then skimmed down to his backside, outlining their contours, memorizing his well-muscled physique.

He feathered kisses over her face, she along his collarbone. He nibbled the undercurves of her breasts, she nipped at the curve of his neck.

His mouth roamed lower. Ailénor splayed her fingers over Garreth's back as he stripped the blankets from between them and bathed her navel with his tongue. He moved lower still, pulling from her touch as he traced a moist line over her taut abdomen. She sank her fingers into his thick head of hair, her breath wedging in her throat, as he paused at the soft curls concealing her womanhood. She flushed hotly as he placed a kiss there, shocked by his boldness as much as by her shameless enjoyment of it.

Ailénor pressed her lashes closed, felt his breath fan her thighs, then felt him move over her once more. Flesh branded flesh as Garreth stretched above her, and she felt the irrefutable proof of his desire.

He recaptured her lips, coaxing her mouth open, while at the same time he parted her legs with the caress of his hand. As his tongue delved into the recesses of her mouth, his fingers slipped into her feminine folds and touched her intimately. Ailénor's heart leapt wildly, and she jolted against him, nearly coming out of her skin. But the movement only served to guide his fingers deeper inside her. She found the sensation too exquisite to deny.

And Garreth would not be denied. He withdrew his fingers partially, then slowly, deliciously began to massage her sensitive core. Lowering his head, he feasted on her breasts, flicking the globes with the tip of his tongue, taking them between his teeth. He continued to stroke her femininity with masterful skill, setting her afire and driving her to an impassioned delirium.

"Garreth, please . . ." Ailénor implored, feeling tension mount between her legs, innocently begging for an unknown release.

Garreth needed no further encouragement, his need for Ailénor so great, his control of self barely existent. As he settled between her thighs, she opened her warmth fully to him. He kissed her deeply, ravenously, as he began to push into her. Almost at once he met the barrier of her maidenhead.

He stilled, a complexity of emotions passing through him, stung with guilt from the knowledge that he would claim her virginal proof. Yet if destiny decreed and conspired that their lives be joined—if, as Ailénor said, all this night was as 'twas meant to be—then was not her maidenhead meant to be his and his alone? She herself offered her treasure. He did not take it lightly. Once he joined with her, 'twould be for now and evermore.

"Garreth . . ." Ailénor pleaded, like to explode. She reached out to him, her hands sliding over his hips and molding his buttocks, urging him to complete their union.

Impassioned, Garreth pushed forward with a single, solid thrust, holding her still as he did so, hearing her sharp intake of breath, and regretting the pain he caused her. He sheathed himself in her, burying his shaft to the hilt. He thought he tasted heaven, so sweet and hot and tight was she. Garreth feared he might lose hold of himself, yet remained very still, allowing her body to adjust to the new sensations, wanting their joining to be perfect for Ailénor.

She also lay motionless, her fingers stabbing into him.

"There will be no more pain, ever, my darling." He brushed kisses against her temples and into her hair. "I vow, only the sweetest pleasure."

He kissed her long and deep until she met him fully. Lowering his head, he seduced her voluptuous breasts with all the skill he owned. As she pressed against him, his hands skimmed the curves of her waist and molded her backside. Slowly he began to move against her, shallowly at first, then with deeper thrusts, unsure how long he could maintain his hold on himself.

Ailénor's body now opened to a world of sensation never before imagined, the feel of his silken rod incredible to her. Her sensitive core craved his touch, and she exulted as Garreth guided her in a joint rhythm.

Ailénor matched his thrusts, instinctively wrapping her legs about him, reveling in the intensified feel of him.

Meeting his passion thrust for thrust, her kisses became as devouring as his. Tension coiled inside her, building to the point of eruption. Just when she thought she could stand it no longer, a sensation shattered through her feminine core, a star burst, sweeping her away. She cried Garreth's name as the tide of ecstasy overwhelmed her and carried her to a dazzling height.

Her intense response triggered Garreth's release. He growled deep in his throat, then vented his passion with a cry as together they exploded in a brilliant, shuddering surrender to destiny.

Bodies and souls joined as one, and fires of passion melded their hearts.

Chapter Six

Ailénor woke abruptly to her unfamiliar surroundings.

"Garreth . . . ?" she called, instantly aware of the bare space beside her.

She shoved herself up onto her elbows and scanned the loft. All lay quiet in the pale glow of morning. No sounds rose from below, nor filtered from without, except the cheery twittering of birdsong. She spied the top of the ladder where it jutted above the end of the flooring.

Had something occurred that prompted Garreth to go below? Or had he simply risen early—in response to nature's urging, or perhaps to seek the miller and their clothes? Their clothes . . .

Ailénor skimmed a quick glance downward by reflex, fully conscious of her unclad state. Jerking the blankets up to her chin, she quickly assessed the situation. Three things impressed themselves all at once. She was alone, naked, and stranded high in the rafters of the mill. No matter the ladder, she was trapped until Garreth's return.

He *would* return, she assured herself, shutting out any dark possibilities. If something had befallen him, surely she would know it in her heart.

Ailénor sharpened her ears for sounds in the building, and listened intently once again. Silence prevailed, broken only by the chittering birds.

She relaxed and eased back down on the pallet. At once she felt a smarting in her muscles, in places never sore before. While her hips and back ached from the hardness of the oak boards, there was a new, unfamiliar soreness between her legs and a decided tenderness to her breasts.

Ailénor held no regrets. Despite the discomfort, she felt radiantly alive, languid yet energized by her lovemaking with Garreth. She looked to the side and skimmed her hand over the blanket to touch the place where he had lain. A smile stole over her lips and through her heart.

Lovemaking. Truly, 'twas that. She loved Garreth and admitted it freely to herself. In his arms, beneath his touch, she had become a woman.

Ailénor inhaled deeply of the loft's cool air, then snuggled down in the cocoon of blankets, feeling much like the caterpillar just turned into a majestic butterfly. Happiness wreathed her, and she basked in the fervid memories of the night before. Her mind detailed the particular intimacy of their joining. Her breasts tightened at the remembrance of Garreth filling her, the feel of him forging against her, she rising to meet him, their bodies rocking together in perfect unison . . .

A noise caught her ear. Her eyes snapped to the end of the loft as Garreth's head and shoulders appeared above the planking, and his gaze merged with hers. She flushed crimson to her toes.

Ailénor glanced away, her lashes fluttering downward as

he climbed aloft and crossed to her. Stealing a glimpse upward, she found his mouth spread in a heart-jarring smile, compounded by a sparkle in his eyes. He looked to be a man supremely content, obviously pleased with their night of shared passion.

She felt her color deepen further. At the same time, pleasure flooded through her, warm and sweet, that she could affect him so.

Garreth consumed Ailénor with his gaze. She looked utterly ravishing, a pretty blush to her skin, her hair tousled about her in fiery disarray. Modestly she avoided his eyes. A place within his heart dilated. He anticipated her shyness this morn, understanding 'twould be difficult for her to face him after their first joining. He wanted to ease any awkwardness she might own.

"Are you all right, my heart?" he asked softly, lowering himself beside her. She gave a nod, but when she still did not meet his gaze, he cupped her chin and raised her face to his. "Ailénor, I do not wish for you to be afraid of me, or ashamed. What we shared . . ."

Ailénor's eyes leapt to his, wide and expressive. ". . . 'twas the most surpassing experience of my life," she completed his sentence in a rush, covering his hand with hers. Her mouth lifted in a smile. "I am not afraid or ashamed. A little embarrassed, mayhap. 'Tis all so new. And somewhat unsettling. Whenever you look on me henceforth, 'twill be . . . well . . . with knowledge of my . . . ah . . . most intimate secrets."

Garreth chuckled deep and rich. "Sweet Ailénor, I have only begun to discover your secrets, and would continue to do so this very moment were it safe to remain in these lodgings." He drew her against him and brushed his lips over her brow and temple. "First I need see you to the protection of the royal city of Winchester. Then I promise to unlock all your secrets."

His lips moved over hers, and he warmed her with a deep and absorbing kiss.

Garreth keenly wished to reveal his intentions to Ailénor concerning their future, but resisted. 'Twas ill-timed. In addition to other complications, she did not yet know the truth of his identity, or aught about the life he would ask her to share with him in England. With the Irish cutthroats at their back, there was no time for lengthy explanations, and those certainly need precede his proposal. Before doing so, however, he must speak with the king.

By choosing Ailénor as his bride, he would, in essence, be rejecting the monarch's kinswomen, Mora and Rosalynd. Not that he had obligated himself to either. Still, the court buzzed with expectation that upon his return from Francia he would betroth himself to one of the king's cousins. He need apprise the king of his decision to wed Ailénor—tactfully, to be sure—along with all that had befallen them.

Having delivered Ailénor from her abductors, and with the approval and support of King Athelstan, Garreth hoped Duke William would find no reason to obstruct the marriage. Naturally he need approach Ailénor's father with his suit, but he wished first to clear all paths concerning the king and duke, for he sensed the greater challenge lay with the Comte de Héricourt.

Ailénor's hands drifted around his neck as she responded beneath his kiss. He groaned with want, but held his passions in check. They need be away. Expecting the king to be in residence, he determined to right things this night. Still, after taking Ailénor's virginity, he did not wish to leave her anxious of his commitment to her.

Ending the kiss, he held her close. "My heart, you are mine. Now and always. We are mated. Never will I let you stray far from my side."

Ailénor's heart overflowed at Garreth's words. He kissed her thoroughly, and she met him fully, joyously. When their lips parted long moments later, they both gasped for the want of breath.

Dropping a kiss to the tip of her nose, Garreth grinned, a beam shining in his eyes. "Unless you intend to travel naked to Winchester, you'd best dress, my sweet."

He grazed one silken shoulder with a kiss, then rose to retrieve her gown from where he had placed it earlier.

" 'Tis rather worse for its ordeal." He shook his head at the garment, then gave it over to Ailénor. "I fear we shall both present quite a startling sight at court."

Ailénor's brows pleated as she accepted the gown, its fabric stiff and scratchy and hopelessly wrinkled.

" 'Worse'? Oh, Garreth, 'tis pitiful." She looked to his tunic and found its condition no better. " 'Startling' is also mildly put." The side of her mouth quirked a smile. "Think you the guards will allow us past the gates?"

"It could prove a challenge," he concurred with a note of amusement. "At least we will have the opportunity to change into more suitable attire before presenting ourselves to the king."

"K-king? We are to meet His Majesty, King Athelstan?"

"Not if you are still wrapped in naught but a blanket." He lifted one brow and eyed her covering, waiting with manifest interest for her to dress.

Ailénor gave him an admonishing look, then matched the lift of his brow and gestured him to turn round.

Garreth's grin deepened. "As you wish, my lady. *This* time."

He listened to the rustle of cloth, then shifted his weight on his feet, chafing with idleness and visions of Ailénor standing naked behind him. He directed his thoughts ahead.

"You will be safe in the fortifications of Winchester," he offered conversationally. "There are over twenty-seven thousand soldiers to keep watch of you and maintain vigil for our 'friends.' Once you are secure in the royal city, we will send a missive to your parents immediately, assuring them of your well-being and alerting them of what has passed."

"Garreth . . ." Unease crept into Ailénor's voice. "Surely word is being spread throughout Normandy of my disappearance. Should Rhiannon's men discover they seized the wrong woman, they will return for *maman*."

"They could not possibly know of it, Ailénor," he comforted.

"Mayhap not yet. But think, Garreth. A kinswoman of

Normandy's duke—abducted? Such news will cross La Manche quickly."

The thought stopped him cold. "I am loath to say it, but as long as they pursue you, my darling, we know they have yet to realize their mistake."

"*Vraiment,*" she agreed in a reflective tone. "*Alors,* let us give them no reason to discover it." Her spirit revived. "I am ready. Let us be away."

Garreth turned to Ailénor and gazed on her with un-qualified approval. "You are very brave, my heart—a woman of true mettle." He took her hands in his and kissed them, then guided her toward the ladder.

Ailénor's grip tightened on Garreth's hand as her eyes drew to the edge of the platform.

"Mayhap not as much 'mettle' as you believe." She took a swallow.

Garreth gave her a reassuring squeeze, then climbed onto the ladder and lowered himself several rungs. Looking up to her, he held forth his hand.

"Trust me, Ailénor. I'll not let you fall."

Many heart-stopping minutes later Ailénor heaved a hugh sigh of relief as she stepped from the last of the cross-pieces and onto the solid floor of the mill. Together with Garreth she passed through the building, descending the two flights of steep stairs to the bottom entrance level. There the miller's children waited by the door.

"Go along with them now," Garreth urged. "Their mother waits for you in their cottage. You can break your fast and make your ablutions. I'll remain here and see if I can be of assistance to the miller."

Perplexed, Ailénor glanced to the machinery that equipped the mill, then back to Garreth. "What assistance would you offer him?"

Garreth read her confusion. "None involving cloth, I as-sure you. The miller is bringing a cart around. He will transport us partway over a bridle path that leads north to the upper Itchen."

"Can we not simply take a boat from Hamwih?" She furrowed a brow.

"Word is about this morn that the storm brought strangers into town during the night. 'Tis unclear whether the reference is only to ourselves or our Irish bloodhounds as well. The miller advises we not chance crossing town to hire a boat. They would likely lurk at the docks. The mill sits on the brink of town. We can set out on the path without drawing notice. The Itchen loops out and turns back on itself like a hairpin. 'Twill be necessary to cross but a short neck of land. We can rejoin the river upstream and engage a boat at the hamlet there. The Itchen flows directly to Winchester—into the city itself—though we will disembark before the gates, of course."

"Of course." Ailénor digested this information.

At that moment the young girl came forth and offered Ailénor a veil to cover her distinctive hair.

"*Merci,*" Ailénor accepted the creamy length of linen, realizing the dark red of her hair would indeed appear a beacon in daylight.

Settling the veil in place, she took leave of Garreth and followed the children's lead. The miller's son paused at the door, verified all was clear, and waved them on. Hastening across the yard—the expanse gone to mud—they gained the cottage.

Ailénor gave herself over to the care of the miller's wife who saw to her needs and laded her with provisions for the journey. She also supplied a worn but serviceable mantle to cover her gown. Barely had Ailénor thanked the woman for her generosity than the miller pulled the horse and cart before the house and summoned her to depart.

Stepping outside, Ailénor found herself quickly ushered to the back of the cart. There Garreth waited, now cloaked in an age-dulled mantle, his features obscured by a hat of faded green felt.

He greeted her with a grin, touching the limp brim of the hat, and handed her up. He joined her, and together they settled themselves in a narrow, open space amidst sacks of barley. The miller banked more sacks around them, then loaded casks of ale onto the back of the cart, further concealing their presence. This done, he climbed onto the seat where the children perched in anticipation. With a click of his tongue and a snap of the reins, the miller sent the nag and cart trundling forward.

Garreth turned a sparkling smile on Ailénor. "Well, my lady, we are off to see the king. What think you of that?"

She wagged her head, eyeing their bedraggled state. "Truly, we make a woeful sight." She sighed and gave a laugh.

"My lady, you wound me," Garreth countered with high cheer. "I confess, however, the state of our dress is the least of my concerns this day. Aside from the curs nipping at our heels, I am still debating how I shall explain to the king the fate of his Psalter."

Ailénor's eyes rounded as she envisioned the priceless and much abused Psalter flying from her hands and sinking to the bottom of the Solent.

"Oh, Garreth. What shall we do?"

As they bumped over the road leading northward, Garreth drew her into his arms.

"We have between here and Winchester to think of something." His smiled with a roguish glint to his eyes.

The tension began to flow out of Ailénor as they approached Winchester.

For hours they had sailed the clear waters of the Itchen, wary of each new vessel that appeared on the river, vigilant for sign of Rhiannon's men. But the day passed uneventfully, and now, as they closed upon a high, conical hill rising to the right, Garreth assured her they neared their goal.

"St. Catherine's Hill," he informed her, some of the tautness diminishing in the set of his shoulders. "You can glimpse the ancient earthworks that crown its top. From there, one has a splendid view of the valley and the city that lies just beyond. When all danger is passed, we should think to make a day's outing there. I believe you would greatly enjoy it." A weary smile touched his face. "Ah, look."

He leaned forward and pointed ahead as the boat skirted the hill.

"The royal lady herself—Winchester," he said with a

note of reverence in his tone. "She was Venta Belgarum to the Romans and Wintocaester to the first Saxons. For centuries now, she has served as the royal and spiritual center of the Wessex kings."

Ailénor's blood stirred at Garreth's words, and she felt her own excitement rise. The city lay on the west bank of the Itchen, nestled in a gap between two steep, wooded slopes.

"The site is highly favored," Garreth apprised. "Not only is the river at its narrowest to ford here, but the old Roman roads converge on the city from all directions."

"Does one lead to Lundenburh or, mayhap, Lindum or Jorvik?" Her interest peaked.

Ailénor's question took Garreth by surprise, but then he recalled her cousin Richard mentioning Lord Rurik's shipping interests in those towns.

"Aye. The northward road passes straight through Silchester and on to Lundenburh. From there, one can catch an additional road, but Lindum and Jorvik lay to a far distance north. Why, minx? Did you wish to travel there as well?"

"*Non.*" She smiled. " 'Tis only that I have heard them described so vividly in my father's and uncle's halls."

Garreth and Ailénor fell to a companionable silence as their boat glided into the settlement that flourished outside the city walls. A multitude of timbered houses and workshops—one and two stories tall—stables, gardens, and fine stone churches lined regular streets, each property defined by ditches. The vineyards, Garreth pointed out to Ailénor, belonged to the abbess of St. Mary's.

As they disembarked near the southeast corner of the city's wall, Garreth released a long breath and stretched as though he had just set aside a great weight. The lines that had etched his forehead throughout the day disappeared, replaced by happier ones radiating from the corners of his eyes as he smiled at Ailénor. On impulse, he drew her against him and planted a sound kiss full upon her lips.

"You are safe now, my darling. No harm will come to you in Winchester."

"Hasty words, sir," Ailénor bantered as she sought to

steady herself as he released her, then darted a quick glance about to see if anyone watched. "We have still to enter the city gates."

"Observe, then, my lady, the strength of arms at hand to aid you."

Garreth directed her attention to the rugged flint and stone wall surrounding Winchester, fronted with defense works—ditches and earth banks. The wall itself bristled with soldiers for as far as the eye could see in either direction.

"*Alors*, but they are an army. I only wish I held your assurance they would aid me on *this* side of the wall should the need arise."

"Be assured," he murmured so low she nearly missed the words. He chuckled then, some unspoken thought lighting the depths of his eyes. "Come. We shall follow the *twichen* and enter by Chingeta, King's Gate. 'Twill lead us directly to the palace complex. Once we are refreshed, we shall see that descriptions of Grimbold and Wimund are circulated amongst the guard and we must compose a missive to your parents."

Ailénor's spirits buoyed as she followed Garreth. He had delivered her unscathed from her plight, and now all was about to be set aright—her mother warned and Rhiannon's creatures hunted out.

The last of Ailénor's fears dissipated, and her presence in England took on the air of a grand adventure. She especially looked forward to meeting the renowned king, Athelstan. She had heard the most dazzling things of both the sovereign and his court. At home she had even once heard him referred to as the "English Charlemagne."

The *twichen* Garreth spoke of turned out to be a lane ringing the city's outer wall and ditches. They followed it westward a short distance along the south wall and came to Chingeta. It occurred to Ailénor that not all persons would be allowed to use what she assumed to be a private entrance, but before she could ask Garreth of it, she found herself standing before the gate looking up at the stone guardhouse atop the entrance.

No less than six guards manned the gate itself. Two came forth with spears in hand. Ailénor did not miss their quick perusal of hers and Garreth's shabby appearance. Mayhap they would turn them both away after all.

To her surprise, as Garreth doffed his ragged hat, both soldiers' faces dropped in obvious surprise. They swiftly reclaimed themselves and snapped to attention, as did the other four securing the gate.

Garreth acknowledged them all with a single nod, then addressed the two soldiers who had first come forth. After a brief exchange the men opened the gate, then filed into a strict line with the other soldiers, and hailed Garreth and Ailénor through.

Ailénor quickened her step beside Garreth, questions sprinting through her mind. She opened her mouth to pose one, then another, but then clamped her lips shut again, so confused was she.

Their reception pleased—nay, it astounded her—as did the ease by which they entered the city. She had presumed days ago that Garreth—as a *thegn* and member of the royal household—was of noble blood. She knew not his precise rank or, apart from his acting as the king's agent in Francia, how he otherwise served the monarch. Obviously Garreth's station was higher than she supposed. Higher than that of the guards, to be sure. Being part of the court, Garreth would likely be known to them. Wouldn't he? Yet, there were so many. And why did they show him such deference?

She held her questions as Garreth ushered her left along another *twichen*, this one running along the inner wall and paved with flint cobbles. They continued to follow the lane west, the ground rising gently but steadily beneath their feet, reminding her the city lay at the base of steep rising hills.

To her right, Ailénor observed large open expanses, and beyond them an immense complex of ecclesiastical buildings that stretched, from what she could tell, back to the city's eastern wall.

" 'Tis Nunnaminster." Garreth gestured toward the easternmost end of the complex, seeing Ailénor's interest.

"St. Mary's, if you will. 'Twas built by King Alfred's queen, Ealhswith, for the women religious. To this end"— he pointed to the buildings directly across from them and slightly west—"you are actually looking at two minsters. They are constructed so close to one another only a slight-built man can walk between. I certainly cannot."

Ailénor marked Garreth's grin. "For shame," she scolded teasingly. "Is this some manly boast?" she squinted back toward the buildings and tried to distinguish two separate roof-lines. "Surely you jest."

"Not at all. Look for the two bell towers. Better, wait until they ring out at compline and the monks of both minsters raise their voices in evensong. They fairly confound one another."

He was chuckling now, but Ailénor continued to concentrate on the distance. Her mouth suddenly dropped open. "There *are* two! And two bell towers."

"Aye. As I said. The smaller one to the fore is Old Minster. New Minster is the grander one that lies behind. 'Twas begun by Alfred, but he and his queen died before either of their minsters could be completed. King Edward, Athelstan's father, saw the buildings finished as well as Alfred's and Ealhswith's remains translated to the New Minster."

"Is that yet another minster to the left? 'Tis magnificent," Ailénor proclaimed as she gazed on the building's solid but graceful architecture.

Garreth followed her line of sight. "That is the royal palace itself. The minsters serve the palace in varied capacities and are closely associated with it. 'Tis why the three were raised within paces of one another. They form an imposing complex, do they not?"

"Monumental. Verily, I am impressed."

Ailénor had not expected to find such architectural sophistication in England. Winchester belied her ideas of the Saxon isle being filled with naught but rustic, timbered halls and simple stone churches. Looking to Garreth, she realized she need learn much more of the homeland of this man who held her heart, for he took obvious pride in it and loved it well.

Dusk began to dim the airs as Garreth conducted her right onto Mensterstret, Little Minster Street. Here shops and tenements lined the way, each occupying generous-sized parcels, marked off by ditches.

She gladly noted that the street stretched in a direct line toward the palace. Tired to the marrow of her bones, Ailénor looked forward to being settled in the palace and hoped, when she could finally seek her rest, she would be afforded a fine feather bed.

The light continued to dwindle, cloaking the grounds in deep velvet shadows as Garreth and Ailénor arrived before the gate of the palace's high enclosure wall. Once more, Garreth's presence brought the guards to rigid attention, and they signaled them through without delay.

The gate opened onto a large, cobbled courtyard where an assortment of people, horses, and carts yet milled in the descending dark. Many a man hailed Garreth in greeting as they crossed the expanse, and Ailénor herself drew more than a little attention. They continued on to the royal residence that rose to a lofty height and where additional sentries lined its stately facade.

Inside, their arrival sparked a flurry of activity. A man who appeared to be a steward of some order hastened forth, greeting Garreth, welcoming Ailénor, and sending the nearby servants scuttling in opposite directions with his orders.

While Garreth spoke with the steward, Ailénor glanced about the palace's elegant entry, then fingered back her tousled hair, increasingly self-conscious of her appearance. Returning her gaze to Garreth, she found a frown weighing on his brow as he listened intently to what the steward spoke.

Ailénor tried to capture the man's words, but as she did, a maidservant arrived—a smiling little woman with apple cheeks and plump as a woodcock. Her lack of height served only to accentuate Ailénor's excess.

Garreth addressed the woman directly, and this time

Ailénor found she could understand most of what he spoke as he bid the maid to prepare her a chamber and bath.

"Lady Ailénor is our guest from the ducal court of Normandy and is the duke's cousin," he informed, causing more than a few eyebrows to rise around them and sending the maid into a bobbing curtsy.

Garreth turned to Ailénor, addressing her in Frankish. "Aldith will see to your needs and bring you to join me once you are refreshed. We can then enjoy a light repast and compose a parchment for your parents."

He smiled and leaned to her ear. "Do not tarry overlong, my heart, for I shall sorely miss you."

Ailénor warmed at his words, her pulse picking up its beat. As she took her leave and followed Aldith along the corridor, she glanced back a final time before passing completely from his sight.

Sending a silent smile across the distance, Ailénor considered herself the most fortunate of women. Tall and handsome, Garreth presented a striking image as he stood engrossed in conversation with the steward. But as Ailénor began to withdraw her gaze, she saw the frown of the moment before return and deepen his brow.

Aldith moved fleetly ahead of Ailénor with swift little bird-like steps. Spying two young maidservants nearby, she clapped her hands, seizing their attention, and sent them scurrying ahead on a string of commands.

Ailénor followed Aldith up a great oaken staircase, adorned with decorated shields and illumined by torches in elaborate iron wall brackets. Reaching the upper floor, they proceeded to an open doorway, partway down the corridor, and entered inside.

There Ailénor found a chamber modest in size but richly furnished. Pillowed benches and fine coffers lined the room's dimensions, while tapestries brightened the walls. A sizable bed occupied one corner, handsomely appointed with patterned bedclothes and matching curtains.

With bustling energy Aldith directed the maid she called Edeva to open the shuttered window for air and to light the small brazier. The other girl, Leflet, she sent from the chamber on an errand. Aldith then turned to Ailénor and, with open hands and a kindly smile, offered to relieve her of her mantle.

It pleased Ailénor that she had understood much of what Aldith spoke. She disliked the thought of being imprisoned by a barrier of language, unable to communicate except through others and having to depend upon their translations.

Her thoughts shifted as she removed the coarse mantle supplied her by the miller's wife, and revealed her ruined gown. Ailénor smoothed a self-conscious hand over its soiled, wrinkled fabric that, for its trials, now hung oddly from her frame. Had Garreth not announced her noble station, none could guess it, she thought to herself.

If Aldith held an opinion of her appearance, she gave not the slightest indication by word or look, but quietly took the cloak and folded it aside.

The girl, Leflet, returned scant moments later with a tray of wine and followed by a small parade of servants bearing a half tub and buckets of hot water.

While Edeva and Leflet supervised the bath preparations, Aldith led Ailénor to a chair and poured her a cup of wine. She then fetched an ivory comb from one of the coffers and addressed herself to Ailénor's hair.

As she sectioned the dark red tresses and worked the tangles free, Aldith cast a comment over her shoulder to Leflet, saying they would need wash Lady Ailénor's hair and instructed she bring out the rose-scented soaps.

Ailénor smiled at the last, then winced as the comb caught in a snarl. Aldith apologized profusely, then worked at the knot more gently, offering small conversation as she did. Ailénor suspected she spoke more to herself, not expecting her to understand Saxon.

"The color of your hair is exceptional, milady. Very beautiful." The comb caught again. "And very tangled," Aldith clucked. "You must have made a difficult journey."

Ailénor fingered the cloth beneath her hand, acutely aware she looked more a scullery maid than the daughter of a *comte*. She felt moved to explain her state—or, leastwise, to attempt to do so, but hesitated, wondering how these women might react to hearing the Danish tongue. 'Twas the Danes who had been responsible for so much grievance in England over the present and past century. Still, 'twas her only means to communicate.

Ailénor gestured toward her hair as Aldith worked another tangle. "Rain . . . storm. At Hamwih."

Edeva and Leflet stopped in their preparations and uttered a simultaneous "ahhh" of comprehension, then quickly chattered something amongst themselves.

Aldith sent them a sharp look, silencing them, but not before Ailénor caught mention of Garreth's name. She shriveled a little inside. How it must appear to them—she and Garreth arriving equally bedraggled, he her sole chaperon.

When the servants who had delivered the tub and bathwater withdrew from the chamber, Aldith motioned for Ailénor to stand so she might unlace the back of her gown.

As Aldith began, Ailénor once more felt the need to offer some explanation of her circumstance.

"Garreth saved me. I was . . ." She cast for the correct word for "abduction" but could not recall it. "I was taken . . . stolen . . . from the court of Duke William in Normandy."

"Ah, Duke William." Aldith nodded, while across the room Edeva and Leflet echoed his name. "Do you understand our Saxon tongue, milady?" Aldith opened the back of Ailénor's gown and began to strip the garment away.

As Ailénor stepped naked from the dress, a horrifying thought struck her. Mayhap the three women could simply look upon her and tell she was no longer a virgin, that she had lain with Garreth. Heat crept into her cheeks, and she fumbled for the question Aldith had just asked. *Saxon—did she understand it?* she remembered a heartbeat later.

"I must listen well. How do you say?—I catch more with my ears than I speak with my lips. 'Tis the same at home. I need practice more." She climbed into the tub and sank into its concealing waters.

"We shall have you speaking Saxon itself and like a

native in no time, Lady Ailénor,'' Aldith cheered, then bid Edeva and Leflet to begin their ministrations.

Ailénor smiled but refrained from comment, unknowing of how long her stay would be in England. The thought halted her. Returning to Francia meant leaving Garreth, but remaining in England meant being severed from her family from whom she had been so abruptly and unceremoniously ripped away.

The realization flew as an arrow through her heart. Garreth had declared he would not allow her far from his side. Yet, as she thought on it, he had made no promises either— not of rings or vows or aught that would bind himself to her in a relationship more licit or permanent. The thought pricked. What plans did Garreth hold for their future?

When the troubling thoughts threatened to bring on a massive headache, Ailénor released her concerns, trusting in Garreth. There had been precious little time to discuss a future of any description. Now that they were safely ensconced in the palace, the luxury of time was theirs. They could speak of it anon and to their hearts' content.

She smiled and sank farther down into the heat of the water, then felt the soreness slowly seep from her bones. While Edeva and Leflet soaped and rinsed her hair, she enjoyed a friendly if limited conversation with them and Aldith. When she asked of King Athelstan, Aldith shook her head.

''His Majesty left Winchester several days past. He rides after the Scots,'' she explained. ''They ever be a thorn in the king's side. This time they have stirred trouble on the border. A little trouble, not much. God willing, King Athelstan shall soon return.''

Ailénor realized 'twas likely the king's absence that had caused Garreth's earlier frown.

Rising and stepping from the tub, Ailénor waited as the maids quickly wrapped her in thick toweling, then followed them to stand by the warmth of the brazier. With additional cloths Edeva and Leflet worked to squeeze and blot the wetness from her hair, drying it as best they could.

Aldith next brought forth a thin linen undergarment for

Ailénor to wear next to her skin. 'Twas what the Frankish called a *chemise*. Aldith, however, pleased to instruct Ailénor with her first word in Saxon, called it a *smoc*.

Ailénor slipped the garment on over her head, then sat at Aldith's request so she might next work with her hair. "'Tis still quite damp." Aldith pursed her lips as she circled Ailénor and considered the length and texture of her hair and the shape of her face. "A braid, I think. Yes. Atop your head."

Without another word, Aldith wove Ailénor's tresses into a single thick braid, then circled it atop her head into a crown and secured it with ivory pins studded with pearls. Her eyes sparkled as she looked on her creation. With a quick waggle of her hand, she motioned for Edeva and Leflet to bring the gowns and prompted Ailénor to stand.

Ailénor found herself at the center of much fussing as the maids helped her into a milky white undertunic embellished with a broad border of gold along the hem. Over this they drew a full-length overtunic, violet in color and trimmed with embroidery. This they bloused up over a jeweled belt, exposing the border of the undertunic.

Leflet brought slippers of soft deerskin with slim bands that fastened elegantly across the ankles. Edeva added a silken mantle, lined in contrasting colors—pale blue against deeper violet. To complete Ailénor's attire, Aldith fastened two filigree brooches to her mantle, one at each shoulder, then covered her hair with a long, light veil.

Stepping back, Aldith clasped her hands together and smiled broadly. Leflet brought forth a mirror. When she held it up, Ailénor found herself startled by the image that gazed back. Her hand fluttered to her throat.

"*Merci*. I—I feel . . . beautiful."

"You *are* beautiful, Lady Ailénor, and you shall claim many a heart at King Athelstan's court," Aldith avowed. She tilted her head and smiled softly. "But then, 'tis probably just one you wish to entrance. Come, milady. Let us not keep him waiting any longer."

*   *   *

Ailénor's heart beat light and rapid as she followed Aldith from the room. The very thought of seeing Garreth made her whole being well with a bottomless joy.

Outside the chamber, she and Aldith stayed their steps as they encountered a palace guard waiting just beyond the portal. Aldith conferred with him, then, by look and gesture, indicated to Ailénor they were to accompany him below.

Descending the great staircase to the entrance floor, they proceeded to a hall, moderate in size but splendid in its trappings. A table—great and round—sat at the room's center surrounded by oaken chairs, one grander than the rest in size and appearance. A forest of pennants lined the walls, each individual and distinct, suspended from lances far above their heads. Ailénor guessed the room to be the king's council chamber.

Continuing across, the guard led them to an arched doorway located at the upper end of the hall. Traversing its portal, they found themselves in a small antechamber that opened onto yet another interior room. There the golden glow of light suggested the presence of others gathered within.

Scarcely a heartbeat later, male voices rose in conversation—one rough and rumbling, the other smooth and pleasantly pitched. Ailénor smiled, recognizing the last to be Garreth's.

As Ailénor stepped toward the entrance, the other man discharged a sharp laugh, followed by what seemed a terse pronouncement. Ailénor could not distinguish whether the man jested, was angry, or whether he and Garreth merely debated some matter in a lively but combative fashion as men were wont to do.

The guard hesitated, seeming reluctant to interrupt, and gestured for the women to wait. Aldith moved back several paces, but Ailénor, hearing Garreth's voice rise on a brisk rejoinder, remained fixed in place.

She peered into the chamber but, from her vantage, could see little more than the opposite wall and the end of a table. The dimensions of the room lay mostly to the right so that she saw nothing of Garreth, nor of the man with whom he spoke.

But even as she craned to catch sight of Garreth, he moved into view, his back confronting her as he addressed the other man. Ailénor concentrated on their words, expecting Garreth was in the course of detailing their adventures from Rouen.

Listening, she began to sense a tension that hung between the two men and wondered if Garreth might, instead, be explaining the unhappy fate of the Psalter. As she caught snippets of the conversation, she realized Garreth spoke of Duke William. To her surprise, his words did not concern her but the Carolingian prince, Louis, and the crown of Francia.

Did she hear aright? she wondered, taken aback. When had Garreth spoken with William? What interest did he have in the political affairs of Francia?

Garreth shifted his stance, his back still to Ailénor and his tall figure blocking her sight of the other man whom he addressed as Cynric. 'Twas this Cynric, she realized, who now spoke.

"William is a predictable man. Ever has been. He and his Normans have struck a deal with the Robertians, and for the price of land, their swords now sing from their scabbards for the Robertians' and Raoul's cause. William will not support Louis's claim without ample reason or for sufficient gain. Mark my words."

"The duke and certain of his barons contend the time is ill-favored to restore the Carolingians," Garreth remarked, "The effort would be doomed."

"It surprises me, Garreth, you did not seek to persuade the duke otherwise. Or might it be possible he has beguiled you to his way of thinking, hoping that you might influence King Athelstan?"

" 'Twas not my place or my mission to persuade, negotiate, or contrive any plans either for Raoul's removal or Louis's return. My charge was solely to gather what information I might. To that end, I would remind you, Cynric, I am accountable to none but the king of my findings in

Francia. Certainly not to you.''

Ailénor froze in place. Garreth, a spy? Nay, it could not be so.

"As the *wicgerefa* of Winchester . . .'' Cynric began.

"As the *wicgerefa* you have no say in such affairs.''

"As a member of the Witan, however, I do. I can assure you, on many a night in your absence we discussed this very matter to great depth, in this very room. The king wants his nephew Louis to wear his rightful crown, and *soon.*''

Cynric moved apart of Garreth and into sight of the table. Taking up the pitcher, he refilled his goblet. As he turned back toward Garreth, lifting the goblet to his lips, his eyes stilled over Ailénor, and he paused midmotion. Slowly he lowered the vessel, his gaze slipping over her.

Cynric proved to be a sharp-featured man of medium height, his hair light brown and cut straight across the brow. His nose was thin and aquiline, accenting angular cheekbones and a well-defined jaw. His fine clothes and jewels spoke of high station. Ailénor suspected him to be a chief minister and confidant of the king.

Yet if that were so, why would he be speaking to Garreth on the matters he did? she reasoned. And how did Garreth's "mission'' of gathering relics connect to Duke William and Louis's throne?

Garreth caught Cynric's look and turned to discover Ailénor. As he faced her fully, her eyes rounded wide.

Garreth stood before her, magnificently attired, his movements setting off the gleam of gold and glint of jewels. His tunic was a rich garnet in color, edged with embroidery, the sleeves fashionably wrinkled over the forearms nearly to the elbow, declaring great cost. The belt about his waist bore richly ornamented clasps and mounts, while a large and resplendent brooch fastened his mantle at his left shoulder. About his neck he wore a gold torque and on his finger a large ruby. A silver-hilted sword gleamed at his side. The man who stood before her was no collector of bones!

The realization jolted. Who *was* Garreth of Tamworth?

Why did he present himself as he did at the court of Normandy?

A wide smile spread Garreth's features, and as his gaze traveled over her, she saw a flash of pride in his eyes. Coming forward, he dismissed the guard and Aldith and, taking her by the hand, led her into the chamber. Before she could utter a word, he made her presentation.

"Lady Ailénor of Héricourt, daughter of Count Lyting Atlison and cousin to Duke William of Normandy."

Immediately Ailénor felt Cynric's close scrutiny. He reminded her much of the Burgundians who had so recently infested the duke's court.

"Lady Ailénor . . ." Cynric bowed over her hand. "Garreth has apprised me of your unfortunate experience. I am Cynric, *wicgerefa*, the High Reeve of Winchester. I must confess I am both enchanted and dazzled by the beauty of Normandy."

"Save your flatteries, Cynric," Garreth clipped out. "Lady Ailénor understands naught of our tongue."

Startled and amused by the testiness she detected in Garreth's voice, Ailénor began to correct his impression of her abilities to communicate when a movement in the shadows caught her eye. There sat another man at the end of the table.

Slowly he leaned forward into the light, his eyes fastening on her. A sense of foreboding rippled through Ailénor. She marked his dark hair and twisted, forked beard. Did she know him? His eyes glittered as he gazed on her, glittered with something akin to hate. Ailénor's heart lurched. She recoiled and stepped toward Garreth.

Cynric withdrew for a moment to speak with the man at the table, then nodded his head in agreement at something the man said. As Cynric returned to Ailénor and Garreth, the other man eased back into the shadows once more, a thin smile playing over his lips.

Ailénor's gaze leapt to Cynric. She wished she could read what she saw reflected in his eyes. Instinct told her to trust him not at all.

He paused before her, smiling the same thin smile as the

other man. "Truly, we are most pleased to welcome you to the royal court at Winchester. You shall be His Majesty's very *special* guest."

Cynric waited as Garreth interpreted his words, then without turning his head or altering his expression, he shifted his eyes to Garreth.

"Well done. I really must congratulate you, Garreth. Very clever. But then you always were one to seize an opportunity whenever it presented itself and turn it to the best advantage."

As Ailénor struggled to make sense of what Cynric said, she felt Garreth stiffen beside her.

"Normandy's duke will be pleased by your valor," Cynric continued, "having so courageously rescued his kinswoman from the hands of cutthroats and brought her to safety." His voice lowered, filled with cunning. "I am sure Duke William will understand completely should Ailénor choose to remain in our company for a time—to acquaint herself with Francia's exiled dowager queen, of course, and provide companionship to Louis. Undoubtedly King Athelstan will be glad to accommodate her until the day Louis is restored to his throne."

Garreth took a quick step forward. "What scheme do you imply, Cynric?"

"Imply? I but state the obvious. 'Tis not the first time you have turned opportunity to advantage. And this time, in delivering the duke's kinswoman to Athelstan, you have provided him a perfect device to force William's hand—a most noble 'guest.' " Cynric's smile spread to a grin as he assayed Ailénor with his look. "Yes, she will be a fine surety for Louis's restoration."

Ailénor's eyes slewed to Garreth. She prayed she misunderstood the meaning of Cynric's words, words he obviously did not expect her to comprehend. Garreth held himself rigid, his face a granite scowl. His hands balled into fists as Cynric continued.

"You can be certain of a reward. But of course you knew that. And the king *always* rewards you well. I'd say your new title as *ealdorman* is well earned this day by bringing His Majesty such a prize.''

"Prize? Nay, you mean hostage.''

Hostage? Ailénor latched on to the word, shock following shock. She was to be used as a pawn, and Garreth was to be rewarded for his part in the event.

Ailénor's eyes narrowed on Garreth. He had betrayed her. By his deed, she would be made a captive of the Saxon court until one throne was traded for another. Anger raged in her breast as he began to turn toward her.

"Deceiver!" she cried and cracked her hand across Garreth's face with all the force she could deliver.

Whirling from him, Ailénor fled the chamber.

Chapter Seven

Ailénor stormed to her chamber, carried on a wave of fury. But the instant she crossed the threshold great tears began to tumble over her cheeks.

Surety. Hostage. Captive. The words resounded in her ears.

Ailénor took hold of the door and slammed it shut, startling Leflet who stood at the bed, tucking in fresh linens. Ailénor swiped at her tears, despising her weakness, but found, once unleashed, she could scarce stanch their flow. The ordeals of the past days now took their toll, all her suppressed emotions rushing forth to overwhelm. Yet for all she had endured, this betrayal she found to be the most unbearable. Garreth had deceived her most cruelly.

Leflet started forward to comfort Ailénor, but before she took two steps, the door burst open, shuddering upon its hinges. Leflet squeaked and scampered back to a corner as Garreth filled the portal and entered in.

Ailénor turned glacial blue eyes on him, then gave him her back and started across the room. But Garreth took a lunging step, caught her by the arm, and spun her around. Ailénor struggled against his hold and smote his chest, but Garreth easily trapped her hands. Jerking her flat against him, he pinned her arms to her sides.

A squeak came from the corner, and Garreth spied Leflet. "Leave us!" he boomed.

"Stay, Leflet!" Ailénor countered.

"Leflet, go!" Garreth leveled a hard-as-nails look at the girl.

Leflet sucked in her breath and, quick as a mouse, scurried past the couple and out the door.

"Let go of me!" Ailénor wriggled beneath his iron-hard grasp but did no more than warm him with her squirming, her breasts, stomach, and thighs being pressed firmly against his length.

Garreth tensed and pulled slightly apart. "Ailénor, stop this. Listen to me."

"*Non.* I have heard enough!" she blurted angrily, tears wetting her cheeks.

"And just what do you think you heard?" he snapped, his temper fraying. "Do you speak Saxon so perfectly?"

"Not Saxon. Danish. And I understand well enough to know by your deceit I am to be held captive at the Saxon court—'surety,' was that not Cynric's word?—to gain Duke William's support for Louis's cause. I understand enough to know you use me to scale the heights of power and profit—at my expense and that of Normandy!"

She aimed her slippered foot at his booted shin. Contacting his ankle, she winced in pain.

Garreth held her at arm's length. "Ailénor, no more, I say. This is madness. Naught is as it seems."

"*Vraiment?* Then I am free to leave? This night? This instant?" she challenged.

Garreth hesitated, and her eyes thinned.

"I thought not. Tell me then. Why *were* you in Normandy? And who are you truly?" Her eyes flickered over his finery and his silver-hilted sword. " 'Tis quite obvious you are so much more than you presented yourself to be in Rouen. Did you deceive William as successfully as you did me?" She stubbornly fought back a tear, but it rolled from beneath her lashes despite her effort.

"William knew precisely my purpose in Francia. 'Twas why I sought an audience with him."

"Yet you departed court so abruptly. Did not your talk with my cousin come to a favorable conclusion? Did he dislike what you had to say? Is that why you sailed from Rouen so suddenly?" A dark suspicion poisoned her thoughts. "Is *that* the reason you asked me to the garden? To seize me yourself?"

"Enough, Ailénor, I'll hear no more!" Garreth barked, seeing where her thoughts led. Next she would accuse him of hiring Grimbold and Wimund himself, a partner to their perfidy, and his bringing her here all an elaborate plot.

He released Ailénor. She rubbed her arms and backed away several steps, distraught and trembling.

Garreth shoved a hand through his hair. It beseemed the whole world reeled about him. When events first exploded in the chamber below, he had been stunned by the turn of things. Scarce did Cynric make his astounding pronouncements when Ailénor came to life and turned on him, striking him across the face. She bolted before he could recover from his shock or comprehend her actions. Now, realizing what had passed, it cut deep that she believed him part to Cynric's schemes. He would brook no more assaults upon his person—verbal or otherwise.

"Ailénor, listen to me. Verily, my mission to Francia was for more than relics and Psalters. Rather, 'twas to garner information. The king wishes to assess, firsthand, which way the wind blows in Francia and where Hugh and William stand concerning the crown. If the Carolingian line is to be restored, 'twill require their aid more than any other to displace Raoul. Despite the king's desire to see Louis crowned, Athelstan is a wise and prudent man. He will not place his nephew in a futile situation. Nor would he hold a woman hostage. 'Tis not the king's way. Nor 'tis mine.''

Ailénor dropped her gaze, avoiding his. ''Still, by what I heard—Cynric's words and yours—it seems events played most advantageously into your hands.''

''There is where your understanding of the language falls short—or at least of its inflections. Obviously you cannot differentiate between that which is stated as fact and that which is spoken with denial or sarcasm.''

''But . . .''

''Hear me out, Ailénor. In no way have I wronged you. I saved you, if you will recall. Saved you from certain ravishment and I dare not think what else. And do not accuse me now of taking advantage of your maidenly virtue. The passions we spent last night were hotly shared. Our futures are bound together, Ailénor. Destiny, you called it, or have you forgotten?''

He took a deep breath. ''For now, I shall consider your words the ravings of an overwrought woman. A woman I cherish. But I ask some measure of faith. Surely you know in your heart I would never bring you harm or unhappiness.''

Ailénor's mouth dropped open at his words. ''*Mais, non* . . . Oh, Garreth, I did not mean . . . What I heard . . . I thought . . .''

Garreth took her hands in his and laid them against his chest. ''Believe me, my heart. We have both been caught in Cynric's web. And Barbetorte's. 'Twas he who sparked the idea in Cynric. Did you not see when he spoke in Cynric's ear?''

''Barbetorte?'' Ailénor's voice rose in amazement. ''Alain Barbetorte, the prince of Brittany—Comte de Cornouaille and Nantes?'' A great light dawned, illuminating all that had foregone.

''You know him?''

''*Of* him.'' Ailénor nodded. ''Two years past he led an

uprising to reconquer his lost lands, crossing over from England at the head of his exiled Bretons.''

Garreth nodded gravely. ''Their attempt failed, forcing them to return into exile.''

''Did you also know William met his challenge in battle?''

''Nay, only that King Raoul awarded parts of the Breton lands to the duke—the Avranchin and the Contentin.''

''*Oui*. Barbetorte despises William. In truth, he despises anyone with Norse blood flowing in their veins. 'Twas the Northmen of the Loire who originally wrested Brittany from Alain's father, Mathuédoi. There was great bloodshed and, as you know, many noble Bretons fled across La Manche. I cannot blame Barbetorte for his feelings, yet I fear he would stoop at nothing to get at William, even through me.''

Garreth held her close. ''Then you do believe me?''

The vision of Alain Barbetorte, his eyes glittering, his detestation palpable as he observed her from the shadows and leaned to Cynric's ear, gave her to believe Garreth's innocence. Concern closed in on her again.

''Surely Barbetorte holds no real influence in the English court.''

''He is Athelstan's godson,'' Garreth apprised. ''He and his Bretons stand ready to assist Louis, hoping to regain Brittany in the bargain. While Barbetorte holds no real power in England, he does have access to the king's ear and holds sway over many of high rank around him—notably, Cynric. Believe me, Ailénor. I am as astonished as you by this contortion of events. Cynric is a powerful man, but I promise you he will not see his plans to fruition.''

Ailénor sank her head against Garreth's chest and released a long, weary breath. ''I have wronged you and I am sorry.''

He lifted her chin with the tip of his finger. ''Shh. You must be exhausted. 'Tis all right. Take some rest now, while I go and confront Cynric. Regardless of the outcome, I shall draft missives to the king and to your parents and see them sent this very night. I cannot go directly through

Cynric's authority, but I can go around it." A smile touched Garreth's lips. "Rest easy, my darling. All shall be set aright, I vow."

He covered her lips with his, drawing her into a deep and healing kiss. Ailénor melted against him, her lips parting and welcoming him further. He stroked the silk of her tongue with his, then allowed his hand to glide slowly along the side of her waist, upward to her ribs and higher still to cup the swell of her . . .

"Milady? Are you all right, milady?" Aldith called as she bustled into the room. "Leflet said . . . Oh, dear. Oh, my, my." Aldith halted, startled and thoroughly flustered by what met her eyes.

Garreth released Ailénor instantly, dropping his hand away. He doubted Aldith saw more than the kiss from where she stood. There was no way to extract himself from this situation comfortably, but he could save Ailénor her embarrassment.

"Lady Ailénor owns no fault here, Aldith. Nor has she been compromised in any way." *Not today*, he added mentally. "Count it as my own weakness. I trust we may rely on your discretion."

Aldith stood pinch-lipped for a moment, then relented. "Aye. That you can. But there will be no more dallying in milady's bedchamber." She wagged a finger.

"Upon my word," Garreth returned. "Now, if you will see that Lady Ailénor is comfortable for the night, I will take my leave."

Turning to Ailénor, he noted the flush in her cheeks. "I shall seek out Cynric. I suspect he prepares his own missive for the king and I shall need to dispatch my own apace."

"And my parents?"

"Aye. I'll not forget them either."

He started to drop a departing kiss to Ailénor's lips but, feeling the maid's heavy gaze, diverted it more chastely to her brow.

Ailénor watched after Garreth, her lips still alive with his kiss. As he disappeared out the door, she realized her questions concerning him had gone unanswered. Who was Garreth of Tamworth?

As Garreth reached the bottom of the great stairs, he spied the manservant, Osbert, and bid him over. Asking of Cynric, Osbert shook his head.

"His lordship has departed the palace with the Breton, Barbetorte. They ride for King's Worthy."

"That could only mean one thing," Garreth muttered, thinking of the royal residence, a short distance to the north. "Osbert, find the scribe and bid him come to my chamber with his parchment and ink pots. I have need of him."

Garreth suspected more schemes to be afoot between Cynric and Barbetorte. Best compose his letters and see them off at once.

Ordering his thoughts, Garreth sought his chamber.

"Milady. Wake up, milady."

Aldith's voice broke through the thick haze of sleep enveloping Ailénor, and she felt a hand gently nudge her arm.

"Milady, you are summoned. Come, you must dress."

"Who . . . ?" Ailénor roused from a slumberous fog and pushed slowly up on an elbow. Dragging open her eyes, she found the room dimly lit with candles.

"Hurry, milady." Aldith assisted Ailénor as she rose from the bed.

Hastily the maid helped Ailénor into a loose-fitting *smoc*, over which she drew a full-length tunic with close-fitting sleeves.

"Who summons me, Aldith?—Garreth?" Ailénor rubbed the sleep from her eyes as the maid laced the back of her dress.

"Nay, milady. A guard waits for you on the orders of the *wicgerefa*."

Ailénor came full awake. "Cynric? What could he want with me at this hour?"

"I know not, milady. Only that he wishes you to come at once." Aldith guided her to a chair, then offered Ailénor a warm, damp cloth to press to her face and took a comb to her hair.

"If it eases your mind, milady, Leflet brought word ahead of the guard that visitors have just arrived at the palace. Mayhap this concerns them."

A heavy rap at the door and call from the guard stirred Aldith anew. Fetching a mantle, she cloaked Ailénor's shoulders and drew the dark red tresses from where they caught beneath the neckline. Aldith gave them a few last strokes of the comb, then bustled over to the door and hauled it open. Outside, a stalwart guard stood at attention, spear in hand.

Unease slid through Ailénor. She found no choice but to comply. Fighting back her concerns, she passed out of the chamber and followed the guard through the torch-lit corridors and down a back stairway. As she went, she wished she had bid Aldith to send word to Garreth.

A cold finger of apprehension traced her spine as the guard brought her before a heavy iron-bound door of a chamber tucked deep in the palace.

The guard preceded her, opening the door and briefly barring her view as he announced her. He stepped aside and gave her a meaningful nod, indicating she should enter.

Filled with misgivings, Ailénor crossed the threshold into the chamber. As her eyes alighted on those within, the door screaked shut behind. Ailénor took a swallow as she found herself trapped with five pairs of eyes fixed on her.

"Lady Ailénor, thank you for coming. And so promptly." Cynric broke away from the rest and came forward full of cordiality.

His eyes skimmed over her, one side of his mouth pulling upward into a thin smile, a smile that stopped short of his eyes. Ailénor did not trust him and would have remained rooted to the spot had he not caught her by the elbow and drawn her farther into the room.

Ailénor's gaze quickly brushed over the others—a lady of obvious station, two youths, and another man, Alain Barbetorte. All, including Cynric, appeared to have just concluded a ride—garbed in heavy traveling cloaks and their faces pinkened by the fresh morning air. Each now partook of a fortifying goblet of wine.

Ailénor returned her gaze to the comely lady who moved to a chair at the room's center and lowered herself onto its cushioned seat. Everything about her seemed regal from the grace of her movements to the noble bearing in the way she sat upon the chair. Her pale flaxen hair was drawn back from her face, overlaid with a translucent veil and crowned with a circlet of gold. Jewels winked upon her gloved hands while the deep blue silk of her gown peeked from beneath her traveling cloak.

To the lady's right stood the plainer of the two youths, about four years and ten in age. With a jolt Ailénor realized she stood before the exiled dowager queen of Francia and her son, Louis, the pretender to the Frankish throne.

Ailénor sank into a deep curtsy and bowed her head. "*La reine* Ogine," she whispered, using the name the Saxon princess Eadgifu had assumed when she became Charles III's consort.

Ailénor kept her eyes fixed to the floor, perplexed as to how she should address the princeling, Louis, who at the moment held no certain title, yet was Francia's rightful—if unhallowed—king.

"M-Majesty," she floundered, then immediately regretted uttering the word. Not only was the term incorrect, 'twas foolish on her part to use it. The lapse might be read as her personal support for Louis's claim.

Eadgifu smiled and gave an approving nod at Ailénor's choice of address. Diverting her gaze past her shoulder, she spoke to Barbetorte who moved now to stand behind her.

"This may be simpler than you led me to believe," she said in Saxon without lowering her voice.

"Which can only be to our benefit," Louis added, glancing toward his mother and the Breton. He started to say more, but Barbetorte raised a warning hand.

"Careful. She understands Saxon to some extent." Barbetorte regarded Ailénor with chilly disdain. "Probably speaks that accursed Norse tongue. She is part Dane, after all. You can see it in her height."

Ailénor tightened her lips against what she would say and lifted her gaze, her heart congested with defiance. Her eyes touched on Barbetorte's left hand where it rested conspicuously on the back of Eadgifu's chair, just above her shoulder. 'Twas a telling gesture, Ailénor thought, declaring his familiarity with Eadgifu and his influence over her—and, presumably, over her son.

"I see." Eadgifu lifted a finely arched brow, considering the Breton's words as she took a sip from her goblet. Her gaze shifted back to Ailénor. "Rise, child. Come into the light," she bid in Frankish.

Ailénor complied, and to spite Barbetorte, she drew herself up, Valkyrie tall, as she stepped forward. Her composure threatened to buckle as she found herself openly inspected by those within the chamber as though she were some prize bauble or rarity.

Eadgifu counseled her features with a sympathetic smile. "I am aware of the distressing events that befell you, Lady Ailénor, and in my brother's absence have come to personally welcome you to his court. Be assured, you are now safe. Our soldiers are alerted with descriptions of your attackers. Should the scoundrels show themselves, they will be seized at once."

"*Merci.*" Ailénor inclined her head, surprised and gratified by Eadgifu's words.

"Your misfortune aside, I confess it pleases me enormously to have a noblewoman of Francia—especially of Normandy—visit our shores." Eadgifu traced her finger around the rim of her goblet. "As you know, 'twas my husband, Charles, who granted Rollo his titles and lands. Rollo expanded his boundaries somewhat, but he was ever loyal to Charles." Her hand stilled, and she held Ailénor's gaze. "The ties are strong between our houses—the Carlings and the Norman dukes. Indeed, the debt runs deep."

The thinly veiled words were not lost on Ailénor, and she wondered where they would lead.

" 'Twould please me to take you into my service, Lady Ailénor, as one of my ladies-in-waiting. When the Carolingian line is restored, I promise you shall remain in my service and enjoy a privileged place—reward for having shared exile with me and proven your loyalty.''

Ailénor stood flabbergasted. The dowager queen wove her web with great skill, making her offer appear a fine and generous one, without a hint of duplicity. Had it not been for Eadgifu's comment to Barbetorte, Ailénor would believe her words most sincere. To the contrary, Ailénor recognized all too well the trap laid before her. To refuse outright would offer grave and perhaps lasting insult. Should Louis indeed come into his own, what retribution might he or his mother exact on her and her family, and perchance all of Normandy?

Ailénor silently fumed. If Cynric and Barbetorte were two of a feather, Eadgifu and her son made four.

''Your Grace,'' Ailénor began cautiously in Frankish, '' 'twould be an immense honor to serve you, and I am deeply flattered. As you know, however, I was abducted from my homeland by men who mistook me for my mother. Most desperately I need apprise my parents of my fate and warn my mother, for she may yet be in danger. In all truth, my heart aches to rejoin my family.''

''I understand, of course,'' Eadgifu said in a silken voice embroidered with compassion. ''You have endured a frightening ordeal and have scarce had time to recover. But fear not. A letter shall be sent to your parents—in due course. 'Tis my fervent hope we can *all* return to Francia, and soon. William can make a difference as to how soon that will be, as can Hugh of Paris,'' she added pointedly. ''Meanwhile, it pleases me—as I am certain it will please William—to accept and honor his kinswoman with a position within my personal retinue.''

Rising, Eadgifu closed the subject. ''As you will learn, the Carlings are long on memory as to the measure of their subjects' loyalty.''

Her meaning hung suspended like a double-edged sword, sharp and clear. Disaffections would be remembered and repaid.

''Are we finished here?'' Louis spoke in rapid Saxon as he strode to a side table and set down his goblet. ''There still be some good hours of hunting left to this day, and I would return apace to King's Worthy." He started for the door, then turned back. "The duke's kinswoman appears satisfactory for our purposes, but even if William conforms to our wishes, I do not trust him a whit. Nor do I trust Hugh for that matter. But then you know my feeling concerning the both of them."

Pivoting, Louis quit the chamber.

As Ailénor drew her gaze from the door, she noted the handsome, fair-haired lad who still stood to one side quietly listening. He shifted uncomfortably and would not meet her eyes.

"You must be exhausted, Lady Ailénor." Eadgifu's voice brought Ailénor's attention back. "Take your rest for the coming days and recover yourself fully. I believe I shall remain in Winchester myself for a time and shop Ceap Stræt and West Gate. When you are up to it, you may join me. There is no place in England quite like Winchester."

With that, Eadgifu whisked from the room, followed out by Barbetorte.

Ailénor turned on Cynric, her ire flaring. "Your king shall know of this. And so shall all of Normandy," she spoke crisply in Danish and hoped he understood. "You cannot succeed."

Cynric closed the space between them, his steps almost swaggering, certainly overconfident. He studied the contents of his goblet, then cut his eyes up at Ailénor.

"Might I assume Garreth has promised you his help?" When she did not answer, he sighed and wagged his head as though she had fallen victim to some folly. "My dear, Garreth of Tamworth is the king's own champion and utterly loyal to the king's wishes. Whatever His Majesty decrees, Garreth will comply, completely and without question."

Ailénor jutted up her chin in defiance to his words.

"You do not believe me? Then you will learn, with some pain perhaps, that the bond between Garreth and the king is strong and, to Garreth's mind, unbreakable. The two were fostered at Tamworth when Athelstan was an *atheling*, a princeling. When King Edward died, Garreth took up his sword and aided Athelstan to his throne. He has helped him secure and preserve it ever since. Garreth is one of England's most renowned warriors, one of the chief officers of the Hird—the King's elite guard. I can promise you, my dear, no pretty head will ever turn Garreth of Tamworth against his king."

Ailénor wavered before Cynric's revelation, and it took several moments for her to regain herself. "He will have no need to act against the king's wishes, for the king will never support this madness," she challenged.

Cynric skimmed a glance to where the young boy stood, then returned his gaze and lowered his voice.

"Oh, but he will. Especially when he realizes just how valuable you are to his purposes."

"And you and the king's sister, nephew, and godson will all be in his ears to convince him of that, is that not so?" she spat. "But Garreth will be there, too, and he will oppose you and appeal to the king directly himself."

Cynric elevated a brow. "Is that so? I have received no word of his leaving the palace thus far."

"He has no need to. He sent missives last night to the king and to Normandy. You shall not prevail in this."

"Did he tell you he would send missives? To the king?"

Ailénor disliked the smugness in his smile or the keen feeling he toyed with her as a cat would a mouse. He turned toward the door where several men waited, servants and possibly court ministers or clerks of some sort, judging by their garments.

"Fulcard," Cynric bid one of the men to enter. "Did any of our couriers leave the palace since my own departure last night?"

"Nay, sire. None save your own." Fulcard made an abbreviated bow toward the high reeve. The man reminded her of a scrawny, narrow-faced weasel dressed in black robes and a skull-conforming cap.

Cynric turned back to Ailénor with a shrug. "I fear Garreth has misled you, my dear. 'Tis not the first time he wooed a maid to his will with pretty words."

Ailénor clenched her hands at her side and bit back the words burning on her tongue. Cynric lied. He was full of guile. Desperately she clung to her trust in Garreth.

Ailénor recognized she could not win a battle of words with Cynric. She could barely keep grasp of them as it was due to the difficulties of language.

"I see no point to continuing this conversation," she clipped out. "Time will prove what has been spoken here. For now I shall retire to my chamber, as the dowager queen suggested." She added the last to override any objection he might shy at her.

Ailénor pivoted and walked briskly to the door where a guard waited, apparently assigned to shadow her every move. She chafed at the constraint. With her freedom of movement curtailed, she was no more than a captive in a golden snare. Boiling, she turned to the right and stalked blindly ahead, running headlong into Garreth.

Ailénor jerked back and stared up at him. God forgive her, but the venom of Cynric's words swarmed through her—of how Garreth "wooed maids to his will with pretty words." The picture that filled her mind's eye was of herself lying naked in Garreth's arms in Hamwih's mill as she gave herself to him.

Unable to bear more, Ailénor shoved past him and fled as fast as her feet would carry her back along the passageway.

From the daggers in Ailénor's eyes, Garreth knew things had run afoul once more. Curse Cynric for his plotting.

"What mischief now?" Garreth boomed as he entered the chamber.

Cynric looked up from where several clerks attended him. He waved them away and fixed his gaze on Garreth. "Mischief?"

"Just now I encountered Eadgifu and Louis with their shadow, Barbetorte. That was after discovering your weasel, Fulcard, intercepted my missives last night."

"Missives? I know of no . . ."

"Save it, Cynric. You arranged for your message alone

to reach His Majesty so you might present matters as you deem fit. You go too far, Cynric. Athelstan shall hear of this in full detail from my lips.''

''Mayhap.'' Cynric's gaze traveled past Garreth's shoulder causing Garreth to turn and look to the far corner. There, to his surprise, he discovered the *atheling* Edred, the youngest of Athelstan's half brothers.

''Your Highness.'' Garreth acknowledged the princeling with a brief bow. ''Do not tell me that you are part to this.''

''The *atheling* decides his own mind,'' Cynric stated imperiously. ''Our plans took form of a sudden, I realize, but we hoped by now you would see the advantage in detaining Lady Ailénor at court.''

''The folly you mean.''

''Folly? How so? 'Tis in Louis's and, thus, the king's best interest, and Lady Ailénor shan't be mistreated. Indeed, she will be granted every courtesy and comfort. At the same time, her presence in England will afford Athelstan leverage with Duke William and underscore his earnestness in restoring the Carolingian line.''

'' 'Tis in no one's best interest save Barbetorte's,'' Garreth retorted. ''One might question where your loyalties truly lie, Cynric. With the king or Alain Barbetorte? What has the Breton promised you?''

''Like you, Garreth, first and foremost I serve my king and thereby this land. Ever shall I strive to do all within my power to advance his interests. That necessarily includes Louis who occupies the king's concerns. Francia's throne is Louis's birthright. His succession remains of grave importance to the king, his uncle.''

''You are blind-sighted, Cynric, and do Athelstan no service. The time is ill-favored to advance Louis to the Frankish throne. Raoul is sure in his power and shall devour the cub like a wolf should he attempt to seize the crown. Even should Louis initially succeed, his throne would be too weak to endure,'' Garreth echoed the duke's words. ''Louis will not find the support he requires among his barons. They look to their own cares.''

Cynric cocked a brow. ''One might question *your* loyalties, Garreth, and what rewards Duke William might have offered for you to dissuade the king with this gloomy assessment. It appears you hold hands rather cozily with the Normans. Or at least with the duke's kinswoman.'' Cynric sneered. ''One must wonder of your relationship with the ravishing Ailénor. You did after all—by your own admission—spend considerable time with her, unaccompanied. What transpired in Hamwih, I wonder, as you waited out the storm? 'Tis something you might not wish the Normans to explore too closely. Or the king, for that matter.''

Garreth gazed on Cynric stonily, silently rebuking himself for having divulged details of his and Ailénor's passage from Normandy. But that was before Cynric and Barbetorte hatched their schemes, and at the time he had suspected no guile.

Cynric only guessed at the intimacies he and Ailénor had shared, Garreth knew. All the same, he would need be careful in his comportment toward her under the watchful eyes of those at court. But for now he need ride directly to the king.

As though Cynric read his mind, he slipped a parchment roll from his tunic and extended it to Garreth.

''The king moves rapidly against the Scots, and our couriers are ever challenged to follow his movements. You need not put yourself to that test. Athelstan has left this charge for you to expedite.''

Garreth took the parchment and broke its wax seal that he recognized as the king's. Unscrolling the piece, he scanned its message. His brows drew together.

A corner of Cynric's mouth curled. ''His Majesty wishes you to fetch his stepmother, the dowager queen, Eadgiva, from Grately.''

Garreth shot a look at Cynric, wondering if this was yet another trap. ''Others of rank can escort Eadgiva to Winchester. Why send an officer of the Hird?''

''Eadgiva herself insisted it be you who fetched her. She repairs to Winchester for *your* ceremonials, after all, to see you elevated to *Ealdorman* of Hamtunscir and make your announcement of a bride.'' When Garreth continued to glower at him, Cynric gave a light shrug. " 'Tis the will of the king.''

Garreth fingered the parchment, deeming it far more important to ride after the king than after the dowager, be it the king's will or not. He looked to the *atheling*, Edred.

"Might I ask where you stand in the matter concerning Lady Ailénor, Your Highness?''

Edred came forward several steps. Dropping his gaze to his toes, he contemplated them a moment before lifting his pale eyes to Garreth.

"I understand your position and argument, Garreth, as I do those put forth by Cynric, Alain, and Eadgifu. As I wish to do no wrong by my brother, however, I believe caution to be the better course and prefer to wait for Athelstan's response to arrive. I'd not risk depriving him of a piece of good fortune, if this be that.''

Garreth found his hands neatly tied. Cynric brought the royal siblings from King's Worthy to outmaneuver him, knowing he would oppose his and Barbetorte's schemes. Garreth posed the greatest threat to their plans, for he himself wielded considerable power and possessed substantial influence with the king.

Though Garreth might challenge Cynric's authority and circumvent him and Barbetorte, he could not override the will of the royal brood—particularly not of this young prince of the blood, a cautious soul, who, in the absence of the king and his older brother Edmund, was the highest ranking royal present—second in line to the throne.

"Time cannot wait, Your Highness," Garreth directed his appeal to the prince. "At least, not for the Comtesse de Héricourt, Ailénor's mother. We need notify her what befell her daughter.''

"That matter must be handled with the utmost care and diplomacy," Cynric interjected. "The initial letter to Normandy must be carefully crafted, for everything else to follow will stand on that. I concur with Prince Edred. We need wait for Athelstan's directives.''

A muscle worked in Garreth's jaw. "And when it arrives, will you abide by the letter of the king's decree? On your honor?''

"I shall. Will you?''

"Have I ever not?'' Garreth tucked the rolled parchment in his belt.

"Then you will be away to Grately?''

"Have I a choice?''

" 'Tis the king's will.'' Cynric gave a satisfied smile. "But in your absence, do not think to issue additional missives. Your efforts shall be wasted, I assure you.''

"You mean I shall be watched? Did you handpick the retinue that will accompany me to Grately? Or are your spies already in place there?''

Cynric did not respond, and Garreth could not read his cold eyes.

"Ailénor best be here when I return,'' he warned. Turning to Edred, he calmed his voice. "Your Highness, 'twould be an act of honor and courtesy to safeguard Lady Ailénor from any further wrongdoing. I will count on your gallantry.''

Sketching a bow, Garreth withdrew. As he heeled back along the corridor, a disturbing thought rose to mind. If the Saxon court held Ailénor hostage, her parents and the duke would never allow him to marry her.

Things were becoming stickier by the minute. Garreth held fast to his faith in Athelstan and in His Majesty's unerring sense of justice.

Supremely frustrated, Garreth made his way to Ailénor's chamber and rapped firmly on the door. He leveled a glance to the end of the passageway and noted a guard posted there.

"Cynric,'' Garreth growled beneath his breath, then knocked on the door again. Moments later it opened a crack and Aldith's face appeared.

"Lady Ailénor is abed.''

" 'Tis pressing I speak with her, Aldith.''

"Sir, the girl is utterly exhausted and has just fallen asleep.''

Garreth stared blankly at the maid. Was he now to be barred from seeing Ailénor?

"Then I take it she found no rest last night?" His tone contested Aldith's words.

The maid faltered. "Lady Ailénor tossed the hours on end, till the guard came for her just before dawn. She will take ill if she does not obtain some sound and proper rest. She asked specifically that none disturb her."

"Including myself?"

"Aye, s-sir." She stumbled over the words, looking greatly discomfited.

Garreth ground his back teeth. He suspected Ailénor to be abed, but very much awake. What falsehoods had Cynric told her? Had she not a crumb of trust in him? He vented a long breath. He could not fight them all and was at the end of his patience.

"Very well." He arrowed a glance through the crack of the door, over Aldith's head, and into the chamber. "When Lady Ailénor rises, inform her I have departed Winchester on orders of the king." He spoke loud enough for Ailénor to hear. "I shall be gone several days, possibly a week. Assure her I continue to do all within my power to aright matters concerning her circumstance and ask her patience and a modicum of faith."

With that, Garreth turned on his heel and left.

Aldith eased the heavy door closed and looked toward the bed. There Ailénor sat upright in the center of its mattress, her gaze lingering upon the door.

"Milady, I can go after him. Milady? Did you hear? He leaves Winchester, milady."

"*Oui*, Aldith. At the bidding of his king."

"Should I go after him, milady?" Aldith fretted.

"*Non.* 'Whatever His Majesty decrees, Garreth will comply,' " she parroted Cynric's words.

Questioning what to believe, Ailénor stretched out on the bed and hugged her pillow, curling into a ball, her stomach knotted in pain.

Chapter Eight

Ailénor glanced up from her needlework to the sundial fixed in the garden wall.

Noting the markings, she dropped her gaze back to her hands lest she draw Eadgifu's notice. Working a flower on the silk, she estimated the hour—no minor task, for, unlike Norman dials that divided the day into twenty-four hours, Saxon dials were divided into eight "tides" and these into three hours apiece. By her reckoning, counting from dawn, it had been eight days and eleven hours since Garreth's departure.

Still no word came from him.

Ailénor continued to sit in companionable silence with

Eadgifu, embellishing one of Her Grace's silk tunics and updating it to a more current look. But as Ailénor plied her needle, her thoughts strayed far from the palace garden.

She regretted not having seen Garreth off. At the time she had been overwhelmed and confused. The days since allowed her to compose herself and reflect over all that had passed since first they met in the ducal orchard of Rouen. Her confidence renewed, she now longed for his return.

It preyed upon her mind that there had been no word or sign these last days of Rhiannon's hirelings. Had they realized their error and returned to Francia? Garreth could not return soon enough, Ailénor thought. She trusted he would set all matters aright, as he promised he would. But when would he come? And would it be in time for her mother's sake?

'Twas her understanding Garreth had traveled to one of the royal residences to collect England's dowager queen, Eadgiva, the third and last of King Edward's wives, and to escort her back to Winchester. Athelstan, Eadgifu, and Edred—King Edward's children—were all half siblings. The late king had sired other children as well, mostly daughters, though there were two living princes of the blood—Edmund, who presently rode with Athelstan, and Edred. Both were sons of Eadgiva.

Edred proved to be the young man who had lingered in the chamber the morn she had been brought before Eadgifu and Louis. She had seen him since, mostly from a distance at morning mass that they attended in New Minster and once, closer up, when the family gathered before the tombs of King Alfred and King Edward. Whenever their gazes met, Ailénor thought to behold in Edred's eyes sympathy tinged with a measure of guilt.

Ailénor directed her thoughts back to her stitches. Eadgifu had been well pleased with her skills and set her to refurbishing an older vermilion gown of which she was very fond. Ailénor found, as she became more acquainted with Eadgifu, that she was neither malevolent nor ill-intended. Rather, she was strong-willed, a tigress looking after her cub and all she deemed rightfully his. What struck

Ailénor most, however, was Eadgifu's unwavering belief that Louis's preemption of the Frankish throne was imminent. To Eadgifu's mind, Ailénor imagined, detaining herself would be a minor sacrifice to ask of a subject.

A movement caught the corner of Ailénor's eye, and when she looked up, she saw a servant hastening into the garden enclosure and dropping into a curtsy before Eadgifu. Ailénor was thankful her grasp of Saxon had steadily improved over the week. Now, as she listened, her heart leapt as she heard the words for which she waited. The baggage wain had arrived from Grately. Garreth had returned.

Eadgifu and Ailénor left their sewing and went directly to the courtyard to greet the dowager and Garreth.

Ailénor's heart skipped with anticipation, her emotions bobbing on a sea of happiness as she emerged from the garden. The courtyard lay in sight. Her eyes lodged immediately on Garreth's tall frame. There before the *charette*, he aided an older woman, presumably the dowager, to the ground.

Unnoticing of Ailénor, Garreth turned back to the conveyance, and Ailénor saw now that it contained two more women. Ailénor looked on as he lifted down one, then the other, not missing how the last woman swayed into Garreth as he set her to the ground so that their bodies brushed, or how the other pressed in and slipped her arm through his.

Ailénor slowed her pace, then stayed her step altogether, feeling suddenly awkward and out of place. She watched from a distance as Eadgifu continued on and joined the others. At her approach, the dowager queen Eadgiva turned and greeted her stepdaughter.

Ailénor noted that the two dowagers—Edward's widow, Eadgiva, and Charles the Simple's widow, Eadgifu—were neither one very old and mayhap only ten years apart in age. Their exchange appeared formal and without great warmth, though to Ailénor's mind, Eadgifu seemed the colder figure, her back stiff, her gestures superficial, spiritless. As Eadgifu concluded the welcoming ritual, she turned and greeted the other women, this time showing surprise and delight at their presence.

As Ailénor glanced away from the scene, her eyes met those of Garreth. A slow smile spread across his face, setting her heart to racing. He withdrew from the others and strode directly toward her. As he did, Ailénor observed the younger women's heads swiveling to follow his movements. The dowager Eadgiva watched also, her brows winging upward.

"My eyes are sore glad to see you." Garreth caught up Ailénor's fingers and gave a slight bow, brushing his lips over them. He straightened, blocking the line of vision between herself and the other women—a conscious thing, she realized. "We need to talk, my heart. Later. Come, you must meet Eadgiva and the king's kinswomen, Mora and Rosalynd."

Ailénor's heart continued to skip as Garreth conducted her across the small expanse. She smiled up at him, supremely happy to be at his side. As her eyes drew to the others, the expressions of the two younger women visibly tightened. If Garreth noticed, he did not reveal it but directed her before the dowager queen.

"Your Grace, I have told you of Lady Ailénor. She is cousin to Duke William of Normandy, and daughter of the Count of Héricourt."

"Lady Ailénor is visiting us for a time," Eadgifu added quickly, before Garreth could say more. "We are greatly pleased to have her. She has endured a most harrowing experience. Fortunate for us all, Garreth saved Lady Ailénor and wisely brought her to Winchester. You must hear the account of their story over dinner."

"*Their* story?" Ailénor heard one of the younger women murmur to the other. They eyed her with cool detachment, giving Ailénor the distinct impression they had just unsheathed their claws.

Ailénor returned her attention to Eadgiva and dipped into a curtsy. She could not read the dowager's expression as she studied her. A moment later Eadgiva smiled—a deliberative smile—and offered her a ringed hand to kiss.

Garreth next presented Ailénor to Mora and Rosalynd, cousins of Athelstan and Eadgifu through their father.

Sisters, Mora and Rosalynd favored one another in looks though not in height. Mora, the shorter of the two, possessed hair the color of darkened honey and clear green eyes flecked with gold. Her face was squarish with a blunt nose, her shoulders broad, and her neck wide.

Rosalynd's increased height made her appear less heavy-boned and stocky than Mora. Her hair was lighter, more tawny, while her eyes, though green, were flecked with brown. The pointedness of her chin softened her squarish features.

Mora and Rosalynd uttered the common courtesies, their eyes raking over Ailénor, needle-sharp, and marking her unusual height with unconcealed disapproval. They appeared to view her as a fly that had just landed in their dish. The two turned in unison to Eadgifu, mentally dismissing Ailénor, and asked of their accommodations.

Ailénor winced as she heard Eadgifu announce they would share her chamber, for she herself had been transferred to Eadgifu's room a few days past to begin her duties as a lady-in-waiting. Ailénor did not look forward to sharing the chamber with these women.

As the group made their way toward the palace, Garreth assisted the dowager queen who moved slowly with the aid of an ivory walking stick.

"We still need to have our talk," Ailénor overheard the dowager tell Garreth.

Ailénor wished to linger and speak to Garreth herself, but Eadgifu bid her to accompany Mora and Rosalynd to the upper chamber and help them settle in before dinner.

Glancing back at Garreth, she sent him a regretful smile and followed Eadgifu and her cousins.

An hour later the horn sounded announcing dinner in the Great Hall.

Garreth looked forward to seeing Ailénor but inwardly blenched at the thought of spending more time with Mora and Rosalynd who relentlessly vied for his attention. Then, too, he chafed at having to constrain his feelings for Ailénor, but he could not risk disclosing their intimate relationship with Cynric and the king's kinswomen watching.

While he did not intend to mislead Mora and Rosalynd, he held no wish to affront them outright. Both were well aware King Athelstan had directed his attention to them as possible brides, and that he had promised to betroth himself upon his return from Francia.

As expected, on entering the Great Hall, Garreth found Mora and Rosalynd lying in wait. Eadgifu stood near the dais with Barbetorte and Cynric. Edred and Louis were also present having arrived from King's Worthy.

Garreth's eyes fell on Ailénor across the room. The sight of her filled his heart with joy. Before he could move three paces, the horn sounded for all to take their places at table. Mora and Rosalynd fluttered instantly to his side, each claiming him to share their trencher.

"Garreth will share a trencher with me tonight," the dowager queen's voice came tartly from behind.

Not to be challenged, she came forward, thumping her ivory stick into the rushes and sending Mora and Rosalynd scuttling away.

"You are on your own tomorrow." She slid a glance to Garreth with a suspiciously wicked smile and took his arm. "I still wish to speak with you, but without those two peahens pecking about!"

"I am at your command, Your Grace." Garreth chuckled.

"Who sent those two flocking to my door at Grately? I wonder." She continued, not waiting for an answer, "The strain of the trip with *them* was enough to upset my humors for months to come."

Garreth grinned, handing the dowager up onto the dais and pulling out her chair. As to who might have notified Mora and Rosalynd of his visit to Grately, Garreth could think of only one name. Cynric. 'Twas another attempt to control the course of events and constrict his movements.

As the dowager settled herself into her chair, she inspected the placement of the table wares—the goblets, spoons, and bowls—and rearranged them to her satisfaction. "You know, Garreth, 'twas I who requested you to fetch me from Grately."

"So I was informed, Your Grace. I have been sleepless ever since, wondering of your reasons."

Eadgiva darted him a look at the jest. Meeting with his wide, teasing smile, her lips twitched with humor.

While a servant filled their goblets with spiced wine, Garreth stole a glance along the table. To the dowager's right Eadgifu sat with Barbetorte. Mora took up a place to the Breton's other side, paired with Louis who appeared less than happy with the arrangement. To Garreth's left, Rosalynd laughed overloud as she settled beside him to share a trencher with Edred. Farther down, Cynric aided Ailénor to a chair.

Garreth silently simmered at the sight.

The dowager plucked at his sleeve, regaining his attention, and bid him lean closer so others might not overhear.

"I asked that you come for me at Grately because I wished to offer you my advisements before your ceremonials and your announcement of a bride. And you know how I like to give advice!" she added with some levity, unaware of his inner turmoil. "I am fond of you, Garreth, and I have no wish to see you form a disastrous liaison by espousing yourself to the wrong woman."

"Am I to understand you have a bride in mind?" Garreth felt genuine pleasure at the dowager's concern for his marriage.

Eadgiva sniffed. "Rather I have two *not* in mind."

Garreth's brows rose at her frankness. He watched as Eadgiva directed her sharp gaze to where Cynric sat with Ailénor.

"Tell me more of Lady Ailénor and this little adventure of yours. You say she was abducted?"

Eadgifu, catching the dowager's last words, quieted the others. "Yes, Garreth, do recount the tale for us all. 'Twill make a fine diversion over supper."

Garreth skimmed a glance toward Ailénor, giving her an assuring look, and as the first course was served, he began to relate their adventure.

Beside him Rosalynd went stony-faced, as did Mora nearby, as they listened to him detail Ailénor's abduction, their perilous crossing, and how he and she had escaped and taken refuge in the half-abandoned village of Hamwih. A needling question from Louis forced Garreth to admit they had eluded the henchmen by hiding overnight in a mill.

"Alone?" Mora sniped.

The dowager quelled her with a sharp look. "Whatever measures Garreth took to save Lady Ailénor, I am sure were noble-minded and above reproach."

Garreth did not miss how Ailénor's hand shook as she sipped her goblet of wine, or the bright spots of color staining her cheeks. Nor did Cynric.

"Actually, we were aided by the good miller and his family." Garreth closed the door on the subject. "We managed to keep from sight and travel to Winchester without encountering the Irishmen. We fear they could still be about, though the guards are alerted with their descriptions."

Cynric leaned forward. "More than that, the guards likewise have Lady Ailénor's description. They have orders to detain anyone inquiring of a woman fitting her description." He leaned back in his chair and leveled a sly look toward Garreth. "I daresay, they might detain Lady Ailénor herself should she take a notion to leave."

The threat was not lost on Garreth who could only sit and clench his hands.

The dowager, Eadgiva, brought the goblet from her lips. "Leave? Oh, we mustn't let her do that." She smiled on Ailénor. "My dear, I do hope you will remain a very, *very* long time, indeed. Why, I am sure the court would be delighted to keep you forever." She added the last with great cheer.

Ailénor's expression fell at the dowager's words, and she looked utterly stricken. She stumbled to her feet, tipping over her goblet.

"I—I . . . Forgive me, Your Grace." Ailénor fled the table, tears tumbling over her face.

Garreth bolted to his feet, swiftly excused himself, and hastened after Ailénor.

The dowager queen looked up and down the table, right to left, enormously upset. "What did I say?"

A moment passed, and no one uttered a word. Eadgiva marked the smirk lining Cynric's lips and a similar one playing over Barbetorte's. Her eyes narrowed.

"I demand an explanation!" She slammed her goblet to the table and thrust to her feet. Turning to her right, she fixed her gaze on her stepdaughter. "Eadgifu. *What* are you keeping from me?"

Ailénor rushed from the hall, aware of someone pursuing her close behind. Heading for the entrance doors, guards suddenly stepped forward and blocked her way, crossing their spears in front of her.

Ailénor came to an abrupt halt, nearly losing her balance and pitching forward. But in the next breath an arm slipped around her waist from behind and caught her up. She heard Garreth utter her name as he pulled her against his chest and held her firm. While she stood in his grasp, her heart thumping madly, he ordered the soldiers to withdraw.

In silence Garreth conducted her toward the staircase but continued past until they came to an alcove.

Ailénor stopped before it and rounded on Garreth. "Truly, I am hostage of the English."

"Nay, Ailénor . . ."

"Then help me. Either get word to my parents or take me back to Hamwih. Put me on a boat and send me to Normandy."

Garreth's jaw tightened. He dropped his gaze to the floor for a moment, then raised his gaze to hers again and held it unflinchingly. "You know I cannot."

"Why?" she cried out.

"We must wait for the king's instructions."

"*We*? Who is 'we,' Garreth? Certainly I am not part of your 'we.' Or have you cast your lot with the others?"

"Nay. Of course not."

"Then help me." She grasped his arms, her fingers driving into them. "Time runs short. There has been no word of Rhiannon's men since our arrival. My mother could be in grave danger. *Please*, I implore you. Either alert my parents or help me return to Francia."

Garreth released a long breath. " 'Tis not so simple as it seems. Did you see the reaction of the guards just now when you neared the door? You are being watched like a hawk. We both are. Cynric has already intercepted my missives to the king and to Normandy. I would not be surprised if he has posted his men at the ports—at least the southern ones—in the event you should escape his grasp. You—we—might both be seized if we went near them."

"You did send missives?"

"Aye, as I said I would. Did Cynric say otherwise?" At Ailénor's nod, he tried to mask his aggravation. "Ailénor, I vow, if word does not arrive from the king within the coming days, I shall go myself in search of him."

Ailénor's heart lurched with a new fear. "You could be in danger yourself if Cynric . . ."

"I shall deal with Cynric and anyone else he might send after me. For your part, I would have your trust . . . in myself and in my king."

Ailénor nodded, her head sinking forward for a moment.

"Oh, Garreth, were it not for circumstances, there would be no urgency for me to leave." A smile brightened her lips as she looked to him. "I would very much like to see more of your land." Her smile widened farther. "And return for a private outing on St. Catherine's Hill."

"And I would love to escort you there." Garreth drew her in his arms. "Lord knows I've missed you," he whispered above her lips, then brushed them with his. Lowering his mouth, he claimed her with his kiss.

A short distance apart Mora and Rosalynd held to the shadows, watching as Ailénor melted against Garreth and welcomed his kiss. Their eyes constricted to catlike slits and their mouths thinned.

Nearby, but farther apart, the dowager queen Eadgiva also looked on, silent and unheeded. She took note of Mora's and Rosalynd's spleenful expressions as they turned to

each other. The dowager then shifted her gaze to the enamored couple. As Ailénor's arms stole around Garreth's
neck, Eadgiva's lips lifted with a smile.

Early the next morning Ailénor shortened her stride to
match the pace of the other women—Eadgifu, Mora, and
Rosalynd—as they emerged from the palace grounds and
made their way north along Mensterstret, accompanied by
a small escort of soldiers.

Ailénor directed her interest to the surrounding sights,
striving to concentrate on something other than Rosalynd's
and Mora's chatter. Sharing quarters with them last night
had proven a quite taxing affair. The two had prattled end-
lessly of their ''splendid jaunt'' from Grately with Garreth,
and how he had charmed and entertained them the entire
way to Winchester. 'Twas as if they sought to make her
jealous, Ailénor thought. *Non*, she reconsidered. 'Twas
more like they were marking their territory and announcing
their claim of Garreth.

Ailénor scanned the sky. 'Twas a pretty, cloudless day
and she was delighted to be outside the palace complex.
Eadgifu wished to visit a particular goldsmith in the West
Gate markets and suggested to her cousins they inspect the
booths of the cloth merchants there for trims and fabrics
for the new gowns they planned.

Ailénor gave over her thoughts to Garreth. She had
hoped to see him before departing the palace this morn;
however, he did not appear in the Great Hall to break his
fast. Presumably he attended to other business. She hoped
it concerned the king.

Ailénor did encounter the dowager queen who apologized for her unknowing remarks of the night before and
went on to enjoy a small conversation with her over their
bread and wine. Ailénor quickly warmed to her and found
herself hoping Eadgiva would accompany them on their
sojourn today.

But the dowager held plans to visit Nunnaminster and
her daughter, Eadburga, who was a religious there. When
she learned the others intended to visit the cloth merchants,

however, she called to Eadgifu.

"Ailénor needs materials for gowns herself. See she acquires enough for several and do so at my expense. Obviously she has naught of her own, coming to the Saxon shores as she did. 'Tis deplorable she should be relegated to borrowed or discarded garments," she reprimanded, mincing no words. "You should have thought of this before now, Eadgifu. See it rectified this day."

Ailénor began to object, but the dowager shooed her on her way, pressing a coin pouch into her palm as she did.

"Purchase something truly stunning—mayhap cloth of emerald-green or sapphire-blue—something that will compliment your extraordinary hair and excite a man's eye!"

Ailénor saw Mora's and Rosalynd's gaiety shrivel.

"Enjoy the day, child." The dowager patted Ailénor's hand. "All will be sorted out. You shall see. And when 'tis, I still hope you will choose to stay with us a time longer in England."

At that, the dowager called for her escort and departed the palace for Nunnaminster.

Ailénor came back to the moment as she and the others arrived at Ceap Stræt, the main east-west axis running through Winchester. As she looked in each direction, it seemed to her the entire length of the wide and cobbled thoroughfare was a veritable marketplace.

Eadgifu directed them across the street to the north side, then turned left in the direction of West Gate. They slowed their progress to peruse the many stalls and shambles. Vendors peddled everything from essentials such as salt, candles, rushes, brooms, and soap, to luxuries—silver from the Harz Mountains and beautiful glassware—blue, green, and amber in color—some extraordinary in their shape and design.

One in particular captured her interest, having large globules ballooning from the lower portion of the glass and wilting to its foot, somewhat like a teardrop only reversed. Owing to the glassblowers' genius, the projections were hollow so that when the glass was filled, so would they be also. Ailénor wished dearly to purchase a matching pair for her parents, but unable to spend the dowager's coins freely, she promised herself to return when she could do so and procure the rare gift.

They continued on past the booths of the shoemakers, leather workers, and wood turners; potters, shieldwrights, needle makers, and, of course, the tables of the moneyers.

Along one section, there were a great many victuallers—butchers, fishmongers, bakers, vintners, and not a few brew houses. Mora wished to acquire something to drink, but Eadgifu urged the women on toward West Gate, insisting she relied on certain merchants there for the finest dye goods.

"The settlement outside West Gate is the city's oldest, largest, and most prosperous," Eadgifu explained to Ailénor, attempting to include her in the conversation that had been dominated by Mora and Rosalynd. "I am particularly fond of its specialized markets. There are also highly skilled metalworkers there—gold and silver smiths, and also bronze workers."

The women's arrival at the walls of Winchester caused some commotion, as the soldiers recognized their royal visitor and scurried to clear the way and offer additional soldiers to augment the women's escort. Eadgifu saw no need for this and proceeded, confident in the palace guard.

Passing through the gate, Ailénor observed that more than a few soldiers took a second glance at her, recognition creasing their eyes. She diverted her gaze and next discovered beggars clustered outside the city gate. One man whose clothes were naught but tattered shreds was blind, his eyes covered with ragged strips of linen.

Moved by pity, Ailénor slipped a coin from the dowager's purse and placed it in his wooden cup. At the dull clunk of the coin against the wood, the man murmured his thanks and blessings.

Seeing the others continued ahead—excepting one stout guard who hovered ever near—Ailénor hurried to catch up.

Wimund dragged the bandages from his eyes and peered after the Comtesse de Héricourt.

Fishing the coin from his cup, he tested it between his teeth, then moved off, shoving the piece into the pouch at his hip. Scant moments later he entered the first stable on Wudestret and located Grimbold mucking out a stall.

"She's here! She's moving toward Athelyngestret."

Grimbold tossed aside his rake and forsook his task, mopping the sweat from his face and his newly grown beard.

"She's not alone. There are guards, though not many," Wimund said in a rush.

"Athelyngestret, did you say? Good. Selida's herb booth stands toward the end of the others. She is not above a bit of silver to help out her 'friends.' Think what she will do for one of our little jewels."

Wimund grunted in agreement at the thought of the wench with melon-sized breasts. Grimbold had renewed his acquaintance with Selida on their arrival in Winchester, plying her first with questions of news of the *comtesse* and secondly with coin to lift her skirts for him. Aye, Selida would do most anything for gain, Wimund had found, even with him.

"What have you in mind?" Wimund asked.

"A potion, I think. Selida has a talent with that. She can devise something to offer the *comtesse,* a drink that will swiftly render her dizzy and seemingly ill. Selida can then offer her a place to sit, guiding her over to her booth. The guards should not object if she rests, and mayhap they will even ease their vigilance. The booth backs up to a coppice of beech trees. We can snatch her from there and disappear before all."

"But what of the guards, Grimbold? Maybe Selida should give them a potion, too."

"She has ways to distract them, do not fear. But should they prove difficult, I shall be prepared to deal with them. Come now. Our time slips away."

Ailénor moved ahead of the other women while they lingered over a table of ribbons and threads.

As she trailed her eyes over harnesses and saddles at the

leather workers' booths, something gnawed at the back of her mind. 'Twas as though something was out of place. Or not quite right. Or . ... She sighed, unsure what the source of the feeling might be.

Her eyes drew back toward the gate where she had given the blind man a coin. Nothing appeared out of the ordinary. People milled about, engrossed in their own affairs. The beggars still crowded the gate. Excepting the blind man.

Ailénor scanned the crowd. He was not to be seen. After a moment she mentally shrugged her uncertainty away. It pleased her to think the man had no more need for begging this day, due to her gift, and had left. Still, her unease persisted.

The day grew warm as Ailénor inspected a diversity of goods, her guard ever near. The jewelry drew her interest more than the cloth goods, but at last she moved toward a stall with brightly colored wool, knowing she dare not return to the palace without material for three gowns.

Around her the humanity of Winchester buzzed, hawkers crying their goods, buyers and vendors arguing over prices, children laughing and darting about the adults, wagons rattling past.

Ailénor smoothed out a length of pretty cloth, the color of pale yellow primroses.

"Cider, milady?" a voice sounded at her shoulder, startling her.

Ailénor turned to find a woman with a tousled mane of dark brown hair and equally dark eyes. Her simple work dress stretched tight over an amazingly bountiful bosom, which, at the moment, was enthralling every male nearby including that of Ailénor's guard.

"Cider, milady?" the woman asked again.

"Non, merci."

"You are with Her Grace's ladies are you not?"

"Oui, yes."

"Her Grace has purchased cider for all the ladies in her company. The day grows warm, and she thought 'twould be appreciated."

"Mais oui. I do appreciate it, truly." Ailénor accepted

the cup, unable to refuse Eadgifu's gracious gesture. She skimmed a glance in Eadgifu's direction, but the woman distracted her once more.

"Drink, milady," she prompted. "And tell me how you like the blend. 'Tis made from three varieties of apples, a balance of mellow and tart."

Indulging the woman, Ailénor raised the cup to her lips.

"What a lovely tone of yellow." Mora appeared at Ailénor's elbow and eyed the cloth in the stall. A half second later Rosalynd joined her. In unison, their gazes fell on the woman next to Ailénor and her startling endowments.

As they continued to gape, the woman stepped away and melted into the crowd.

"Is that cider?" Mora stared at Ailénor's cup. "I should like some. Where did you get it?"

Before Ailénor could answer, Rosalynd interrupted, holding up the cloth.

"Would you really wish to wear yellow for your betrothal gown, Mora?"

"And what is the matter with yellow?"

"'Tis rather garish."

"And I suppose you would prefer black for yours. 'Tis a festive occasion, Rosalynd. I would rather look like a spring blossom than a dried weed."

"You are making a gown for your betrothal, Mora?" Ailénor interjected, fearing the squabble was about to escalate. "How wonderful."

"Actually, I am also," Rosalynd added, glaring at Mora, challenge in her eyes.

"What great fortune that you are both to wed. Congratulations." Ailénor lifted her cup to them in their honor, then set it to her lips.

The sisters exchanged glances, then shared a small laugh as though they harbored a secret.

Ailénor paused as her upper lip touched the cider. She lowered the cup once more. "Have I said something amusing?"

They exchanged another look. Mora pursed her smiling

lips as though to keep them from divulging something she would love to say.

"Is it to be a double wedding?" Ailénor smiled at the thought. "May I ask whom you are to marry?"

Rosalynd replaced the cloth on the table and turned to Ailénor, a gleam in her eyes. "Why, did Garreth not tell you? He is to choose between Mora and myself, betrothing himself to one of us just after the ceremony investing him as the *Ealdorman* of Hamtunscir."

Ailénor's heart rammed against her ribs. She fought to keep the shock from her face, but knew she failed miserably.

How could this be? her mind reeled. Garreth had made love to her. He took her virginity, deflowered her, knowing full well he would soon wed another—Mora or Rosalynd. He had promised to keep her always at his side. But as what? His concubine?

For a moment Mora's and Rosalynd's faces swam before her eyes. But then her anger erupted. Disgusted, Ailénor passed her cider off to Mora.

"Forgive me. I must return to the palace. I find I do not feel well of a sudden."

Turning on her heel, Ailénor hastened back toward the gate and, entering the city, hurried toward the palace with tears in her eyes.

Eadgifu, seeing Ailénor's sudden departure, nodded to one of the soldiers to follow her, then joined her cousins.

"Whatever passed between you and Lady Ailénor? She looked stricken."

Mora and Rosalynd struggled to conceal their triumph.

"She seems to have taken ill," Mora said, full of innocence.

"I am not surprised. She is still recovering from her journey." Eadgifu turned to the yellow cloth spread on the table and began to examine it.

Mora shared a conspiratorial smile with Rosalynd. Exultant, she lifted the cup to her lips and downed the cider.

*   *   *

Short of breath and with an ache in her side, Ailénor forced herself on at a brisk pace and entered the palace.

She heard the clip of the boots of the guard following behind her but dismissed him from her thoughts and headed for the staircase. As she gained the first step, she heard Cynric's voice call her name.

She stayed her foot, clenching her fists at her side. She held no wish to suffer the man. Not now. Not when her heart was breaking.

"Lady Ailénor," Cynric called again. "I thought you would wish to know—a letter has arrived from the king."

Slowly Ailénor turned in place. Cynric stood a short space apart, a parchment grasped in his hand, a look of victory in his eyes. Ailénor steeled herself.

"King Athelstan concurs that you should remain for the time as a guest of his court. He wishes to greet you himself on his return. Furthermore, he believes you will be more comfortable at the royal estate at Andover and has instructed for your immediate removal there."

Ailénor's heart beat high and rapid at his words. She was to be a prisoner, then. Where Garreth held every confidence in his king, that same king now failed her.

She notched her chin defiantly. "Does Garreth know of this?"

Cynric's lips curled in a smile. "My lady, Garreth has agreed to lead the baggage wain himself for your transferral to the fortifications at Andover." At her look, he came forward. "I tried to warn you. Garreth will follow the king's wishes in all matters . . . even those concerning you."

Ailénor felt as though a knife had just been plunged through her heart and twisted. She pivoted and escaped up the stairs. As she reached the top of the flight, she heard a commotion from below.

Casting a quick look back down, she saw two soldiers carrying Mora into the palace. 'Twould appear she had passed out in a dead faint.

*   *   *

Garreth took the stairs two at a time, having only now received word of Ailénor's return. Unfortunately Cynric had already spoken with her.

When Garreth reached the chamber, it was bustling with activity. Through the open door he glimpsed Mora, moaning on her pallet while Rosalynd wrung out a wet cloth and laid it to her head.

Aldith caught sight of him and bustled over to the door. "The ladies can have no visitors now, I am sorry." She began to close the door.

He thrust out his hand, preventing Aldith from closing the door. "I need to speak with Ailénor. 'Tis a matter of some urgency."

"Lady Ailénor has taken to her bed and does not wish to see anyone."

"Is Eadgifu present?"

"Nay."

"Then I strongly suggest you stir Ailénor from her bed unless you wish me to do so myself."

"Sir!" she sputtered, aghast. "You wouldn't! Why, milady has not a stitch on beneath the covers."

Garreth smiled grimly. "Then I suggest you hurry to see her dressed."

Aldith's eyes rounded. She snapped her mouth shut and disappeared inside the chamber. Minutes later Ailénor appeared at the portal. She had been crying, Garreth realized as he observed her reddened eyes. He vented a long breath.

"Could we speak a moment?" he asked quietly.

Ailénor nodded in assent and joined him outside the room.

"I am surprised as you are at the king's missive, though not entirely. 'Tis my belief Cynric misrepresented matters to King Athelstan. I intend to ride personally to the king and confront him."

"Is that before or after you deliver me to Andover?"

Garreth winced, not realizing she knew this.

"And what next?" she pressed on. "Will you collect laurels from the king? And a bride of royal blood?"

"Bride? What are you speaking of?"

Inside the chamber, Rosalynd eased beside the partially opened door and listened.

"Do you deny you are to betroth yourself to one of the king's cousins—Rosalynd or Mora?"

"Who told you this?" Garreth growled.

"Does it matter? Tell the truth, Garreth. Are you to choose one of them as your wife?"

"No. Yes. Both."

"You cannot have it all ways," Ailénor argued, slipping into Frankish. She lowered her voice. "You claimed my maidenhead, knowing full well you would pledge yourself elsewhere."

"That is not the way of it," he blurted in Saxon, then transferred also to Frankish. "No commitments have been made, formal or informal. The king only suggested I consider his royal cousins. I met them on two previous occasions and those for a very limited time. The only pledge I made was to announce my choice of a bride upon my return from Francia. And that I still intend to do."

Ailénor swallowed hard against his words, then dashed a tear from her cheek. She began to turn from Garreth, unable to hear more. He held her fast, however, and would not allow her to move away.

"I intend to announce my choice is you, Ailénor," he said more gently.

Ailénor's gaze leapt to his, emotions conflicting within her, his words joyous and bittersweet within her heart.

"Yet you would banish me to Andover. You would lead me there yourself and leave my mother endangered due to Saxon duplicity. Mayhap this offer of marriage is but another way to bind me here."

"Nay, you are wrong, Ailénor. All is not as it seems. I believe the king sends you to Andover with good reason. It lies roughly thirteen miles to the north and upon the same road that I will need to travel to reach him. By sending you to Andover, he also removes you out from under Cynric's authority. It may be a signal he suspects something is amiss in what Cynric related to him."

"And if it is not? What if the king agrees with Cynric

and intends to keep me his captive, installing me where my own people cannot easily find me?''

''I cannot believe that.''

''Then prove me wrong. Help me reach a ship that will take me to Normandy. If the ports are watched, then take me to Lundenburh where I can board one of my uncle's vessels. *Then* you can have your talk with the king.''

''That I cannot do, Ailénor.''

''Cannot or will not?''

''I am bound by oath and loyalty to my king.'' *And by ties you cannot possibly understand.* ''Had I been able to deliver you back to Normandy before the matter was submitted to the king, I could have acted of my own accord. But once Cynric's message went out, I was bound to wait. To do otherwise would be tantamount to supplanting the king's authority and imposing my own will.''

Cynric's words flowed back to Ailénor. Garreth would faithfully follow the king's biddings, no matter what. Her heart sank.

Garreth reverted to Saxon though he appeared not to realize he had. ''The king's missive requires you to remain in England. To that end, I will conduct you safely to Andover, fulfilling his instructions. Afterward, however, I shall personally go in search of him to settle this matter. Then we will speak of the future and what we will share.''

Inside the bedchamber Mora lifted her head a trifle from her pillow. ''What do they say?'' she gritted out against a raging headache, yet aware Ailénor had joined Garreth outside the door.

Rosalynd came away from the portal and changed the cloth on Mora's forehead. ''Ailénor is to remain at court, no telling how long,'' she spoke quietly so Aldith would not hear. ''Garreth is to escort her to the king's estate at Andover.''

''Remain? But she can't!'' Mora blurted and immediately regretted it as pain seared through her head. ''Oh, Rosalynd, Garreth is sorely affected by her. I think she has placed a charm on him.''

Rosalynd bit the nail of her thumb, turning her thoughts.

She looked up of a sudden, her eyes flashing.

"When was the last time you visited Andover?"

Streaks of pink lightened an otherwise slate-gray sky, as the baggage wain assembled at dawn.

Ailénor waited upon a brown roundcy, preferring to ride horsed than to be enclosed with Mora and Rosalynd in the covered *charette* for the duration of the journey. She still wondered at their insistence to accompany her to Andover. Mayhap they really did have relatives there, but Ailénor believed their sudden friendliness toward her to be wholly feigned.

Eadgifu, pleased by Athelstan's command, graciously yielded up her new lady-in-waiting, having no wish to travel to "windy" Andover herself. Late yesterday she repaired to King's Worthy to rejoin Louis and Alain Barbetorte.

The dowager queen Eadgiva decided to entrench herself at Winchester and wait for her stepson Athelstan. She declared she had a few choice things to say to him, and not a few included the high-stepping *wicgerefa*, Cynric.

The last of the spare wagons arrived from the West Gate stables and were loaded with furniture and goods for the journey. Like most royal palaces, Andover stood barren when the royals were not in residence.

Garreth traveled along the full length of the entourage, making his last inspection of the horses, wagons, and accompanying retinue. Satisfied, he turned his horse and returned to the head of the line where he joined Ailénor.

She had spoken no more than a handful of words to him for the last two days. Now she looked straight ahead and would not look at him. Garreth longed to reach the king and right this matter, setting it behind them.

Shouting out a command, he signaled the entourage forward and conducted them toward North Gate.

At the end of the baggage wain, Wimund grumbled beside Grimbold as they manned one of the wagons.

"I tell you, we have lost too much time. Princess Rhiannon warned she would hire others and give the treasure to them if we tarried too long.''

Grimbold rolled an eye to Wimund, weary of his constant fretting. He clicked his tongue and twitched the reins, prodding the animal ahead.

"We have little choice as I see it. But this time we should be able to get inside the royal compound at Andover. You need learn patience, Wimund. Why do you think I sought employment at one of the largest stables that serves the palace? Sometimes 'tis necessary to bide a little time and keep one's ears to the ground for the best opportunity. Right now, ours appears to be Andover.''

"But the treasure," Wimund whined. "By the time we reach Ireland with the *comtesse*, Rhiannon will have promised it elsewhere.'' He thought a moment, his great eyes darting about as if to catch a thought. "But she doesn't know we are here, does she? Mayhap if she did, and that we have the *comtesse* in sight and the reasons for our delay . . .'' He spun on his seat, intense with emotion. "Do you think I should catch a quick craft to Ireland to tell her and join you later at Andover?''

At the end of his patience, Grimbold gave Wimund a long look. "Is that what you wish to do—go to Ireland?''

Wimund nodded rapidly.

"Mayhap 'tis best after all," Grimbold conceded. "Take the old Roman road from West Gate straight across to the coast to the Severn. Catch a boat there. Return the same way, only at Sarum take the branch that leads north and east. You'll soon come to Andover. 'Tis on the same road that leads to Lundenburh.''

Grimbold slowed the wagon, and Wimund scrambled down. As he pulled ahead, Grimbold shook his head, thinking of what the princess would do to Wimund when he appeared empty-handed. It didn't really matter if Wimund returned. His luck lay at Andover, he could feel it in his bones. In the coming days, Lady Ailinn of Héricourt would be his. And so would be the treasure.

*   *   *

The baggage wain departed Winchester, passing beneath the stone church that spanned the North Gate bridge overhead. To the north the land opened out to rolling meadows, dotted with wooded coppices and bounded by the River Itchen to the east.

Ailénor glanced up as skylarks winged their way ahead. What great advantage they had, Ailénor thought, to see the whole view of things at once, even what lay ahead of them before they even reached it. How she wished she could view her world as they. And look ahead to the path that lay before her in the days to come.

But she could not wait on kings or on the man she loved. If she was to get back to Normandy in time to warn her mother, she must rely on herself. When Garreth departed Andover, she would find a way to escape and find her way to Lundenburh.

Chapter Nine

Lyting marked the center of the target, drew on his bow, and with unerring aim sent the arrow hissing to its goal to crowd four other shafts. Without a wasted movement, he nocked another arrow, pulled, released, and added a sixth.

God help the whoresons who took Ailénor, he thought darkly. If any harm came to her, he would personally . . .

"Lord Lyting!" a servant cried, hastening toward him. "Lady Ailinn asks you to join her in your chamber at once. There are arrivals from Valsemé." The servant came to a halt, panting for breath. "Lady Ailinn says 'tis urgent."

Lyting handed off his bow and headed for the keep. Long minutes later he climbed the stairs by twos to the upper floor where his and Ailinn's chamber lay. He arrived at the door just ahead of his brother, Rurik, who approached from the opposite end of the gallery.

As they entered, Ailinn turned and looked up from where she sat with Brienne and their visitors. Lyting directed his gaze to the couple who were now rising to their feet, and immediately recognized Ailinn's stepcousin Lia.

Ailinn and Lia were as close as sisters, having been raised together from their youth. During the raid on Clonmel, they had been seized along with their kinswomen and transported to the Danish market town of Hedeby. 'Twas there Lyting first set eyes on Ailinn. And there an old friend, Ketil, discovered Lia being sold as a slave. Ketil purchased her freedom, and together with his wife, Aleth, brought her to Normandy. Lia later married one of Rurik's men-at-arms and made Valsemé her new home.

But 'twas not her husband who accompanied her this day. Lyting did not recognize the man. Whomever he was, he appeared neither Frankish nor Norse by the look of him.

As Lyting greeted Lia, he could feel a fine tension layering the room. Ailinn appeared alarmingly pale, and fine lines etched Brienne's forehead. Mentally he steeled himself, wondering what news Lia bore that could be so urgent.

"May I present my kinsman, Comyn of Clonmel," Lia began. "He brings remarkable news from Ireland. Rhiannon is alive. She returned six months ago from the East."

Lyting's eyes leapt to Ailinn. She dropped her gaze, sealing her lips against the emotions she plainly felt. As Lyting returned his gaze to Lia, he wondered how she felt of this news. Rhiannon had been responsible for the death of Lia's sister, Deira. He himself had witnessed the act. Try though he did, he could not save Deira from the fierce rapids of Gelandri. It had haunted his soul ever since.

Lia's voice netted his attention. "When I heard the full of Comyn's story, I knew we must come at once. I fear it may have some bearing on Ailénor's disappearance."

Lyting exchanged a look of surprise with Rurik. "How so, Lia?"

She turned to Comyn and spoke with him briefly in Gaelic. Again she looked to Lyting and Rurik. "Comyn does not speak Frankish, but I will translate his words for you. 'Tis a long tale. Mayhap you wish to seat yourselves."

Lyting shook his head but crossed the expanse to stand behind Ailinn. He placed a calming hand upon her shoulder while she in turn slipped her hand overtop his. Rurik, meanwhile, joined Brienne.

Softly, in Gaelic, Lia bid Comyn to begin, and then rendered his words in Frankish.

"One day, six months past, Rhiannon arrived in Clonmel, bringing with her a barbarian of the Steppe, a man with the devil's mark upon his face. At the time, Mór, her father, lingered on his deathbed. He was jubilant to find Rhiannon had survived, having thought her to be dead these many long years. Rhiannon, too, was overjoyed, thinking Mór had died during the Norse raid on Clonmel.

"In the days that followed, Rhiannon described how she and the barbarian, Varya, had gained their freedom. It seems a missionary discovered them—one of the itinerant monks who devote their lives to converting heathens and seeking enslaved Christians so they might buy them out of bondage."

Lia paused as Comyn said something very rapidly, gesturing expressively with his hands.

"Comyn says to this day no one understands the nature of Rhiannon's association with Varya, only that she convinced the monk to bargain his freedom as well as hers, claiming him to be agreeable to conversion and taking baptism. From what can be surmised, Varya never received the holy waters. Nor is it clear what became of the monk. But over the last year, Rhiannon and the barbarian made their way west to Ireland.

"The Eóganachts welcomed Rhiannon, though privately they remained wary of the heathen. Soon she showed her true grain, stirring untold trouble within the tribe. Then, when some of the cattle mysteriously died and unseasonable storms descended on Clonmel, some even feared she and her devil-man practiced the dark arts. While Comyn did not know Rhiannon in her younger days, he says she is now a hard and bitter woman with frightful scars and a twistedness in her mind. A twistedness, he believes, rooted in the deep hatred she carries in her heart.''

Lia paused to quench the dryness of her throat with a swallow of wine, then continued.

''When Rhiannon learned of my recent visit to Clonmel, she began to question the others intently. When she discovered Ailinn had also survived her captivity and lives in Normandy, it obsessed her mind till she could speak of naught else. The women who attended Rhiannon overheard her boast to Varya of how she would have Ailinn seized and brought to Ireland so she might take her revenge on her.

''Meanwhile, Mór died. Some say Rhiannon hastened him to his grave. Scarce had he been laid to his rest when Rhiannon and the barbarian disappeared, taking with them Mór's personal treasure that he had long kept hidden in an ancient underground *souterrain* of which she knew. The tribesmen who tracked them say Rhiannon and Varya traveled to an abandoned hill-fort named Cahercommaun, on the southwest coast of Ireland.

''Comyn confesses the men did not confront them. The tribe preferred to leave Rhiannon and her barbarian to themselves, wishing nothing more to do with them.''

Comyn stood up, speaking animatedly, appealing in his Gaelic tongue directly to Lyting and Rurik.

''He says Rhiannon is evil, driven by her hatred and her desire for revenge. In Clonmel, Comyn and the others began to worry. With such wealth as she now commands, Rhiannon may be capable of almost anything. They especially worry over the threat concerning Ailinn and felt an urgency to warn us.''

Silence fell upon the group as they considered Comyn's disturbing words. At last, Ailinn spoke, her voice trembling, tears in her eyes.

''We have been searching Francia in vain. Ailénor must

have been taken in my stead, by mistake.''

"We do not know that for certain,'' Lyting said gently.

"Mayhap we do.'' Rurik rubbed a thumb along his jaw in thought. "Mayhap like a piece of broken pottery, we have been holding all the pieces but not fitting them together correctly. What do we know thus far? Ailénor was seen near the kitchens just before dawn and seized soon after in the garden. Her cloak and brooch confirm that. About the same time, two servants disappeared from their duties, and later a cart of rushes was found abandoned outside the west gate.''

"Assuming the men *were* Rhiannon's hirelings, and that they believed 'twas Ailinn they had seized,'' Lyting reasoned aloud, "their quickest escape would have been by ship, downriver, toward the coast and open waters.''

"Only one ship left that morn in the direction of La Manche,'' Rurik rejoined. "Aside from the boatswain, 'twas reported two men sailed with Garreth of Tamworth. Do we have their description?''

"*Nei*, but I know who claimed to have seen them.'' Lyting departed the chamber long enough to send for the man, then returned to comfort Ailinn while they waited. When he entered the room, the others were discussing the two missing manservants.

"They were said to be coarse-looking,'' Brienne was saying. "But do we know something more specific than that? Some detail that might help identify them as the men in the ship?''

"One had monstrously large eyes,'' Lyting offered. "The other's face was scarred as if he once suffered the pox.''

Stunned, Ailinn swiveled in her chair to look up at Lyting. "You did not tell me this before now. I saw them. We all did. In the alcove by the stairs. I remember, they seemed menacing somehow, and for a moment I thought . . . but I believed my mind played me a trick.''

"Thought what, *elskan mín*?'' Concern filled Lyting's eyes.

"I thought they meant me harm. I was alone with them

for a moment. Brienne cleaned her dress above stairs, and I went down ahead of her. The men were in the alcove, and when they saw me they started to move toward me as though cornering quarry. But then you and Rurik appeared." Ailinn reached for her husband's hands and gripped them tightly. "Oh, Lyting, I heard one of them speak Gaelic!"

Rurik stood to his feet. "I remember them as well, though I didn't see their features clearly. I thought it odd that they should stack trestles behind the stairs."

Lyting, too, remembered the men in the alcove. "My God, Ailinn, they came very near to seizing you."

"Now they have our Ailénor instead." She looked at him with doleful eyes.

Lyting comforted Ailinn while Rurik and Brienne spoke further with Comyn and Lia. At last one of the guards ushered in a man called Gervase.

Gervase doffed his hat, turning it nervously in his hands as he sketched a bow, obviously unsure why he had been summoned to the ducal palace. Lyting quickly put him at ease, then asked several pointed questions of the men who had sailed from Rouen the fateful morn Ailénor had disappeared.

"They came to the docks just as the skies were breaking," Gervase recalled. "Wanted to cross La Manche, they said. I was sailing for Paris myself, so I sent them to speak with Turold the Saxon, two ships over. He was about to make that run."

"Do you recall anything in particular about the two men? What they looked like?"

Gervase scratched his ragged beard. "They both were hooded. Couldn't see their features well in the lingering dark. There was something strange about one of them, though. Something not quite right about his face. 'Twas his eyes, actually. They looked . . ."

"Large?" Lyting supplied.

"That's it! Huge, like a bug's eyes."

The others exchanged glances.

"Did you see what the men loaded onto the ship?"

Gervase shook his head. "No trunks or other goods, if that is what you mean. Nothing but a grain sack."

"Think carefully. Could it have contained a person?"

All expression drained from Gervase's face as he recognized what they truly asked. "*Oui*, Lord. It could have been a maid."

Ailinn's hands flew to cover her mouth, and she squeezed her eyes together in quiet anguish. Brienne quickly slipped an arm around her.

"Faith, Ailinn. We must not forget Garreth was aboard. Mayhap he was able to aid her."

"There were reports of a wicked storm that kicked up that night on La Manche," Gervase warned. "At least two ships are known to have been lost. 'Tis impossible to know if their ship reached land or even where they might have been when the storm hit. The storm likely drove them off course as well."

Rurik caught Lyting's gaze. " 'Twill take too long to check the individual ports along the coast. It might be best to sail directly for Lundenburh. One of Valsemé's ships is there now. We could pick up news from the crew and others along the wharf. 'Tis a starting point. We can put in elsewhere if need be."

"It might also be helpful to know from Comyn exactly where they would have been headed," Lyting rejoined, then turned to Ailinn.

Ailinn's heart clutched as she rose from her chair, knowing that he was about to leave her. She shook her head against his unspoken words.

"I will not be left behind, Lyting. I am sailing with you." Startled, he tried to object, but she grasped his arms. "Many years ago, you promised to take me back to Ireland *whenever* I wished. I pray we need not journey so far as that, but I refuse to remain here waiting for word. 'Tis me Rhiannon seeks, and what led to this sorrow. Please, my love. I cannot remain here."

She could see Lyting debate the matter in his mind. Knowing him, he held no wish to put her at any risk.

"For our Ailénor," she pleaded softly, placing a hand over his heart.

Lyting slipped his hand over hers and nodded his agreement.

Brienne started to say something to Rurik, but he stayed her. "I will need you at Valsemé, *ástin mín*. Take the children there, *all* of them, and Felise, too. I will send word to you there. Meanwhile, we three will take the ship and crew with which we sailed to Rouen. I will go now and advise William of what passes and ask that he provide you and the children an escort to the barony."

Giving Brienne a swift kiss, Rurik looked to his brother. "Lyting, I shall need a hand readying the ship."

Lyting looked to Ailinn. "Are you sure you wish to make this journey, *elskan mín*?"

Ailinn's thoughts went to Ireland, and she sensed deep within her, even should they find their daughter, the matter would not see its end until she confronted Rhiannon directly.

"Elskan mín?" Lyting asked again when she did not respond. "Are you certain you wish to do this?"

Ailinn took a deep breath. "I must."

CAHERCOMMAUN, IRELAND

Rhiannon's eyes glazed as Varya brought her to the brink of release, then held her there, sustaining the moment on a fine edge as he sucked gently, then drew his tongue away from the swollen fruit of her womanhood to caress a less sensitive area.

Reaching up, he gave a small tug to the fine golden chain draped across her belly, each end affixed to gold rings fastened through her nipples. She felt the burning, embraced it. Pain and ecstasy, the two must become one to attain the most intense and explosive of sensual experiences.

Varya drew his hand downward, cupping the soft mound of her femininity and kneading it with his palm. At the same time, he slid his tongue up again to her sensitive core, and with a gentle nip signaled he was taking her. His tongue danced over the silken flesh with precise, rapid movements as he brought her to the pinnacle of pleasure and sent her hurtling beyond. Rhiannon fragmented, exploding with fierce convulsions, fire shooting through her veins.

She panted as she descended from the orgiastic heights, aware of Varya shifting to his knees and drawing up her parted legs. He placed her feet on his shoulders, then entered her with a swift, solid thrust. He still wore the ivory cock-ring that was part of their earlier play. It encircled the base of his manhood and now, as he pressed against her, its large inset pearl kissed her nerve-rich nub.

Varya moved against her with brisk, powerful thrusts. The pearl grazed Rhiannon's sensitive flesh, but again she welcomed and relished the pain. That, too, was an art.

A growl rumbled from Varya's chest, building to a full-throated roar as he threw back his head and, grinding against her, purchased his own climax.

Rhiannon watched his features constrict with pain, pleasure, ecstasy. Finishing, his black eyes sought hers. She smiled and nodded. He pleased her, and he need know that. Varya, too, had his pride.

As her Avar lover left the bed, Rhiannon stretched out, catlike, her gaze flowing over his naked, iron-hard body. She watched as he worked the ivory ring from his male member. Her lips curved upward. Varya had a devil's tool to match his devil's face. In him she had found not only a formidable protector, but also a worthy mate. Best of all, he would do anything she asked of him. Anything at all.

Rhiannon rose from the bed and crossed the room to her clothes chest, with a slow, confident stride that set the slim golden chain swaying from her breasts to gently buffet her taut stomach. Varya's dark gaze followed her. Rhiannon took further pleasure in that and allowed him his fill. Her face might be scarred, but her body was that of a young woman, faultless in its shape.

She drew on a loose gown and took up a comb, setting it to her disheveled hair. Behind, she heard Varya move about the room as he collected his clothes.

How far they had come, she thought to herself. How much they had endured. And survived. Now they were free. With her sharpness of mind, Varya's barbaric power, and her father's treasure, life was at her command. Indeed, they had come far.

Her thoughts drifted back to a day, eighteen years past, when a fierce Petcheneg bore her across the golden expanse of the Steppe. The Petchenegs were a vile, loathsome people. A woman of lesser spirit would have broken under their domination. But her own will was indomitable. It proved her greatest strength, and her salvation.

Many a time she had tried to escape. Many a time she had been punished. Only to try again. Why they did not kill her, she was unsure. Mayhap they liked her too well in their beds. Whatever their reason, they tired of her in time, and at one of the crossroads on the Baltic, they traded her to a group of Avars. 'Twas then she met Varya.

Varya was born of an Avar warrior and a slave woman. As a healthy male child, his father could have freed him from slavery and raised him up as a warrior as well. But because of the blight that covered half his face, Varya was not given the honor. Instead he lived reviled by all, even the lowest of slaves.

Heathens, Rhiannon had found, were as superstitious and fearful as Christians when it came to a man with the devil's mark. Thus Varya grew from childhood, knowing naught but beatings and hard work and no tenderness in his life, except perhaps once a mother, who had died or been sold long ago.

Rhiannon first saw Varya from a distance, alone and crouched before a fire, his unblemished side toward her. She thought him to be a favorable-looking man, ruggedly hewn with muscles that looked to be of rock. In him Rhiannon saw great potential. She looked closer and guessed him to have seen about twenty years at the time. She had seen thirty.

Rhiannon found it odd that he sat isolated from the others. By the wide paths they made around him, she intuited they feared him. He looked toward her then, and she discovered their reason—a purplish-red stain that cursed him and sealed his fate. Rhiannon did not flinch, but held his gaze steadily with hers. If she could gain his loyalty, he would make an excellent protector in captivity.

First she strove to gain his trust. She treated him fairly, not with softness or kindness, which would be viewed as weakness amidst the harsh life of the Steppe. Instead, she was humane where others were not. Also, she neither avoided looking on his mark nor reminded him of it with open stares. She trained herself to look beyond it and treat him as any other. In time, she truly no longer saw the stigma when she gazed on him.

Once one of the older slave women caused him to trip and spill an armload of wood, sending the logs rolling into the cookfire and upsetting a bubbling pot of broth. The woman clouted Varya about the head with the hot ladle, but Rhiannon stayed the wrathful slave and told her to see to the vessel herself. The woman spit at her, but Rhiannon held no care. Varya looked at Rhiannon strangely, as though uncomprehending why anyone should come to his aid. Whatever his thoughts, he did not communicate them, but remained behind his mental wall.

Time passed, and Rhiannon saw little progress. One day she angered one of the Avars, and he set a knife to her throat, intending to kill her. Varya, who had never spoken to her knowledge, roared a frightening sound as he came forward at the man, seemingly out of nowhere. The pressure of the Avar's hand slackened, and though he did not stop the path of his knife, it did not cut as deeply as he intended. Dropping Rhiannon in a heap, the Avar quickly retreated, fearful of the crazed devil-man.

Varya tended to her wounds and fostered her back to health. Somehow he stanched the bleeding, though he knew nothing of the stitching of such wounds. He did, however, know of herbs and poultices and was able to keep the wound free of infection. The scar that formed was grotesque, but Rhiannon owed him her life and made no complaint. From that time forth, their bond grew. The others left them alone, fearing Varya more than ever, wholly unsure of his capacities when roused.

During that time Rhiannon took him as her lover, something no woman had ever done. And Varya was extremely grateful.

Over time, Rhiannon learned the rudiments of his language and taught him some of hers. For five years they plotted their escape. Then fate intervened. While at another of the market crossroads, a traveling missionary discovered them.

They were free now, and the world was theirs. But first, above all, she would right the wrongs done her, beginning with her wretched stepcousin Ailinn.

A rap at the door jolted Rhiannon from her thoughts. At her bidding, a nervous bent stick of a maidservant entered and announced a visitor—a man named Wimund.

"At last." Rhiannon's pulse quickened.

Tossing a mantle about her shoulders, she preceded Varya from the room, her expectations rising as they entered the adjoining chamber that served as the hall. Inside, Wimund waited alone.

Rhiannon cast her glance about the room, then spun on Wimund who had the audacity to smile at her.

"Where is she?" Her temper flared, and she advanced on him. "Why have you returned empty-handed?"

Wimund's smile fell. "I—I came to report . . ."

"I do not want a report. I want Ailinn here, now."

"Princess, we seized Lady Ailinn in Rouen and crossed the Channel, but there was a fierce storm, and there has been a delay."

"What?" Rhiannon screeched. "Where is she? And where is Grimbold?"

"They are in England. Grimbold follows her from Winchester to a place named Andover."

"*Follows* her? You mean she slipped your grasp?" Her fury multiplied, and she closed the space with a menacing step.

"There was a Saxon noble aboard, and he . . ."

"Give me no excuses," she shrieked as she clawed her

fingers and raked them across Wimund's face, drawing blood.

Varya moved behind him, clamped him on the shoulders, and hauled him up on his toes. Rhiannon plucked the dagger from the sheath at Wimund's hip and held it to his throat.

"Listen to me, you miserable little insect of a man. I do not wish to see your face unless Ailinn is in your possession. Now, go back to England and bring her to me."

She withdrew the blade and motioned for Varya to release him.

Wimund backed toward the door, bobbing in short, rapid bows. "Yes, Princess. At once." He stumbled in his haste to leave.

"One thing more," Rhiannon called after Wimund. "Varya will accompany you this time."

An hour later Rhiannon stood on the wall of the hill-fort, looking out over the steep drop to the sea as Varya and Wimund's ship departed.

"You shan't escape your fate, Ailinn," she promised on the wind. "Not this time."

Chapter Ten

ANDOVER, ENGLAND

Ailénor's heart dipped when she saw the fortifications of Andover. Defended by earthworks, stockade, sentry walks, and a guardhouse that spanned the entrance gate, she knew there would be little chance of escape.

Guiding her small rouncy behind Garreth's larger courser, she entered the compound at the head of the baggage wain and reined her horse to a standstill. As she began to dismount, Garreth appeared at her side to assist her.

Their eyes met and held. She knew in her heart their time together now dwindled to its close. Placing her hands on his broad shoulders, she allowed him to lift her down. She gazed into his beautiful, dark brown eyes, making no move to withdraw her hands from him. Nor did he withdraw his from her. They stood locked together for a moment in time. It tore at her that their paths must part.

"I pray thee, do not leave me here, Garreth," she appealed softly. "Help me."

A sadness, a wearied frustration, flickered across his eyes. "That is what I am striving to do."

His look pleaded for understanding. But Ailénor knew understanding alone would not protect her mother. Nor would he change his course of action.

She dropped her gaze. "Then 'twould seem there is nothing more to say."

Drawing her hands from his shoulders, she stepped from his hold. She must rely on herself. The English king, she believed, would uphold his earlier decision ordering her detainment. If so, she doubted not at all what Garreth would do. Cynric had been very clear. Were Garreth faced with a choice between his king and herself, she would lose.

However she could accomplish it, she must escape Andover and find her way to her uncle's ship in Lundenburh.

Dispirited, Ailénor glanced aside and caught sight of Rosalynd and Mora whose eyes were fixed on herself and Garreth. She guessed them to be the only ones who sincerely wished for her to leave court. It gave her no joy, knowing when she did she would be leaving Garreth to the wiles of these two felines.

Garreth's gaze lingered over Ailénor as she looked back along the baggage wain, his emotions drawn taut as a bowstring. Was he doing right by her? He had asked himself that question a thousand times. And a thousand times he found no answer that could be held free of doubt.

One thing remained, however. His steadfast faith in the wisdom and justice of Athelstan.

A bright patch of color caught his eye—Mora's scarlet sleeve as she waved for him to help her and her sister from their covered *charette*. Garreth glanced at Ailénor, wishing to offer some encouragement, but as his gaze met her stiff back, he knew she was right. There was nothing more to say. Nothing more until he conferred with Athelstan face-to-face.

Garreth strode from Ailénor's side to assist Mora and Rosalynd. They flushed and twittered and fawned as he lifted them one by one to the ground, stretching his nerves all the tighter. In silence he escorted the women to the timbered hall, leaving behind the courtyard abuzz with activity as members of the retinue saw to the horses and the unloading of the wagons.

Inside the rustic building, they were met by the palace staff who had been informed of their coming and also by the reeve of the royal estate of Andover, a man known to Garreth as Rannulf.

While servants conducted the ladies to their chambers, Garreth conferred with the reeve concerning the king's missive. He then repaired to the quarters he customarily occupied on his annual visits with the monarch. After refreshing himself, he next joined the women in the main hall for a goblet of wine and to make his farewell.

"You are leaving?" Mora gasped. "But we just arrived."

Rosalynd shared her sister's surprise, her mouth dropping open. Ailénor simply looked away.

"I go to the king on a matter of some urgency," Garreth explained. "I trust you will understand."

Ailénor pressed her lashes shut as though blotting out his words. Mora pouted petulantly but in a way meant to dissuade him from leaving. Rosalynd pleaded for him to remain. Unable to bear more, Garreth placed his goblet on the table and sketched a shallow bow.

"Ladies. If you will excuse me, I must see to obtaining a fresh mount."

Quitting the hall, Garreth headed for the stables, more anxious than ever to reach the king and resolve this whole affair.

The stables proved to be a bustling, congested scene. The last of the pack and wagon horses were being unhitched, rubbed down, and walked about the yard, and the sundry conveyances lined up beside the building.

The commotion extended to inside the stable as well, where stablehands stalled and fed the horses and others cared for and stored the gear. His gaze fell on one of the workers hanging up the heavy horse collars.

"Have you seen the groom named Warrin?" Garreth called above the racket.

The man, darting a brief look to Garreth, shook his head, then turned back to his work. Garreth thought he recognized him as one of the men in the baggage wain who had just made the journey from Winchester. He possessed small, hard eyes and a scrubby beard that covered his lower face.

Garreth crossed to the stalls to examine the choice of horses. He required one trained for long distances, having stamina and standing to a suitable height, able to accommodate his own size. What he would give for one of the large Norman horses he had seen at the ducal palace at Rouen.

As he began to examine the horse in the first stall, it flinched and sidestepped, throwing its head up and away from Garreth's touch. The horse's eyes showed a large amount of white, an indication the animal was skittish. Definitely not a good choice for the task set before him—scouring the countryside for a king.

Garreth moved on to a dark bay courser in the next stall that looked promising. He diverted his gaze momentarily to the bearded man hanging up the tack. There was something indefinably familiar about him. But Garreth could not pinpoint just what that was.

Returning his attention to the bay, he ran his hand down the animal's leg, feeling for heat or swelling that might indicate inflammation or joint problems. He next checked the hooves, making sure they were clean and free of small stones. They were. The groom had done his job.

Garreth straightened and, rubbing the horse's muzzle, checked its eyes. As he did, he allowed his gaze to drift once more to the bearded man. He sat conditioning a saddle, rubbing it with lanolin-rich sheep's wool.

Something jabbed at the back of Garreth's mind like the point of a bull's horn. He concentrated on the man's profile, narrowing his eyes. Just then, the groom, Warrin, appeared at his side and interrupted his thoughts with a hearty greeting.

Warrin quickly caught Garreth up in conversation, agreeing with his assessment of the one horse while assuring the bay was sound and dependable. They looked over several more mounts, but Garreth settled on the bay.

While Warrin saddled the horse, Garreth again considered the bearded man, though he was no longer in sight. Many minutes later, as Garreth led the courser from the stable, his thoughts remained clogged as to why he should be afflicted with the nettling feeling.

Progressing across the courtyard, another thought supplanted that of the stablehand. Ailénor. He craved to see her before his departure, yet given her coolness since their arrival, he believed she held no wish to see him.

Filled with regret, he set his foot to the stirrup and swung up into the saddle. But as he started to turn the bay toward the gate, Ailénor appeared unexpectedly, hastening from the hall.

She halted, gazing at him across the expanse.

Garreth read the pain and conflict in her eyes. How he wished to ask her trust of him. Wished to vow his love for her. But words would no longer suffice.

Impulsively he touched his heels to the flanks of the horse, spurring it forward. Coming alongside Ailénor, he reached out and swept her up in one arm, then kissed her boldly, possessively, without care to who might watch.

Setting her once more to the ground, he touched her cheek, memorizing her features, then turned his horse across the courtyard.

Ailénor felt her heart rent in two as Garreth galloped through the gate. She pressed her fingers to her lips, a tear sliding from the corner of her eye.

No matter the outcome of his meeting with the king and despite her love for him, God willing, she would no longer be at Andover when Garreth returned.

*   *   *

Ailénor sat with her stitchery in the ladies' bower with Mora and Rosalynd, her needle idle in her hands, her thoughts far away.

She needed to act swiftly if she was to escape, yet her heavy-heartedness threatened to overwhelm her. Thinking of Garreth, then of her dear *maman* and the dangers that threatened, wrung Ailénor emotionally to the core.

She staved her tears, swiping the moisture from her lashes and drawing Rosalynd's attention.

"Does aught distress you, Lady Ailénor?"

Rosalynd appeared genuinely concerned, but Ailénor did not trust her motives. Still, she desperately needed help. If Rosalynd and Mora truly wished her gone from court, mayhap her hope of escape lay with them.

"I was thinking of my mother," Ailénor returned.

Mora glanced up from her handwork. "Is she not well?"

Ailénor realized the sisters did not know she had been abducted in her mother's place. Garreth had related the tale over dinner at Winchester, but he had omitted that detail. Before she could decide how much to reveal to them, Rosalynd spoke.

"Has no word come from Normandy?"

Ailénor's gaze jumped to hers. "In truth, my parents and the ducal court have no idea what has become of me, or even that I am here in England."

"What?" Mora gasped.

"How can that be?" Rosalynd leaned forward. "Has no missive been sent?"

Ailénor hesitated, fearing they might not wish to help her if they realized she was being detained as a political hostage. "The high reeve, Cynric, would not allow it without conferring with the king . . ."

" 'Tis ludicrous," Mora blurted, interrupting Ailénor and relieving her of further explanation. "I have always said that man was a cockscomb. Don't look at me so, Rosalynd. You know he is that and much worse."

Ailénor's gaze flicked between them. "Forgive me. I

mean no offense to the king's hospitality, but I fear greatly for my mother's well-being.''

Ailénor thought it best if they believed her mother ailed. Yet knowing the truth and the dark possibilities that might befall her mother if she failed to warn her seared her heart. Ailénor crumpled the embroidery in her lap, purposely catching a sob in her throat.

''I *must* return to Normandy before 'tis too late. Before she . . . If only I could reach my uncle's ship in Lundenburh.''

Rosalynd moved to Ailénor's side to comfort her, though Ailénor saw that her eyes glinted with cunning. ''And so you shall.''

''You can help me?'' Hope flooded Ailénor's voice.

Rosalynd raised her chin proudly. ''Not only have Mora and I relations in Andover, but being of royal lineage, we are not without means *or* connections.'' Her lips curled into a smile. ''Leave everything to me.''

Garreth sat at the scarred table over a goblet of cold ale and a joint of venison, considering the words he would use when he met up with the king.

His progress thus far had been favorable. Yesterday he had reached the burh of Chisbury, and today that of Cricklade. The burhs were part of the fortification system begun by King Alfred, none being more than twenty miles apart and offering defense and communication points throughout the land. 'Twas Garreth's intention to travel by way of the burhs as far as he might toward Scotland, collecting what information he could of the monarch's movements.

With an early start on the morrow, he expected to arrive at Cirencester before midday. From there he would head north to Tamworth. He suspected the king and his troops had passed through the Mercian stronghold before heading on. With luck he would encounter them on their return, perhaps at Bakewell or Manchester, and have no need of tracking them to the Scottish border itself.

As Garreth sat working through his thoughts, a man entered the lodging—a man with a scar running alongside his eye, downward over his cheek, and into his scrubby beard.

The nettling feeling he had experienced two days before now returned fresh and every bit as disturbing.

What was it about the man? Garreth gave his concentration to him. He did not know the man, nor did he appear a threat. Still, the disquieting feeling would not subside.

Garreth took another bite of venison. Chewing it slowly, he traced the line of the man's scar to where it disappeared into his beard. Except it didn't disappear wholly. There was a visible path where the hair would not grow along the scar.

The thought jarred, bringing with it the memory of the bearded stablehand at Andover. 'Twas the beard that had bothered him. It seemed somehow odd and did not suit the stablehand's face. 'Twas a fairly new growth, curly and briery, yet uneven—spotty in its sproutings—as though the skin beneath was damaged, scarred.

Garreth suspected the scars to cover the greater portion of the man's cheeks. He would have to have been slashed badly with a knife. Or suffered a disfiguring disease. Like the pox.

Garreth bolted to his feet, realization slamming through him. ''Grimbold,'' he spat out.

Tossing down the meat, he abandoned the room.

Ailénor waited inside the horse litter for Rosalynd to join her.

Thus far, their plans had unfolded smoothly. It played to their advantage that neither Rosalynd nor Mora had visited Andover for many years, having lived mostly between the family estates at Boscombe and Eashing and joining the court for seasonal celebrations at other royal residences.

Over time, most of the staff at Andover had changed. The maidservants now attending them were among the newest and had never before met Rosalynd or Mora. Nor, of course, had they met Ailénor. 'Twas a fairly easy matter to confuse them as to who was who. Ailénor and Mora assumed each other's identity, ''correcting'' the maids' earlier perceptions formed at their arrival.

The first eve, Rosalynd dispatched a swift rider to her

cousin Gilbert at Kingsclere, arranging for her and Mora to visit there in the coming days and requesting he fetch them with a small escort.

Rosalynd also informed the reeve Rannulf of their intentions so he would expect their departure. What he did not know was that Ailénor would assume Mora's place. Once at Kingsclere, Ailénor would ride on to Silchester and Lundenburh with Gilbert as her escort. Gilbert, Rosalynd claimed, owed her more than a few favors and could be trusted. She offered no further explanation, but judging by her look, Ailénor did not doubt her.

Gilbert arrived midafternoon of their third day at Andover, and when he met Ailénor face-to-face, he appeared more than happy to accommodate Rosalynd's request. Too happy. This did not give Ailénor great ease, as he impressed her as a carefree, flirtatious sort of man. Yet he seemed sincere and honorable. Ailénor believed he would truly endeavor to safeguard her to the best of his capacity.

'Twas going to be an interesting journey.

For her part, Mora took to her bed over the last days and feigned illness. She jested that she had only to think of her recent malady in Winchester to effect it, then set about convincing the young maid she was, in fact, Ailénor. The sisters insisted they take their meals in the bower and tend their friend, thus keeping them all from the sight and scrutiny of others, especially Rannulf.

Rosalynd now stood several feet away from the litter, speaking with Gilbert as servants finished loading the packhorses. Rannulf appeared suddenly from the hall and strode toward them.

Ailénor quickly adjusted the veils swathing her head and throat and concealing the color of her hair. She heard Rosalynd offer her regret that she must leave "dear Ailénor" abed and ill, though much improved, and asked the reeve to assure the servants provided her every comfort.

Exactly what Rosalynd planned beyond Ailénor's escape remained somewhat blurred. 'Twould seem she intended to return within days to Andover, send the maids to the family's more distant estate at Eashing, and, if asked, claim she and Mora knew nothing of what had become of Ailénor, having both been absent from Andover.

The blame for Ailénor's disappearance would fall ultimately on Rannulf's shoulders. Ailénor felt no small amount of guilt for this. In all likelihood, he would forfeit his position as reeve. But she could not count the cost as too high if 'twould save the life of her mother. Mayhap her father or Duke William could right the situation or recompense Rannulf in some way.

All that lay in the future. For now, they must successfully leave the fortifications of Andover. Seeing Rannulf step toward the litter and peer inside, Ailénor averted her face, looking out the opposite window, toward the stable.

The doors stood open to the building. Just inside, shrouded in shadow, stood a bearded man staring straight at her. A chill spilled down her spine as she felt the stab of his eyes. Shifting well back in her seat, she withdrew herself from view.

"You must excuse Mora." Rosalynd addressed Rannulf outside the litter. "She broke out in a rash this morning—a reaction to the eel sauce served at supper last night, I fear. She is quite sensitive." Rosalynd lowered her voice. "Mora is mortified for anyone to see her in such a frightful state. Especially you, Rannulf," she fairly purred.

Ailénor's jaw dropped at the last of Rosalynd's comments, and she dared a small glance in their direction. The reeve was an attractive enough man, but did Rosalynd have the gall to flirt with him in the same moment she was deceiving him?

She heard Rannulf offer his concern regarding Mora and vow to see Lady Ailénor well cared for. Guilt assailed her further, but Rosalynd was already in the process of climbing into the litter assisted by Gilbert.

The horses started forward, and the moments stretched out. Ailénor's stomach knotted along with her nerves, as she bore each moment, fearful of discovery. When the small escort passed at last through the gates undelayed and headed north, Ailénor released her breath and shared a small, victorious laugh with Rosalynd.

The party continued at a comfortable pace, the early-morning sun still rising in the east. Late afternoon they closed on Kingsclere. Before they came into sight of the defense works surrounding the estate, they stopped, and Ailénor descended from the litter. One of Gilbert's men gave over his horse to her, then joined Rosalynd.

As Ailénor mounted the animal, Gilbert smiled. "I see we should have brought you a larger steed, my lady, but the mare has plenty of heart. Shall we ride?"

Ailénor waved to Rosalynd in parting, grateful for her help and amazed at her artfulness in conceiving and implementing so clever a deception. Rosalynd's gift for intrigue was truly astonishing.

Ailénor followed Gilbert's lead, heading north for Silchester. They pressed their animals for speed. The trip to Kingsclere had already brought them three quarters of the way to their destination. At Silchester they would stop overnight and, at first light, take the road east for Lundenburh.

They continued on at an even pace, making good progress over the next few hours. Gilbert looked back, as he often did, checking on Ailénor and casting her a smile. But this time his smile stilled, then faded as his brows pulled together over his nose. Several more times he snatched glances past his shoulder.

"A horseman," he called out.

Ailénor took a glance back as well and beheld a dark-cloaked figure on an equally dark horse. He maintained his distance for a time, but as they came upon a forested area, the horseman whipped his steed and began to close the space between them.

"Ride, my lady!" Gilbert shouted. "Silchester is not far ahead. I fear the man to be a brigand."

Ailénor leaned into her horse, requiring no further encouragement. The ground blurred beneath her as the thunder of the horses' hooves filled her ears.

The horseman gained steadily upon them. Gilbert dropped back, allowing Ailénor to move ahead, then drew his sword to protect her.

Ailénor raced on at his bidding. Casting a glance back, she caught the flash of metal as the horseman bared a knife from his belt. She looked again and saw him move along Gilbert's left side, placing him at a disadvantage for Gilbert wielded his sword right-handed.

Before Gilbert could turn to take his first stroke, the horseman hurled his knife with deadly precision and caught him in the back.

Gilbert wrenched in pain, twisting in his saddle and taking his horse down with him.

The horseman lashed his mount forward, centering the full of his interest on Ailénor.

Her blood ran cold. Digging her heels into her horse's flanks, Ailénor strained the animal to its limits.

Garreth rode fast and furious along the road to Silchester.

On his return to Andover, he had discovered Ailénor gone. Mora disassembled under his forthright questions, then confessed in a flood of tears to the women's collusion.

She and her sister still had much to explain. But now he bore down on his steed, anger rolling through him that Ailénor should leave the safety of Andover and place herself in peril.

He was also angry with himself for not foreseeing this event and having left her to her own resourcefulness.

He galloped on, his thoughts in a boil, fixed so intently ahead that at first he did not see the bulk in the road or the horse grazing off to the side.

Garreth hard-reined his horse, realizing 'twas a man sprawled facedown, a knife projecting from his back.

Ailénor drew on all her skills. Gilbert had been right. The mare had heart. Though showing signs of tiring, when asked she put on an extra burst of speed.

Ailénor managed to keep ahead of the horseman. She flattened herself against the horse's neck, calling encouragement in her ear. But for all the horse's valiant efforts, the horseman continued to narrow the distance.

"Come on, girl," Ailénor cried, then stole a glance back.

Her breath sealed in her throat as a new terror appeared—
a second horseman.

Garreth drove his mount hard as he held Grimbold and
Ailénor in view. Thank God Ailénor was the skilled horsewoman she was, or Grimbold would have overtaken her by
now.

Gradually the distance diminished, and Garreth con-
verged on the two. Pulling alongside Grimbold, he unsheathed his sword.

Grimbold cast Garreth a black look. Yanking the reins
of his horse, he drove his beast into Garreth's bay, forcing
him toward the edge of the raised road. But as the horses
collided, the bay stumbled slightly, jolting Garreth forward
in his saddle.

Grabbing a fistful of mane, Garreth held fast and reseated
himself. The bay fell back, provoked and fractious, its ears
flattened. As Grimbold lashed his horse in pursuit of Ailénor, however, Garreth charged the bay onward. With no
more than a touch to its flanks, the horse reached out and
lengthened its stride.

From the corner of Ailénor's eye she saw the dark shape
of the horseman move alongside her. She swallowed her
panic and urged the mare on, though fearful the intrepid
little animal might drop beneath her at any moment.

Daring a glance at her assailant, she met his small, hard
eyes, cold and gleaming. Her heart lurched as she recognized Grimbold.

Tightening her grip on the reins, she jabbed her heels
into the mare, but the horse was spent. Grimbold began to
reach for her reins. Just then, the second horseman gained
on them.

Ailénor's pulse pounded in her veins. Certain 'twas Wimund, she snatched a sideward glance. To her astonishment
she found Garreth bearing down on Grimbold. He advanced
steadily forward, the head and shoulders of his horse moving in line with the hindquarters of Grimbold's.

Ailénor's heart swelled with joy at the sight of Garreth,

but her joy turned to horror as Grimbold veered, ramming his mount into the bay. In a blur she saw the shock and quiver of horseflesh as the beasts slammed together. Their legs instantly entangled—hind leg with foreleg—causing them to spill. Screaming in pain and outrage, the horses plunged from the road, rolling in a chaos of hooves and legs and taking their riders with them.

Garreth heard Ailénor's scream as he flew free of the tumult and crashed to the ground, the wind leaving his lungs in a painful rush.

Dazed, he lay unmoving a moment, vaguely aware of a sticky wetness on his forehead where a hoof had grazed him.

Close by, the horses struggled frantically to right themselves and climbed to their feet. Through their stir of legs, Garreth spotted Grimbold thrusting to his own feet and seizing upon the sword where it lay gleaming in the dirt.

Before Garreth could rise, Grimbold came at him, slicing the blade in a downward arc. Garreth pivoted onto his left hip, feeling the whoosh of air as the sword slashed behind him and bit into the ground. Without wasting an instant, he rolled back and locked his legs with Grimbold's. Blocking the shin of one and kicking into the back of the knee of the other, he took him off balance.

Grimbold pitched forward, dropping the sword and barely catching himself with his hands. As he groped for the hilt, Garreth hard-booted him in the side and sent him sprawling.

Garreth thrust upward and grabbed for the sword. But before he gained his feet, Grimbold hurled himself at Garreth. Together they thudded to the ground, rolling into the midst of the jittery horses and losing the sword once more as they came apart. The animals shied, snorting and stepping nervously, white showing in their eyes.

Garreth scrambled to his feet and flung himself at Grimbold who had not yet risen. But even as he did, Grimbold slipped a knife from his boot. Seeing the flash of metal, Garreth twisted aside and took the impact on his shoulder.

Grimbold immediately sprang atop him, aiming the blade for Garreth's heart.

Garreth trapped Grimbold's wrist, forcing it back. But Grimbold moved his other hand over the knife's hilt as well and put the full of his weight behind the blade.

Sorely disadvantaged, Garreth's arms trembled as he pitted his strength against Grimbold's. Muscles straining, he slowly angled the knife away from his heart and off to the side. Slackening his hold abruptly, Garreth caused Grimbold to fall forward and drive the knife into the ground just above his shoulder.

Grimbold snarled and started to rise, but Garreth drew up his feet and caught Grimbold in the abdomen. Using the strength of his legs, Garreth heaved Grimbold off of him.

Grimbold yelped as he landed on his spine and rolled in a backward somersault, stopping a short space apart of the horses. He clawed to his feet, fury in his eyes as he fixed them on Garreth.

Garreth grabbed for the knife and pressed to his feet. As he did, the glint of steel caught his eyes, coming from the grass between the skittish animals.

Grimbold, too, spied the sword. Without heed, he shouted at the horses and shoved venomously at the one blocking his way. It capered, moving aside and opening a path to the sword where it lay by the bay's hindquarters.

Garreth drove toward Grimbold. But Grimbold, seeing his advance, lunged for the blade and startled the horse. The bay kicked back, catching Grimbold straight on in the face with both iron-shod hooves. As Grimbold pitched to the ground, the panicked animal trampled back over him.

When Garreth reached him, Grimbold lay twisted, his neck and head bent at an awkward angle, his eyes staring open but unseeing toward the sky.

Ailénor urged her horse from the road and moved toward Garreth. Her stomach churned, and her heart still battered against her breast. Garreth stood over the body, heaving for breath, but catching sight of her, he stayed her with an upheld hand before she drew too near the grisly sight.

"There is little time," he panted. "I will see to Grimbold if you can calm the horses."

Ailénor nodded, glad to be useful. Dismounting, she moved slowly toward the animals, speaking in soft, soothing tones. When they allowed her close enough, she gathered their reins.

Garreth, meanwhile, wrapped a blanket about Grimbold's mangled body and lashed it onto the horse that had been his. After checking the bay for injuries, he mounted and caught up the reins of Grimbold's horse and turned southward.

"Come. We must ride apace."

Ailénor reined her horse, believing he intended to return to Andover and her short-lived freedom to be at an end.

Garreth's brow darkened. "Do you tarry while a man lies bleeding on the road, presumably on your behalf?"

"Gilbert?" she gasped in surprise. "He is alive?"

Garreth leveled her a forbearing look. "We shall discuss your association with this Gilbert at a later time. For now, we need tend to him before his condition worsens. I could do little for him, pressed as I was to come to your aid. Now let us reach him before he no longer has need of us."

Ailénor and Garreth traveled the distance in silence. Mercifully Gilbert still lived, though he suffered considerable pain. Ailénor assisted Garreth in dressing and binding his wounds.

"Can you ride?" Garreth asked Gilbert when they finished. He gave a weak nod in affirmation, and Garreth looked to Ailénor. "We cannot move him far. Silchester lies nearest. We shall ride there for tonight and discuss the matter of this folly tomorrow."

Judging by the fine lines raying his eyes and the tension about his mouth, Ailénor realized how thoroughly upset Garreth was by the incident. He had every right to be, she reflected as they mounted once more. Her escape had wrought disaster.

Garreth took it upon himself to lead the horse bearing Grimbold, while Ailénor offered to guide Gilbert's horse. Heading north, they progressed undelayed toward Silchester.

Chapter Eleven

In queenly splendor, Silchester crowned the soft breast of a hill, her high, towered walls gilded gold in the setting sun. She reigned over a pleasant but empty landscape, a mantle of green and a wealth of jewel-bright flowers spread at her feet.

As the small party approached the city, Ailénor's interest drew to the thin stone slabs raised alongside the road. Letters, numerals, and decorative medallions incised their surfaces. She tossed a questioning glance to Garreth.

"Grave markers," he informed before she could ask. "Roman. Like Winchester, they built Silchester centuries ago. 'Twas their custom to bury their dead outside the walls.'' His gaze traveled to the horse behind him and its lifeless burden. '' 'Twould seem we need continue the practice. I know of a man in the city who can see it done.''

Garreth offered no further comment as he directed his attention ahead to the south gate and its bastions. Ailénor looked to Gilbert. He appeared pale and much weakened.

''Hold fast, friend. We shall see to your care and comfort directly.''

Urging her mare forward, Ailénor gave her interest to the sturdy walls and defense works surrounding Silchester. 'Twas eerily quiet. No soldiers lined the ramparts or manned the watchtowers as they did at Winchester. Nor was there a bustling settlement outside the city or crowds of people flocking about the gates.

She forbore comment as she followed Garreth's lead onto the railed, wooden bridge. Guiding her mount and Gilbert's across the center of the structure, she kept her eyes fixed firmly ahead and away from the yawning ditch below. Gaining the opposite side, she passed beneath the gate's double archway and through impressively thick walls.

Inside the city the streets stretched straight and broad in the Roman fashion, reminding Ailénor of Winchester's. But unlike Winchester's, they stood choked with weeds. And empty.

Garreth continued on, seemingly untroubled by these details. Ailénor swept her eyes left and right, then started at the sight of crumbling buildings and vacant fields, overrun with brambles and bushes.

''Is Silchester a place of the living or the dead?'' she muttered aloud, causing Garreth to look back.

''Forgive me, Ailénor. I neglected to warn you. The city has been abandoned for centuries.''

Ailénor skimmed another glance over the shells of stone and mortar. They stood in various states of ruin, some still roofed with tiles, most only fragments of walls.

''I do not understand,'' she said as they turned onto an adjoining road westward. At the same moment a woman appeared in the doorway of one of the hovels.

''Silchester's inhabitants fled or were killed during the

Saxon invasions,'' Garreth explained, slowing his horse to allow Ailénor to come alongside him. "The other cities suffered like fates and were deserted as well.''

They picked their way along the ill-kept road, passing the remains of a small temple, raised on a marble platform, its once-colonnaded porch now a ghostly file of bleached and broken pillars.

Ailénor looked to Garreth. "Did not the Saxons occupy the cities?''

He shook his head. "They seemed wholly averse to dwelling in the open and established their villages off tracks in the woodlands. 'Twas centuries before the cities were reinhabited. Silchester, however, has remained forsaken to this day.''

Ailénor tilted her head. "Yet Winchester flourishes.''

"Winchester enjoys ready access to water. Silchester has none. Still, the main roads converge here. Armies, pilgrims, wayfarers, and such must pass through her streets to join other routes—in particular, the one to Lundenburh.''

The road ended, abutting another. Once more, they turned northward. Here and there among the ruins, Ailénor spied small cookfires and people clustered about them.

"Are those travelers, then? Pilgrims?''

Garreth followed her gaze. "Mayhap. But one must be wary of thieves or wantons waiting to plague the unsuspecting or attach themselves to passing troops.''

Ailénor remembered the woman in the doorway.

At her frown, Garreth smiled. "Come. Silchester does boast a few establishments—to point, a stable and an inn. We will see to Gilbert's needs and the horses' care and, with luck, find suitable lodgings for the night.''

Seeing more fires and figures sprinkled amongst the rubble, she sincerely hoped so.

Prodding the horses to pick up their pace, they proceeded past the relic of a once grand and sprawling complex and turned west again. After progressing a short distance, Garreth turned off the road and led them into a spacious, if scrubby, courtyard dotted with sky-blue succory and bright yellow tansy.

Ailénor ran her gaze along the aged edifice that surrounded the yard on three sides. It rose two levels high and possessed a covered walkway all the way around. Only one wing appeared in good repair, and 'twas here Garreth directed them. Dismounting, he moved to her side.

"Stay with Gilbert. I will locate the innkeeper and bring help."

With that, Garreth disappeared inside, returning minutes later with a stout, bearded man and two helpers. They hastened to Gilbert's aid and helped him from his mount. The younger men carried Gilbert inside, while the older man stepped to the horse bearing Grimbold's body. Garreth and he spoke in low tones, then seemed to come to some agreement. Taking the horse by the reins, the man led the animal away.

Garreth returned to Ailénor. "That was Ebrard, the innkeeper. He and his sons will attend to Gilbert and care for him until he is able to travel back to his estate. They will also bury Grimbold. In recompense, I have given them Grimbold's horse."

Garreth raised his hands to Ailénor. She leaned toward him and allowed him to lift her down from her mare.

"Will we stay here tonight?" she asked, hopeful, having no desire to sleep in the open among weeds and ruins.

"Nay, I fear not. The inn is full, as it commonly is, with three men to a bed. A space is being made for Gilbert in the loft, but there is no suitable place for a lady."

"Oh," she voiced softly, wondering what "suitable" place they might find amidst Silchester's crumbling buildings.

"The wing opposite has been converted into a stable." He gestured across the courtyard. "We can leave the horses to be rubbed down, groomed, and fed, then see what Ebrard has to offer two hungry travelers."

Ailénor accompanied Garreth, conducting the horses toward the stable. She glanced over the building.

"The inn is so large. Can we not stay in another part of it?"

"'Tis unsafe. This is the original *mansio*. Excepting

what has been restored, the upper wood floors have deteriorated, and what roof remains threatens to collapse. But do not worry. We shall not be without shelter tonight. There is a place I often use when passing through Silchester. It even has a roof and a door with a bar.'' He slipped her a smile and added, ''Thanks to Ebrard.''

At the stable, Ailénor waited as Garreth gave over the horses to the groom and made arrangements concerning Gilbert's mount. With that done, he rejoined her, and they traversed the courtyard once more, stopping at the inn's door to inquire of Gilbert and request a platter of meat and a small jug of ale. This they shared, sitting on the portico in the dwindling light.

No sooner had they finished than one of Ebrard's sons materialized from the direction of the stable, pushing a cart. He stopped before them, smiling and pointing to the cart's contents. ''Hay, blankets, lamp, bowl, cloths . . .'' he enumerated.

Garreth gave a nod of approval and rose. Taking Ailénor by the hand, he drew her to her feet as well.

''Ebrard remembers my preferences. He is a good host. Come. Let us seek our rest for the night.''

Following the innkeeper's son, Garreth and Ailénor crossed the street and continued down partway until they came to a small building, seemingly in good repair. 'Twas not until she passed beneath its pillared porch and entered that she suspected 'twas a church.

Columns divided the central space into a nave and two narrow side aisles. The nave ended in a semicircular apse, empty now, though large enough for an altar to occupy. There, too, the building extended out to either side in two truncated arms giving it a cruciform shape.

Ebrard's son lit a lamp, allowing her to better see the mosaic patterning on the floor and the fragments of painted plaster that still clung to the wall. The song of a bird drew her eyes upward, and she discovered a large portion of the ceiling open to the heavens.

''This is the city's only Christian church,'' Garreth said at her ear, confirming her thoughts. ''It fell to disuse long

ago. I have found that ne'er-do-wells generally do not
bother the church—fearing to bring a divine curse upon
themselves if they do, I suppose. Sometimes pilgrims seek
refuge here, and I must share its privacy, but tonight we
are alone.''

By the time Garreth led her to the tiny chamber that lay
at the rear of the church, behind the altar area, Ebrard's son
had already arranged the hay and covered it over with one
of the blankets, creating a pallet on the stone floor. He left
briefly, taking the bowl with him, and returned it filled with
water. Setting the cloths out beside it, he then took his
leave, taking the cart with him.

Garreth closed and bolted the door. Ailénor saw 'twas
new and guessed it to be Ebrard's handiwork. She looked
also to the ceiling and saw the room indeed was roofed.

"We should be safe here," Garreth said as he unbelted
his sword and laid it beside the pallet. Sitting down, he
loosened the laces at the neck of his tunic, then reached for
a linen cloth and dipped it in the bowl of water.

"Here, let me," Ailénor said, moving to the pallet and
taking the cloth from his hand.

Kneeling before him, she wrung it out and set it to his
forehead, covering his wound where his horse had grazed
him. He flinched, but she was unsure whether 'twas from
the cold of the water or the pain of the injury.

Ailénor withdrew the cloth and rinsed it out, then lay it
to his forehead once more. Garreth grew quiet as she tended
him and cleaned away the last traces of blood and dirt.
Drawing away the linen, she studied the bruise darkening
his forehead, then felt the heat of his eyes.

Garreth could not take his gaze from Ailénor as she
cleansed his wound. He could feel the warmth radiate from
her body, so close was she. He inhaled her mingled scent
of flowers and sunshine while her breasts enticed scant
inches from his mouth as she shifted, lifting up one moment, then sitting back the next.

Sweet Ailénor, the mistress of torment. She had stirred
his passion and played upon his heart since she first fell
atop him, and a multitude of times since. The night they

made love she spoke of destiny, and he believed her words
to be true. She was his life mate, his soul mate. To think
he nearly lost her this day for all eternity. The thought
convulsed him and shadowed his mood.

He started to move and stretch out his legs, but winced
as pain shot through his shoulder where he had taken the
earlier fall. He rotated his shoulder, attempting to work the
soreness from the muscle.

"*Alors*, are you wounded there, too?" Anxious, Ailénor
tried to open the neck of his tunic to better see his shoulder,
but to no avail. She then caught the hem of his tunic and
began to draw it off.

"Ailénor, I am all right . . . I . . ."

Garreth could not stay her persistent hands and relented,
allowing her to remove the shirt and inspect his shoulder.
As she bent over him, her breath fell warm on his suddenly
chilled skin. When she placed her hand to his shoulder, her
touch was as fire.

Garreth caught her hands and stilled her movements.
Tension boiled inside him, churning between wanting to
scold her for scaring him half to death earlier and wanting
to make fierce love to her at the same time. His emotions
neared to bursting as the events of the day surged once
more to mind, as did the memory of the peril in which she
had placed herself.

"Christ's toes, Ailénor," he blurted gruffly. "What possessed you to slip away like that? You knew the dangers."

She stiffened, lifting her chin a notch. "I had Gilbert to
rely on."

"And a great deal of help he proved to be."

"Oh, unfair, Garreth! He risked his life for me and nearly
lost it."

"He would have had no need to had you remained at
Andover."

"You know I could not," she cried, shoving to her feet.

Garreth rose and caught her by the arms. Spinning her
around, he pulled her against his body.

"Do you know what would have happened had I not
arrived on the road when I did? Have you any idea what

the sight of Grimbold overtaking you did to me? It nearly caused my heart to stop and shortened my life by years."

"As the sight of you spilling over with the horses did to me! I feared you to be dead at first, then I watched helpless while you fought Grimbold, blood on your head." Her eyes suddenly teared up, and she shook her head with a look of shameful guilt. " 'Tis my fault, I know—what befell you, Gilbert, Grimbold."

"Shed no tears for Grimbold. He brought his fate upon himself. But you . . . you should have never left Andover."

"What else could I do? You were not going to help me."

"Not going to . . ." Garreth choked on her words. "Why do you think I was riding to the king? And why do you think I rode back as though hell snapped at my heels when I realized 'twas Grimbold I encountered in the stables at Andover? I feared for your life."

Ailénor paled at his revelation. "So. 'Twas unsafe at Andover after all." Ailénor pulled from his arms. "And still you intend to return me there. Do you not? To comply with the king's commands?"

Garreth vented an impatient breath. "I have explained what I believe to be His Majesty's reasons."

"Reasons no longer matter—the king's or yours. Do you not see? I *must* get back to Normandy. You know I must."

"And you will try again?"

She looked away as the events of the past two weeks rushed up to overwhelm. Tears stung at the back of her eyes as she turned to the man she loved.

"Ah, Garreth, we have been caught in a terrible web— spun first of revenge, then of intrigue. Whatever comes, know I admire you for your loyalty and I understand the course of your actions, but you must understand mine as well. You say you hastened to my rescue for fear of my life. I hasten to my mother for fear of hers. Wimund yet prowls somewhere. Even should he fail at his task, from what I know of Rhiannon, I cannot believe she will rest until she exacts the retribution she seeks. She will send another and another to seize the Comtesse de Héricourt. I must protect my mother, as she would me."

Garreth gazed on Ailénor a long, silent moment, then enfolded her back into his arms, resting his cheek atop her head.

"Dear God, I do understand and love you all the more for it, my brave and beautiful Ailénor. Truly, we are caught in a web, but not wholly entrapped by it. We will deal tomorrow with what course we might take. For now, only one thing matters—that you are safe."

"Two," she corrected, leaning back and smoothing a dark lock of hair from his forehead. "I could not bear it if anything happened to you. You are my very heart, and I love you most truly."

Garreth warmed at her words. Lowering his head, his lips moved over Ailénor's, hot and sweet. He trailed kisses to her eyes, cheeks, jaw, and throat, then upward to her temple and brow. Ailénor's arms slipped about his neck, her ardor rising to match his as their lips met again.

Their kisses grew fevered as they sank to their knees on their mean pallet, their bodies pressing tight together, their mouths devouring.

Garreth tangled his fingers in her thick tresses and drew her down to the pallet atop him. She pulled her lips from his to spread kisses over his muscled chest and its flat nipples, moving lower to his stomach, as her hands reached toward his *braies*.

When her fingers brushed his rigid arousal, Garreth caught her wrists and rolled her onto her back. Covering her mouth possessively, he explored her sweet recesses with his tongue, teasing hers in a sweet delirium. He felt her become fluid beneath him, giving herself to him willingly, eagerly.

When his hand began to cup her breast, she arched toward him, filling his palm, inviting his touch. He caressed her through the cloth until he felt her nipple harden. Craving to feel her flesh against his, he fumbled blindly at the laces at the back of her dress. Following his lead, her hands sought the ties of his *braies*.

Frustrated by their lack of progress, Garreth drew Ailénor up to a sitting position and turned her around. Working at the laces, he opened the gown and bared her back. Pressing kisses to her shoulders and the back of her neck, he drew the gown downward, stripping it away to her hips.

He slipped his hands to the front, filling them with her warm, bare breasts, fondling them gently, teasing their firm buds. Ailénor let her head sink back on his shoulder, thrusting her breasts forward and exposing her neck.

Kissing the curve of her neck, Garreth continued to caress one breast as he slid his other hand downward, seeking the sweet, hidden secret between her legs. Ailénor moaned as he claimed her and seduced her with his touch.

Drawing her back onto his lap, he turned her and bent his head to her breast, taking her nipple in his mouth and laving and suckling it. Ailénor tightened her grip on him as he continued to savor her and shifted her from his lap. Laying her gently on the pallet, he cherished her other breast, then drew his tongue on a downward path toward her abdomen, pausing long enough to strip away her gown from her legs and dispense with his leggings and *braies*.

He shifted upward to move over her, but as he did, Ailénor lifted her hand and enclosed him in the warmth of her palm. He sucked in his breath as her fingers began to explore him and smoothed her thumb over the tip of his manhood. Growling, he moved fully atop her and drew her hand away, settling himself between her legs.

He took her nipple into his mouth greedily and plundered her sweet flesh with his lips and tongue. Reaching downward, he slipped his fingers inside her, seeking her core. He massaged her tenderly as she opened herself to him. At her invitation, he covered her mouth again. Their tongues danced wildly, rhythmically, matching the rhythm he set below. Feeling her swelling response, he withdrew his hand and slipped his shaft into her, continuing to build the momentum as he moved against her.

Ailénor moaned at the contact, then again as he increased his rhythm. Wrapping her legs tightly about him, moving in perfect unison, she drove him toward an eager climax.

Garreth's name burst from Ailénor's lips as her contracting waves grabbed him. Garreth joined her in his own fierce release, groaning mightily as he thrust deeply, repeatedly, spending himself thoroughly as he filled her with the gift of himself. Exhausted, he sank atop her, panting for breath.

He smiled and dropped kisses over her nose, her eyelids, the corner of her mouth, along her jaw. "Are you all right, my heart?"

She sought to steady her own breath as she smoothed her hands over his muscled back. "More than all right when I am in your arms."

In the lamplight he saw the worry steal back into her eyes. "Garreth . . ."

"Shhh, love. We'll find a way through this."

Rolling from her, he curled his body around hers, draping an arm over her waist and drawing her even nearer.

Later, in the depths of the night, when he caressed her breast and trailed kisses along her shoulder, Ailénor stirred. Turning toward him, she welcomed his love and met him fully. After their lovemaking, she slept soundly beside him, secure in his embrace. Garreth, however, remained awake, disparate emotions warring within him, making it impossible to sleep.

The main routes passed through Silchester. He could travel south and return Ailénor to Andover, thus complying with the king's commands. Or he could head north and seek the king directly, taking Ailénor with him. But a third possibility beckoned. The east road to Lundenburh.

Deep in his soul, he found it a most disturbing thought. Disturbing because he sensed it to be the right path to take, yet he knew not how to reconcile that course of action.

Through the long hours, he lay unsleeping, torn between his love for this woman and his loyalty to his king.

Garreth knelt on the chilly floor in the nave of the church facing the empty sanctuary where an altar once stood.

Instinct rode him hard to deliver Ailénor to Lundenburh, while a voice from the corner of his conscience decried it as a preemption of royal command, misuse of power, and a betrayal of the king's own person.

His thoughts continued to chase each other in a dizzying

cycle, as reason and instinct vied with unconditional loyalty and ties that ran as deep as an oak's tap root.

The misdirection of Cynric's actions was fueled by the motives of the grasping Breton, Barbetorte, and the king's half sister Eadgifu, anxious to see her son wear Francia's crown. Garreth strongly believed matters had been misrepresented to the king, that if Athelstan knew the entirety of the matter, he would have none of it.

Yet Garreth could not be certain beyond doubt. The issue concerned a hallowed throne and the sovereign's blood nephew. And what of the king's missive itself, officially ordering Ailénor's detainment? His mind argued every facet, every point of contention, until mentally exhausted he banished the thoughts altogether and stilled his mind.

Garreth pressed his eyes shut and bowed his head, inhaling deeply as he rested a moment. His thoughts floated without form, then of their own accord stretched back across time. Back to Tamworth and his first encounter with Athelstan.

When twelve-year-old Garreth entered the lower end of the hall that afternoon, he found it wrapped in quiet and virtually empty except for a few servants moving about in the lull that preceded the supper hour.

Voices drew his attention. Looking right, he discovered three young nobles standing in a knot, all taller, older, and more strapping than he. They chuckled and whispered amongst themselves as though conspiring some mischief. The object of their interest proved to be a small servant girl, making her way from the kitchen passage.

No more than five or six, the child progressed slowly, bearing a tray with bowls of mustard to the sideboard where the meats would soon be sauced. As she neared her goal, one of the nobles shifted his stance and tripped the child apurpose. The young men then burst into a spate of laughter as the bowls flipped into the air and upended their contents into the rushes.

Stricken, the child could only stare, fat tears beginning to roll down her cheeks. The noble youths taunted her all the more, commanding she scoop the sauce from the rushes and refill the bowls.

But another promptly countered the other's charge. "Nay, the sauce cannot be served. 'Tis fit only for the dogs now. Make the chit eat it."

Infuriated, Garreth stepped forward, planting himself betwixt the child and her tormentors. "Eat it yourselves."

Taken aback by his sudden appearance and defense of the girl, the nobles narrowed their interest on their new prey.

No match for them and their more seasoned skills, Garreth knew he dared much, but he would not tolerate such abuse, no matter the person, station, or place. That much he brought with him from Aylesbury. Closing his hands to fists at his sides, he put on a bold face.

"You dishonor Mercia's lord and lady, maltreating children under their care."

"Ho, and who are you?" asked one.

"Is he not the Kentish pup who just arrived a few days past?" remarked another.

"Gangly, isn't he? And in need of some lessoning, I'd say," said the third.

"And I'd say *you* are the ones in need of lessoning," a fourth voice boomed, its owner unseen.

The young nobles parted their ranks, revealing a flaxen-haired youth of approximately their age, average in height yet well muscled, and possessing piercing blue eyes.

Those eyes now bore into each of them as he stepped into their midst. "Shall we do it, then? Right here and now. Or wilt you get down on your hands and knees and lap the rushes yourselves?"

"We did not mean . . . Just a bit of fun . . . We are sorry . . ."

But the flaxen-haired youth would not be appeased. Drawing the little child up by her hand, he kept her at his side while commanding the three to their knees. Reluctantly they did as told, but hesitated over the mess in the rushes.

"Well?" The young man's eyes were as chips of ice.

Garreth watched in utter amazement as the nobles bent

to the rushes and began to lick the mustard, sickly grimaces contorting their faces. The flaxen-haired youth held them to this long enough to satisfy his sense of justice.

"Enough!" he barked. "Take the bowls and tray and present yourselves to the pantler for more mustard. And see you reimburse the steward for the cost of what was lost."

Chastised, the nobles left, coughing and sleeving their mouths. The young man then sent the child to the kitchens with calming words. He turned to Garreth.

"You honor the house of Mercia this day. On behalf of Lord Athelred and Lady Athelflaed, I thank you."

Garreth recognized at once a kindred soul in the flaxen-haired youth. But he glimpsed something more beyond his boldness and fairness—a force of spirit and personality that bespoke of courage and some other intangible essence more rare.

"So you are the Kentman. I had not the opportunity to meet you before now. Saint's bones, but you have pluck and are a fine champion of innocents. Mercia can use more like you. Come. Have you seen a *lanthorn* before? I have just finished fashioning one."

Garreth followed the young man across the hall to a side niche. There he picked up a handsome, boxlike affair, its frame of wood, its sides and door of thinly shaved ox-horn, translucent as glass and milky white. Inside it contained a fresh candle fixed on a spike.

"See," the youth said as he gestured to the box. "The horn allows the light to flow through without loss of brightness, yet drafts cannot disturb the flame or snuff it out. 'Tis my grandfather's invention," he added proudly. "I thought to use it tonight to go in search of frogs. Would you like to join me?" A gleam appeared in his eyes. "Of course, we cannot let Lady Athelflaed know."

Their instant and easy camaraderie closed the gap of their years, and Garreth found himself much at ease with the young noble as he happily agreed and examined the innovation.

"Your grandfather is a very clever man. Who is he?"

"He was King Alfred." A smile spread the young man's

features as he held forth his hand. "And I am Athelstan. Welcome to Tamworth."

Stunned, Garreth clasped forearms with the prince, and in that grip the first strands of their friendship were bonded.

From that time forward—and after a successful night of sacking frogs—they enjoyed a close fellowship, open and honest and, on Garreth's part, filled with increasing respect for Athelstan.

Garreth's happiness at Tamworth was soon darkened, however, by the death of his mother. Within several years his father, too, lay dead, but not before he had remarried and sired two more sons. Scarce had he grown cold than the widow challenged her husband's first union so that she might disclaim Garreth and seize the titles and lands for her own offspring.

The woman's actions inflamed Mercia's lady, Athelflaed, who upheld Garreth's cause with a passion. But in it, Garreth knew, she also read disturbing parallels with the prince's own lineage.

Shadows enshrouded the marriages of Garreth's and Athelstan's parents alike—both mothers being Mercian noblewomen, both finding their eternal rest in the same abbey grounds. Upon their mothers' deaths, their fathers had remarried, each to a grasping woman. One threatened to steal the legacy of Kent's high reeve of Aylesbury, the other the crown of the West Saxon king.

Athelflaed read the signs with deep foreboding and guarded the young men's interests as was within her power. But 'twas not enough.

Garreth's stepmother contested the validity of his parents' vows, alleging the cleric who performed the ceremony to have been an excommunicant. Though 'twas recalled in Kentish memory the priest once suffered the ban—unjustly so and soon rescinded—the unhappy episode occurred in roughly the same period surrounding the nuptials. The precise dates of the ban's duration hung in question, and lucklessly the priest had died on pilgrimage long past.

The second wife, who sprang from one of Kent's most powerful families, gained the support of her kinsmen—including a few high-placed ecclesiastics—and successfully seized her late husband's inheritance for her sons, proclaiming Garreth bastard-born.

Athelflaed, accepting none of this, placed Garreth directly under her protection. Repudiated by the Kentmen, Garreth adopted the house of Mercia as his own.

Athelstan, also enraged at such injustice, took Garreth under his wing, and their comradeship deepened even further. The prince kept Garreth ever near and helped him hone his skills with lance and sword. Garreth soon joined Athelstan on campaign, and together they fought for Mercia's cause against the Danelaw.

Athelflaed's concerns for her nephew, Athelstan, did not abate when King Edward's second wife died and despite her approval of his choice of a third bride. Already rumors spread claiming Athelstan's mother to have been no more than a low-born consort—a beautiful shepherdess—but not a lawful wife and never a hallowed queen. No matter that she had died before Edward's accession, or that whilst she lived she had been clearly accepted at court by King Alfred and his queen, Ealhswith. No matter that King Alfred favored his grandson, Athelstan, and bestowed on him the symbols of kingship—a cloak of royal purple, a Saxon sword and belt.

Athelflaed did not live to support Athelstan at the critical time of his succession. When King Edward died six years after she, her fears proved to have been well founded. The first crisis Athelstan bore was that of his right of succession and the question of his legitimacy.

Garreth took up his sword for Athelstan and embraced his cause as his own. Aelfweard, Athelstan's half brother, appeared prepared to give challenge but died sixteen days after their father of wounds received in the same battle. Next, Edwin, the second son of the second marriage, gave opposition. While the Mercians elected Athelstan their king at Tamworth, the West Saxons supported Edwin.

But in the months to come, the councilors transferred their loyalty to Athelstan, recognizing him to be the more seasoned warrior and most capable of defending the kingdom. Angered, Edwin attempted to blind Athelstan, but Garreth foiled the plot with Athelstan narrowly escaping.

On the fourth day of September in the Lord's year 925, Athelstan was crowned at Kingston. He went forth to secure the peace of his kingdom and began his climb to a glorious ascent.

Garreth rode at his side, his sword ever faithful and at the king's command. At Jorvik they drove out the Norse-Irish king, Sihtric. Next, they moved against the Northumbrians at Bamburgh, then successively wrought the submissions of the kings of the Scots, the Cumbrians, the Welsh, and the Britons of Cornwall.

Three short years after his accession, King Athelstan reigned as *Rex To Bri*—King of all Britain. 'Twas the first time since the days of the Roman conquerors that the Isle had been brought under one rule. Offa had envisioned it, Alfred had lain the footings, but Athelstan brought it into reality. Such was his glory.

Yet Athelstan was much more than mere victor. Courageous and skillful in battle, he was also gracious and generous with men, humble yet bold where needed. He bore a keen sense of fairness and justice and inspired others to noble action and deeds.

Still, he possessed a quality that set him apart from other men—what Garreth had only glimpsed that first day at Tamworth, but which came to full flower in the years of Athelstan's kingship. 'Twas what others called *magnanimitas*—a greatness of soul.

Garreth's admiration flowed for his king and friend even as he knelt in the abandoned church in Silchester. He basked in the light of his thoughts, but a shadow quickly moved through it. Edwin.

Earlier this year, the king's half brother sought once more to overthrow him. But once more Garreth put Edwin to rout, pursuing him to the coast. Edwin seized a ship but drowned in his flight across the Channel. When Garreth received the news, he rode immediately to the king.

Garreth considered now, as he knelt in the tiny church, how much he had worried that Edwin's death might be used by the king's enemies to stain his reputation. Yet what would they do if they learned Athelstan now held the kinswoman of Normandy's duke as his captive? Surely they would use it to advantage to tarnish his crown. And what retributions might the Normans themselves take against him?

Garreth's pulse thudded in his veins. He must protect the king's interests and reputation as well as Ailénor's. Yet what to do? The king might not share his views.

Again thoughts of Edwin intruded. When Garreth informed the king of his half brother's death, they had sat awake the entirety of the night speaking of it. It had been the king who brought up Edwin's earlier attempt to blind him and how Garreth had thwarted his efforts. Garreth had warned at the time to keep Edwin far away, even to exile him, that no good would come from Edwin.

"I should have listened to you," Athelstan told Garreth that night as they spoke of Edwin's death. "For as long as I have known you, your instincts have served you well."

"Your instincts serve *you* just as well," Garreth returned, then smiled. " 'Tis only your *magnanimitas* that gets in the way and obscures it sometimes. 'Tis well to forgive, my king, but sometimes, as in Edwin's case, you trust too greatly."

"Then you must stay near and advise me, friend." The light returned to Athelstan's eyes. "Trust and follow your instincts, Garreth. Surely they are your best guide."

Ailénor awoke to a cold and empty pallet.

Looking toward the door, she found it open. Beyond, the soft glow of morning washed the interior of the church.

Hastily she drew on her gown and slipped from the chamber. She had taken no more than a few steps when she halted abruptly.

The first rays of dawn streamed through the open roof, bathing Garreth and the vacant sanctuary in a golden light. Soundlessly, trying not to disturb him, she approached where he knelt. But as she neared, his eye caught her movement, and he turned his head to look at her.

Ailénor's breath caught as she read his utter exhaustion. He looked to have waged a great battle this night, within the very depths of his soul.

"We must be away," he said quietly, rising to his feet.

At his sober look, Ailénor's heart dipped. "So you return me to Andover after all, captive of the English."

"Nay, love. We ride for Lundenburh."

Ailénor blinked, disbelieving her ears. No words would form on her lips.

"I shall see you safely aboard your uncle's ship and under sail for Normandy," Garreth continued. "Then shall I ride to the king directly and explain my actions and all that has gone before."

Still stunned, Ailénor gripped his hands and searched his eyes. In helping her, he set himself directly against his king's wishes and strained the ties that bound them. Yet 'twas exactly what she had asked of him time and again. How much better for Garreth had she been able to reach Lundenburh without his aid. No one could hold him to blame for her escape from Andover.

"You risk much on my account, and I truly regret that."

"There is risk in the very act of living, dear Ailénor." A faint smile touched his lips, then disappeared. "But that must not stop us, especially when the cause is just and we need protect those we love and care for deeply."

Garreth stroked back a strand of hair from her face, his expression grown solemn again.

"Whatever comes, I will stand fully accountable and accept any consequences that might result. My faith remains in the king's wisdom and sense of justice. As soon as I can, I shall come for you in Francia. We must face the possibility, however, that the king will take grave exception to my countering his commands and authority. He could dispossess me completely if he so chooses, and I could arrive in Francia reduced in standing to no better than a *ceorl*. I would have naught to offer you, and your family might forbid a union between us. Already I am not high in your duke's favor."

"I shall accept you however you come to me, Garreth."

Her fingers reached out to stroke the fatigue from his face. "And I shall wait for you faithfully."

Garreth shifted her fingers to his lips and pressed them with a kiss. "Upon my vow, I will come for you. I shall not rest until you are again at my side. Ailénor of Héricourt, before God I pledge you my troth, my love, and my fidelity. And I wait impatiently for the day I can bind myself to you and make you my wife in fact—to love and to treasure all the days of my life and an eternity beyond."

Garreth's words filled Ailénor's heart to overflowing, and she found herself gazing on him through a haze of tears.

"And before God do I plight you my troth and my love, Garreth of Tamworth. I am yours, and yours alone, now and for always. You are the keeper of my heart. I shall wait no matter how long the days. No matter whether you come to me acclaimed or bereft, I shall accept you. May these, our vows, rise straight to heaven and find favor there."

Garreth drew Ailénor into his embrace. Lips melded and hearts mingled and love joined two as one.

Chapter Twelve

Ailénor maneuvered her mount around one of the rubble-filled holes potting the road, then moved alongside Garreth's bay once more.

An assortment of travelers, wagons, and packhorses accompanied them, some having journeyed the full distance from Silchester, others having increased their numbers along the way as they passed a village here and a sprinkling of cottages there. Forests lined much of the old Roman causeway, broken sporadically by clearings. But more and more as they neared the city, the countryside opened up to land under tillage.

"Just ahead the road bends toward the Thames." Garreth

indicated with a tilt of his head. "We should be able to catch sight of Lundenburh in a moment."

The horses progressed at a moderate pace. As promised, glimpses of the city's pale walls appeared through the screen of trees. Ailénor's heart rose, picking up its beat in anticipation, so near was their goal. Again the road crooked northward. In time they emerged from the cover of the greenwood.

Ailénor now saw they advanced along the crest of a hill. A stream sprang to life off to the left, sparkling cheerily and keeping their company until it and the road alike plummeted from sight. As they verged on that point, Garreth brought his horse to a halt, allowing the wagons to rattle past and begin their descent down the steep incline.

"We are atop Old Bourn Hill," Garreth informed her with a smile, then lifted his hand to point. "There, across the ravine and the River of Wells, lies Lundenburh."

Ailénor raised her gaze from where the road dropped away, and glanced to the lower-lying hill opposite. She drank in the expansive view, her gaze flowing over the thick, sentry-lined walls and into the city itself. The late-afternoon sun fired the thatched roofs to a reddish-gold, and she caught the distant din from within.

Lundenburh proved as alive as Silchester was dead, yet a far different sort of city from that of Winchester, her life contained solely within her walls, with no settlements without. Still, even at this hour, people jammed the gate, demanding entrance.

Ailénor reined her mount behind Garreth's and began to descend the slope. At the bottom he waited for her, then together they crossed the timbered bridge and advanced up the opposite and, thankfully, less arduous side. Rejoining the crowd, they pressed steadily forward till, amidst the crush, they squeezed through the gate's constricted opening.

Inside, they entered onto a narrow street cramped with houses and teeming with activity. Vendors hawked wares, carts clattered over the paving stones, and a pig rooted through refuse near one of the merchants' food stalls.

Garreth led Ailénor to an adjoining lane and turned southward toward the River Thames.

"There is good lodging on Candlewick Street," he called back. "We should first visit Thames Street, however, and attempt to locate your uncle's ship. My guess is we will find it docked at Downgate. The ships from Francia tend to favor the quays there. Are you certain 'twill be in port at this time?"

"*Oui*. If it has not already sailed," Ailénor returned.

"Will you be able to recognize it?" Garreth called once more.

Ailénor flashed him a smile. "I believe so. My father designed the craft. Its lines are more Norse than Frankish, and it sails under the sign of the falcon, my uncle's emblem."

Garreth snatched a glance over his shoulder, the corners of his mouth lifting. "The sail will not be raised, Ailénor."

"*Vraiment*, but the ship has certain modifications—such as a falcon head rising from the prow rather than that of a serpent."

Picking their way through Lundenburh's congested streets, they soon arrived at Thames Street. As they neared the river, the pungent scents of fish and salt water weighed the air, mingling with the more fragrant and appetizing aromas of the cookhouses. Ailénor's stomach rumbled, but Garreth was already turning his bay into another side street.

"This alley leads directly to Downgate," he called. "Take care as you follow."

Ailénor understood his warning scant moments later. Dark and exceedingly narrow, the alley fell in a sharp decline to the waterfront, an uneasy footing for their horses. As they emerged at the bottom, they found the quays swarming with seamen and clogged with vessels. Salt, fish, horses, furs, and more laded the ships and barges, while bales of wool and casks of wine loaded the wharves, stacked high and in abundance.

From her vantage atop her mare, Ailénor studied the various ships tied up in the slips, her face brightening with a wide smile as she sighted the merchant vessel of the Comte de Valsemé.

Prodding her mare forward, this time 'twas she who bade Garreth follow. At their approach, one seaman, possessing a head and jaw full of coppery curls, dropped the line he coiled, recognition and confusion colliding simultaneously in his eyes.

"L-Lady Ailénor?" He inclined his head, his brows butting together as he puzzled over her presence.

"Gunnolf! I am sore glad to see you," Ailénor proclaimed as she slid from her mare and hastened toward him.

Garreth quickly joined her while other crew members also abandoned their tasks and gathered round. Another familiar face appeared—that of Einar. She had last seen them at the long Christmas celebrations at Valsemé. Gunnolf was one of her uncle's chief shipmasters and Einar an important mate, soon to command his own ship in her uncle's growing fleet.

Recovering from their shock at the sudden appearance of their employer's niece on the wharf of Lundenburh, Gunnolf and Einar inundated Ailénor with questions.

Garreth strained to understand their rapid exchange, attuning his ear to the heavily accented Frankish the Norman sailors spoke. As he groped for their meaning, he better appreciated Ailénor's trials communicating these past weeks.

If the men of Valsemé displayed surprise at Ailénor's arrival, then they viewed him with blatant suspicion, eyeing him closely. Garreth restrained his tongue while Ailénor related a much abbreviated version of their adventures and spoke only of her abduction, his intervention, and their flight from Rhiannon's men. She now introduced him more fully, presenting him as a member of King Athelstan's royal court and an officer of the Hird, then expressed the urgency of her returning to Normandy—danger still threatened her mother, and her family was still unknowing of her whereabouts.

The men comprehended the gravity of the situation and vowed to see her safely there.

"The cargo is only partially loaded and cannot be abandoned," Gunnolf explained. "The men will need at least another day to complete the task. We should be able to depart Saturday morn, shortly after dawn. Will you be safe until then?"

Grasping the seamen's words and their concern, Garreth's hand moved instinctively to rest on his sword hilt.

"You can count on it," he averred, slowing his Frankish so the men would understand. "I will secure lodgings for Ailénor away from the riverfront, up on Candlewick Street, and guard her myself. If the man Wimund comes sniffing about, you will know him by his grotesquely large eyes."

Relieved and thankful at having found the ship still in port, Garreth and Ailénor took their leave, promising to check on the crew's progress on the morrow.

Leaving the Downgate quay, they proceeded directly to Candlewick Street. There Garreth secured lodging from an elderly widow from whom he often leased when visiting the city. For a modest amount, she let out to them the upper floor of the tiny row house adjoining her own—the property of her perpetually absent son.

The accommodation enjoyed a separate back entrance and sparse furnishings—a table and chairs and, what Garreth appreciated most, an extra-long bed with a wondrously soft mattress. The lodging fee included fresh linens and a candle for each night's stay. But for an additional sum the widow provided a modest meal, tonight a small roast capon, plum and currant tartlet, and a pitcher of cold ale.

While Garreth stabled the horses at the end of the street, Ailénor waited with the little repast in the upper room. Waves of tiredness washed over her. With their safe arrival and successful contact with Valsemé's ship, it seemed a huge weight had lifted from her. What remained in its absence was an acute realization of how truly tired she was.

Overcome with fatigue, Ailénor rose and moved to the bed. Pulling off her gown, she started to slip between the covers, but at the rumbling complaint of her stomach, she wrapped a sheet around her and returned to the table. When Garreth entered the room moments later, she was in the course of nibbling a diminutive drumstick.

"I am sorry. I could not wait." She looked up to him and smiled sleepily.

Garreth came to stand before her. Lifting her chin with his strong hand, he gently traced the dark circle beneath her left eye with his thumb and smiled his understanding.

"I am the one who is apologetic for I did not mean for you to wait for my return."

Joining her at the table, he stretched out his long legs and took a swallow of ale. They ate in quiet companionship, the capon dwindling to bones and the tartlet to crumbs. Ailénor covered her mouth, unable to stifle a yawn.

"Why don't you rest, Ailénor?" Garreth submitted softly. "I'll finish the ale and join you in a moment."

Ailénor rose, then paused to lean forward and gift Garreth with a kiss. "*Merci*, my love. Thank you."

Garreth's gaze followed her as she crossed to the bed and drew off her sheet, seemingly forgetful of her nude state. He took another mouthful of ale, fully appreciating her feminine perfection, her smooth back, the curve of her waist where it nipped in, her pleasingly rounded behind, long slender legs, and, as she turned toward him, her full rose-tipped breasts.

Ailénor stretched out across the bed, sinking into its softness.

"Mmm." She nestled into the mattress, then felt for the sheet and drew it partway up. "Do you realize, Garreth," she murmured, drowsy and content, "this is the first time we shall actually share a bed?"

Garreth's smile spread. Downing the rest of the ale, he rose and crossed to her, an ache in his loins. But as he came to stand over her, he found she had already drifted into a deep and much needed sleep.

Garreth reached down and gently outlined her face with the tip of his forefinger, then trailed it to one round breast and circled her nipple. Feeling his own weariness and seeing its claim on Ailénor, he released a long breath and withdrew his hand.

Disposing of his own clothes, he climbed into bed beside

her and adjusted the sheet. Conforming his body to hers, he cradled her and looped his arm over her waist.

Exhaustion traveled through him, claiming him inch by inch. Content and comfortable, wrapped around the woman he loved, Garreth allowed it to carry him away into a dreamless sleep.

Early the next morning, Ailénor awakened to find Garreth holding open the door to a procession of people with an exceptionally large tub, linens, soaps, and buckets upon buckets of hot water.

As they prepared the bath, Garreth strode to the bed bearing small loaves of warm fragrant bread and spiced cider. He sat beside her, grinning.

"Today is ours, my love. And I intend we enjoy it to the full."

Ailénor pushed to a sitting position, holding the sheet high against her throat as the other occupants of the room continued to fuss over the bathwater. While Garreth and she waited, they partook of the bread and ale. He then rose as the others finished and the last departed, and barred the door.

Garreth returned to Ailénor's side and began to divest himself of his mantle, tunic, leggings, and *braies*. Ailénor looked on as she finished the last of the bread, drawing her gaze slowly downward over his powerful physique.

Laying aside his garments, Garreth reached for the sheet Ailénor still clutched to her breast. Drawing it slowly from her fingers, he pulled it free entirely. His gaze lingered over her naked form a moment. Then, without a word but smiling, he bent and lifted her in his arms, carried her to the tub and stepped in.

"Garreth?" Ailénor slipped her arms about his neck. "Garreth!" Her voice echoed her surprise as he sank into the heated waters with her firmly in his grasp.

To her further astonishment, Garreth shifted her to face him, causing her to straddle his hips, for there was barely enough room. She gasped, feeling his manhood poised at the entrance of her womanhood, ready to invade. But he did not. With a wicked smile he reached for the soap, slowly lathered his hands, and spread the creamy foam over her breasts.

"Garreth . . ." Ailénor's voice broke. She moaned with his seduction, tilting back her head as she luxuriated in the feel of his hands moving over her breasts, now cupping, now fondling, arousing her to a fine madness.

"Ah, Garreth, how you do possess me so." She lifted her head to look at him, her heart beating a quick rhythm. She moistened her lips and smiled. "But the seduction cannot be yours alone," she whispered huskily.

Taking the soap from him, she lathered his chest generously. "As you said, love. Today is ours. Let us enjoy it to the full." Her smile spread as her hand slid downward, disappearing beneath the water and causing Garreth to straighten instantly.

"Wench!" He growled, surprise and approval rumbling in his voice. He seized her lips hungrily with his, then rinsing the soap from her breasts, he lifted her upward to him and feasted on her splendid offering.

Hours later, after an impassioned, sometimes more leisured, morning of lovemaking, they emerged from their lodging and headed toward Downgate at an unhurried pace.

At the wharf they spoke with Gunnolf who assured them the ship would sail on the morrow. As Garreth and Ailénor climbed the steep alleyway to Thames Street, Garreth saw her pensive, unsmiling look. At Gunnolf's confirmation of the ship's departure, he, too, felt the heavy reality of their separation pressing upon them, dampening the remainder of their time together as well as their spirits.

Garreth slipped his arm about her. "The hours are ours until dawn, Ailénor. Lundenburh has much to offer, especially on Fridays."

She lifted her gaze to his.

"Sweet Ailénor, let us fill the next hours with as much happiness as our last ones, so we might carry them with us with warm remembrance."

At his words, a smile touched Ailénor's lips, and she

lifted her hand to his cheek. "*Oui*, Garreth. Let us fill them to overflowing."

Garreth caught her fingers and filled her palm with a kiss, then escorted her north and west along the streets.

When they came to Cheapside Street, they slowed to peruse the many craftsmen's and merchants' stalls with their wondrous variety of goods and luxuries. Garreth purchased Ailénor a flower garland for her hair, and they enjoyed roast joints of meat and cups of ale acquired from street vendors.

From there they moved north through the metalworkers' lane where goldsmiths, silversmiths, and jewelers displayed their wealth and skills. Emerging near the northwest wall of the city, they headed for Aldersgate. There, amidst considerable traffic, they passed through the gate and arrived at a wide-open field that proved level and smooth.

"This is Smoothfield, or Smithfield as some have begun to call it," Garreth apprised as they threaded through the crowd gathered there. "Horse markets are held here each Friday and races in the afternoon. With your love of horses, I thought you might enjoy seeing them."

" 'Tis like a fair," Ailénor noted happily, glancing about, for musicians, jugglers, and hawkers wove through the assemblage. Around the field, horses were being displayed and put through their paces. To one corner, however, a different sort of market was taking place. There, pigs and cows were being sold as well as plows and other farm equipment.

Garreth and Ailénor spent the next hour looking over the various steeds. They especially enjoyed watching the palfreys, for these horses were trained in a special gait, bringing both legs down on one side at the same time, thereby giving an exceptionally smooth ride.

They moved on to see the fleet-footed coursers and lively, high-stepping colts, then on to the plow mares, many with bellies swollen with young, and lastly the strong-legged packhorses.

When the races commenced, Ailénor expressed her surprise to Garreth that 'twas stable lads who rode the spirited steeds without benefit of harness or saddle but only with bits to curb the animals' mouths and reins to guide them. The horses were raced in twos and threes, the riders urging and switching them on to the cries and exhortations of the crowd.

At the close of the races, the crowds did not dissipate. Indeed, it seemed the city had emptied out to enjoy the Friday festivities. Round dances now formed, the dancers holding hands, circling and singing to the accompaniment of the vielle and bells. Ailénor and Garreth enjoyed cups of spiced wine as they watched, then joined in the merriment.

As the approaching eve drew its veil over their day and the light diminished, Garreth and Ailénor started back for Candlewick Street. They walked in silence, pleasantly tired from the day's activities. They could no longer ignore that their time was fast coming to an end, however. Garreth looked at Ailénor and saw the melancholy that had enveloped her earlier had returned.

"I wouldst have a smile from the lady who keeps my heart," he cajoled.

"Garreth, the hours advance so quickly now. Soon 'twill be . . ."

"Shhh, love." Garreth stopped, putting a finger to her lips. "The hours are still ours. Let us not waste one precious minute on fretting or laments."

Noting their location to be near the lane of the goldsmiths, he led her a street over and partway down its length to one of the shops. Coming to the door of a jeweler, Garreth pounded heavily upon its oaken surface.

"Good fellow, forgive me for disturbing your peace," he called out. "Tomorrow my lady and I must part for many a month, and I desire to purchase her a keepsake." He looked to Ailénor. "Something pleasing, to remind her of myself and proclaim my love whilst we are apart."

Ailénor smiled at Garreth and slipped her arm in his.

From within, they heard the tread of footsteps, followed by a scraping sound as the bar was removed from the door. Seconds later it screaked open revealing a diminutive man with wiry gray hair. He looked up at them, looking none too pleased by the disturbance. But as he noted the quality of their clothing that marked them as well born, his mood brightened.

"You are to be separated, you say?" His eyes went to Ailénor, and a sparkle appeared in his eyes. "Well, young man, if I was your age and had such a beauty waiting for me, I'd wish her to carry my token, too. Mayhap a ring would best serve. One she can place on her fourth finger that is connected to her heart."

The jeweler disappeared to the back of his shop and returned moments later with a tray of gold and silver rings, some incised with flowers and engraved with sentiments inside.

"They are lovely," Ailénor praised and took one up.

Garreth rubbed a thoughtful finger over his lip, however, not wholly satisfied. "I wouldst have something with gems or pearls for my lady."

Ailénor's eyes widened, reflecting her surprise at Garreth's extravagance. The jeweler's countenance also lit up once more, as he realized the profit to be made off this late transaction. He considered Ailénor's dark red hair and the length of her slender fingers.

"I believe I have something most suitable for your lady. Step inside, step inside," he bid, heading back into the shop.

Garreth and Ailénor moved inside the door and waited. When the jeweler returned, he bore a small velvet pouch. Opening it, he withdrew an exquisite gold ring mounted with a large pearl with four amethysts surrounding it, of a deep purple hue. He held it up for Garreth's and Ailénor's approval.

Garreth nodded and relieved the jeweler of the ring. Slipping it onto Ailénor's finger, he found it to fit perfectly as though made especially for her and for this night.

" 'Tis beautiful," Ailénor whispered.

"Then 'tis yours." Garreth lifted her hand to his lips, placing a kiss on the ring and her finger all at once.

Turning to the jeweler, Garreth bartered the price and in the end gave him most of the contents of his coin purse and the fine silver brooch that secured his mantle.

Ailénor started to object and remove the ring, but Garreth caught her hand. "Nay, love. Keep it upon your finger where I have placed it. Let it be the symbol of our love and faithfulness and the pledge we took at Silchester."

Ailénor's love shined in her eyes. "*Merci, mon amour.* I shall not remove it and each time I gaze upon it, I shall think of you."

Turning to the jeweler, she praised his talent and thanked him, then accompanied Garreth down the lane.

Garreth pressed a kiss to the softness of her hair. "Come, love. Let us return to our lodging. I wish to hold you till the dawn."

Neither spoke as they entered the row house and climbed the narrow stairs to the upper floor.

Inside, Garreth flamed their last candle, placing it on the table, then turned to Ailénor. His gaze lingered over her for a long silent moment. Closing the space between them, he lifted his hands to her mantle and slipped it from her shoulders.

"For the time left to us, I would ask a wish, Ailénor." He placed a kiss beneath her jaw, then brushed his lips over her ear.

"You have but to name it, love." Ailénor drew a quick breath as he outlined the shell of her ear with the tip of his tongue.

"From now until dawn, I would ask you wear but one thing for me."

"One only, Garreth?" She closed her eyes, a shiver of desire running through her as he trailed kisses along her neck to the curve of her shoulder.

"Mmmm. Your ring alone."

Ailénor opened her eyes and met his dark and smiling ones. "And am I to be afforded the same wish?"

"I have no ring, Ailénor." His smile widened to a grin.

"Ah, *domage.* A shame." She rose on her toes and kissed the base of his throat, then stroked it with her tongue. "Mayhap you can manage without one."

"I will certainly try." He captured her lips. Together

they tasted and teased, their appetites growing.

Garreth pulled slowly apart, breaking the kiss. He gazed on her in the candle's glow, his smile fading to a more solemn look. Ailénor saw the passion firing his eyes, felt their heat as they remained fixed on her.

Reaching for the flowered garland, he withdrew it from her hair and laid it aside. He next threaded his fingers through her tresses and spread their wealth about her shoulders.

His mouth claimed hers once more, his tongue delving, tracing the recesses, drawing her into an impassioned but unhurried kiss as he gathered her to him. At the same time his hands moved to the back of her gown, and he worked the lacings free.

The cloth separated beneath his hands, and Garreth smoothed his palms down over her spine, reaching farther still beneath the material to splay his fingers over the curve of her buttocks. His hands traveled upward again, spreading the gown open even farther.

His mouth left hers, and he shifted back, his gaze pulling from her lips to the top of the gown as he drew it downward, baring her shoulders and breasts.

Ailénor gave a delicate shiver as the cool air touched her skin, but 'twas the force and heat of his gaze that caused her breasts to tighten almost painfully. Garreth pushed the cloth to her hips and sent it in a puddle to her feet.

Ailénor flushed from her hairline to her toes as his gaze moved to the triangle of curls concealing her femininity and rested there. After a moment his gaze slipped lower, grazing the length of her legs, then slowly upward again as though he memorized every detail.

"And did you have another wish?" she whispered, her throat gone dry.

"That you are mine tonight in every way."

"I already am."

Ailénor took his hands and lifted them to her breasts. As he began to massage and knead her, she began to unbuckle his belt. Her hands trembled as her excitement grew. Laying aside his sword and belt, she tugged up his tunic, and with his help drew it off.

She leaned into him, pressing her warm skin against his, her breasts pillowing against his hard, hair-roughened chest. Garreth coupled her mouth with his, melding her tongue with his in long silken strokes.

His lips left hers to savor her breast, while the hand it replaced slipped down between her legs. Ailénor welcomed his touch. She gave herself to his mastery a moment longer, then drew away and urged him to sit on the chair.

At his confused look she leaned forward, brushing his lips with her nipples, then bent to pull off his boots, one and then the other. Garreth's gaze flowed hotly over her, coming to rest time and again on her swaying breasts and on the treasure that awaited him.

She sank to her knees, naked before him and well aware of the evidence of his arousal beneath his *braies*. She began to remove his leggings, unavoidably touching his legs in the course of her movements with an arm, a hip, a thigh, and sometimes the curve of a breast. He suddenly leaned forward and completed the task.

"You torment me to sheer madness, sweet Ailénor," he said, standing to rid himself of his remaining garment.

Ailénor sat back on her heels appreciating the view, but as he sat once more he caught her hands and pulled her to her feet. He urged her to move forward. Suddenly uncertain, she hesitated.

"I would have you in all ways," he reminded, seeing her surprise and unease.

With firm but gentle hands he coaxed her to move over his lap and straddle him. Doing so, she found herself fully opened to him and felt more vulnerable than she had during their loveplay earlier in the tub. But for her trust she was rewarded in the next instant as Garreth guided her down, joining himself to her and filling her completely. The position brought her breasts to his mouth level, and he lost no time, circling her nipples with his tongue, then covering one with his mouth to suckle it gently erect. Ailénor sank her hands in his hair, reveling in all the delicious sensations.

"Garreth, is this allowed?" she whispered hoarsely, shocked at the bold, variant position but loving each glorious moment of it.

"Yes, my darling. Ride me now." His strong hands rocked her hips against him in an even rhythm, then he moved to her other breast and laved it. Flicking his tongue over her wet nipple, he blew upon it, suckled it, and lavished it some more.

Ailénor rolled back her head, giving herself to his seduction, relishing the sensations spiraling through her. She caught her breath as Garreth rose to his feet, with her in his arms and still joined to her. Ailénor wrapped her legs around his waist as he carried her to the bed and lay down with her in the middle of the mattress.

His mouth fastened on hers, and their tongues coupled and caught on fire. He began to move against her, and she found the contact exquisite, commanding. He brought her to the brink of release, then eased back, altering between deep and shallow thrusts, delaying their pleasure.

But Ailénor burned with desire and had no wish to wait. Loosening the grip of her legs on his waist, she slid her feet down over his legs and locked them behind his knees and calves.

"Now, Garreth . . . can't wait," she gasped as the first wave of pleasure touched her feminine center.

"As my lady wishes," Garreth ground out, nearing his own climax.

He moved against her with strong, even strokes. Fastening his mouth over hers, he mated her tongue with the same driving rhythm. They moved together, faster and faster.

Ailénor heard her name rip suddenly from Garreth's throat. At the same moment a tide of sensation overcame her, bursting through the center of her being and deluging her with wave after wave of shuddering, pounding, convulsive release. She became a part of him as he did of her. Transported to rapturous heights, passion consumed them in a fiery sea of ecstasy.

* * *

Garreth glanced back at the row house where Ailénor still rested, then scanned the lane in the early-morning light, hoping to find a street crier peddling hot breads and spiced cider as he had yesterday.

Several houses down, a youth hawked his toothsome goods, trudging slowly away. Garreth fell into long, deliberate strides, calling out and bidding the boy wait. When he caught up with him, Garreth purchased several loaves and a small pitcher of drink, arranging for the lad to retrieve the vessel later.

Seeing a merchant raise his stall a little farther down at the street's corner, Garreth thought of purchasing a pretty hair ribbon for Ailénor's exceptional hair.

Heading there, he saw the streets of Lundenburh were already astir with people, busy about their diverse purposes as they started their day.

'Twas an intriguing town, he reflected. Like Silchester, 'twas Roman in origin but abandoned in the face of the Saxon aggression. Curiously, 'twas the subsequent invaders—the Danes—who had revived it as a center of commerce, trading with European markets, and this only recently. The king encouraged such traffic, despite who fostered it. England profited even more so now that Athelstan had brought her under one rule.

Though Garreth personally preferred Winchester to Lundenburh, here, with so many ships from distant ports, one enjoyed more diverse and interesting sights.

The same thought invaded his concentration minutes later as he stood undecided, choosing from three ribbons. Garreth was startled by the sight a short distance away of a barbaric man of a breed apart from any he'd seen before.

Unusual for the early-morning bustle, people maintained a wide space around the man, murmuring and parting before him as he tread slowly along the street. True, he was bare-chested and hard-muscled, with a fell sword gleaming at his side. But what startled most was his shaved head with its single shock of black hair tumbling down his back. That jolted, and one thing more. A purplish mark covering half his face.

Unease rose in Garreth, his instincts prodding him to return to Ailénor. Acquiring all three ribbons, he quickly headed back to join her.

Climbing to the upper floor, he found her sitting in bed, waiting for his return. He held forth his offering.

"I thought you might be hungry this morn."

Her smile lifted to his and spread. "Famished is closer to the truth. I hold you responsible, Garreth of Tamworth."

Garreth chuckled and gave a quick bow. "Blame accepted, my lady."

Settling himself on the edge of the bed, he handed her a loaf of bread and presented the cider. Quiet descended upon them as they partook of the simple fare.

Garreth watched as Ailénor licked the last crumbs from her fingers. She gazed up at him, and their eyes locked with knowing looks. Their time together was at an end.

They both started to speak at once, then stopped. Garreth slipped his hand over hers.

"Once I see you safely away from the docks, I will ride straight to the king. My confidence remains in his judgment. It is my hope we shall be reunited with his blessing very soon."

"Then 'tis best I be away so we might be together all the sooner." Ailénor attempted a smile but failed.

Garreth pressed a kiss to her forehead, concurring with a small nod. They finished the last of the cider, then Ailénor rose and dressed in silence. Garreth laced the back of her dress and gifted her with the ribbons. She happily received them and selected the green one to tie back her hair.

By the time she was ready, Garreth saw that her heart had grown heavy again. She kept her lashes lowered to keep him from seeing how her eyes brimmed with unfallen tears. He lifted his finger to the corner of one eye and caught a droplet about to fall.

"'Tis time," he whispered softly.

"*Oui* . . . oh, Garreth . . ." Ailénor's voice broke as her emotions overcame her.

She stepped into his arms, and he embraced her at once, his lips closing over hers, her hands slipping upward around his neck. They held one another tightly, sharing a last bittersweet kiss, filled with aching and longing and the sheer misery of parting.

As Garreth released her, Ailénor fingered away the stream of tears slipping over her cheek.

" 'Tis time," she said in a soft, shaky voice.

Fortifying herself with a breath, she preceded Garreth out the door.

Seeing Ailénor had forgotten her mantle, Garreth caught it up from the chair, then crossed the room to follow, and descended to the street.

Emerging from the building, he lifted his eyes to seek Ailénor, then jarred to a halt. The barbarian stood before him with Ailénor held against his chest, one muscled arm across her body, the other hand clamped upon her mouth.

Garreth read terror in Ailénor's eyes, her gaze traveling past him.

"Ailénor!" He lurched forward, his hand going to his sword hilt.

Scarce did his fingers touch the cool metal than a bolt of pain ripped through the back of his skull and darkness overtook him.

Gagged and bound, Ailénor lay beside Garreth's unconscious form in the bow of a small and shallow ship.

The vessel rode the swell and pitch of the Thames as it departed the quay and began its journey downriver. Gulls shrilled and cartwheeled overhead against a marbled sky.

Ailénor sliced a look to Wimund who sat amidship. She cursed him silently, for 'twas he who had struck Garreth from behind, and she with naught but a look to warn him.

The fierce heathen who had seized her now sat astern, near to the boatswain, a seedy-looking man with few teeth. She could only presume all three were creatures of the woman who wished her mother harm—Rhiannon.

Ailénor glanced up to the flaxen sails overhead. Uncommonly, the ship possessed two—both square, the one to the fore smaller than the one aft, each bearing a crimson cross upon its billowed surface, like the Celtic high crosses her mother had so oft described.

Fleetingly Ailénor wondered whether Rhiannon's miscreants had stolen them from some monastery. Probably so, she decided. Why else would they sail beneath so holy a symbol?

She closed her eyes, the crimson crosses burning into her mind's eye, knowing in her heart they sailed for Ireland.

The *Sea Falcon* swept up the River Thames beneath a sail of midnight blue, its great silver falcon heralding the arrival of the Comte de Valsemé.

Rurik personally manned the tiller as the ship closed on the quays of Lundenburh and his crew prepared to dock. Lyting and Ailinn stood at the prow of the ship gazing shoreward, drawn taut with anticipation and worry.

Rurik raised a hand and pointed toward the wharves. "There is Downgate. We will put in there."

Ailinn's grip tightened on Lyting's arm as they looked toward the quay. A ship momentarily blocked their view with its double sails but then moved swiftly past.

"Gunnolf's ship is still in port," Rurik called out once more. "Let us hope he will have news for us."

Ailinn's attention drifted from the sight of Lundenburh's shore, drawn to the double sails of the ship that had just passed. They bore a sight she had not seen in decades— the Celtic high crosses of Ireland.

Chapter Thirteen

WEST IRISH COAST

The stiff Atlantic breeze tossed Ailénor's hair in a wild and fiery dance. Her hair ribbon had loosened and blown overboard days ago, somewhere off the English coast.

Ailénor shuddered beneath her mist-sodden cloak. The damp of the open sea had seeped into everything, reaching its cool fingers down to the very bone.

"Lean against me," Garreth whispered at her ear, his breath falling warm upon her as he shifted nearer.

"I thought you were sleeping." She graced him with a soft smile.

"Only napping. Conserving my strength. You need do the same, Ailénor."

Tiredness lined his features, yet the cool beam in his eyes and hard set of his jaw spoke of his determination to win them free.

Ailénor eased herself against his chest and listened to the steady rhythm of his heart. She knew it irked Garreth no end that he had fallen victim to Wimund's wiles and for a second time. The little wart of a man had a penchant for slogging people from behind, and Garreth blamed himself for not being alert to his dangerous presence. That their circumstances were now no better than when they first made the crossing from Francia galled Garreth all the more.

But Ailénor had also witnessed how he steeled himself with a warrior's resolve—biting down on his frustration and biding the time, counseling they meet each hour and each minute as they came, prepared to seize whatever opportunity might present itself.

As Ailénor rested against Garreth's solid chest, she leveled her gaze over the ship's side to the spectacular coastline with its soaring cliffs and rock-strewn shores. Colonies of kittiwakes and razorbills populated ledges along the cliff face. A small flock of the latter now flew in a low line above the water, distinguishable by their thick beaks and necks and black-and-white bodies.

As she continued to watch, the striking silhouette of a solitary peregrine rose above the cliff, its flight strong and swift, its wing-beats fast, giving itself occasionally to gliding. Seeing the peregrine, Ailénor thought of her sister and her hawks, thought of her family and of Héricourt. They seemed so far away. Dismally she wondered if ever she would see them again.

She must keep faith, she told herself with stiff resolve. In God, in Garreth, and in herself.

She slid a glance to the others. The fearsome barbarian remained astern near the boatswain. He seemed a stony island unto himself, never exhibiting the least emotion. He did, however, appear to be interested in the boatswain's steerage of the ship and watched his movements closely, as now.

Wimund, on the other hand, had wallowed in a superior mood since departing the docks of Lundenburh. Compared to the barbarian, he seemed absolutely loquacious at times. Carrying her gaze to him, Ailénor gave a start to find his enormous eyes fixed on her. They glowed with nervous anticipation—a greedy, possessive look that made her cringe.

She shifted uncomfortably, masking her revulsion. His great eyes roamed over her as they had so often during this journey. As before, his gaze paused where her hands disappeared behind her back.

Ailénor knew he coveted the pearl and amethyst ring upon her finger. He had spied it during their first day at sea and had eyed it numerous times since. Quickly she worked the ring around her finger, turning the pearl and stone settings to inside her palm, then closed her fingers tight over them. All too vividly, she remembered Wimund prying the gems from the precious Psalter, desecrating it. He'd not have the ring Garreth had given her.

Wimund continued to stare at her, grinning like the cat that caught the mouse. He wiped his lips, then gave a sniggering laugh and moved forward.

"Thought you could slip away from ol' Wimund, did you? He's got big eyes. Doesn't miss much. Got a sharp sniffer, too." He thumped his forefinger against the side of his nose that seemed to jut out even farther from his face due to his lack of chin.

Ailénor strove to ignore him, her gaze following the elegant passage of a string of low-flying kittiwakes, snowy white with black-tipped wings. But her slight of Wimund only encouraged him to sidle closer. Ailénor felt Garreth stiffen.

"Didn't take much to pick up Grimbold's scent and follow his track. Was to meet him at Andover. They were all astir when I arrived. That reeve, Rannulf, he was in a fine fettle, too. Discovered you had slipped away, right under his nose. The stablehands remembered Grimbold, though, and thought he had headed north.''

Wimund stabbed a stubby finger at his chest. ''Now, I figured he left to follow you. Varya and I traveled all the way to Silchester before finding anything. Then what should we see as we approached the city but a fresh grave?''

He took another swipe at his lips for he had a tendency to dribble from the corner of his mouth. ''Not many people in Silchester. But the innkeeper, he got real chatty once he got an eyeful of Varya and his sword. 'Twasn't hard to track you from there.''

Wimund's lids drew partially together over his huge eyes, giving him a squint akin to that of a toad.

''Lundenburh was more crowded. But the waterfront never sleeps. Lots of eyes along the docks, and luck was with us. People remembered a pretty, redheaded woman.''

He reached out and fingered Ailénor's hair, causing her to shrink back.

''Leave her be,'' Garreth snarled.

Wimund's countenance suddenly changed, a menacing look entering his eyes. ''For now, mayhap.'' His gaze prowled down Ailénor's arm. ''But I'll have that ring.''

Grabbing for her hand, Wimund fumbled at her fingers. Ailénor fisted her hand and twisted away, pressing into Garreth's chest. But Wimund's persistent fingers dug into hers, and he started to pry them loose one by one.

''I said leave off her, cur!'' Garreth barked, trying to kick out with his bound feet, but Ailénor leaned across his chest and lap, frustrating his efforts while Wimund tore at her fingers.

''Mine, now. Give it to me!'' Wimund demanded as his grappling movements rocked the boat. Ailénor gave a cry as he yanked at the ring.

Suddenly a thunderous growl rolled from stern to prow. The heathen, Varya, rose and came forward. Clamping down on Wimund's shoulders, he jerked him back, jamming him onto his seat. Varya then uttered low guttural sounds—possibly words—but more like those of a maddened beast.

Wimund glowered and sulked, knifing glances over his shoulder at the barbarian who resumed his seat and sat stonily, arms crossed over his wide chest. Turning back to Ailénor, a nasty gleam appeared in Wimund's eyes.

"Keep the ring. I'll be having another prize from you, *Comtesse.*" He emphasized her title. "The princess promised." He glanced shoreward and scanned the coast. His lips pulled into a smile. "And ol' Wimund will be enjoying it very soon now. We are there." He pointed a blunt finger toward the shore. " 'Tis Cahercommaun."

Ailénor's breath shortened, her stomach clenching. Her eyes sought Garreth's, then together they looked to the dramatic cliff towering above the waters.

Flocks of black crowlike choughs occupied its ledges, some circling just off shore—ominous specters, shrilling their high-pitched "kiahs" in welcome.

Lifting her gaze to the cliff's summit, Ailénor beheld the ponderous walls of the ancient hill-fort. Rhiannon's lair.

"Princess. The *bàrc* arrives. Princess, wake up."

Rhiannon stirred as the words seeped through the fog of sleep and settled in her brain. She felt her arm jostled once, then twice. Levering open one eye, she peered at the spindly servant girl, Blinne. She thought to box the girl's ears for disturbing her rest. Instead, Rhiannon turned to her other side and burrowed into her pillow.

"Be gone, or I shall take a stick to you."

"The *bàrc*, Princess. Varya returns."

Rhiannon came fully awake, her heart jolting. Shoving upright, she rolled back and grabbed Blinne by the fleshless rail that was her arm.

"Did you see them? How many are there aboard?" Rhiannon demanded, dragging the girl half onto the bed.

Blinne's features crumpled with visible pain as Rhiannon's fingers dug to the bone. "Please. I did not count. Mayhap four, five."

"Is there a woman with dark red hair, the shade of the trees afire in autumn?"

Blinne's head bobbed up and down in quick affirmation, tears collecting in her eyes.

Rhiannon released her hold, triumph soaring through her veins. "My robe. Hurry!" She gestured to the chest where it lay.

Blinne scrambled to retrieve the rich garment, then held it out as Rhiannon stepped naked from the bed. Too anxious to dress further, Rhiannon belted the garment and hastened from the chamber.

Hurrying out into the large, circular courtyard, she rapidly crossed its expanse and headed for the west wall that backed to the cliff's edge and overlooked the sea.

On bare feet she mounted the rough steps that flanked the inner defense wall, climbing to a height of fifteen feet to stand atop the thick drystone construction.

Rhiannon's robe billowed in the wind as she scanned the waters below. Farther down the coast, along a narrow strip of land, she beheld a ship putting into shore and recognized its twin sails bearing crimson crosses.

She could not see the faces clearly but made out Varya easily enough, then spied a woman with the distinctive auburn hair that could only belong to her reviled stepcousin. 'Twas true, then. 'Twas she. Ailinn of the Érainn.

Rhiannon's elation swelled, her joy unbridled. She raised her hands and boasted to the heavens. "I have won! The victory is mine! And so will be the vengeance."

She threw her head back, venting a laugh that came from a place deep in her soul—a black hole that contained all the pain she had ever known—all the misery she believed Ailinn had caused her—a place that cried for retribution.

Again Rhiannon looked to the small figures disembarking below. They headed toward the steep path that led to the top of the cliff.

Rhiannon twirled in a small circle, jubilant as a child, then skipped fleetly over the steps. She would meet them, she decided swiftly. Yes, she would wait at the top of the cliff in cool and queenly splendor while Ailinn clawed her way up the miserable little trail. Her coddled stepcousin would arrive sweating and panting with her heart hammering in her chest. And when she reached the top she would find herself at Rhiannon's feet—Rhiannon, back from the dead.

Rhiannon hurried back to her room, shouting Blinne's name. Inside, she flung open her chests, pulled out a scarlet gown of silk and a brocaded mantle edged with martin. She adorned herself with a heavy golden torque, jeweled rings, and finely wrought bracelets. Finishing, she swathed her head and neck in a filmy veil, carefully arranging the folds to conceal her scars.

Rushing out again, she passed from the inner courtyard through a linteled gate. Cahercommaun possessed three defense walls in all, the innermost nearly a complete circle, the outer two semicircular in design, each ending at the edge of the cliff that plunged to the sea.

The hill-fort's design delayed Rhiannon now, for she was forced to run along the inner ring to a second linteled gate that opened onto the outer ring. Reaching the third and outermost gate, she quickened through it and hastened along the rim of the cliff, stopping now and then to check on the party's progress down the shore.

Her feet carried her on until she reached the top of the path and stood catching her breath. Rhiannon waited, her breaths evening out. She smoothed her gown and adjusted her veils, her heart pounding with high anticipation.

Soon heads and shoulders appeared. Again Rhiannon glimpsed the deep, rich red of her stepcousin's hair. Her excitement multiplied.

At last the others neared the top. Wimund came first, followed by Ailinn. Unexpectedly, 'twas not Grimbold who came next, but a tall, dark-haired man. Rhiannon could not yet see his face, but Varya followed with his sword gleaming at the man's back.

Rhiannon could not concern herself with his presence at the moment. Ailinn was within her grasp. Rhiannon refused to allow anything to distract from or spoil this moment.

She waited triumphant at the crest of the cliff. Waited to

see the shock in Ailinn's golden-brown eyes when she beheld who had ordered her abduction—Rhiannon, who had been abandoned in the Steppe to die.

Laughter, dark and rich, bubbled through Rhiannon's veins, but she restrained herself from voicing it and quickly fingered the folds of her veil a final time.

Wimund gained the top first, heaving for breath. Catching sight of Rhiannon, he nearly fell backward in surprise. He secured his footing, then grinned and began babbling.

"Princess! I have brought her. Just as I promised. The *comtesse* for the treasure. Grimbold is dead, so the treasure belongs solely to me now. Though I'll be taking my pleasure on her before I leave, as you said I could."

Rhiannon's anger spiked when the scab of a man continued to block her view of her old adversary. Taking a swift step forward, Rhiannon shoved Wimund aside as though he were no more than a bothersome insect.

Rhiannon's lips stretched into a broad smile as her stepcousin raised her face and her eyes widened with shock.

Rhiannon gloated, her green eyes boring into those of crystal blue, the face familiar yet possessing the youthful bloom of one who had yet to see her twentieth year. Rhiannon's face fell.

"Wha-a-at?!" she shrieked. "What have you done?" She reeled on Wimund, choking with fury. "Who is this?"

Wimund shrank back. "W-why the *comtesse*, L-Lady Ailinn."

"Fool! 'Tis not *she*! 'Tis not Ailinn of the Érainn."

The young woman suddenly jutted up her chin. "*Ní hea*," she proclaimed in Gaelic. "I am not Lady Ailinn. I am her daughter, Ailénor of Héricourt."

The girl met her gaze evenly, defiantly, so much like her despised mother. Rhiannon hissed, fire crackling through her veins.

"Her daughter?" Rhiannon's nostrils flared. She rounded once more on Wimund. "Her *daughter*?" she repeated, her voice rising several notes higher. Rhiannon clouted Wimund alongside the head. "Imbecile! Half-wit! What do I want with the daughter?"

Wimund hunkered down, covering his head. "I . . . we . . . she looked like . . ." He wet his lips nervously. "P-perhaps all is n-not lost, Princess. I-if you possess the daughter, surely the mother will do all in her power to save her child. E-even exchange places."

"Silence!" Rhiannon seethed. "I want none of your excuses."

She slashed her eyes over the dark-haired man who stood silent behind the girl.

"Varya," she snapped. "Take these two to the *souterrain*, then come to my chamber. You can apprise me then of what passed and explain why this man is here."

She glanced at Wimund's quivering form. "And you, you misbegotten maggot, I will deal with you directly. You best hope this situation is salvageable."

With a curt nod, she signaled to Varya. "Take them below."

Turning on her heel, she stalked from the cliff.

Ailénor leaned her head back against the cool stone of the cave wall, her lashes pressed shut as she recalled the past hours. One image haunted more than any other—that of Rhiannon as she waited atop the cliff.

Even now, chills crawled through Ailénor to think of the witchlike creature—a shock of white streaking her dark hair, nails sharp as talons, her skin aged and leathery from years of harsh exposure, and the scars—dear God, the scars. The veil had scarce concealed those upon her cheek, but when Rhiannon's anger overtook her, the cloth fell loose, revealing yet another, more hideous scar upon her neck.

But more than anything, Ailénor could not forget the woman's eyes. Their green depths burned with fire. And hate.

So this was Rhiannon, her mother's stepcousin. It both revulsed and incensed Ailénor to think this foul being wished to harm her mother. Her mother, who was filled with naught but goodness and beauty and grace. She was like the light of day, and Rhiannon the pitch of night. Her mother was like a luminous pearl, and Rhiannon, blackest obsidian.

"Ailénor," Garreth spoke softly to her right, catching her attention. "We were right. Look."

Ailénor glanced toward him, then saw a little bird near Garreth's foot, strutting a circle and cocking its head with curiosity at his boot.

The scent of fresh air and the distinct sound of bird cries had given them to suspect the tunnel opened out onto the face of the cliff. Now they were sure.

On a whir of wings, their little visitor left as easily as it came, disappearing down the low-ceilinged passageway in the direction of the sea.

"If only we could be rid of these." Garreth pulled his leg against the ankle iron and chain that anchored him to the wall.

Ailénor looked to her own chain and to the ropes that bound her wrists.

When they first put into shore, their captors had retied their hands in front of them so they might better climb the steep path up the side of the cliff. On being taken to the underground passage, their ankles were then shackled with cuffs and chains, the latter attached to rings embedded in the wall. Garreth and she were spaced far enough apart that neither could reach the other, nor anything else in the *souterrain*.

Wooden chests, baskets, ropes, and sundry supplies lined the walls. If they held implements that could free them of their bonds or facilitate their escape, there was no way to lay hold of them.

"Ailénor," Garreth prodded her from her thoughts. "Do you know aught of Ireland? Did your mother ever speak of its western parts? 'Twill be best to know which way to flee when the time comes, over land or by sea."

Garreth's confidence heartened Ailénor, and she appreciated that he allowed no room for "ifs."

"Mayhap this is the Kingdom of Thurmond. *Maman*

talked of its sheer cliffs and wild, desolate beauty. 'Tis a barren, rocky region with few trees and little water. 'Tis strewn with caves, and peat bogs come up right to it, some like quicksand. They can suck even a strong man straight under.''

Garreth grimaced. ''The sea sounds more appealing. Do you think we could handle a two-master?'' The corners of his mouth pulled upward, a light sparkling to life in his eyes. ''Of course, we can always rig it as a one-master, if you like. You obviously know more of ships and sailing, and I do not mind at all placing myself under your very skillful hands.''

He grinned outright now, and Ailénor could not keep her own lips from stretching into a smile. He hadn't lost his sense of humor. For that she was thankful. It soothed her nerves and cheered her spirits, giving a breath of hope that all would yet be right.

As she gazed on Garreth, her heart warm with love, the heavy tread of boots sounded on the passage stairs off to her left.

Turning, Ailénor's smile froze upon her lips. The formidable barbarian, Varya, stood at the bottom of the steps. He was a fierce, savage-looking man—a rock-solid mass of muscle with merciless black eyes. His hand moved to his hip and he unsheathed his curved, gleaming sword.

Ailénor swallowed.

A shadow moved out from behind Varya and scurried ratlike down the last steps and straight toward Ailénor. Instinctively she pulled back, then saw 'twas Wimund. His great eyes glowed with his excitement as he squatted beside her.

''The key, the key,'' he demanded impatiently, twisting to look back at Varya. The heathen removed the key ring from his wide belt and tossed it to Wimund.

Wimund uttered a gleeful laugh as he took hold of Ailénor's ankle and jabbed the key into the iron lock. Mumbling happily to himself in Gaelic, he removed the manacle, but then couldn't resist running his hand upward over her calf and back down again.

''Nice. Nice.'' He bobbed his head, then began to pluck her gown from her other ankle.

Repelled, Ailénor drew in her legs, but as she did, a shadow fell across them. They looked up into Varya's glowering face. Wimund scuttled back under the heathen's cold glare.

Reaching down, Varya took hold of Ailénor by the upper arm and hauled her to her feet. He continued to hold her firmly at his side as he gestured with his sword point for Wimund to unlock Garreth.

Wimund scrambled over to Garreth and worked the lock. As he took off the restraint, Garreth thrust to his feet, knocking Wimund off balance.

Garreth stood tall and stony-faced, riveting Varya with his eyes alone—a hard, unyielding look that warned no harm should befall Ailénor.

Ailénor trembled to her toes, fearful for Garreth as he dared to maintain his stance, rigid with challenge, yet with his wrists still bound.

Scuffling to his feet, Wimund slipped out a knife and pointed it at Garreth's ribs. But Garreth rounded on the rodent, causing Wimund to fall back a pace. Nervously Wimund flashed the knife before him.

''Garreth! *Non*, do not tempt them,'' Ailénor pleaded.

Garreth looked at her, and their eyes locked and held. As he eased his posture, Wimund gave forth a cackling laugh, pleased with the little victory.

But in the next moment Varya cut through Wimund's gaiety, rumbling a command in his coarse, growling voice.

Wimund shoved Garreth toward the steps, carping in Gaelic. Ailénor knew Garreth could not understand his words. She, however, caught each one.

''Get on. Get on,'' Wimund jabbered. ''Princess Rhiannon waits. Not wise to make her wait. Not wise at all.''

As Ailénor and Garreth emerged from the *souterrain*, Ailénor saw that the color had left the sky, leaving everything dusted in shades of gray.

'Twas much later than she had imagined. Days were exceptionally long in the summer months in Ireland and the nights comparably short. Even now, though it be past Lammas Day and pressing late into August, the days remained lengthy.

From the look of the sky, Ailénor guessed it to be well past compline and nearer to matins, the midnight hour. That Rhiannon summoned them at so late an hour surprised her not at all. To such a woman, day and night would hold no meaning.

Following Wimund, they approached the largest of the buildings in the courtyard. He hastened to shoulder open the iron-studded door, then setting his knife to Garreth's back once more, he ordered them inside.

Sputtering torches greeted them, casting poor light and shifting shadows upon the stone walls and emitting an acrid odor. Ailénor followed Garreth and Wimund deeper into the hall with Varya immediately behind her. She coughed as the smoke touched her lungs and brought tears to her eyes. It layered the room in a thin haze, drifting slowly upward to an opening in the ceiling.

Ailénor scanned the sparse trappings displayed on one wall and noted the ornamented chest that stood against it. Joining Garreth where he stood at the room's center with Wimund, she glanced up to him but found his gaze fixed to the far end of the chamber. Following his line of sight, she discovered Rhiannon.

Rhiannon sat upon a thronelike chair, richly carved and cushioned. Her bright scarlet dress appeared bloodred in the torchlight and her dark robes an inky black. She reminded Ailénor of a queenly spider waiting in her cave. Waiting to trap and consume her prey.

Ailénor saw how Rhiannon's gaze strayed over Garreth, her interest obvious. But at Ailénor's movement, Rhiannon's eyes shifted.

A shadow passed through Rhiannon's expression, and her eyes glittered, filling with such venom and a look so chilling, Ailénor thought her blood would never flow warm again.

Ailénor forced herself to stand firm and not yield to the

powerful instinct to draw back. Clearly Rhiannon saw in herself her mother Ailinn. Ailénor and she shared a strong resemblance, one that the poor light would serve only to enhance. One that could not help but stir Rhiannon's darkest feelings toward her mother. Indeed, Rhiannon's hatred was palpable.

Ailénor's throat suddenly felt dry as sand. She pulled her gaze from Rhiannon and looked to Garreth to see if he was as affected by the woman's malevolence as she.

"*Suidh.*" Rhiannon's voice cut like a knife through the heavy silence, drawing Ailénor's gaze back. Raising a long, jeweled forefinger, Rhiannon pointed to a place behind them.

"She says to sit," Ailénor interpreted for Garreth in a hushed tone.

Turning, they found a rough bench had been brought forward. Without a word, they crossed to it and seated themselves there. Varya took up his stance behind them, his sword remaining drawn.

Wimund, meanwhile, hovered near Rhiannon, as though hoping to gain her attention. But at her black look, he scrabbled back and took a place on a low stool in the corner.

Several painfully thin servants materialized from a side door and moved wraithlike about the hall. Quickly they assembled a trestle before Garreth and Ailénor, then spread it with a crisp white linen that was wholly incongruous with the setting. Unlocking the ornamented chest, they drew forth fine goblets and silver plate chased with gold, again not in keeping with the stark surroundings but obviously part of Rhiannon's private hoard.

Garreth leaned ever so slightly toward Ailénor. "I wonder how she acquired such wealth. Do you suppose she stole it?"

"Naught would surprise me of a woman who has survived the Steppe and tamed a barbarian," Ailénor commented dryly.

Varya rumbled something from behind, presumably ordering them to be quiet.

The servants next appeared with pitchers of wine and platters of food, attending first to their princess, then to the captive guests, Ailénor and Garreth.

Rhiannon sipped from a magnificent jeweled goblet and ate from a plate of silver and gold held by a servant. Ailénor noted that she partook of the same simple fare served herself and Garreth—fish, bread, cheese, and wine.

Yet for all the impressive finery, the wine was cloudy with sediment, and a servant had to cut away the mold on the cheese at a side table before it could be presented. The bread, in turn, proved coarse and stale. Only the fish was fresh and of merit, having been smoked over a fire.

Rhiannon finished her portion and rinsed it down with the murky wine. She then lifted her jeweled goblet as if to salute Garreth and Ailénor.

"Let it not be said my hall lacks hospitality. Even my enemies are fed."

From the corner of her eye, Ailénor saw Garreth look to her for the meaning of Rhiannon's words, but she did not wish to miss the opportunity of the moment.

"If we are your enemies, Rhiannon, you have made us so. We did not ask to be brought here."

Rhiannon lowered the goblet, her eyes firing at Ailénor's boldness. Just as quickly Rhiannon shuttered the look, a thin smile unfurling across her lips. She rose slowly in place. Holding out her goblet, she waited while a servant refilled it, then advanced toward the couple, her strides long and rhythmic.

"True. You did not ask to come here." Rhiannon's voice flowed smooth as silk. "And yet, here you are."

Coming to stand beside Garreth, she trailed a hand over his broad shoulders, then brushed her fingers through his dark hair.

"Now, I am faced with the question of what exactly to do with you."

With one of her talonlike nails, she traced a line from behind Garreth's ear, across his throat to beneath his chin.

Ailénor shivered inwardly for its path was identical to that of the scar on Rhiannon's throat.

"I have no quarrel with your companion," Rhiannon purred. "But his presence does complicate things." Her gaze slid to Ailénor. "As for you, my dear, I find myself in agreement with Wimund. You have a very definite use to me."

Wimund's eyes brightened. He abandoned his stool and scuttled forward. "Yes, Princess. She is most useful. Most useful, indeed . . ."

Rhiannon quelled him with an incisive look, sending him scuffling back.

Ailénor seized the moment, daring to rise to her feet and confront Rhiannon. She heard Garreth utter her name but ignored the concerned warning in his voice. Boldly she stood fast, her hands tied and a heathen at her back.

"Confess it, Rhiannon, your plans are already spoiled, and you have lost your advantage. You cannot hope to have another opportunity to seize my mother. My father will protect her with his lion's heart and eagle's eyes." Her gaze went to Wimund. "Neither this creature nor anyone else you send has a prayer of getting near my family. Meanwhile, all Normandy searches for me, and when they find . . ."

Rhiannon broke out in discordant laughter. "My dear, your kinsmen have no idea where you are or who abducted you." Rhiannon narrowed a look at Wimund. "Unless that, too, was bungled."

Wimund came forward quickly and solicitously. "No, Princess. Not bungled. They have no way of knowing."

A gleam of satisfaction appeared in Rhiannon's eyes as she turned her gaze on Ailénor once more.

"As to ensnaring your mother, Wimund is right. I have no need to abduct her. She will come most willingly to sacrifice herself and exchange places with you—her oh-so-precious daughter."

Ailénor seethed. The woman had the heart of a viper and a soul full of poison.

"Do not underestimate my parents. Either of them," Ailénor grit out, making no effort to veil her contempt. "But, most especially, do not underestimate my father. Christian though he may be, he *is* a full-blooded Norseman—a great warrior and fiercely protective of his family. You and your vermin are no match for him. Do you really wish to face *his* retribution?"

"Ahh, your father. Of course, I have not forgotten the courageous Lyting Atlison. A very handsome, very desirable man." The corners of Rhiannon's mouth tilted upward, memories tempering the harsh light in her eyes. "So, he succeeded in freeing Ailinn from our Norse captors. He had to have killed Hakon to do so. For that I am grateful."

Beholding Rhiannon's look, Ailénor realized this Hakon must have been the man who had enslaved and abused her. For a scant moment, she felt a twinge of pity for the woman and the horrible plight she had endured. But then Rhiannon's eyes welled with loathing once more.

"Judging by your age, 'twould appear it did not take Ailinn long to entice Lyting between her thighs. Did she seduce him on the banks of the Dnieper? I suppose, in good conscience, he felt compelled to marry her."

Ailénor's temper flared. At the same time it surprised her to hear the twin notes of jealousy and envy in Rhiannon's voice. Had Rhiannon lusted after her father those many years ago?

Ailénor lifted her chin proudly. "They were wed in Constantinople amidst great splendor and with the emperor himself in attendance. I was begotten after my parents' marriage in the Imperial City."

"So they told you." Rhiannon smirked.

"So I know. The months can be counted easily enough. The depth of their love is obviously beyond your comprehension and something you prefer to deny."

Rhiannon's eyes flamed. "What I comprehend is that because of your mother my life has been ruined. I will be avenged!"

"Ruined? How? Because she was not raped in your

place? Or abducted by the tribesmen in your place? Or simply did not die when you wished her to, for your own selfish reasons?''

Rhiannon hissed, raising a clawed hand to Ailénor's face, ready to slash and disfigure her. At the threat, Garreth bolted to his feet, knocking back the bench and shouldering in front of Ailénor.

In a heartbeat, Varya kicked the bench away and lunged forward, leveling his sword at Garreth's neck, the blade's honed edge kissing the place just beneath his jaw.

"You shall pay for those words," Rhiannon snarled in Ailénor's face. "Just as your mother shall pay for her offenses."

Anxious, Wimund shifted from foot to foot and wrung his hands, his great eyes rolling from Rhiannon to Ailénor to Varya and the deadly sword at Garreth's neck.

"Yes, yes, Princess. She shall pay," he soothed. "But we need the daughter now to snare the mother and lure her here. I will deliver the missive myself."

Rhiannon rounded on him, looking ready to swallow him whole and spit out his bones. He cowered beneath her glare, and a long moment passed. Then, unexpectedly, she vented a breath and turned her interest to Garreth. Signaling Varya to withdraw his sword, she considered Garreth closely.

Wimund started to retreat a step, but Rhiannon's arm shot out. Seizing him by the front of his tunic, and without so much as a sideways glance, she hauled him back.

"What more can you tell me of this Saxon? Varya said only that he was with the girl in Lundenburh, and you insisted he be spared and brought here. Something about a ransom."

"Aye, aye. A fine ransom." Wimund nodded vigorously. "He is a nobleman, a *thegn*. He was at the court of Rouen and sailed the Channel with us. The boatswain claimed him to be connected to King Athelstan's court. Gave us a good bit of trouble, he did, too. Escaped with the girl and took her straight to the palace at Winchester. Don't know his status among the Saxons, but by his fine garments, I'd guess he ranks high enough to bring a fat purse.''

Wimund rubbed his chest as Rhiannon released him.

"Can't let him go without some gain." He darted a nasty look at Garreth. "After all, he is responsible for Grimbold's death.''

"Is he really?" Rhiannon closed the space between herself and Garreth. Smoothing a hand over his chest, her interest sharpened. "Do you have a name, Saxon?''

"The girl calls him Garreth," Wimund supplied hastily, interrupting.

"Garreth." She rolled the name on her tongue as though it were a savory morsel. " 'Tis a pleasing name. I would know more about him. Much more." Rhiannon dragged her gaze from Garreth's features. "Varya, take our Saxon guest to my private chamber and bind him to a chair. I wish to question him further. You can then return the girl to the *souterrain.*''

Ailénor stood appalled yet found no opportunity to explain the exchange to Garreth. She saw that Varya's look had hardened, tension lining the muscles in his body. When he remained unmoving, she feared what the barbarian might do. To her relief, he only gestured toward a door at the back of the hall and shoved Garreth toward it.

But just when her worries were allayed, Garreth heeled around on Varya, unwilling to leave Ailénor.

"*Non*, Garreth. Please." Dread wrung Ailénor's heart. He stood not a chance against the barbarian with his hands tied. Varya could fell him with one swift stroke of his blade. "Go with him. Rhiannon desires to question you." Ailénor did not expand on her suspicions. "I will be all right. Truly."

Garreth looked unconvinced.

"They dare not hurt me if they are to use me to lure my mother here, as is their plan. Now, please go. Do not bring harm on yourself." She sent him a small smile. "How could you help me, then?" she reasoned, hoping he would accept her logic.

Garreth's jaw hardened, a muscle leaping there. But at

last he tore his gaze from Ailénor and allowed Varya to conduct him from the room.

Ailénor turned to Rhiannon whose eyes followed Garreth with a look that was a mixture of triumph and anticipation.

"He does not understand Gaelic," Ailénor clipped.

"Does it matter?" Rhiannon smiled cattily, then traversed the room to resume her place on her chair and bid a servant to refill her goblet.

"Princess." Wimund followed after her and sidled close, nervously licking his lips. "Ol' Wimund has already risked a lot. Made a mistake, 'tis true. But the *comtesse's* daughter is still of great value and the mother has already suffered much anguish at her disappearance."

"What is it you want, little man?" Rhiannon snapped impatiently.

He licked his lips again. "Surely the girl is worth part of the promised treasure. And . . ."

"And?" Rhiannon's voice rose, her temper flashing.

"And you promised ol' Wimund could pleasure himself on the *comtesse*. Why not on the daughter, then? 'Twill aggrieve Lady Ailinn all the more to have her daughter violated in her stead." His look grew avid, and he pressed closer. " 'Tis something that can never be repaired."

Rhiannon mulled his words, her eyes slanting to Ailénor. A malicious smile spread over her lips.

"Very well."

Varya reappeared just then, his scowl still in place. Looking to him, Rhiannon rose to her feet.

"Varya, take the girl below to the *souterrain*. Chain her and let Wimund have her as he will. When he is finished, he will need be rewarded with what is rightly due him. Do you understand?"

Alarm sleeted needlelike through Ailénor at Rhiannon's words. Still, she did not miss the look that passed between Rhiannon and the barbarian, a private, knowing look.

She saw how Rhiannon transferred a domed ring from her right forefinger to the opposite hand—a signal of some sort. Ailénor could only wonder at Rhiannon's true intentions toward Wimund, but knew it would make no difference to the fate about to befall herself.

Rhiannon started across the room toward her private chamber, then stopped and glanced back over her shoulder.

"If it pleases you, Varya, you can have the chit as well."

Chapter Fourteen

A fresh wave of terror crested through Ailénor's heart.

Wimund hastened promptly to her side and gripped her arm. "She's mine first," he muttered blackly to Varya and forced her across the hall.

Varya ignored him, remaining fixed in his stance, not a muscle flinching as he watched Rhiannon disappear into her private chamber and close the door. He waited several heartbeats longer, staring at the barrier, then drove his sword into its scabbard. Seizing a torch from the wall, he heeled after Wimund and Ailénor.

Tremors racked Ailénor as she stepped into the pitch-dark courtyard, flanked by the two men who would defile her. Desperately she harnessed her fears. To cry out and alert Garreth would bring him certain death. 'Twas clear Varya would like nothing better than to terminate any efforts Garreth might make to reach her, and permanently so, whether he still be bound or not.

Wimund propelled Ailénor forward. She gave each man a sharp, quick glance, then instantly regretted it. Torchlight exaggerated their features, Wimund appearing eerily grotesque and Varya even more spine-chillingly brutish than before.

Her stomach roiled. Fine beads of perspiration broke out on her forehead as she and her captors continued toward the entrance of the passageway. Gulping a lungful of air, she lifted her eyes to the black bowl of the sky overhead. There the stars watched like a thousand eyes.

Did Heaven see? Did Heaven listen? Did Heaven care that she was about to be ravaged?

A prayer rose from her heart like a dove on wings. She beseeched the Almighty for deliverance, then His host of saints, especially those most dear to this isle at the edge of the world—Patrick and Brigid and . . .

"Get on with you," Wimund grumbled when her step faltered.

Ailénor's breath caught to see they stood before the mouth of the *souterrain*. Sending a final appeal heavenward, she entered its jaws and began the descent.

Varya held the torch high so that its light tumbled down the steps and illumined the path to the appointed place of her ravishment. Hope deserted her that she might yet escape this bitter lot.

She *would* survive, she told herself firmly and clung to the thought as Wimund pulled her farther down the throat of the passage. 'Twas not these men's purpose to slay her.

Wimund gave an eager, chuckling laugh, his excitement increasing as they reached the bottom of the stairs where the light pooled. He smiled at her, his toadlike eyes staring, and ran a grimy hand along her arm. She shrank inwardly and tried to jerk away, but he gripped her all the tighter and hauled her toward the wall where the iron chains waited.

Ailénor's heart raced as the cruel moment closed in on her. She darted a glance about the cave, seeking an escape or something to lay hold of to protect herself, but knew 'twas in vain.

Wimund chuckled again, drawing his knife and setting its point to her side. Ailénor stiffened at the menace.

"Down on the floor with you." He prodded her with the tip of the blade when she failed to move.

Ailénor winced as it pricked her through her gown, but before she could respond, Wimund fisted a handful of her hair and yanked her down to the cave floor.

Pain shot through her knees, the heels of her bound hands burning as she caught herself on the rugged stone. She gasped as Wimund dragged her back by her hair and forced her to a sitting position as he knelt beside her. He continued to anchor her by her hair, pressing the knife to her back, directly in line with her heart.

"Put the irons on her," Wimund barked at Varya though his eyes remained lodged on Ailénor. " 'Twill go easier for you if you don't fight ol' Wimund. Hate to have to bruise you up. Give ol' Wimund a good ride, and he won't need to."

Wimund's grin widened as he eased closer. Ailénor's nostrils filled with his stale, unwashed odor. Snatching a sideways glance of him, she saw the intensity of his look and the drool forming in the corner of his mouth. Her stomach turned. Utterly repulsed, she looked to Varya where he placed the torch in an iron bracket.

He turned and approached her, then crouched at her feet. Taking up the iron cuff, he shackled her right ankle, chaining her to the wall. Ailénor's gaze met his as he fastened it in place. Varya's black eyes appeared dispassionate pebbles of jet. Yet she perceived a flicker of thought behind the stone.

Varya's expression did not alter as he stood and withdrew several paces. Crossing his arms over his thickly muscled chest, he remained locked in his stance, his sword gleaming at his side. He waited. And watched.

Wimund chuckled at Ailénor's ear. Her skin turned to gooseflesh as he freed her hair and rubbed his hand up and down her arm.

"When I'm done with her, I'll be wanting to see the treasure the princess promised," Wimund informed the barbarian.

Varya acknowledged with a brief nod of his head but did not move otherwise. Noting this, Wimund's eyes narrowed.

"Ol' Wimund doesn't need any help here."

Varya remained stock-still.

"You want to watch? Is that it? Take a few lessons?"

Wimund's grin faded when Varya gave no response.

"Hrmmp. Well, suit yourself." He returned his attention to Ailénor. "Now, my sweet, let's see what you've got waiting for ol' Wimund."

Ailénor felt the knife tip catch the lacing at the back of her gown and cut through. Before she could react, Wimund fisted her hair again and forced her onto her back, immediately lurching atop her. He locked his lips on hers and thrust his tongue into her mouth, delivering a wet, gagging kiss. Revolted, Ailénor shoved at him with all her strength, kicking out at the same time and toppling him off of her.

Wimund scrambled back, a vicious look slashing his features. He gripped her by the throat, high beneath her jaw, and drove his fingers brutally into her flesh, squeezing off her breath as he held the knife before her eyes.

"We can do this your way or my way. Easy or rough—doesn't matter. I'll enjoy it either way."

Incensed by his words, Ailénor gave him a fierce look, worthy of her Norse-Irish blood. Surprise sparked Wimund's great eyes as she continued to cleave him with the look. He maintained his suffocating hold on her a moment longer, until she began to slip into a faint. Then, releasing her, he left her choking for air and drew away.

Spots still danced before Ailénor's eyes when Wimund reappeared with a fresh length of rope in his hands. Forcing her arms back over her head, he fastened the rope to her already bound hands and ran it through the second iron ring affixed in the wall where, earlier, Garreth had been moored.

This done, Wimund scrabbled back to Ailénor's side. He gave a chortling laugh as she lay virtually immobilized on the floor.

Sheathing his knife, he then straddled her waist and pinned her down, making it impossible for her to dislodge him with her free leg.

"Now, you'll not be giving ol' Wimund any more trouble. Just pleasure."

His lust surging, he grabbed her breasts with greedy hands and began to knead them roughly.

"Aye, a lot of pleasure, my lovely. That's what you'll be giving ol' Wimund."

Coarsely he crushed her breasts, causing her to wince in pain. She bit her lower lip to keep from crying out and tried to twist free of his grasp, but to no avail.

Reaching to the neck of her gown, Wimund jerked it open. Ailénor's flesh crawled, and she could not control the shaking that overtook her as Wimund spread kisses and spittle along the curve of her neck.

Looking to the ceiling of the cave, she beseeched Heaven once more to help her.

Cool air touched her shoulder as Wimund dragged the cloth farther down. As his lips slid over her skin, tears sprang to Ailénor's eyes. On a desperate, inexplicable impulse, she looked to Varya.

Rhiannon flamed a slim taper over the oil lamp, then transferred it to the golden grains of incense waiting in the censer. She held it there until the resinous substance began to smoke, diffusing a dense, musky odor.

Snuffing the taper in a glazed vessel of sand, Rhiannon turned and gave the room a cursory glance. It pleased her well. A dozen small oil lamps bathed it in a soft glow, heightening the sheen of the fabrics that draped the walls. To her right, the wide bed waited, deliciously inviting, its dimensions strewn with an extravagance of pillows.

Her gaze came to rest on the Saxon where he sat bound to a straight-backed chair, his arms and hands secured behind him and his legs tied separately to those of the chair.

Rhiannon's blood warmed in her veins, pulsing a steady beat. Such a handsome man to have fallen into her lair. The winds of fate blew capriciously at times, bringing the most unexpected—and pleasurable—surprises. She would not question her good fortune or waste fate's offering. Not tonight when the gift was so very desirable. So exceptionally virile.

Rhiannon turned away, giving the Saxon her back as she drew the veil from her throat and exposed her scars. The dim light helped obscure her disfigurements. Still, she did not wish to draw attention to them and risk quenching the Saxon's lusts before she had even the chance to stir them.

Loosening her hair, she shook out its length, then began unlacing her gown.

Let him first fill his vision with her best assets, she thought. Her body was firm and shapely, pleasing to look on even at the age of five and thirty. The Saxon could not be that much younger—five, maybe six years less than herself.

Sliding her gown downward, she let it pool at her feet, then stepped naked from its crimson folds. Leisurely she moved to the bed and caught up a silken robe. Slipping into it, she crossed the material low on her hips and cinctured it with a silver belt.

Turning once more to the Saxon, she found he stubbornly kept his eyes averted. Rhiannon pursed her lips, then smiled, undaunted. She liked a good challenge. And he appeared worthy of the effort for the delights she would take from him this night.

With a slow, easy gait, she moved to the ornamented chest that lined the side wall. Retrieving an ivory comb from its depths, she smoothed her hair, arranging its wealth over her shoulder so it shrouded the scar on her neck and most of those on her cheek.

Men were all the same, she reflected briefly. None of them would ever willingly pass by an opportunity to rut. She thought of the Irish lads she had once favored with her body in Clonmel, then of the Norsemen and tribesmen of the Steppe who enslaved her and ravished her repeatedly.

Yes, men were all the same in her experience. *All.* Save one.

Rhiannon's brow twinged at the long-repressed memory. Immediately she shut out the image of the silver-haired warrior. Taking a deep, refreshing breath, she focused her thoughts on her current prey—Garreth of Tamworth, trapped in her web.

Rhiannon retrieved a small vial of fragrant oil from the chest, then moved to stand before him. Why shouldn't she take advantage of this man while he was in her power? Had not men done so to her over the past eighteen years and without regret? Now the moment was hers. She ran an eye over the Saxon. Given the right stimulation, he would respond. After all, men's responses *were* largely involuntary. He would have little choice.

Rhiannon stepped closer to the Saxon, her movements drawing his eyes. Yes, he would come around. He was just a man. Like all the rest.

Rhiannon ran her fingers along the opening of her robe, drawing his eyes. Holding his attention, she parted the cloth, exposing the creamy mounds of her breasts, the fabric barely covering her nipples.

Drawing the stopper from the vial, she traced its wet end between her breasts, then outlined their curves before returning the stopper to the vial.

She smiled on the Saxon as she strode toward him, giving a rhythmic tilt to her hips. Stepping in close to him, she rubbed her leg against his inner thigh and brought her breasts level with his mouth and nose. When he refused to look at her directly, Rhiannon lifted his face with her long-nailed fingers.

"Do you like the scent I wear? 'Tis a combination meant to stir the senses," she purred.

He lifted cold eyes to her, then glanced away.

"But of course, you do not understand Gaelic. Fortunately there are other, more pleasurable languages we might speak."

Opening the vial once more, she placed several droplets

of the fragrant rich oil on her fingertips, then slipped her hand into his tunic and spread the oil over his hard chest.

"Feel how it warms your skin and makes it tingle. Think of it anointing your entire body." As she withdrew her hand, she lightly raked her nails over his flat nipple.

Straightening, she withdrew her leg from between his and circled around to stand behind him. Pressing closer, she cradled his head, pillowing him between her breasts. He jerked forward violently.

Rhiannon ignored his resistance and smoothed her fingers down over his neck, massaging his corded muscles.

"You are so tense, my Saxon. You need something to relax you."

Shifting slightly to one side, she bent to his ear, aware of how her robe gaped from her breasts. She gave a small laugh and caught his lobe between her teeth, rasping it slightly as she let it go and moved away with her languid, practiced strut.

Galled, Garreth watched the witchlike creature cross to the open chest. Did she actually think to seduce him? To rape him? He, a *man*? 'Twas ludicrous beyond imagining.

As he sat immobilized by Varya's handiwork with the ropes, he rapidly explored the possibilities for escape. And found none. There was but one door—little good it would do him though, tied as he was. Dare he play along with Rhiannon's seduction so that she might free him, allowing his escape?

Churning the thought in his mind, he surveyed the few devices displayed on the wall—a flail with metal tips, a length of chain, and leather tethers hanging from pegs, all in sharp contrast to the seductive opulence of the room. Garreth gave a small start as he realized these items were not weapons, but instruments for some kind of dark diversion in which Rhiannon, and likely Varya, indulged.

Something deep in his gut warned him not to underestimate Rhiannon or her appetites. As Ailénor had put it, naught should surprise him coming from a woman who had survived the Steppe and tamed a barbarian. She could be capable of just about anything—or at least think she was—

including seducing a man and stealing his seed against his will.

Rhiannon removed a pouch of herbs from the chest. Taking a pinch of the blend, she sprinkled the particles into a gem-studded goblet, then filled it with wine.

"I believe you will enjoy this." She bore the goblet to the Saxon. "At least you will before the night is through. Of course, you will remember little, and quite probably, you will suffer a generous headache. But then, I have a potion for that, too."

Rhiannon held the drugged wine before the Saxon, knowing he had not understood one word. It mattered not. This was one of her best mixtures, designed to make a man lose all resistance. The Saxon would slip into a relaxed, enamored state, and she would then command him.

" 'Tis my experience it takes little to rouse a man's lust, most especially those in their prime. They are always ready. And you most definitely are in your prime."

Rhiannon tipped the goblet to the Saxon's lips.

"Drink," she encouraged, looking forward to the coming hours.

But the Saxon resisted, clenching his jaw so that the liquid dribbled over his mouth and chin. Rhiannon gave a laugh at this futile challenge and bent to lick the wine from the corner of his mouth. She then ran her tongue across his lips and seized them with her own. He stiffened beneath her aggression and jerked his head free.

"So resistant, my Saxon," Rhiannon teased in a throaty voice, drawing her eyes over his handsome features. "Come now. Drink your fill and let us both be satisfied."

Again she held forth the goblet, but he fought her, turning his head from side to side whenever she tried to press the rim to his lips. She persisted, but suddenly his brows drew together, and he whipped his head back, knocking the goblet with his chin and sending it flying into the rushes.

Rhiannon narrowed her eyes to slits, her breasts rising and falling with her quickened breaths. She circled the Saxon, deciding what tactic to employ. Coming to stand in front of him, she sank to her knees, then placed her hand on his. Slowly she slid her palms along his inner thighs, then retracted them, only to slide them forward again, this time a little farther. She repeated the movement, the third time running both hands over his groin and up to his waist.

Outrage blistered his dark eyes, and he jumped the chair back. Rhiannon smiled darkly.

"Yes, my Saxon. One emotion can excite as well as another—anger as well as lust."

She rose and climbed onto his lap, straddling his legs. In doing so, her robe parted, but she cared not at all. Instead, she rubbed her breasts catlike against his chest and pressed her hips against his groin. Moving against him, she caught his lower lip with the edge of her teeth, then captured his mouth with hers.

Garreth tried to free himself from Rhiannon's assault, but she clung fast. Twisting furiously, he finally broke his lips from hers. Undeterred, she spread kisses down his neck and smoothed her hands over his chest. Drawing one hand lower, she reached toward his groin, then covered him and began to stroke him.

Garreth gave a great roar. Coming forward on the balls of his feet, he tipped forward, dumping Rhiannon onto the floor. He nearly lost his own balance but barely regained it and managed to right the chair.

Rhiannon toppled into the rushes, hitting her head. Her mood veered, anger flaring in her eyes, turning them from green to gold.

She started to rise and come at him, but Garreth tilted forward once more and pressed onto his forefeet. Swinging his body and the chair in a single movement, he caught Rhiannon with the legs and sent her reeling back into the rushes. He joined her on the floor a moment later.

Rhiannon clawed onto her hands and knees, glaring at Garreth. As he lay before her, unable to move, she looked to him like a demon possessed. In the next breath, she pressed to her feet and started for him.

"Witch," he bellowed, seeking some way to make her understand he wished nothing to do with her. He spat at her when she continued toward him again, then spat once more so there could be no misunderstanding. Garreth glared at her, filling his look with all the loathing in his heart.

Rhiannon stopped cold before the Saxon's contempt. He looked on her with the same depth of contempt she had beheld in only one other man—Lyting Atlison, when she stood naked before him on the banks of the Dnieper and offered herself to him. And he had rejected her.

Something snapped deep inside of her, an unholy rage surging forth that any man should spurn her. Who did these strutting cocks think they were to turn away from her? As if they were better, superior. How dare they reject her, Rhiannon, princess of the Eóganachts!

On the Dnieper, she had been able to do naught about the shining Norman lord. But tonight this Saxon's insults would not go unpunished.

Varya saw the plea in the girl's eyes.

The bug, Wimund, crawled atop her, wetting her face and throat with his slavering kisses and tugging at the strings of his pants.

Wimund was less than a bug, Varya decided. He was a slug.

Again Varya looked to the girl. All his life had he witnessed women raped and brutalized—young, old, beautiful, ugly. It mattered not to the rutting warriors of the Steppe. They violated the slave women over and over, shattering their spirits until they were no more than shells.

Varya watched Wimund fumble in his excitement. How easily a man could force himself on a woman like an animal and take his pleasure at will.

He himself had never known a woman carnally before Rhiannon. Even the women slaves reviled him for the blight upon his face. But, in the end, he deemed himself more fortunate than all the rest, free and slave alike. For Rhiannon had opened a world of sensation to him and taught him there was more to be attained than a moment's fleeting pleasure. With her he had known the fulfillment of joining two willing bodies and exploring each other's deepest desires.

Looking to the girl, he thought of her spirit crushed. It set ill with him.

Since his birth, others had tried to break his own spirit. Except Rhiannon. As a slave, he had been badly abused, but from the first Rhiannon had looked on him not as the devil's spawn but as a man.

This one—Ailénor—was beautiful, unblemished. In truth, he had not witnessed the rape of a woman since he had been freed two years past. Memories rushed back, sharp and clear. As his eyes met with the girl's once more, her silent plea touched something deep inside of him.

She knew that he, too, was to have her. Yet she appealed to him for help. In so doing, she chose him over Wimund. She feared him, Varya was sure, but not once had she recoiled from him or shown revulsion over his marked face.

Varya gazed on Wimund as he yanked up the girl's skirt and plucked himself from his pants.

Slug, Varya thought again. Not fit for the pretty Ailénor. Rhiannon had ordered Wimund killed. Why not now, instead of later? 'Twould make no difference. Except to the slug. And the slug didn't matter.

A cry escaped the girl as Wimund kneed open her legs. He rammed against her with his puny member but to no avail, for she twisted and bucked. Wimund's knife flashed as he seized it from his belt and pressed it against the unmarred flesh of her throat.

The image coupled with another in Varya's mind—that of Rhiannon, on a day long ago, when others had sought to kill her.

Varya roared his contempt, seizing Wimund by the back of his tunic and hauling him off Ailénor. Without pause, he dragged him deeper along the passage to where it opened onto the cliff. Wimund thrashed at the end of Varya's arm, protesting loudly and bellowing a string of vicious names.

Closed-lipped, Varya freed his sword and with a single swift stroke sliced Wimund's throat. Hurling him out from the face of the cliff, Varya watched the body fall the distance, plummeting like a sack of grain and spilling over the rocks below.

Ailénor shook violently as she lay on the cold stone floor, stretched out, bound hand and foot with her skirt bunched up to the top of her thighs.

She stilled as she heard footsteps. Varya's, by their heavy clip. She heard none other. As he came into view, she saw the sword in his hand and the blood staining its edge.

Panic swarmed through her as her heart catapulted to her throat. She had heard Wimund's clamoring protest from deep in the passage. And then abrupt silence.

Wimund was dead, and Varya had killed him. What would he do now to her?

Ailénor trembled in terror as Varya squatted beside her. Several tears slipped uncontrolled down her cheeks, so frightened was she. Still, despite her fears, she forced herself to look on him. To her amazement, he did no more than reach out and wipe a droplet from her face with the pad of his thumb.

Ailénor knew not what to think. Did Varya mean to ravish her or not? Surely 'twas in his mind, for even now his black eyes roamed downward, over her bare legs. But having done so, he turned to gaze in the direction of the stairs.

Seeing his long, pensive look, Ailénor realized his concerns lay more with Rhiannon and Garreth and that which transpired between them than with herself. 'Twas startling, but Ailénor believed Varya to be jealous. As she considered this, the truth of his and Rhiannon's relationship became apparent.

Varya's eyes drew to Ailénor once more. She held her breath, uncertain of his intent, then watched as he lowered the tip of his blooded sword to a place above her head. She felt the slight tug of the ropes as he severed the bindings and freed her hands. He rose then and started for the stairs, leaving her leg chained.

Ailénor's relief quickly turned to dread, and a black anguish swept through her. As she watched Varya mount the stairs, his sword in hand, she knew his mark now was Garreth.

With brisk, purposeful strides, Varya entered the hall and headed directly toward Rhiannon's bedchamber.

Converging on its door, he determined to break it down with his bare hands if he must. Naught would stand between him and the two inside.

Casting a glance to the battle-ax bracketed on the wall, he thought to hew through the wood with a few determined strokes. But before he could lay hold of the implement, the door flung open, and Rhiannon stood framed in the portal, her green eyes blazing.

Surprise flickered across her features to find him standing there, but she instantly recovered herself.

"Varya. Remove this Saxon dog from my presence. Take him out into the Burren, as far away as possible—to one of the caves, mayhap, or, better still, the peat bogs. Dispose of him and leave no trace. Should his royal friends come looking for him, we need be sure they will never find any remains." Her eyes flashed fire, and her voice rose. "Do you understand? Take him far off and kill him!"

Varya looked past Rhiannon's shoulder, into the room where the Saxon lay on the floor, still trussed to the chair. His lips parted over a full row of teeth.

"Varya understands."

Chapter Fifteen

Light chased shadow beneath the crackling torch fires, capering over stone and rushes, staining them red-gold.

Ensconced upon her highseat, Rhiannon slowly sipped from her jeweled goblet, contemplating how best to bait her trap for Ailinn of the Érainn.

How she loathed to wait even another day, another hour, before exacting her revenge. 'Twas Wimund's and Grimbold's incompetence that fouled her plans and cost her this delay. The two deserved their fates.

She lifted the goblet to her lips just as the ragged reed of a girl, Blinne, burst into the hall and rushed across the room.

"Norsemen! Norsemen come! From the south. Oh, Princess, what shall we do?" she wailed, dropping to her knees at Rhiannon's feet.

Rhiannon's grip tightened upon the goblet. Leaning forward, she seized the girl by her arm and dragged her upward. "Norsemen? Are you sure, Blinne? How many ships did you see?"

The girl squirmed under the pressure of Rhiannon's fingers. "O-one ship, Princess. It rides sleek and low to the water like a dragonship. What could they want here, Princess?" Blinne sniveled. "There be no monasteries to plunder. Only a barren land."

Rhiannon considered the girl's words. Truly, Blinne was correct. The Burren offered naught but a desolate landscape with few trees and little water. Mayhap they would sail on. Or mayhap her tribesmen had set the wolves upon her to seize her treasure. And yet the Eóganachts would not traffic with the Norse. Not even to steal her father's treasure. She was sure of it.

Rhiannon narrowed her eyes. "I will see for myself. But warn the others not to run. They are safest in the walls of Cahercommaun."

Releasing the girl, Rhiannon hastened from the chamber. Traversing the courtyard, she climbed the stairs of the west wall and, on gaining the top, gazed southward, out over the sea.

The sight that met her eyes jarred, the familiar lines of the Norse ship calling back dark memories. And yet, on second glance, she realized the vessel was smaller than a Norse warship and the lines dissimilar to those in which she had ridden.

Upon the mast, the ship carried a great square sail of deepest blue. Its emblem reflected the first rays of dawn, and she now saw it to be a great silver falcon.

As the ship continued its approach, she espied a man and woman standing at the bow, his hair snow-pale, hers dark red, tossing in the wind like tongues of fire.

A dark joy spread through Rhiannon. She would have her revenge this day after all.

"At last, Ailinn," she spoke to the figure at the prow of the ship. "We meet again. This time, there shall be no escape for you. For this time, the day is *mine*."

Rhiannon turned and descended the rough steps. Her mind raced, afire with swift plotting and calculating. Those in the ship still need put into shore and make the long climb to the cliff's top. When they did, she would be more than ready for them.

Varya. Where was the man? her thoughts darted. *Had he yet to return?* She started in search of him. Then changed her mind and headed toward the *souterrain*.

His hands bound before him, Garreth made his way across the crevassed beds of limestone, their bone-white surfaces tinged pink with the first blush of dawn.

He paused momentarily, but the barbarian prodded him with a staff from behind and grunted for him to move on.

Garreth continued to pick his way eastward, avoiding the turf-filled fissures that could easily trap a foot or twist an ankle. Rhiannon's words had required no translation. She had ordered Varya to kill him. Now, Garreth wondered, where in this forsaken place did the heathen propose to fulfill the deed? Or, leastwise, attempt it.

Garreth readied to give challenge. Though without benefit of a weapon and his hands tied, he must not fail. Should he die, so might Ailénor.

Garreth scanned the surroundings as Varya shoved him onward. Not far ahead, the limestone plain gave way to a low-lying field, blanketed with scrubby vegetation. Off to the right, a stream sparkled against the bleak landscape, obviously issuing from the distant hills.

Verging on the edge of the field, Varya brought him to a halt and drew his sword. Garreth tensed. To his surprise, Varya moved around him and, taking his long blackthorn staff, stabbed at the ground before gesturing Garreth forward.

The earth sank beneath Garreth's feet, spongy beneath the bracken. A peat bog, he realized as he took another step.

Garreth watched the blackthorn staff, its knobbed end where the root once grew, bobbing at the air as Varya methodically jabbed at the ground. Slowly they progressed deeper into the bog land, the cool air of the Burren now turning moist.

Garreth glanced again to the stream and saw how it disappeared into the earth short of reaching the field. 'Twould likely feed the peat field from beneath, creating a treacherous mire. Ailénor's words sprang vividly to mind—the bogs could *suck even a strong man straight under.*

Realizing Varya's plan to inter him in the bog moor, Garreth steeled himself and waited to seize the most favorable moment. If he misjudged, there would be no second chance. Even now, as Varya tested the bog, he held his sword ready for any sudden move on his part.

Garreth studied the barbarian's movements. He deemed he held but one advantage over the tribesman in this more than unequal situation. Before he could think further on it, the blackthorn staff sank deep into the bog, the suction proving so strong, Varya had to wrest it free with considerable effort.

Garreth braced himself, every muscle battle-tense, as Varya turned toward him. The heathen's black eyes smiled as he brought up his sword.

Alarm rippled through Ailénor as Rhiannon appeared in the passage, her hair streaming about her shoulders, her eyes bright and fierce with excitement.

"Bind her," Rhiannon snapped out, sending the two bony servants who trailed in her shadow scrambling to Ailénor's side.

Dragging her to her feet, they forced Ailénor's hands to her back and rapidly tied her wrists. Then unlocking the manacle that cuffed her ankle, they hauled her before Rhiannon.

Ailénor twisted against the servants' hold and glared at the scarred woman before her. "Where is Garreth? What have you done with him?"

Rhiannon's lips curled, malicious as a snake's. "He accompanied Varya for a walk in the Burren. I expect Varya to return any moment.'' She added the last with obvious relish, enjoying the grief she inflicted. ''But now, Ailénor of Héricourt, 'tis your turn to take a short walk.''

Rhiannon's gaze sliced to the servants. ''Bring her!'' Pivoting, she ascended the stairs, her cloak billowing behind her.

The servants hastened Ailénor up the steps, shoving her roughly and causing her to stumble time and again. Emerging from the *souterrain*, they drove her across the courtyard no less gently, following Rhiannon to the far wall that loomed above the sea.

Rhiannon stopped before the stairs and rounded on Ailénor. Unsheathing the jeweled knife at her waist, she seized Ailénor and pressed the blade to her side, sending the servants shambling back.

''Come.'' Her eyes glittered, filled with dark purpose. ''A surprise awaits you. At the top.''

Ailénor's thoughts reeled as Rhiannon compelled her up one step, then another. Did the woman mean to toss her from the ancient wall to the rocks and sea below?

Higher they climbed, Ailénor finding each step more difficult than the last as a deep foreboding invaded her soul. Rhiannon prodded her on with the knife's deadly point, until many anxious minutes later, they gained the top and stepped onto its uneven surface.

Ailénor's blood froze as her gaze spilled over the edge and down the plummeting cliff. Her stomach rolled, and her head swam while an encroaching blackness filled her vision. Feeling herself sway, she caught herself but found her footage perilously unstable with her hands bound behind her.

Ailénor shut her eyes against the nightmare, but found that only made her feel much worse.

''See who rushes to your aid,'' Rhiannon hissed at her ear and gave her a shake.

Ailénor cracked open her eyes against her fear, her heart drumming in her breast. Snatching a glance below, she saw naught but hungry, churning waters. But as she cast a sec-

ond glance southward along the shoreline, her eyes met
with a sail of silver and blue. Her eyes widened as she
recognized her uncle's ship putting into shore where she
and Garreth had disembarked the day before and where the
other boat still remained.

Hope swelled bright and sweet, then darkened, choked
with fresh fears. What wickedness did this madwoman
plan?

As though hearing her thoughts, Rhiannon dragged Ailénor farther along the wall, then held her fast before her,
displaying her for her parents to see.

Ailénor's foot slipped on loose rubble, sending the pieces
hurtling off the wall and leaving her foot overhanging the
edge. She went rigid beneath Rhiannon's grasp, but the
woman took no notice.

"Behold your daughter, Ailinn!" Rhiannon cried out to
the ship, as though those below could hear her. "Come for
her if you will. And trade your place with hers."

Rhiannon gave forth a cackling laugh, the sound of it
chilling Ailénor to the marrow. Braving a glance to her
parents, she found and met their gaze.

Ailénor dreaded to think what they might attempt in order to save her. Dreaded to think what Rhiannon might do
to reap her revenge. Dreaded to think what might have already befallen Garreth in the forbidding plains of the Burren.

"Merciful God," she whispered, her heart raw with anguish. "Deliver us. Deliver us all."

The heathen's eyes remained fixed on Garreth as he leveled
his sword at Garreth's chest and dropped aside the blackthorn staff. Slowly, purposefully, he stepped from the edge
of the peat mire and began to encircle his prey.

Garreth turned in unison, never allowing him his back,
never taking his gaze from the barbarian's face.

Varya continued to maintain the distance between them
as he circled, maneuvering Garreth ever closer to the deadly
mire. Coming to a standstill, he planted his feet shoulder

width apart and motioned for Garreth to kneel amidst the bracken.

Garreth stood immobile, holding the heathen's gaze. He presumed Varya intended to either decapitate him or run him through, a cold execution without challenge or sport—quick, clean, final. He could not allow it.

Once he knelt, Garreth knew he would forfeit his maneuvering capability. Bound as he was, his sole advantage lay in his agility. Varya might be iron-muscled and strong as an ox, but his movements were stiff and systematic. Garreth's hope lay in his own quickness. And mayhap in the unpredictable element of surprise.

Again Varya motioned him to his knees. Garreth saw but two options—to feign he did not understand or to refuse outright to follow Varya's biddings. He chose the latter and shook his head.

Varya's look darkened at first, but then changed altogether. A fire lit the depths of his eyes, spreading through the black pools. 'Twas evident the barbarian found pleasure in the unexpected challenge. And welcomed it.

Again Varya began to circle. Casting his sword from hand to hand, he drew Garreth's gaze, then caught the sword hilt in his left palm and whirled the length of steel in a flashy display. Without pause, he reached with his free hand to the back of his belt and produced a slim-bladed dagger. Varya smiled, carving the space before him, his blood rising for the kill.

Garreth ignored the heavy drubbing in his veins and shut out all distraction, sharpening his concentration on the barbarian.

Varya continued to circle—slowly, deliberately, swinging and slicing the sword blade through the air with a flourish meant to mesmerize. Meanwhile, his other hand posed the dagger, ready for the sting. Alert to his cunning, Garreth knew he would need take Varya off balance, striking low beneath the threat of the blades for Varya's most vulnerable point, his knees.

Garreth shifted his stance to remain facing the barbarian, but as he stepped back a pace, he felt a strong pull at his boot, as though a hand had reached from the bog and trapped it, towing it down. Quickly Garreth retracted his foot and glanced over the ground covering. 'Twas impossible to tell where the treacherous parts of the bog lay. Only a few rocks surfaced above the scrubby growth, indicating more solid ground.

Varya's movement recaptured Garreth's attention. Having seen the mishap, the heathen's eyes now shined all the brighter. He licked the dagger's blade and set it between his teeth. Emitting a low, animallike growl, he issued a challenge and closed on Garreth, spinning his sword from hand to hand.

Garreth braced himself. In the corner of his vision, he glimpsed the blackthorn staff lying amidst the bracken. As Varya pressed in, he edged toward it. Once within reach, he gauged the moment, then dove for the staff, knowing Varya's sword would swiftly follow.

Falling atop the staff, Garreth clamped hold of it with both hands and instantly rolled. The sword slashed downward, whoosing past his head and shoulder, scarcely missing him.

Again Garreth rolled. As he came onto his back, Varya snatched the blade from his teeth, flipped it over, and hurled it. Garreth's eyes widened as the knife lodged in the staff, separated from his face by only a few inches of wood.

Without losing the moment, Garreth curled upward and struck out for Varya's knees. The staff vibrated in his hands as it made contact with the iron-forged barbarian, hitting him a fraction too low.

Varya grunted but did not budge, Garreth's attempt serving only to provoke him. As Varya turned toward him, Garreth brought up the staff to direct a second blow, but Varya swept down his sword and sheared off its end.

Garreth swallowed his surprise and, before Varya could raise his blade, rammed the staff into his abdomen. The heathen hunched forward. Quickly Garreth brought up the staff's reverse end, clouting him hard aside the head and with enough force to send him staggering backward.

Rapidly Garreth rolled onto his stomach, anchoring the

staff with his weight. Bringing up his wrists, he set the ropes against the knife's blade, where it still protruded from the shaft. He sawed at the bindings, but before he could cut through, Varya came at him, both hands clenching his upraised sword. As the blade hewed downward, Garreth rolled apart of the staff and knife.

Varya kicked the staff away and stalked him, blood trickling from his cheek. Hoisting his sword, he slashed for Garreth's back. Garreth lurched aside, unharmed. But when he started to lift up, the blade sliced crosswise, grazing the top of his hair as it whished past in a breeze of cool air.

Garreth shot a glance to where the blackthorn staff and knife now lay. He need make a try for them. But again Varya struck downward. And again Garreth wrenched back and watched the sword bite into the ground. Astonishingly it sank into the bog, rooting in a pocket of mire—all the deeper with Varya's weight pressing upon it.

Varya straightened, yanking and twisting hard upon the hilt, then staggering back as it came free. Taking advantage of Varya's instability, Garreth drove upward, slamming into Varya's rib cage and heaving him backward a short distance.

The sword dropped from Varya's hand as he pitched back and thudded gracelessly to the ground. Garreth lunged atop it. Catching the blade between his hands, he propped it up and pressed the wrist bindings against its keen edge. The ropes fell away, and he shifted back, his hands closing about the sword's hilt.

Without warning, Varya rushed him. The barbarian's foot caught him below the ribs like a battering ram, stealing his breath and sending him sprawling, his grip loosening on the sword.

Varya stepped past the weapon, a ferocious look upon his face. Reaching down, he grabbed Garreth just beneath the jaw and hauled him to his feet. Straight-arming him, Varya raised Garreth to his toes, then slowly compressed his fingers, squeezing off his supply of air.

Garreth gripped Varya's hand, trying to pry the fingers loose. When he made no progress, he locked his hands together and struck down on Varya's arm, hammering at the joint of his inner elbow.

Varya's arm bent beneath the blows. Seizing the opening, Garreth came immediately across Varya's face with his own elbow, quick and sharp, driving across the barbarian's cheek and nose, the latter giving way with a snap and gush of blood.

Varya staggered back, his grip slackening on Garreth's throat. Garreth heaved for breath, but Varya brought up his other hand and joined it with the first, wrapping it around Garreth's neck.

As the heathen increased his pressure, Garreth grabbed for his wrists, then yanked them hard and to one side, managing to open Varya's side to him. Swiftly Garreth brought up his knee and rammed it into Varya's gut, causing him to lurch back several paces. The barbarian dragged Garreth with him, his grip on Garreth's neck holding fast. Again Garreth kneed him, driving him back several more paces.

Infuriated, Varya pressed Garreth upward, still gripping him by the throat, then, twisting his body, attempted to toss Garreth from his hip and throw him to the ground. But Garreth twisted, too, realizing Varya's intent to trap him beneath him and finish his deed. Together they toppled into the bracken and rolled.

Suddenly Garreth felt the bog give under his side, a nightmarish feeling of the earth turning soft as custard and opening to swallow them whole. Using all his strength, he carried through on the roll, ensuring when they stopped that Varya lay beneath him.

Eye to eye with Garreth and hate in his glare, Varya maintained his crushing grip. Garreth countered, seizing Varya's thick neck with both his hands and squeezing tight. Slowly they sank in the mire, strength pitted against strength—all the while the bog discharging a hideous stench as their bodies displaced the peat.

Garreth shifted his weight forward, pressing down on Varya and forcing his head to sink more quickly into the bog. Alarm touched the heathen's eyes as he realized they were descending into the bog. Focusing back on Garreth, the hate returned to his eyes, coupled with a determination to take Garreth with him. Varya held Garreth with a death grip. At the same time Garreth bore down and watched the barbarian's features disappear into the thick, brown mire.

Pain centered in Garreth's chest, his need for air crucial. Still he maintained his hold and pressure on Varya, resolving that even should he die, the heathen would not rise to bring harm to Ailénor.

Spots mottled Garreth's vision as he sank farther with Varya, the cool mire beginning to encase him. His chest burned, and his thoughts began to close off one by one. Still he pressed down on the heathen, holding before his eyes the vision of the woman he loved.

Unexpectedly, Varya's grip loosened. Air rushed into Garreth's lungs, and he gasped it greedily. As he did, the strength drained from Varya's fingers. They trailed down the front of Garreth's tunic, then fell away, his hand slowly disappearing into the bog.

Garreth continued to heave for air, his grip still firm on Varya, assuring he would pose no more of a threat. But Garreth realized he, too, was fast sinking. Reason told him he could not be far from more solid ground. Yet as he considered the bracken surrounding him, he wondered where it lay.

Spotting the blackthorn staff several yards away, he believed it to be at least partially on safer ground. Carefully he spread out his weight, then slowly rolled toward it, away from where Varya lay entombed in peat. He remained motionless on his back, allowing the mire to flow around his arms and legs, waiting to see if he would sink. When he did not, he slowly—very slowly—rolled once more.

Again he lay motionless. Finally, reaching out for the staff, he brushed it with his fingertips. On a second riskier try he caught hold of it.

Using the blackthorn's knobbed end, Garreth probed the ground, trying to find something to catch on to. The shallow roots of the plants gave way under his attempts, ripping from the bog. Garreth tested the ground further, thinking to perhaps dig into the spongy peat enough to pull himself forward. Just then the staff knocked against something hard. A rock.

Garreth rejoiced. Hooking the end of the blackthorn onto it, he painstakingly pulled himself, inch by inch, toward firm ground.

Ailinn gripped Lyting's hands, their gazes riveted to where Rhiannon held their daughter atop Cahercommaun's wall, crowning the towering cliff. Ailinn thought her heart would cease beating altogether, so terrified was she for Ailénor.

Rhiannon cried out something from above, disturbing the birds perched on the ledges there. Inky-black choughs lifted from the dark sandstone cliff and winged out to sea, ominous specters against the dawning sky.

"Could you grasp what she said?" Lyting pressed, having no real knowledge of Gaelic. "Do you think she threatens to harm Ailénor should we begin the climb?"

Ailinn shook her head. "*Non*, 'tis precisely what she wants. She is waiting. For me."

Releasing her hold on Lyting, she started to step away, determined to face her stepcousin and bring this torture to an end. But Lyting caught her at once and pulled her back against him.

"You cannot think to confront her alone, *elskan mín*."

Lyting looked at his wife with consternation. He had not revealed to her what his keen sight allowed him to see—a glint of metal, a knife, in Rhiannon's hand, held to their daughter's side. Rhiannon's treacherousness did not surprise him, but he wondered if she could be expected to act sanely.

"Once you step into her trap, there is naught to keep her from harming you both. And mayhap no way I can help you. I'll not risk you both."

Anguish lacerated Ailinn's golden-brown eyes. "Oh, do you not see, my love? This has ever had to do with me alone, not Ailénor. Neither she, nor any of our children, will be safe until Rhiannon and I come face-to-face and put an end to this enmity."

Lyting shared her pain—and her unspoken fury—for all

that Rhiannon had visited upon their child and family. Gathering Ailinn close, he pressed his lips to her hair.

"I cannot deny the truth of what you say, my darling. But we shall face Rhiannon together and devise some way to save Ailénor. I expect your presence will prove a great distraction to Rhiannon. One we should be able to use to advantage."

At Rurik's approach, Lyting eased his hold on Ailinn and met his brother's somber gaze.

"The crew are seeing to the ship and will join us forthwith." Rurik halted beside them, then lifted his gaze to the clifftop. A muscle worked in his jaw, then he slowly scanned the wall, his eyes the color of polished steel, their blue having drained long ago. "Have you seen evidence of a guard? I have yet to spy even one armed man."

"*Nei,*" Lyting returned. "If Rhiannon retains any, they must be few or they would have given some show of force."

"Unless 'tis a trap."

Lyting concurred with a nod. He refrained from adding there was also no sign of Garreth. From what they had learned in Lundenburh, Garreth had been seized along with Ailénor outside their lodgings. He might now be dead or incapacitated. In either case, he would be of no help to them. Witnesses also spoke of a barbarian fitting the description supplied them previously by Lia's kinsmen. The barbarian, Lyting noted, was also in absence.

"Ailinn and I intend to confront Rhiannon directly," he apprised Rurik. "Mayhap you and the crew can follow behind, keeping from sight. You'll need ropes and grapples." He glanced to the fortifications topping the cliff. "There are three distinct defense walls visible. 'Tis likely Rhiannon will permit only Ailinn and myself inside the gates." His gaze shifted to Rurik. "Are you up to scaling walls, *broFir*?"

Rurik rubbed his jaw, looking from Lyting to Ailinn and back again to Lyting.

"Actually I was about to ask you the same question. I have a suggestion as to how we might free Ailénor."

*   *   *

Lyting paused in his steep climb up the rocky cliff, then gestured to the crewmen below him to do the same. Glancing toward the top, he watched Rurik help Ailinn up the last of the difficult path. The two disappeared as they stepped away and headed toward the hill-fort.

Lyting signaled the men to advance, then resumed his climb. Rurik's plan required they exchange places. He held no qualms in entrusting Ailinn to Rurik, or relying on his brother's ability to save Ailénor should the chance open to him. It only grated on him that he could not be immediately present to his wife and daughter.

Lyting leaned into the climb, adjusting the bow and quiver of arrows slung to his back. Rurik was right, of course. Given Rhiannon's capacities, they must assume the worst—she would not free Ailénor and might spitefully end her life. 'Twas plain what they must do—disable Rhiannon before she could injure Ailénor.

The weapon of choice was, naturally, a bow and arrow with which Rurik and he were both proficient. Lyting's aim and skill were more consistently accurate than Rurik's, however, and his exceptional sight a much needed advantage. The only concern was whether Lyting was emotionally meet for the task, being 'twas his own daughter who was at risk. Lyting avowed he was.

'Twas agreed Rurik would accompany Ailinn and pose as himself. Eighteen years had intervened since Rhiannon last saw him, and his and Rurik's features were so similar they felt confident they could fool her. 'Twas only Rurik's golden hair that might betray him, but that was easily covered.

Meanwhile, Lyting would infiltrate the fort and take up a position where he could mark Rhiannon. As she and Ailinn confronted one another, Rhiannon would, Lyting hoped, step for a moment from Ailénor's side. To that end, Ailinn would attempt to draw her out. Lyting would be ready.

Long ago, Rhiannon's cankered soul cost another young girl her life—her sweet cousin, Deira. Upon his sacred vow, this day, she'd not have Ailénor, too.

*   *   *

Reaching the clifftop, Lyting kept low and carefully peered over the edge. Ailinn and Rurik stood before Cahercommaun's gate, Rurik's hood now drawn up, concealing his hair.

Half of the massive door drew open a crack, and a gaunt man in coarse clothes emerged. Obviously a servant, his eyes rounded as he took in Rurik's stature and warrior's physique. With a trembly hand, he gestured to Rurik's sword, indicating he should disarm himself.

Rurik stared down at the man, causing him to shake all the worse, but gave no real resistance. Lyting presumed Rurik's thoughts ran with his own. Even if Rhiannon maintained no armed force to oppose them, she did hold Ailénor, quite literally, and could kill her on a whim.

Lyting watched as Rurik unbelted his sword and unsheathed two knives, laying them on the ground. Ailinn added her eating dagger, then held open her mantle for the servant to see she carried naught else. Satisfied, the man ushered Rurik and Ailinn inside the fort and closed the gate.

Waiting several moments longer and continuing to skim the area for watchful eyes, Lyting finished the climb and motioned the men to join him. Together the small group hastened to the defense wall, pressing into the shadows and doffing their gear. As the men readied the grappling hooks and ropes, Lyting gauged the height of the wall.

"Save your strength, my lord," the man Torfi whispered at his elbow. "I'll go over and see the door open."

"Have a care, then, friend," Lyting rejoined. "When you reach the top, keep low lest you be seen. Rhiannon herself might have a clear view of you from her position on the farmost wall."

Torfi nodded his understanding, then turned to where the others—Hamar, Geir, and Lars—worked at securing the grapple in place. Hamar swung the iron claw overhead, measuring out the rope. At the precise moment, he let it fly and succeeded in hooking it over the wall.

With a stout yank to assure 'twas lodged fast, Hamar passed the rope to Torfi. Torfi made quick work of scaling the wall on his short, bandy legs. Gaining the top, he flattened himself upon the stone and glanced about, then signaled Lyting and the others all was clear. At that, Torfi disappeared from sight only to reappear moments later when he opened the gate.

Slipping inside, Lyting and the others immediately encountered a second defense wall, as tall as the first and equally uninviting. This time 'twas Lars who offered to mount the wall. A strong and able young man, he accomplished the deed with quick efficiency, again finding no opposition, and opened the door without incident. Passing through, Lyting and the men faced the third innermost wall protecting the very heart of Cahercommaun.

Lyting ran a hand through his hair, frustrated and anxious to know what transpired within. "I'll take this one," he said, handing over his bow and quiver of arrows to Hamar.

Gripping hold of the rope, he climbed the wall, pulling himself up, hand over hand, and "walking" the full height to the top. There he dragged himself onto the ledge and stretched out. Below, a handful of buildings lined the inner wall. In the courtyard beyond, Ailinn and Rurik stood facing the west wall where Rhiannon now held the knife to Ailénor's heart.

Rage roared through his Norse veins, ferocious and devouring. Had he his weapons and a clear shot, he'd drop Rhiannon this instant. Lyting beheld the stark fear in his daughter's eyes, then realized as she looked to Ailinn and shook her head that Ailénor's fear was for her mother.

Lyting pressed his lashes shut and took hold of himself. God's might, he must not fail them. Opening his eyes, he studied the yard below and observed several thin servants clustered at the end of one building, watching the events beyond. Rhiannon shrilled something, sending them darting back inside. Perusing the grounds further, he still found no sign of any guards or of the barbarian.

Lowering himself to the ground, Lyting moved to the gate and withdrew the heavy bar. As the men joined him, they sought cover behind the nearest building. Lyting retrieved his bow and quiver from Hamar and quickly strung the stave. He then directed the men to spread out and keep from sight.

Like a shadow, Lyting melted along the lengths of the buildings, moving cautiously from one to the next, seeking the best vantage point from which to sight the she-devil, Rhiannon. His heart pumped hard. Any moment he half expected to be discovered or to come upon Rhiannon's barbarian companion.

Moving behind a small stone structure near the west wall, he found the position well met his needs. Seizing a handful of arrows from his quiver, Lyting stabbed them into the ground next to him for instant access, then nocked one in place.

Sighting Rhiannon down the shaft, he narrowed all thought to his target. Marking her, he drew on the string and waited for an opening to fell her without risking his daughter.

As he bided the moment, Ailinn stepped from Rurik's side to boldly confront Rhiannon. But as Lyting sharpened his ear to her words, he heard instead a boot fall, off to his right.

Swiveling, he drew full upon the string and marked the half-crouched figure, covered in filth and carrying a curved sword. Lyting readied to discharge the arrow, but the man halted, and their eyes met.

Garreth froze in his boot prints as he saw Lord Lyting's deadly arrow drawn on himself. Dropping the sword, he held up his hands. To his enormous relief, Lord Lyting directed the weapon aside and to the ground and allowed the string to slacken.

Ailénor's father looked every bit as stunned as he did to see him. In truth, he thought the man standing with Lady Ailinn in the courtyard to be Lord Lyting. He realized now 'twas Lord Rurik and was astonished Ailénor's family had been able to track them here.

Joining Lord Lyting, Garreth crouched down behind the stone cell—the entrance chamber leading to the *souterrain*—and exchanged a brief nod of greeting.

"I feared you to be dead," Lord Lyting whispered.

"Nearly so, but for the grace of God."

Garreth edged to the corner of the structure and glimpsed the scene in the courtyard. He started to rise at the sight of Rhiannon pulling Ailénor along the wall to the top of the steps, pressing the cold steel against her flesh.

"Easy, son." Lyting stayed him, gripping him by the shoulder. "Patience. Lady Ailinn will try to lure Rhiannon from Ailénor's side. If I can get a clear shot, I'll take Rhiannon down. Meanwhile, Rurik is prepared to do what he must. Our crewmen are in position as well."

Garreth glanced again to Ailénor and saw her terror. He could not sit idly by and wait.

"An underground passage lies below. It opens onto the cliff's face. With luck, I can scale it. If Rhiannon can be drawn down the steps, I might be able to approach her unseen from behind." Seeing a look of concern cross Lord Lyting's features, he held up a hand. "I'll not risk Ailénor or place her in further peril. Upon my oath."

Lord Lyting agreed but signaled to one of his men. "Take Hamar with you. He has the ropes and grapples that saw us over the walls."

Garreth started to turn, then seeing the sword lying where he had dropped it, he caught it up and gave it over to Lord Lyting.

"Mayhap this will be of some use to you. 'Twas Varya's, Rhiannon's barbarian consort."

"*Was*?"

"Was," Garreth confirmed. Bidding Hamar to follow, he slipped around to the cell's entrance and descended into the *souterrain.*

Ailinn suppressed her horror at the sight of her daughter being held, her hands bound behind her, a knife at her heart. Suppressed her shock and outrage at the sight of Rhiannon, scarred and witchlike, holding the blade there.

Ailinn blocked the images from her mind and armored herself for the trial at hand. Iron-hearted, she stepped from Rurik's side to the center of the enclosure.

"I have come, Rhiannon." Her voice rang out in the courtyard. "Ailénor is innocent of anything that lies between us. Let her go."

Rhiannon pulled Ailénor along the wall to the top of the steps, her green eyes burning into Ailinn, fever-bright, her look triumphant. A shrill of laughter rose from her throat.

"Ailinn of the Érainn!" she exulted. "Long have I awaited this day."

"As have I," Ailinn returned, steel in her tone. "Ever since your men seized Ailénor."

The words brought Rhiannon up short, and an unreadable look flickered across her eyes. She lifted a brow.

"A mistake," she tossed lightly with no real remorse. Her smile turned reptilian. " 'Twas you they sought."

"And I am here. But Ailénor is not part of this. Release her. Then shall we see this to an end, the two of us."

"Yes," Rhiannon hissed, forcing Ailénor down another step. "Yes. The two of us. To an end."

Again Ailinn moved forward, stopping a short distance from the stone steps. Rhiannon's eyes glittered with anticipation, and she began to compel Ailénor down yet another step. But Ailénor suddenly braced her feet against the stone and resisted Rhiannon's prodding.

"Non, maman!" Ailénor cried out. "Stay back! She will kill you!"

Rhiannon's piercing laugh filled the air. "How touching," she exclaimed with venomous delight. "The mother seeks to save the daughter. And the daughter the mother." Her eyes cut to the hooded man. "Has the father naught to say?"

Not waiting an answer, she broke into fresh laughter. But her laughter died as abruptly as it had begun, her mood shifting tempest-quick. Securing her grip on Ailénor, she slashed Ailinn with eyes that had turned to daggers.

"Look on me! I am back from the dead. I have endured a living hell these many years on the Steppe. But I refused to be conquered and I lived for my revenge. Now I am returned, and this day shall I take it and savor it to the full.

"Look on me!" she repeated, turning her head to expose

the scars marring her cheek and neck. "Look on me! I was enslaved, violated, disfigured, and abused in ways you cannot begin to imagine. The lot I bore should have been yours!"

Ailinn recoiled before Rhiannon's vehemence. Never had she understood the seeds of Rhiannon's hatred for herself. Seeds that were present from the beginning, manifest in the first moments they met, long ago in Clonmel.

Rhiannon had nurtured her hatreds and denied reality as it suited her, possessing a great capacity to twist things to justify and believe whatever she wanted. But over these many years, Rhiannon's hatreds and self-deceptions had ultimately driven her to madness as she continued to blame everyone else for her misfortune.

Non, Ailinn corrected. Rhiannon blamed all her ills upon herself—Ailinn of the Érainn—alone. How could she reason with a madwoman?

" 'Twas not I who caused you to be enslaved, Rhiannon. We were *all* captured that day in Clonmel and lost our power over our destinies. On the Dnieper, when the horsemen attacked, you were not chained with the other women and easily carried away."

"No! No! It should have been you! I pushed you into their path that they might take you. But again you defied fate. Then, and earlier with the Norsemen. You alone were spared their lusts. You bewitched them, as you did my people—you and your mother—with your temptress looks and manipulative ways, both of you naught but lowly Érainn. I spit on you!"

Garreth and Hamar worked apace, securing a length of rope through the iron rings embedded in the wall and fastening its end about his waist. Additional rope had been found in the storage chests, lining the passage wall, and proved amply long to make the climb.

The women's voices sounded from above, but Garreth could understand naught of their Gaelic tongue. He stepped toward the cave opening, wondering whether Rhiannon had yet moved from the wall.

"Mayhap this will be of use," Hamar said behind him, offering him the grappling hook. "Mayhap you can hook the witch's foot and drag her over."

Garreth declined with a shake of his head. " 'Twould be too risky for Ailénor's sake."

Frustratingly, like Lord Lyting, Garreth found himself trapped in the moment, waiting upon circumstance. He hoped Lady Ailinn and Lord Rurik would be successful in luring Rhiannon from Ailénor's side.

Grasping on to the wall at the cave's opening, he leaned out slightly and glanced up the face of the cliff. 'Twas rugged with little on which to grab hold. Mayhap 'twas sheer madness to attempt the climb. He had no solid plans even should he reach the top.

Ailénor's voice sounded from above, a desperate and pleading cry, followed by Rhiannon's shrill laughter. Garreth's whole being went rigid. He could not waste another moment. Somehow he must reach her.

Ailénor sucked in her breath as Rhiannon's nails bit into her arm and the knife pressed into her flesh. The woman continued to rant at her mother in a stinging voice, her words filled with loathing but lacking rationality.

Ailénor dropped her glance over the edge of the stone steps, ignoring the leap of her pulse, and visually measured the distance. She and Rhiannon still stood high above the ground. If only they descended a few more steps, she might be able to wrench from Rhiannon's hold and jump free. But with her hands tied behind her, she could not use them to break her fall. Likely, she would only succeed in breaking her neck.

Ailénor looked to her mother and then her uncle. Rhiannon was not wise to their deception. Somewhere near, her father waited, she was sure of it. She could sense his presence. But not Garreth's. Anguish tore at her heart afresh. God in heaven, what had become of him?

Rhiannon forced her down another step. "You stole my rightful place!" she blazed at her mother.

Suddenly Rhiannon fell silent—too silent—and shifted

behind her. Ailénor rapidly scanned the courtyard to see what could be amiss. Her gaze fell on her uncle. His hood had slipped back slightly, enough for the morning's rising sun to gild the bright golden hair framing his face.

"What trick is this?" Rhiannon shrieked, hauling Ailénor backward, up several steps. "Who are you? Who? I say." She raised the knife from Ailénor's chest to her throat.

"I am Rurik Atlison. 'Tis my ship that brought Ailinn here to Cahercommaun."

As Ailénor rendered his words to Gaelic, her uncle stepped to her mother's side.

"And where is Lyting Atlison?" Rhiannon snapped. "The two of you are obviously kinsmen. Do not lie to me and tell me he is not here. I saw him standing on the shore below."

When neither Rurik nor Ailinn immediately replied, Rhiannon scrutinized the courtyard, twisting right and left, holding Ailénor firmly in her grasp.

"Come forth," she bellowed, "or the girl dies!"

Lyting stepped into view, emerging from behind the stone structure that led to the *souterrain*. He remained there, not joining the others.

" 'Tis over, Rhiannon," he called out.

Ailénor conveyed his words to Rhiannon. She hissed as additional men stepped forward from the shadows of the buildings. Ailénor recognized them to be seamen in service to her uncle. Disappointed, she realized Garreth was not among them.

"Naught is over!" Rhiannon retorted. "If you wish your daughter to live, you will do as I say."

"Varya!" Rhiannon called out. When he did not appear, she shouted all the louder. "Blinne! Send Varya to me."

"Varya is dead," Lyting proclaimed.

Ailénor had yet to translate his words when her father reached behind the stone structure and brought forth the curved sword of the barbarian. He held it high for Rhiannon to see.

"Dead."

Rhiannon screeched at the sight of the sword, knowing as did Ailénor that Varya would never part with it unless he was truly dead.

But if he was dead, what of Garreth? Ailénor agonized. And how had the sword come into her father's possession?

Rhiannon spewed a string of curses and oaths, then abruptly broke into a keening wail, only to stop again and scourge those below with her tongue.

Again Lyting spoke, this time Ailinn rendering his words. "There is no one to protect you now, Rhiannon. Varya is dead. You have no guard and are outnumbered. There is no escape. Release Ailénor unharmed, and no harm will befall you."

"Harm? Hah!" The words vaulted from Rhiannon's throat. "Do you think your punishments worry me? What pain can you possibly inflict that I have not already endured? Pain is naught to me. Nor do I fear it."

Rhiannon drew Ailénor with her up the last step and onto the wall. "But I will not be denied my revenge. Ailinn must pay. And so must you, Lyting Atlison, for spurning me on the banks of the Dnieper."

The tone of Rhiannon's voice changed again, growing strained, tormented. "I am Rhiannon," she protested to the heavens. "Princess of the Casil-Eóganachts, daughter of the great *ruri ri* Mór, once destined to sit at Domnal's side as Queen of Cashel."

Again her mood shifted, her grip tightening on Ailénor as her choler returned. " 'Twas your fault, Ailinn, that I was ruined that day. The Norsemen mistook you for me, sparing you and despoiling me. It should have been you they defiled. I *wish* it had been you! Why should you, a lowly Érainn, dwell in luxury while I was cast into darkness?

"I have waited for my revenge and I shall have it," she continued bitterly. "And 'twill be an even better vengeance than first I planned. I can torture you for a time and kill you but once. But both your souls shall writhe in ceaseless agony and die ten thousand times when I take your daughter's life."

"And the moment you do, Rhiannon," Lyting's voice sounded, "your life will be forfeit, too."

Ailénor dared cast a glance in her father's direction, moving only her eyes. She beheld him with his bow raised and drawn taut, his arrow anchored on its target with deadly precision.

Rhiannon gave a derisive laugh as Ailinn related Lyting's warning. "Surely I shall die. But not by any of your hands. The day *is* still mine. I'll not be robbed of my revenge."

For a hair's breadth of a moment, the knife blade slackened at Ailénor's throat, but at the same time Rhiannon hooked her arm through Ailénor's and stepped back. Ailénor's feet jerked from the stone wall, and together they plunged through the air, Rhiannon dragging her down like an anchor, the cliff face blurring before Ailénor's eyes.

Pain shot through Ailénor—feet, legs, hip, and shoulder—as something solid broke her fall and she crumpled atop it. A bird flapped away at the invasion, and Rhiannon grunted near her feet.

Ailénor gasped for breath but otherwise remained motionless, astounded she was still alive. Gazing heavenward to the top of the cliff, she saw they had not fallen as far as she thought.

Carefully she turned her head. And instantly froze as she realized she lay on a narrow shelf, jutting from the cliff's face high above the sea. Ailénor pressed back against the cliff, wholly petrified.

Lying facedown at Ailénor's feet, Rhiannon raised herself partially, spitting grit out of her mouth. She took her bearings, then drew her gaze toward Ailénor. Slowly she braced herself up on her elbows, bringing into view the knife she still clutched in her hand. Rhiannon smiled a thin serpent's smile, one of victory.

"You cannot escape me," she rasped, then coughed, an unpleasant, wheezing sound. "The day . . . is yet mine."

With a fevered look, Rhiannon thrust upward, raising the knife and lunging for Ailénor. But as her weight shifted, the shelf crumbled. Rhiannon clawed for Ailénor but caught only air as she plummeted from sight. Her scream echoed down the cliff. Then ceased altogether.

Ailénor forgot to breathe. Paralyzed with shock and fear, she remained flattened against the cliff wall, her heart pounding in her chest, certain the remaining shelf would dissolve beneath her any second. She closed her eyes, terrified for what was to come.

Truly Rhiannon would yet reap her revenge this day.

Garreth leapt back as something hurtled past the opening of the cave. Dropping to his knees, he leaned out and looked down. His heart skipped to his throat as he beheld Ailénor and Rhiannon lying on a narrow projection.

As he watched, Rhiannon rose up, a knife flashing in her hand. But in the same instant, the ledge broke apart. Garreth almost lost his grip on the edge of the cave floor as chunks of the cliff and a figure he knew to be Rhiannon hurtled to the sea.

But where was Ailénor? He could not catch sight of her. He searched the waters below, then glanced again to the cliff face. His heart jolted once more as he saw her—just barely—pressed against the cliff on a tiny lip of stone.

"Hamar, quickly," he called.

Hamar joined him in an instant and glanced down. Just as rapidly, he rose and took hold of the rope, measuring out a liberal length and anchoring it about his waist. "I'll feed the line to you," he said hastily as he moved to the wall and gripped the iron rings. "Go! *Allez, allez!*"

Garreth took a firm hold of the rope tied about him. Standing with his back to the sea, he leapt backward out of the mouth of the cave and dropped through the air. As the rope went tight, Garreth swung back toward the wall, cushioning the impact with his legs.

"*Allez!*" Hamar shouted from above.

Again Garreth pushed off and felt the rope slacken as Hamar released it from the top. Garreth dropped dozens more feet, jolting to a stop just below Ailénor. She lay on a ledge off to his right, her eyes squeezed tight. Bit by bit, the shelf was disintegrating, its rubble falling like dark, gritty hailstones to the sea below. 'Twould give way any moment.

Planting his feet firmly on the face of the cliff, Garreth gripped the rope tight and "ran" across the rock to the left, picking up momentum. When he had gone far enough, he kicked out and swung back to the right. Passing wide of Ailénor, he grasped at the irregularities of the cliff's surface to slow his speed and pull himself closer to its face. His direction reversed, and he began to skim left. As he came in line with Ailénor, he reached out and seized her about the waist, snatching her from the shelf just as it dissolved.

Ailénor screamed, her eyes flying open, as they swung through the air and began to spin. Garreth held her locked in his muscled strength as they continued to whirl, using his legs to keep them from slamming against the rock.

"I've got you, love. I've got you," he avowed, panting for breath. "I'll not let you fall. Not ever, my darling. Trust me."

Stunned and disoriented as they hung suspended in air, Ailénor focused on Garreth. Her eyes went wide, then began to spill great tears.

"Garreth, you're alive! You're alive!" She lay her head against his chest and wept for joy.

As Garreth held tight to Ailénor, Hamar called from above, saying the others had joined him and promising to draw them up in no time. With so many devoted to the effort, Garreth and Ailénor found themselves rising swiftly up the escarpment. Garreth looked skyward and now saw that Lady Ailinn and Lord Lyting watched them from Cahercommaun's wall.

As they verged on the mouth of the cave, a half-dozen hands lay hold to them and pulled them to safety—the two strongest proving to belong to Lord Rurik. The men lifted Garreth and Ailénor as one into the passage. Rurik immediately cut the bindings from Ailénor's hands.

"Have you any sharp pain anywhere, Ailénor? Have you broken any bones?"

"*Non*, Uncle," she replied in a small, whispery voice.

"Though I am bruised to the bone and more than a little shaky."

"As well you should be. Quiet now."

Rurik turned his attention to Garreth and, together with Hamar, helped him unlock his arms from Ailénor. Garreth gritted his teeth at the pain and stiffness his muscles harbored for having been tested so long.

Easing Ailénor from Garreth's side, Rurik bid Hamar and Torfi to attend him, then examined his niece's injuries.

"Ailénor! Ailénor!" Ailinn's voice echoed in the passage.

Ailénor looked up as her parents appeared and rushed to her side.

Gently Ailinn enfolded her daughter in her arms. "My child. Oh, my child," she whispered brokenly.

Lyting stroked Ailénor's hair and uttered endearments, then, overcome with emotion, slipped his arms protectively around both his ladies.

After much embracing and shedding of tears, and effusive praise and thankfulness to Garreth for his courageous efforts in saving Ailénor, the party abandoned the *souterrain*, their joy unbounded.

Once in the courtyard, Rurik dispersed his crew to seek those dwelling in the hill-fort, then suggested they inspect the various buildings. Ailénor visibly paled.

"I have no desire to return inside Rhiannon's lair." She drew her arms about herself as though chilled.

"Nor do I," Garreth added solemnly, then looked to her parents. "I shall accompany Ailénor outside the walls and wait with her by the outermost gate." A smile touched his lips. "We would welcome the rest."

Lyting nodded his understanding, then turned to Ailinn. "Do you wish to join them while I assist the others?"

"*Non.*" Her eyes darkened with her thoughts. "Long ago, certain belongings of my mother disappeared. I always suspected Rhiannon to have taken them. Mayhap we shall find them here, among those things she brought from Clonmel. I should like to look for them."

As the couples parted, and Garreth escorted Ailénor toward the gate, Ailinn's gaze lingered after them with motherly interest.

She had not missed the warmth that appeared in her daughter's eyes each time she looked on Garreth. Now, as the two passed through the gate, she observed Garreth lifting his hand to Ailénor's waist. 'Twas not an impersonal gesture bred by good manners, but a protective, possessive one. The corners of Ailinn's mouth drew upward in a meditative smile.

"*Elskan mín*, do you come?"

Ailinn glanced to Lyting and found him holding out his hand to her.

"*Mais oui.*" She joined him at once and, taking his hand, entered Rhiannon's hall.

Outside the hill-fort, Ailénor and Garreth settled down in the shade of its wall. As they waited, Ailénor grew quiet, somber. Slipping an arm about her, Garreth drew her against him.

"Does something trouble you, my heart?"

A single tear slid over her cheek. "Oh, Garreth, I thought you were dead. I thought Varya . . ."

"Shhh, now," Garreth soothed, dropping a kiss to her head. " 'Tis a long, unpleasant tale that can wait for a later time." Garreth glanced down at his ruined clothes, covered with peat, then at Ailénor's. "Ah, my heart. Look what I have done to your gown."

Ailénor likewise glanced at her sullied clothes, the front darkened with the peat.

"A small price for so gallant a rescue." She smiled up at him and fingered away a tear. "At least, since 'tis already soiled, you will have no worry holding me." Her gaze dropped to his lips. "And I feel greatly in need of being held . . . and kissed . . . just now."

Garreth's heart warmed with love. "Let it never be said I denied my lady."

As his mouth moved over hers and tasted her sweetness, Ailénor's arms stole upward around his neck.

*   *   *

While Rurik and the crewmen spoke with the servants, informing them they were now free, Lyting and Ailinn explored Rhiannon's chambers. The search yielded naught of the brooches and rings Ailinn sought, but she was content to have looked for them and know she did not leave them behind.

As Lyting collected his weapons, Ailinn paused at the portal in the hall. Finding her deep in thought, he placed an arm around her shoulder.

"Elskan mín?"

Ailinn continued to gaze into the courtyard and smiled softly. "I have a feeling Ailénor and Garreth care for one another in a special way."

"A special way?"

She brought her eyes to his. " 'Tis not surprising, my love. They were drawn to one another from the first, when they met in Rouen, and they've spent considerable time since. 'Tis natural their feelings should blossom."

"Blossom?" Lyting's brow deepened.

Ailinn gave a light laugh and, raising on tiptoe, kissed Lyting's cheek. *"Blossom,"* she repeated with certainty.

Lyting slung his bow and quiver of arrows to his back, then caught up the barbarian's sword from where it rested, propped against the framework of the door.

"Garreth should have this," he said pensively, changing the subject.

"He might not want the reminder." Ailinn gave a shudder at the wicked-looking blade.

"Still, I should offer it."

"Bien. Why don't you ask him? They are outside the gate. I'll see if Rurik and the men are ready to leave. I shall also convey our thoughts concerning the wealth of Rhiannon's possessions—that they should be distributed among the poor souls forced to serve her. I am certain the others will agree 'tis the compassionate thing to do."

Lyting traversed the courtyard and passed through the triple gates. As he emerged from the last, his feet took root. Garreth and Ailénor were consumed in a passionate kiss—she lying partially atop Garreth, he with his hand resting intimately upon her backside. Garreth caressed her, but rather than shrinking from the familiarity, Ailénor pressed against him with a moan of pleasure.

Lyting roared an oath in Norse, his bellow sending the two jolting apart.

Ailénor flushed furiously. "Father, I . . . we . . ."

The guilty looks they both wore told Lyting all he needed or wanted to know. Ailénor was no longer a virgin, and the man before him was the one who had made it so!

Furious at the discovery and already taxed beyond his limits this day, Lyting shouted back terse orders to the crewmen who were just now emerging from the gate. Surprise lit their faces, but they obeyed his commands, unsheathing their blades and hastening to surround Garreth.

Rurik and Ailinn hurried to join them, shocked to see the events unfolding. But Lyting would brook no interference in the matter, his paternal sensibilities outraged.

"*BroFir*, I enjoin you to sail with Ailénor and her mother for Valsemé and await my arrival. I shall take the ship we found grounded on the shore below and Lars and Geir to help man it. I shall also take Garreth. 'Twould seem Ailénor fared little better among the Saxons than the Irish."

Raising the barbarian's sword, Lyting signaled the men to conduct Garreth toward the cliff path and lead him down to the sea. He then turned on his heel, his jaw set like granite.

"Garreth is my captive now."

Chapter Sixteen

Never in his life had Garreth sailed at such great speed. But never had he sailed with the man called Sjorefurinn, the Sea Fox. And, at the moment, Sjorefurinn—Lord Lyting—was one very angry father.

The ship slipped down the southwestern coast of Ireland and skimmed across the Celtic Sea, fleet as an arrow. On it raced, gaining the Channel waters as it passed the tip of the Penwith Peninsula and pressed relentlessly onward.

With consummate skill, Lord Lyting commanded the ship from his position at the tiller. Ingeniously he had rigged the sheeting lines through the oar holes, running them astern and enabling him to control the sails from where he sat. At the same time, he navigated the ship with the steering board.

Garreth had never seen the like. He also recognized that the presence of the two other seamen aboard was likely more to guard himself than to assist Lord Lyting in any points of sailing.

Time skipped past, and soon the ship closed on Francia's coast and entered the mouth of one of its rivers. Well into the night of the second day, it docked beneath a high bailey wall of pale limestone.

As they disembarked, a half-dozen men-at-arms hastened to meet the count, giving Garreth to realize he stood now before Chastel de Héricourt. On Lord Lyting's orders, the soldiers removed Garreth straightaway to a chamber, high in Héricourt's tower keep. There Garreth remained, locked and guarded, while Ailénor's father presumably cooled his fury elsewhere.

Garreth found little rest during the remainder of the night. As little, it would seem, as Lord Lyting. From the chamber's window slit, he saw the count pace the sentry walk in the twilight just before dawn. At sunrise, Lord Lyting rode out and galloped along the river, not to return until many hours later.

Midafternoon, the guard opened the door long enough to set a platter of food and skin of wine inside. Garreth chafed at his confinement, but not until nightfall did the guard again unlock the door. This time he conducted Garreth to the keep's main chamber, one level below.

Lord Lyting awaited Garreth in the stark room, pacing its confines. The keep, being a defensive stronghold and storehouse for times of siege, held few furnishings. Two chairs had been positioned in the center of the room, facing one another. The count gestured for Garreth to assume one of them, though he himself crossed to the window and looked out. For a moment he stood silent, turning his thoughts. When he finally spoke, his gaze remained fixed to the distance.

"Ailénor's mother was once a captive, carried off from

her home by Danish raiders and enslaved.''

Whatever Garreth expected the count to say, 'twas not this. ''Ailénor has told me some of the story and how you sailed with Lady Ailinn to the east and freed her.''

Lyting nodded, then turned from the window and met Garreth's gaze with solemn eyes.

''Understanding the realities of captivity and its darkest aspects as we do, I cannot begin to describe for you our anguish when Ailénor disappeared. At first we even considered you might have taken her.''

The comment took Garreth aback. Before he could reply, Lyting raised his hand and forestalled him.

''We quickly concluded you did not. Still, we know little of what actually befell Ailénor at the ducal palace, and nothing beyond the time she vanished from Rouen. I would hear that tale now.'' Lord Lyting left the window and seated himself on the chair opposite Garreth. ''Shall we begin with what drew Ailénor to the garden at dawn?''

Garreth cleared his voice, once more caught short by Lord Lyting's questions, but glad for the opportunity to explain what had occurred.

''My business in Rouen concluded rather abruptly. With little time for farewells, Ailénor and I agreed to meet in the garden, just before I was to sail.'' Garreth avoided mentioning their powerful attraction to one another. ''When I arrived, Ailénor was not present, nor did she appear. Much later, I learned she had already been seized by Rhiannon's men.''

Lyting listened intently as Garreth described the events that unfolded—Grimbold's and Wimund's presence aboard ship when he arrived at the docks, his later discovery of Ailénor in the hold, their crossing, and the sudden, violent storm that overtook them and proved to be their salvation.

''We escaped into the village of Hamwih and took refuge in a mill on the edge of town. 'Twas three-storied and had a loft high in the rafters. We climbed up and passed the remainder of the night there.''

The count's brows drew slowly together. Garreth silently

rebuked himself for calling attention to the loft. By Lord Lyting's look, 'twas obvious he surmised correctly 'twas the very place he had deflowered Ailénor.

"With Rhiannon's hirelings breathing down our necks, we needed to find a place to hide ourselves away," Garreth added hastily. "It seemed the best solution at the time."

Lyting held Garreth with an unblinking gaze, his look inscrutable. "My daughter, did she . . . ?"

Garreth stiffened, his every instinct vaulting to protect Ailénor. "Sir, what passed between your daughter and myself in the loft . . .'twas not her fault."

Now Lord Lyting did blink, and his brows deepened as well. "You are admitting you seduced her?"

An image of Ailénor eager and passionate and oh-so-willing in his arms flooded Garreth's mind.

"The seduction was mine, sir. She is innocent. I pray you hold her to no blame."

Lord Lyting rose, pondering Garreth for a prolonged moment, his lips compressed, his hand flexing at his side.

" 'Twas not my intent to question you about what transpired in the loft. With Ailénor's fear of heights, I only found it surprising she would attempt such a climb. But now that you have opened the matter of having been intimate with her, I would know if there is aught else you wish to say."

Garreth steeled himself against Lord Lyting's eyes as they bore into him. Garreth gained the distinct impression he waited for him to voice something in particular. But what more could he add? Garreth drew a bracing breath.

"Sir, I have led your daughter astray. I stand ready to take complete and sole responsibility for my actions."

A coldness settled over Lord Lyting like a mantle, and his eyes cooled to chips of ice. "Indeed, you shall." Plainly unsatisfied with the answer, his anger returned.

At his signal the guards came forward and removed Garreth, returning him to his chamber above and leaving him to wonder of the new source of the count's displeasure.

*   *   *

Once again, in the early-morning hours, Lord Lyting frequented the sentry walk, then rode out at dawn.

Garreth glimpsed him in the field outside the wall, working his horses—magnificent animals, more impressive than the best of England's stock. At times the count would look up toward the keep. Garreth could feel the bite of his eyes and felt certain the count could see him standing at the slender window.

The day lengthened, and Garreth was left to himself to ponder his transgression. As the skies deepened, the guard appeared and unlocked the door. Once more, Garreth found himself escorted to the chamber below.

Torches blazed in iron brackets, causing shadows to chase over the walls and around the edges of the room. The two chairs from yesterday remained in the center of the floor, this time with trestles set between and upon them a large gaming board.

Lord Lyting sat over the board, setting out hefty playing pieces on its field of squares, these of alternating colors. He appeared composed, his mood tempered. Garreth could only hope the count had alleviated his anger in his earlier physical exertions. Mayhap 'twas why this meeting and the one before took place so late in the day. Ailénor's father was, after all, a born and bred Northman, a Dane. Garreth could think of few men more dangerous than an irate father with Norse blood boiling in his veins.

Lord Lyting motioned Garreth to sit.

"This is the game of *shah*. I brought it with me from Constantinople. 'Tis a Persian game. A war game, actually. *Shah* in Persian means 'King.' The object of the game is to capture the opponent's king. The board shall be our battlefield."

Something in the way Lord Lyting said the last made Garreth look up. He wondered what the count was about. Were they to execute their personal battle upon the board? Was the count testing him in yet some other way? Or might he be using the diversion to further hold rein on his temper? Garreth found little choice but to oblige him and attempt the game.

Lord Lyting finished positioning two ivory "armies"—
one white, one gold—on opposite sides of the board and
explained the movements each piece might make.

"You will learn best by experience." The count demonstrated leading out one of his foot soldiers.

The first game ended four moves later as Lord Lyting
devoured Garreth's men on the board. On the second try,
Garreth concentrated more fully, wondering again why they
were engaging in the game, but appreciating its complexi-
ties that duly tasked one's mental abilities.

During the brief course of the second game, he got a
rough feel for the moves of the pieces, and even though
Lord Lyting trounced him thoroughly, Garreth found he
looked forward to another try, enjoying the challenge. His
confidence building, they began a third round. Garreth
reached for one of his foot soldiers.

"I know from my brother your true purpose in coming
to Normandy." Lord Lyting spoke with calm deliberation.
"As you have admitted to being intimate with my daughter,
I believe, as her father and guardian, I am entitled to know
just exactly who you are."

Garreth's concentration splintered, and he set the gaming
piece down randomly on a square. He raised his eyes to
the count.

"I am no *ceorl* if that concerns you. As to my lineage,
my father was *heah gerefa*, high reeve of Aylesbury. I am
a *thegn* of high station, one of the select officers of the
Hird, the king's elite guard. I am also soon to be elevated
to *Ealdorman* of Hamtunscir, if 'tis of any consolation.
Ailénor did not lose her maidenhead to a commoner."

" 'Tis no consolation for a daughter to be seduced by a
man of any rank," the count said bluntly, then removed
Garreth's foot soldier with his horseman. Silence hung
thick between them. "Why did you send no word from
England once you eluded Rhiannon's men?"

Again Lord Lyting's question came swift and to the
point. Garreth moved another piece upon the board as he
began to describe Ailénor's and his flight to Winchester and
the incidents that occurred thereafter.

He had not intended to reveal as much as he did in the end, but Lord Lyting continued to fire question upon question, deftly prying the answers from him. 'Twas as though, for Lord Lyting, doing two things at once—playing the mentally demanding game and interrogating Garreth— served to sharpen his mind to a keen edge. For Garreth's part the experience was mentally exhausting. 'Twas a mind game Lord Lyting played as move by move, play by play, question by question, he extracted information from his opponent.

In the course of things, Garreth disclosed Cynric's part and how he himself had come under suspicion for embracing Duke William's and Lord Rurik's view on the question of restoring young Louis to the Frankish throne. He went on to explain how his attempts to contact Normandy failed, and how he felt bound to wait on the king's decision, averse to circumventing his sovereign's authority. He hoped the count appreciated his position.

As the game pieces disappeared from the board— mostly Garreth's, but a number of the count's as well— Garreth began to detail Ailénor's removal from Winchester to Andover, her escape, and how they came to be in Lundenburh.

In disclosing the king's order to transfer her to Andover, Garreth quickly defended his king's action, stating his belief 'twas Athelstan's intention to distance her from Cynric's authority and examine the matter when he returned. But when Mora's and Rosalynd's part came to light—how in their jealousy they had arranged Ailénor's escape—Lord Lyting came forward in his chair.

"Jealous? How so? Do they have legitimate claims on you?"

"In their minds alone," Garreth assured. "They believed I would choose one of them for my wife."

Fire flashed in Lord Lyting's eyes. "You had *two* other women waiting at the altar when you seduced my Ailénor?"

"'Twas not the way of it at all," Garreth countered hastily, then explained the circumstances that had entangled him with the king's kinswomen. The tension eased visibly from the count's shoulders, and judging by the twitching around the corners of his mouth, Garreth believed Lord Lyting found his predicament more than a little amusing.

Garreth continued his story, telling of the second near abduction of Ailénor on the road to Silchester and of his overcoming Grimbold. He skipped ahead in his story and told of his decision to help Ailénor leave England and of their abduction in Lundenburh and transferral to Ireland. But Lord Lyting returned to the subject of Silchester and their stay in Lundenburh, leveling a volley of shrewd questions until Garreth again fell into the trap of revealing more intimacies with Ailénor.

" 'Twas not a single seduction then, but many?'' Lord Lyting raised a questioning brow. Garreth attempted no reply. "I assume Ailénor was a willing participant?"

"She owns no fault in the matter," Garreth returned stoutly, chafing under the ceaseless questions, angry at himself for having revealed so much, and his patience worn thin. He recognized Lord Lyting pressed him apurpose, trying to wring from him some further confession, but he knew not what he sought.

They both sat over the board in frustration. A muscle worked in Lord Lyting's jaw as he studied the board.

Weary, Garreth broke the silence, hoping to bring the discussion to a close. "I believe you know the rest—except perhaps that Rhiannon ordered Varya to kill me. Suffice it to say, we had an encounter with a peat bog. Varya lost."

Lyting directed a glance at Garreth's grimy clothes. "Is that what that is?"

Garreth nodded. "As I said, you know the rest."

"Except that which I need know most of all."

Garreth vented a breath. "I have told you everything and more."

"Not *everything*." Lord Lyting moved his empress piece obliquely along three squares. "Watch your *shah*."

Garreth flicked a glance over the king, then returned his gaze to the count, supremely frustrated, a headache throbbing at his temples. He was tired of playing games.

"You pick my brains for hours, then tell me I have not told you that which you wish to hear?"

Garreth shoved to his feet and held the count with a hard gaze.

"I've admitted to seducing Ailénor. I've vowed to take full responsibility for my actions and whatever punishment you deem proper. What more do you seek? My regret? I do not regret having made love to Ailénor, and I would do so again and again. I love her, more than life itself. And she loves me. We pledged ourselves to one another in the church at Silchester. It had no altar and was a crumbling ruin. The roof was open clear to the heavens. But God heard our vows, of that I am sure. And he knows our hearts. Do to me what you will, but my love for Ailénor, and hers for me, will remain, burning pure and bright in our hearts."

Lyting slowly rose to his feet, his gaze locking with Garreth's. He studied him closely.

"You will accept full responsibility for your actions, no matter the cost?"

"No matter the cost."

"So be it."

Lord Lyting reached down toward the board and displaced Garreth's king with his empress.

"*Shah mat,*" he said. "The game is at an end. Your king is forfeit."

Lord Lyting turned to the guards by the door, speaking rapidly in Norse. Garreth barely grasped the words but believed he called for pen and parchment.

The count started for the door, energy and purpose in his step. "We sail at dawn," he declared as he closed on the portal. He suddenly halted and turned back, tossing a glance to Garreth, then addressed the guard beside him.

"But before then, see he has a bath."

VALSEMÉ

Ailénor gazed out the window in her aunt's solar, scanning the view of verdant hills rolling in the distance, and a portion of the River Toques that sparkled with sunlight. It appeared as though a thousand diamonds had been scattered over its surface.

She rested her head against the side of the window, her thoughts reaching to Héricourt and to Garreth. What was her father doing to him?

"Come, darling," her mother spoke softly, moving to her side. "Join us for some perry. 'Tis sweet and cool and will refresh you."

Ailénor brought her eyes to her mother, her heart aching. But before she could speak, her mother lifted a hand to gently touch her cheek.

" 'Twill be all right, sweetheart. You will see."

"But, *Papa* . . ."

"Your father loves you deeply, Ailénor. Nothing can change that."

"But what of Garreth? Oh, *Maman*, *Papa* must be very angry with him. With us both. Do you think he would . . ."

"I think we must trust your father's judgment. He will strive to do only what is best for you."

"But not so for Garreth, I fear."

Ailinn slipped an arm around her daughter and gave her a hug. "I know of no man as just and fair as your father. Except, perhaps, your uncle. It may be more difficult for him to battle through his anger for he is very protective of his family, especially of his ladies. Have faith in him. Has he ever failed us?"

Ailénor wiped the moisture that had slipped from her eyes and shook her head. *"Non, maman."*

Ailinn gave her another squeeze. "Come, then, and see Marielle's needlework. She has almost finished the border on her new gown."

Ailénor followed her mother and rejoined the others who gathered in the solar with their sewing. Her Aunt Brienne and cousin Gisèle worked edgings on pillow casings, while Marielle put the finishing touches to the hem of her rose-colored dress.

Ailénor's sister Etainn did not join them, of course, being

too impatient to work a needle. Instead she had taken Lucán and Michan to the mews to instruct them in falconry. Felise tended the youngest of the children outside in the fresh air of the garden. Adelis and Brietta, however, sat together, each with a small square of cloth, working daisies and stems with basic stitches.

Since returning to Normandy, Ailénor had kept to herself for the most part, finding it difficult to face the ceaseless questions and attention of others. Only her mother, Uncle Rurik, and Aunt Brienne knew of her embarrassment—that she had lain with Garreth—and what had happened betwixt him and her father in Ireland.

Ailénor lifted the cup of perry to her lips just as a knock sounded at the door and her Uncle Rurik stepped inside the chamber.

"There is word," he said, his tone sober.

Ailinn clasped her daughter's hand in her own while Brienne quickly rose and went to Rurik. His eyes brushed hers, then he cast his glance toward Ailinn.

"Lyting requires Ailénor to be dressed and ready to face him by evenfall. He will make known his decision concerning Garreth then."

Brienne laid a hand to Rurik's arm as he started to leave. "Is that all?"

"For now," he returned, covering her hand with his and giving it a reassuring squeeze. "I have already ordered bathwater heated for Ailénor. It might be wise to search her coffers for something suitable for her to wear. I shall return when 'tis time."

With that Rurik dropped a swift kiss on Brienne's forehead and departed.

"Time for what?" Brienne called after him, mystified, then turned, her gaze seeking the others. "And suitable for what?"

Ailénor shifted her glance from her mother to her aunt as dread perched in her soul.

Ailinn rose, drawing up Ailénor and patting her on the hand. "I have no idea to what he refers. But I think in the face of the unknown, the best advice for a lady is to meet it looking her best!''

Brienne flashed a smile. ''I brought both of Ailénor's coffers from Rouen. Surely we will find something 'suitable' in them.''

''Given Lyting's temper when last I saw him, I think we need do far better than 'suitable.' '' Ailinn joined Brienne at the door. '' 'Fabulous' would be more helpful.''

''Certes. Fabuleuse,'' Brienne agreed. ''The gold gown is beautiful on Ailénor, do you not think? Of course, emerald-green would be striking.''

''Or blue, the color of sapphires,'' Ailinn submitted, caught up in the moment. She stopped, suddenly realizing Ailénor had yet to join them. ''Are you coming, darling? We really cannot begin without you.'' She gave a small, bright laugh, her first in weeks.

As Ailénor started to join her mother and aunt, Gisèle leaned toward Marielle.

''Father said Uncle Lyting made a decision concerning Garreth. Whatever did he do?''

Ailénor felt the heat rise from her toes to her cheeks. Without looking back, she hurried from the room.

Shades of lavender and orange streaked the evening skies as Lord Lyting's ship closed upon its destination.

Garreth looked to the stalwart tower looming in the near distance above an imposing fortress wall. As the ship put into shore, he could only wonder if he would next be immured in this bastion. Certainly this was the place Lord Lyting intended to mete out his judgment.

The count's dozen retainers aboard ship disembarked, joining a complement of Norman soldiers who waited fully armed upon the dock. At Lord Lyting's charge, Garreth rose and preceded him. The moment he stepped onto land, the soldiers surrounded him.

Lord Lyting shouted out an order, then side by side with Garreth accompanied him in the direction of the keep. For the moment the brooding tower was the only thing Garreth could see past the soldiers' helmeted heads and bristling spears.

As they continued, a buzz of voices swelled beyond the ranks. Garreth glimpsed a crowd collected there, straining to catch sight of him. His stomach rolled over. Obviously some spectacle was about to take place, and judging by their expressions, they did not intend to miss a second of it.

Garreth steeled himself. He knew little about Norman justice or what punishment might be demanded of a man who had ravished a nobleman's daughter. Might he face a simple flogging? Or something more untidy and permanent, like being put to the sword or even beheaded? He recoiled at the thought. Surely the Normans adhered to the more civilized system of *wergilds*, fines, for misdeeds. Did they not?

The land rose beneath his feet as the armed escort moved steadily in the direction of the bailey and keep. For a crowd who came to witness a public discipline, possibly torture or even death, Garreth thought them subdued—excited to be sure, but not unruly, as one might expect. When they arrived at what seemed to be an open area, a courtyard of some kind, the soldiers came to a halt, and the crowd fell silent. 'Twas that silence that sent an icy chill skidding along his spine. Garreth prepared himself for the worst.

Lord Lyting stood solemn beside him, gazing straight ahead as the soldiers parted their ranks and formed two straight lines, creating a passage with only one possible exit. Garreth glanced right and left at the expectant faces, then, drawing a breath, cast his glance to the very end of the line, expecting to find a flogging pole or some imaginative device for torture.

Garreth's heart catapulted as his eyes fell upon the fate that awaited him—Ailénor, a vision in sapphire and gold, standing upon the steps of a stone church. She looked every bit as shocked as he.

Beside her stood an aged churchman gripping his mass book in shaky hands, and to either side of the steps, Lady

Ailinn, Lord Rurik, Lady Brienne, and an assortment of Ailénor's siblings and cousins, even the maid Felise.

He returned his gaze to Ailénor and melded his eyes to hers. He thought her as entrancing as the day he first set eyes on her, if not more. Dear God, how he loved her.

Garreth remained rooted in place until Lord Lyting spoke beside him.

"You are not going to balk now, are you?"

"Balk?"

"You said you would accept full responsibility, *no matter the cost.* I expect you to marry my daughter."

Garreth struggled to find his tongue, incredulous at his great fortune. "And that I shall, sir. Upon my vow, I most definitely shall."

Garreth could no longer suppress his smile as he started forward, his pace quickening as he closed on the steps and leapt up them to join Ailénor. Before he could move to her side, the churchman positioned himself between them and cleared his throat noisily.

Ailénor's heart beat so fast she thought it might leap from her breast. Tears stung the back of her eyes, so happy, so relieved was she.

Beside her, Brother Bernard cleared his voice once more, raised his missal, then paused a moment and cut his eyes over the display of weapons with sharp disapproval. He started to object, she thought, but reconsidered when his gaze fell on her father who stood rigid and unyielding in his stance.

"Arms at a wedding," Brother Bernard muttered, then began the rites in his deep, gravelly voice.

Ailénor's eyes misted as she listened to the words of the ceremony and saw that Garreth's eyes shone as well as they pronounced their vows, their happiness overflowing.

"And now the ring," Brother Bernard opened his hand to Garreth.

Garreth faltered and glanced to Lord Lyting whose stern look changed to one of surprise, then chagrin as he realized he had forgotten this important detail. The wedding halted as those gathered sought a solution, looking to their hands for rings they might remove and lend the bride. Their own wedding bands, of course, would not suffice. Lord Rurik offered to return to the keep in search of one, but Ailénor stayed him.

"Wait, I have a ring. The perfect ring." She held forth her hand displaying the pearl and amethyst ring Garreth had presented her in Lundenburh the day they were to part—the symbol of their unremitting love and fidelity.

Slipping the ring from her finger, she gave it over to Brother Bernard. He, in turn, blessed the ring and passed it to Garreth.

Garreth's smile expanded as wide as his heart as he captured his bride's outstretched hand and slid the ring onto her fourth finger. He then closed his hand around hers, having no intention of releasing her.

Brother Bernard, noting his resolve, quickly pronounced them husband and wife.

As the words sank into Garreth's brain, he realized he was not without authority. Ailénor was his wife now and *he* her guardian. None could gainsay him in matters concerning her. Taking full advantage of his new status, Garreth pulled her toward him, causing Brother Bernard to take a pace back, and drew Ailénor into his arms. Covering her mouth with his, he claimed her in a deep and intentionally bone-melting kiss.

Garreth continued the kiss, aware of the murmurings and shiftings of those gathered about them. Ailénor dissolved against him, her arms sliding upward, circling his neck. 'Twas the churchman's forced coughing that prompted Garreth to finally end the kiss. When he released her, he had to support her by the waist to keep her upright. Looking up, he found the soldiery grinning wide, not to mention Lord Lyting and Lord Rurik.

Brother Bernard led the couple and the counts' families and friends into the church to complete the service with mass. Sometime later Garreth and Ailénor emerged to the jubilant ringing of Valsemé's bell and, amidst much gaiety and jollity, headed toward the keep.

As Rurik and Brienne issued from the church, they paused

outside the doors. Brienne looked up at her golden lord.

"It seems impossible, but twenty-one years past we exchanged our vows on this very step, my dearest."

Rurik caught up her hand to his lips. "And my love shines as bright for you this day."

Lyting and Ailinn materialized from the church just then, along with Lia and her family.

"Ho, brother," Lyting called, full of cheer. "Was it not at Ketil's wedding that I could barely pass around the two of you embracing on the steps? Need I remind you yet again there is serious feasting to which we must attend?"

Brienne looked up and scanned the church's facade with a happy sigh. "There have been so many occasions of joy in this church over the years—weddings, baptisms . . ."

"And I am certain we shall see many more." Rurik smiled, then looked to his brother. "What happened at Héricourt? I expected you far sooner and was beginning to think you had truly done something dire to the Saxon."

Lyting's lips curved in a pensive smile as their small group left the church. " 'Tis sore difficult to get some men to admit they love a woman. I satisfied myself Garreth was worthy of Ailénor in other ways, but I was not about to condemn her to a life of misery if he had simply taken advantage of her with no true care for her."

"I take it he passed your trials?" Rurik smiled once again.

"Passionately, when he finally admitted it. He was too busy defending her honor at first." Lyting tossed a glance to Rurik, humor stealing into his eyes. "But now that Garreth is a member of our family, I can tell you one thing. We need work on his skills at *shah*."

"Oh, Lyting." Ailinn laughed, slipping her arm in his. "You didn't draw and quarter him with questions over *that* game, did you? 'Twould drive a sane person mad!"

Laughter rippled through the group as they followed the procession toward the keep.

Garreth and Ailénor assumed the place of honor at the high table on the dais and presided over their hastily prepared wedding banquet. Many questions still remained unresolved for Garreth as to what might await him in England, or whether his new Norman in-laws intended to detain him further in Normandy.

He set the matter firmly aside. This night, of all nights, he would allow nothing to occupy his mind save his enchanting bride and the promise of the hours that lay ahead. He leaned toward her and dropped a kiss behind her ear.

Ailénor tingled to her toes at the warmth of Garreth's lips. 'Twas impossible to concentrate on the minstrel's song. Impossible to concentrate on anything save Garreth. Glancing up at him, she met his adoring eyes. Ailénor thought her heart would burst with happiness.

The feasting continued well into the night with everyone relaxed and in good cheer. Ailénor was glad to share her happiness with her family and those she had long known at Valsemé. Surprisingly, when the time for the bedding ceremony arrived, an unexpected shyness stole over her. She blushed profusely to everyone's delight as the ladies in the hall led her away.

Lord Lyting attended to Garreth, seeing that he was plied liberally with beer. Rurik, meanwhile, brought out a special flask of a crystal drink from the East and insisted all should partake of a round.

"Careful, Garreth, 'tis potent stuff," Lyting warned, then took a bracing swallow. He rolled an eye to Rurik. "Did we not indulge in a like drink on your wedding night, brother? Look to where it led—a hall filled with children."

"You should talk! What staggers the mind, though, is trying to imagine you as a *grand-père*." Rurik grinned in high spirits and topped off Garreth's cup. "Garreth, here, looks man enough for the task. I wouldn't be surprised if you gain your grandfatherly status in the coming year."

Garreth took a swallow of the liquor, then held his breath as it blazed fire to his stomach and set his veins aflame. "In truth," he choked, "I suspect you two are trying to disable me. Is a man really supposed to be able to function after drinking this?"

"He's right." Rurik clapped his cup down on the table. "We must deliver him while he is still conscious."

Lyting relieved Garreth of his cup. "Indeed, and from the looks of him, we better see to it quickly."

Lyting signaled to the men gathered about. Garreth next found himself seized off his feet, hoisted in the air, and delivered to the bridal chamber amidst happy, raucous song. By the time they arrived he was stripped to his *braies*. Unceremoniously his companions divested him of the rest and deposited him in bed with Ailénor to the gasps of the ladies.

After more good-humored teasing, they withdrew from the chamber, leaving Garreth and Ailénor alone at last. In unison, the couple breathed a sigh of relief, then sat in silence.

Garreth looked to where their toes nearly met the end of the bed. A grin stole over his features. "I'd say we fill the bed rather well, my heart."

Ailénor followed his gaze, then her lashes fluttered downward. "I am overtall for a woman," she tossed lightly.

Garreth caught the thread of embarrassment beneath her teasing tone. "And I'd have you no other way, my heart." He turned to his side and reached to pick up a tendril of dark red hair that lay on her shoulder. "I knew from the first we were meant for each other." He kissed the end of her hair, then her silken shoulder.

"And how is that, love?" Ailénor murmured as his lips moved along the curve of her neck, causing her pulse to leap and her thoughts to disassemble.

"Because when we rolled down the orchard hill together and came to a stop just so . . ." He rolled her onto her back and moved atop of her, simulating the incident. "I knew our parts would fit perfectly together."

"Garreth!" Ailénor's eyes flew wide as he filled her.

"And I was right." He grinned wickedly, then kissed her lips, her throat, her breasts. "Whatever has gone before, sweet Ailénor, you are my captive, now and forevermore."

"Garreth," she purred as he covered her nipple with his

mouth and lavished it with an exquisite kiss. Drawing up one of her long legs, she wrapped it high over his buttocks and legs, forcing him tight against her, so that his manhood pressed deep within her and he growled with delight.

She caught his earlobe playfully with her teeth and nipped it gently. "Who is whose captive now?"

Epilogue

"Cricket's going to fall," Michan fretted, squinching his eyes against the bright sky as he stared into the upper branches of the aged apple tree.

Ailénor tipped back her head and spied the white ball of fur perched there, its round, golden eyes pleading. The fur-puff gave a doleful "mew."

Ailénor knotted her hands at her side. "Now, Michan, we both know Cricket can manage quite well. She will climb down by herself when she wishes to."

"You wouldn't want Cricket to fall and go splat like an overripe plum, would you?" the boy persisted, nettled at her unwillingness to fetch the kitten down.

Ailénor gave her brother a patient eye that he promptly met with a pout.

"If Richard and Kylan were here, they'd . . ."

"They'd say your sister is right," a masculine voice sounded from behind. "Cricket can back herself down."

Ailénor and Michan turned to find Kylan, his mouth spread with a grin as he came to stand beside them. He gave Ailénor a sparkling wink and glanced at young Michan.

"Your sister has had enough excitement of late, wouldn't you agree? Besides, now that she is married, she mustn't do anything so unbefitting her new station as climbing trees."

Ailénor sent Kylan a smile of thanks. He glanced to the kitten, then back again to her.

"I'll remain here and oversee Cricket's deliverance. But you, my lady, are requested to come to the hall forthwith." She gave him a quizzing look. "A courier has just now arrived."

"From the duke?" Ailénor thought this odd for Duke William had already dispatched a message congratulating Garreth and herself on their marriage and inviting them to Rouen. She suspected her father and uncle had something to do with winning his approval.

"*Non.* The courier arrives from England. He bears a missive from King Athelstan."

Ailénor swallowed. "*Alors.* I knew this moment must come. His Majesty has learned what Garreth has done." She snatched a quick glance of her cousin. "Garreth aided my escape to Lundenburh when the king instructed I be held at Andover. I fear what his judgment will be on Garreth. Surely 'tis what the missive contains."

The side of Kylan's mouth slanted upward into a curious smile. "Actually, the missive is for your father. The messenger sought him first at Héricourt, then, on discovering he had departed for Valsemé, followed him here. They are speaking now."

"I see," she said softly. Her brows knitted together. "*En vérité*, I do not see. But I shall hurry." Ailénor gave a quick squeeze to Kylan's arm. *"Merci, cousin."*

Hastening from the orchard, Ailénor headed toward the bailey and, once through the gate and defense walls, proceeded to Valsemé's great manor house.

As she quickened her pace she thought how extraordinary that King Athelstan should direct his message to her father. How could he know of the Comte de Héricourt?

Except by Cynric's missive, came the answer. The one issued from Winchester, twisted in its accounts to advance Cynric's—and Barbetorte's—purposes.

Tendrils of fear twined about her heart. Cynric was no admirer of Garreth. She shuddered to think what lies he—and the Breton—might be now whispering into the royal ears.

Would Athelstan strip Garreth of his titles and position? Might he order him shackled should he return, or exile him permanently?

But did the king even know Garreth was here? If his and her movements had been traced to Lundenburh, perhaps the king presumed Garreth sailed with her to Normandy, not knowing of their abduction to Ireland.

The more Ailénor pondered the matter, the more she dreaded the tidings the missive carried.

Her heart thrumming in her chest, she mounted the steps of the manor and entered the main hall. There servants moved quietly and efficiently about, setting up trestles for the coming meal. At the far end, Garreth stood with her mother and aunt and uncle.

Ailénor whisked a glance over the hall but saw no sign of her father. Presumably he still secluded himself with the courier.

Crossing the distance, she drew the gazes of the others. She could read naught in their looks—not in her maman's, nor her Aunt Brienne's nor her Uncle Rurik's. But as Garreth turned, her breath caught at the somber intensity in his eyes. In their dark brown depths, she read the torment tearing at his soul.

Ailénor moved quickly to his side and slipped her arm around his waist, offering up a solacing smile. For all the world, she wished she could ease his cares and assure him everything would be all right. But how could she know the mind of a king or that which he might decree?

The sound of boots drew Ailénor's attention. She saw her father emerge from a side chamber, followed by the royal messenger.

Her father's smooth features did not betray his thoughts, but for one brief instant his gaze shifted to her. Some concern shadowed his clear blue eyes and immediately gave her unease. Joining them, he directed his gaze to the others. Still, for a moment he did not speak.

"Well, *broFir*," Rurik said in his deep, rich voice. "Are we to stand here the day, strung taut with curiosity? What says the king?"

Lyting skimmed a look to Rurik, then to the ladies and Garreth.

"I believe some explanation is first due on my part. Before leaving Héricourt to, ah, *accompany* Garreth to his wedding, I dispatched two missives. One, of course, to you, Rurik, apprising you of my decision and requesting suitable preparations be made."

"And see the bride readied and waiting on the church steps," Rurik added with a decided grin.

A smile touched Lyting's lips as well. "*Já*. That, too. But I also felt compelled to inform the English monarch of the impending marriage of his royal *thegn* and sent a second missive to King Athelstan."

Ailénor and Garreth exchanged startled glances, but Lyting continued.

"Though I offered no explanation for the suddenness of the ceremony, I did recount for him the events that preceded it—beginning with Ailénor's abduction from Rouen. The missive detailed what I had learned from Garreth, particularly that of Ailénor's detainment at Winchester and those involved. I also included why, to my understanding, Garreth chose to contradict his sovereign's direct orders and took her to Lundenburh with the purpose of freeing her and sending her back to Normandy."

Lyting faced Garreth, meeting his gaze evenly. "Providentially, my missive reached the king at Winchester without difficulty. I can tell you, by his reply, he was most gratified to receive its contents. He also includes in his letter a pronouncement concerning yourself. Rather than my restating his directives, 'tis best you hear the king's own words.''

Stepping aside, Lyting motioned the courier forward.

As the young man unscrolled the parchment, Ailénor felt Garreth stiffen beside her, steeling himself to receive his king's judgment. She glimpsed his rigid stance, then gave her attention back to the courier who at the moment was reciting the formal salutations and wishes for God's blessings. Her father bid the young man to skip to the heart of the letter.

'' '. . . God preserve you always . . . indebtedness for enlightening . . . solved many perturbing questions . . .' '' He fumbled through the lines.

In exasperation, her father pointed to where he should begin. The courier cleared his throat.

'' ''Tis my hope, when this letter finds you, it will likewise find Garreth still in your company. I would ask that you give him to know, when first I received word of events at Winchester—as related by the *wicgerefa* Cynric—I found them sorely perplexing. Doubly so, having received no word from Garreth himself. In ordering Lady Ailénor's transference to Andover under Garreth's escort, 'twas my intent to remove them both from the direct authority of the high reeve, providing them the protection of a royal decree. When still no word came from Garreth, I further distrusted the situation. Having finished my purposes in the north, I headed with my troops for Winchester, believing Lady Ailénor to be safe at Andover.

'' 'As to the matter of Garreth's countermanding my orders, I have decided to address that particular transgression by issuing a new charge—one that he is warned not to ignore, but to follow without deviation.

'' 'I would ask you to convey unto him that, as his sovereign lord, I, Athelstan, King of all Britain, do command Garreth of Tamworth, royal *thegn* and officer in the Hird, to return to the royal palace at Winchester where, in my presence, he will immediately relinquish his place at court and rank in the Hird . . .' ''

Garreth pressed his lashes tight.

" ' . . . that he might thereupon be elevated to the distinguished position of *Ealdorman* of Hamtunscir and endowed with those lands and titles entailed. At that time he shall also be conferred a place in the Witan. Long have I desired to reward him in this manner for his years of faithful service and many deeds of valor, yet never has it been more deserved than now.

" 'Again, I enjoin Garreth to come with all speed to Winchester, that these honors might be bestowed on him and that his bride might be graciously welcomed and their union fittingly celebrated.' ''

The courier paused and looked to Garreth. "Sir, there is an added note of a more personal nature. Would you prefer we step aside?''

"No," Garreth's voice came roughly. "You may read it here. But do so in Saxon.''

"As you will." The young man cleared his throat once more and began. "King Athelstan writes thusly: 'Most worthy and loyal friend, your instincts continue to serve you well. Thank you for your ordeals on behalf of Lady Ailénor and my crown. Your unswayable opposition against the intrigues at court and your many pains to right the circumstances have, with no doubt in my mind, averted direct conflict with Normandy. It may interest you to know that Cynric oversees new duties on the Welsh border, and that my sister, nephew, and Alain de Barbetorte have withdrawn to distant estates for an indefinite time.

" 'One thing more need be stated, my friend. Long has it grieved me that, even as king, by law I could do naught to restore your birthright, so unjustly taken from you. Be satisfied in the knowledge that no Kentman in this time— including those who have aggrieved you—have gained such distinction or worth as you. You have eclipsed them all—in honor, lands, title, and wealth. And in matters of what is right and virtuous, you stand heads above them. I am constantly amazed at how much keener is God's brand of justice than man's—mayhap not always what we expect, but ever brimming with surprises and a thousand times more satisfying in the end. I wait expectantly for your return, Garreth, and look forward to you and your bride beginning your new lives together as Lord and Lady of Hamtunscir.

" 'Given this day at Winchester, August 31, in the year of our Lord 933. Athelstan, *Rex To Bri.*' "

Ailénor wiped the moisture from her eyes and saw that Garreth's eyes shone as well. He stood silent a moment, absorbing the missive's words. She wondered if he yet realized that she—and likely her father and uncle—could understand the last of it.

Just then, he raised his eyes to hers. She could not help but meet his look with a brilliant smile. Garreth smiled, too, then gave a relieved laugh. Impulsively he swept her off her toes—his hands at her waist—and twirled her twice around before setting her to her feet again. He then proceeded to kiss her soundly and joyously on the lips before all.

Breathless, Ailénor tottered momentarily, holding on to her husband's arm, her heart overflowing with happiness for him. Her parents and aunt and uncle quickly offered Garreth their congratulations, then others came forth who had been silently gathering in the hall.

As everyone was caught up in the exuberance of the moment, well-wishing Garreth, Ailénor looked on, excited that all had come to such a happy conclusion. She anticipated accompanying Garreth to England where they were to become the "Lord and Lady of Hamtunscir," and oversee lands . . . across the waters.

The thought struck Ailénor like a thunderbolt. Suddenly she understood with painful clarity the earlier look in her father's eyes. No longer would she dwell in Normandy, but on the other side of La Manche, leaving her family and homeland.

The moment turned bittersweet. Ailénor's gaze stole to her father, and she found his eyes already upon her. He gave her a nod as if to say he understood. Ailénor felt a piercing in her heart as she faced the full ramifications of her marriage. Why during the blissful week since her wedding had she not once thought on this inevitability that would change her life forevermore?

The thought consumed her as she looked upon the beloved face of her *maman* who smiled happily now as she spoke with Garreth. Not wishing to spoil the moment, Ailénor lifted her smile back in place. She loved Garreth with all her heart and would willingly make her life with him wherever that might lead. Still, she would miss her family terribly.

The excitement carried over through dinner, which became an occasion for more feasting. As Ailénor sat beside Garreth at their place of honor on the dais, she looked out over the hall.

Many relatives and friends gathered there, having arrived at Valsemé throughout the past week of festivities. She gazed on the familiar faces of those she had known all her life and with whom she had grown up—her brothers and sisters and many cousins and, of course, dear Felise.

There were also Ketil and Aleth, long-time family friends, arrived from Ivry. With them sat Lia and her husband and children. Nearby, Brother Bernard appeared to discuss the merits of the wine with Richard and Kylan. The youngest children shared the end of one trestle—Brietta, Adelis, and Ena huddling together over one trencher, Michan enjoying his own, and the infamous Cricket peeking from beneath the hem of the table linens.

A lump formed in Ailénor's throat. As her gaze drew to the high table—to her parents and aunt and uncle—emotion overcame her. She felt heartsick at the prospect of being severed from them all and living so far away. Her eyes misted.

In need of fresh air and time alone to deal with her melancholy, Ailénor rose, explaining she wished to stretch her legs with a brief walk. Concern filled Garreth's eyes, but she bid him stay and finish his conversation with her father, for they had been engrossed discussing the horses of Hamtunscir. Masking her true feelings with a smile, she made her way from the hall.

Garreth's gaze followed Ailénor as she departed the hall. Something troubled her, but he was at a loss as to what that might be. Excusing himself, he left the dais and quit the hall.

Stepping outside, he spied her immediately, standing at the base of the *motte*, an immense mound of dirt from which Valsemé's great keep rose. Ailénor gazed up the long flight of steps that stretched to the tower's entrance on the second level. To his astonishment, she began to mount them.

"Ailénor! What are you doing, my heart?" he called out, catching up with her moments later.

She smiled softly as he joined her. "I thought to climb to the top of the keep."

"Is this your way of 'stretching your legs'?" He flashed her a grin, though in truth her words took him totally aback. "What of your fear of heights?"

The corner of her lips curved upward. "When I was trapped on the cliff ledge, I realized something I have known deep inside all along. 'Tis more a fear of falling I possess than a fear of heights. I also learned that from such an elevation one can see to a fabulous distance. And just now I would like to see all I can of Normandy . . . before I must leave it."

Garreth began to understand her mystifying mood. "Of course," he said gently. "I would like to see it with you."

Garreth took each step with her, placing an assuring hand at the small of her back. Whenever he felt her tense, he whispered distractions in her ear, speaking lightly of diverse things and encouraging her to keep her gaze uplifted. On gaining the top, they entered the imposing tower and mounted the interior stairs. These Ailénor managed without difficulty.

Moving ever upward through the various levels, they came at last to a small low-ceilinged room in the very top of the keep. There a ladder stood braced in place, rising to a small door in the ceiling. Garreth mounted the crosspieces and opened it, then stepped back down. Looking to Ailénor, he held out his hand.

"Are you sure you will be all right, love?"

"*Oui.*" She placed her hand in his. "Just hold me tight, Garreth."

As Ailénor and Garreth emerged on the top of the keep, the sweeping view took their breath away. Layers of clouds stacked the sky, while the evening's long light fell across the green rolling hills. In the distance the River Touques coursed westward, a sparkling silver thread that would soon carry them to their future in England.

Garreth stood behind Ailénor, his arms wrapped securely about her. At first she held herself stiff as a column. But as they continued to absorb the beauty and serenity of the scene, she gradually relaxed against him.

"Did I tell you I was born at Valsemé and raised here the first years of my life?" she asked quietly, reflectively. " 'Twas before Duke Rollo awarded my father the lands of Héricourt."

Again she fell silent and when after several minutes she still did not speak, Garreth shifted to look at her.

"Does something trouble you, love?"

She bit her lower lip, then finally lifted her hand and pointed toward the hills.

"See how the trees are touched with crimson and gold? Summer draws to a close. As do my days in Normandy."

Comprehension seized him fully, brilliantly. Ailénor belonged to a large, close-knit family, something he had never enjoyed. At Rouen she had been abruptly ripped away from them. Now, having barely returned, she must leave once again, but this time in a more permanent way.

He had not thought of the effect all this would have on her. Or what it cost her. While his life would continue in much the same vein, her entire life was taking a new direction. Garreth chose his next words with care.

"Consider, love, the trees will leaf and blossom again. 'Tis nature's promise. And a foretoken that we, too, shall return here. And often, I promise you."

Ailénor turned in his arms and searched his eyes. He

embraced her with the warmth of his smile.

"Has it escaped your notice, love, how much time your father and I have spent in conversation these past days? 'Twas our intent—before the courier arrived—to tell you our plans this eve. We are entering into a joint venture, so to speak—breeding horses. 'Tis my own hope to improve the horse stock in England that runs to the small side. Your father is gifting us with a stallion and six mares."

Smoothing a wisp of hair from her brow, he gazed earnestly into her eyes. "I hope you will grow to like your new homeland. 'Twill require some adjustments, I know. But do not fear. We shall travel back and forth to Normandy quite frequently, as will your parents to England." He gave her a wink, eliciting a smile. "In truth, considering the size of your family, I would not be surprised if we need enlarge our hall to accommodate their many visitations."

"Oh, Garreth, is all this true?" A bright smile replaced the pain in Ailénor's eyes, and she hugged him mightily.

"Upon my oath. 'Tis my intent to make you the happiest woman in England."

"I shall be happy wherever you are, my husband." She slipped her arms around his neck. "My home is with you."

"And there may it ever remain." Garreth embraced Ailénor, his lips descending over hers. He kissed her slowly, thoroughly, and deeper still.

Their hearts entwined, their love reached out toward all the tomorrows and beyond.

AUTHOR'S NOTE

Restoration of the Carolingian throne: Louis d'Outremer gained Francia's throne in 936 A.D. with the support of William Longsword, Duke of Normandy, and Hugh, the Count of Paris. Rather than being grateful, the young king remained distrusting and suspicious of both men. When William Longsword was assassinated in 942 A.D., Louis kidnapped William's son and successor, ten-year-old Richard I. Thanks to the gallantry of the duke's squire—who escaped with the boy in the dark of night and raced back to Rouen—Richard survived the ordeal and ruled until 996 A.D.

Place names: Translations for the Anglo-Saxon names (in King Athelstan's day) are as follows: Lundenburh—London; Lindum—Lincoln; and Jorvik—York.

The dowager queens, Eadgiva of England and Eadgifu of France: To ease confusion in the text, I have used a variation of Eadgifu (Eadgiva) for the English dowager queen, King Edward's widow. In reality, both she and her stepdaughter, Charles the Simple's queen, bore the same name.

*If you enjoyed this book,
take advantage
of this special offer.
Subscribe now and get a*

FREE
Historical
Romance

No Obligation (a $4.50 value)

Each month the editors of True Value select the four *very best* novels from America's leading publishers of romantic fiction. Preview them in your home *Free* for 10 days. With the first four books you receive, we'll send you a FREE book as our introductory gift. No Obligation!

For if any reason you decide not to keep them, just return them and owe nothing. If you like them as much as we think you will, you'll pay just $4.00 each and save at *least* $.50 each off the cover price. (Your savings are *guaranteed* to be at least $2.00 each month.) There is NO postage and handling – or other hidden charges. There are no minimum number of books to buy and you may cancel at any time.

*Send in
the Coupon
Below*

To get your FREE historical romance fill out the coupon below and mail it today. As soon as we receive it we'll send you your FREE Book along with your first month's selections.

Mail To: **True Value Home Subscription Services, Inc., P.O. Box 5235
120 Brighton Road, Clifton, New Jersey 07015-5235**

YES! I want to start previewing the very best historical romances being published today. Send me my FREE book along with the first month's selections. I understand that I may look them over FREE for 10 days. If I'm not absolutely delighted I may return them and owe nothing. Otherwise I will pay the low price of just $4.00 each: a total $16.00 (at least an $18.00 value) and save at least $2.00. Then each month I will receive four brand new novels to preview as soon as they are published for the same low price. I can always return a shipment and I may cancel this subscription at any time with no obligation to buy even a single book. In any event the FREE book is mine to keep regardless.

Name _____

Street Address _____ Apt. No. _____

City _____ State _____ Zip _____

Telephone _____

Signature _____
(if under 18 parent or guardian must sign)

Terms and prices subject to change. Orders subject to acceptance by True Value Home Subscription Services, Inc.

11699-8